# Lady Emily's EXOTIC JOURNEY

# LILLIAN MAREK

sourcebooks
casablanca

Published by Sourcebooks Casablanca, an imprint of
Sourcebooks, Inc.
P.O. Box 4410, Naperville, Illinois 60567-4410
(630) 961-3900
Fax: (630) 961-2168
www.sourcebooks.com

Printed and bound in Canada.
MBP 10 9 8 7 6 5 4 3 2 1

# *One*

*Constantinople, March 1861*

CONSTANTINOPLE HAD LOOKED SO PROMISING TO Lady Emily when they arrived this morning, with the city rising up out of the morning mists, white and shining with turrets and domes and balconies everywhere. The long, narrow boats in the harbor all sported bright sails. It had been so new and strange and exotic.

Now here she was, walking with Lady Julia behind her parents on Wilton carpets. Wilton carpets imported from Salisbury! When even she knew that this part of the world was famous for its carpets.

She heaved a sigh. They had traveled thousands of miles to finally reach Constantinople—the Gateway to Asia, the ancient Byzantium, the capital of the fabulous Ottoman Empire, a city of magic and mystery—and for what?

To be tucked up in the British Embassy, a Palladian building that would have looked perfectly at home around the corner from Penworth House in London.

She understood that it was British and represented the Queen and the Empire and all that, but did it have to be so very *English*?

The doors at the end of the hall were flung open and a butler, dressed precisely as he would have been in London, announced, "The Most Honorable the Marquess of Penworth. The Most Honorable the Marchioness of Penworth. The Lady Emily Tremaine. The Lady Julia de Vaux."

They might just as well have never left home.

Emily smiled the insipid smile she reserved for her parents' political friends—the smile intended to assure everyone that she was sweet and docile—and prepared to be bored. She was very good at pretending to be whatever she was expected to be. Next to her, she could feel Julia straighten her already perfect posture. She reached over to squeeze her friend's hand.

"Lord Penworth, Lady Penworth, allow me to welcome you to Constantinople." A ruddy-faced gentleman with thinning gray hair on his head and a thinning gray beard on his chin inclined his head. "And this must be your daughter, Lady Emily?" He looked somewhere between the two young women, as if uncertain which one to address.

Emily took pity on him and curtsied politely.

He looked relieved and turned to Julia. "And Lady Julia?" She performed a similar curtsy.

"My husband and I are delighted to welcome such distinguished visitors to Constantinople," said the small, gray woman who was standing stiffly beside the ambassador, ignoring the fact that he had been ignoring her.

Emily blinked. She knew marital disharmony when she heard it. She also knew how unpleasant it could make an evening.

"We are delighted to be here, Lady Bulwer," said Lord Penworth courteously. "This part of the world is new to us, and we have all been looking forward to our visit." He turned to the ambassador. "I understand that you, Sir Henry, are quite familiar with it."

"Tolerably well, tolerably well. I'm told you're here to study the possibility of a railroad along the Tigris River valley. Can't quite see it myself." Before the ambassador realized it, Lord Penworth had cut him out of the herd of women and was shepherding him off to the side.

In the sudden quiet, Lady Penworth smiled at her hostess and gestured at the room about them. "I am most impressed by the way you have managed to turn this embassy into a bit of England," she said. "If I did not know, I would think myself still in London."

Lady Bulwer looked both pleased and smug. She obviously failed to note any hint of irony in Lady Penworth's words. Emily recognized the signs. Her parents would out-diplomat the diplomats, smoothing over any bumps of disharmony in the Bulwer house-hold, and conversation would flow placidly through conventional channels. Boring, but unexceptionable. And only too familiar.

Then Julia touched her arm.

Still looking straight ahead, and still with a faint, polite smile on her face, Julia indicated that Emily should look at the left-hand corner of the room. Emily had never understood how it was that Julia could send these messages without making a sound or even moving her head, but send them she did.

In this case, it was a message Emily received with interest. Off in the corner were two young men pretending to examine a huge globe while they took sideways glances at the newcomers. This was much more promising than the possibility of trouble between the ambassador and his wife. Refusing to pretend a lack of curiosity—she was growing tired, very tired, of pretending—she looked straight at them.

One was an extraordinarily handsome man, clean-shaven to display a beautifully sculpted mouth and a square jaw. His perfectly tailored black tailcoat outlined a tall, broad-shouldered physique. The blinding whiteness of his shirt and bow tie contrasted with the slight olive cast of his skin. His hair was almost black, and his dark eyes betrayed no awareness of her scrutiny. He stood with all the bored elegance of the quintessential English gentleman. Bored and probably boring.

The other man looked far more interesting. He was not so tall—slim and wiry, rather than powerful looking—and not nearly so handsome. His nose was quite long—assertive might be a polite way to describe it—and his tanned face was long and narrow. Like his companion, he was clean shaven, though his hair, a dark brown, was in need of cutting. While his evening clothes were perfectly proper, they were worn carelessly, and he waved his hands about as he spoke in a way that seemed definitely un-English. He noticed immediately when she held her gaze on him and turned to return her scrutiny. She refused to look away, even when he unashamedly examined her from head to toe. His eyes glinted with amusement, and he gave her an appreciative grin and salute.

The cheek of him! She laughed out loud, making Julia hiss and drawing the attention of her mother and Lady Bulwer. Sir Henry must have noticed something as well, for he waved the young men over to be introduced to Papa.

They both stopped a proper distance away, and the handsome one waited with an almost military stiffness. Sir Henry introduced him first. "This is David Oliphant, Lord Penworth. He's with the Foreign Office and will be your aide and guide on the journey. He knows the territory and can speak the lingo. All the lingoes, in fact—Turkish, Kurdish, Arabic, whatever you run into along the way."

Oliphant bowed. "Honored, my lord."

Lord Penworth smiled. "My pleasure."

"And this young man is Lucien Chambertin. He's on his way back to Mosul where he's been working with Carnac, digging up stone beasts or some such."

"The remains of Nineveh, Sir Henry." Chambertin then turned to Lord Penworth with a brief, graceful bow and a smile. "I am most pleased to make your acquaintance, my lord, for I am hoping you will allow me to impose on you and join your caravan for the journey to Mosul."

He spoke excellent English, with just a hint of a French accent. Just the perfect hint, Emily decided. Sir Henry was not including the ladies in his introductions, to her annoyance, so she had been obliged to position herself close enough to hear what they were saying. This was one of the rare occasions when she was grateful for her crinolines. They made it impossible for the ladies to stand too close to one another, so she placed herself to the rear of her mother. From that position, she could listen to the gentlemen's conversation while appearing to attend to the ladies'. What's more, from her angle she could watch them from the corner of her eye without being obvious.

"I cannot imagine why you should not join us," Lord Penworth told the Frenchman. "I understand that, in Mesopotamia, it is always best to travel in a large group. You are one of these new scholars—what do they call them, archaeologists?"

Chambertin gave one of those Gallic shrugs. "Ah no, nothing so grand. I am just a passing traveler, but I cannot resist the opportunity to see the ruins of Nineveh when the opportunity offers itself. And then when Monsieur Carnac says he has need of assistance, I agree to stay for a while."

"Well, my wife will certainly find the ruins interesting. She has developed quite a fascination with the ancient world."

Oliphant looked startled. "Your wife? But surely Lady Penworth does not intend to accompany us."

"Of course." Lord Penworth in turn looked startled at the question. "I could hardly deny her the opportunity to see the ancient cradle of civilization. Not when I am looking forward to it myself."

"I'm sorry. I was told you were traveling to view the possible site of a railway."

"I am." Penworth smiled. "That is my excuse for this trip. General Chesney has been urging our government to build a railway from Basra to Constantinople. His argument is that it would provide much quicker and safer communication with India. Palmerston wanted me to take a look and see if there would be any other use for it."

The ambassador snorted. "Not much. There's nothing of any use or interest in that part of the world except for those huge carvings that fellows like Carnac haul out of the ground."

The handsome Mr. Oliphant looked worried. Before he could say anything, dinner was announced, the remaining introductions were finally made, and Emily found herself walking in to dinner on the arm of M. Chambertin. He had behaved quite correctly when they were introduced and held out his arm in perfectly proper fashion. He said nothing that would have been out of place in the most rigidly proper setting imaginable. Nonetheless, she suspected that he had been well aware of her eavesdropping. There was a decidedly improper light dancing in his eyes.

She liked it.

About dinner she was less certain. The oxtail soup had been followed by lobster rissoles, and now a footman placed a slice from the roast sirloin of beef on her plate, where it joined the spoonful of mashed turnips and the boiled onion. The onion had been so thoroughly boiled that it was finding it difficult to hold its shape and had begun to tilt dispiritedly to one side.

"This is really quite a remarkable meal," Lady Penworth said to their hostess. "Do you find it difficult to obtain English food here?"

"You've no idea." Lady Bulwer sighed sadly. "It has taken me ages to convince the cook that plain boiled vegetables are what we want. You can't imagine the outlandish spices he wants to use. And the olive oil! It's a constant struggle."

"And in that battle, the food lost," muttered Emily, poking the onion into total collapse.

A snort from M. Chambertin at her side indicated that her words had not gone unheard. After using his napkin, he turned to her. "You do not care for *rosbif*?" he asked with a grin. "I thought all the English eat nothing else."

"We are in *Constantinople*, thousands of miles from home, and we might as well be in Tunbridge Wells."

He made a sympathetic grimace. "Perhaps while your papa goes to look at the railway route, Sir Henry can find you a guide who will show you and your friend a bit of Constantinople. You should really see the Topkapi—the old palace—and the bazaar."

"Oh, but we aren't going to be staying here. Julia and I are going with my parents."

Mr. Oliphant, who had been speaking quietly with Julia, heard that and looked around in shock. "Lady Emily, you and Lady Julia and Lady Penworth are *all* planning to go to Mosul? Surely not. I cannot believe your father will allow this."

Emily sighed. She was accustomed to such reactions. *Lady Emily, you cannot possibly mean... Lady Emily, surely you do not intend...* All too often, she had restrained herself and done what was expected. She intended this trip to be different. Still, she was curious as well as annoyed. Was Mr. Oliphant about to urge propriety, or was there some other reason for his distress? "Why should we not?" she asked.

Mr. Oliphant took a sip of wine, as if to calm himself. Or fortify himself. It was impossible to be certain. He cleared his throat. "I fear Lord Penworth may not be fully aware of the difficulties—dangers, even—of travel in this part of the world. The caravan route through Aleppo and Damascus and then across the desert is hazardous under the best of circumstances, and these days…" He shook his head.

"My friend does not exaggerate," added M. Chambertin, looking serious. "Although the recent massacres in the Lebanon seem to be at an end, brigands have become more bold, and even the largest caravans—they are not safe."

"But we are not planning to take that route." Emily looked at Julia for confirmation and received it. "We are to sail to Samsun on the Black Sea, travel by caravan over the mountains to Diyarbakir, and then down the river to Mosul. And eventually on to Baghdad and Basra. Papa discussed it all with people back in London when he and Lord Palmerston were planning the route. So you need not worry." She smiled to reassure the gentlemen.

M. Chambertin and Mr. Oliphant exchanged glances, trying to decide which should speak. It fell to Mr. Oliphant. "I do not question your father's plan, Lady Emily. These days that is by far the safer route, though no place is entirely safe from attacks by brigands. However, he may have underestimated the physical difficulties of the trip. The mountains—these are not gentle little hills like the ones you find in

England. They are barren and rocky, and we will cross them on roads that are little more than footpaths. It is impossible to take a carriage. If they do not go on foot, travelers must go on horseback or on mules. And this early in the year, it will still be bitterly cold, especially at night."

"You needn't worry," Emily assured him. "We are all excellent riders, and I am told that the cold is preferable to the heat of the summer."

M. Chambertin smiled at her and shook his head. "I do not doubt that you are a horsewoman *par excellence*, and your mother and Lady Julia as well. However, the journey over the mountains will take weeks. We will encounter few villages, and those we find will be most poor. There will be times when we must sleep in tents or take shelter in stables. Nowhere will there be comfortable inns where ladies can refresh themselves."

Emily and Julia looked at each other, sharing their irritation. Male condescension was obviously to be found everywhere.

"I believe you misunderstand the situation, gentlemen." Julia spoke in her iciest, most superior tones. "We are not fragile pieces of porcelain. We are grown women, and English women at that. I do not think you will find us swooning at the sight of a spider. Or, for that matter, at the sight of a lion. Since Lord Penworth has determined that we are capable of undertaking the journey, I see no need for you to question his judgment."

Mr. Oliphant flushed uncomfortably. "I assure you that no insult was intended either to you or to Lord

Penworth. It is simply that ladies do not normally undertake such a journey."

Julia's tone grew even icier. "*Ladies* do not? Are you suggesting that there is something improper about our taking part in this trip?"

His flush deepened. "Not at all. I would not…I assure you…my only concern is your safety."

"You need not worry about that either," said Emily, waving a hand casually in the air. "Harry—that's Lady Julia's brother, Lord Doncaster. He's married to my sister Elinor. He has provided each of us with a revolver."

There was an odd, choking sound from M. Chambertin.

Emily turned to him. "Are you quite well, monsieur?"

"Quite well." His face, when it reappeared from his napkin, was slightly red. "And the Lord Doncaster, he has no doubt taught you how to shoot these revolvers?"

"Of course." Emily smiled rather smugly. "In fact, I am becoming quite a good shot. Would you care for a demonstration? Not here in the dining room," she assured Mr. Oliphant, who was looking more and more distressed.

M. Chambertin, on the other hand, was grinning broadly. "No demonstration will be needed, I assure you. I begin to think that this will be a most interesting voyage. *Bien intéressant.*"

❧

Lord Penworth, wrapped in his comfortable old brown dressing gown and seated in the comfortable armchair in the chamber he and his wife had been given, watched Lady Penworth brush out her hair. He had enjoyed this ritual for more than thirty years, and it had yet to pall. His wife's hair was still thick and lustrous. The few gray hairs only highlighted its inky darkness. She was still the most beautiful woman he had ever known. And the least docile.

"Anne, my dear…"

"Yes?" She met his eyes in the mirror.

"Now that we have come too far to turn back easily, are you going to tell me why we are all here?"

"Now, Phillip, you know that Lord Palmerston asked for your opinion on this railway proposal."

He noticed with amusement that her eyes evaded his just as that answer evaded the question. His Anne disliked telling fibs. "Yes, I know that, and I could have told him it was a foolish idea without leaving my own fireside."

She drew the brush rhythmically through her hair. "Well, I have been worried about Emily lately. She's been bored."

"Really? She seems busy enough."

"Yes, but she has been busy with social events that do not truly interest her. Boredom can be dangerous. She needs a challenge, something new before she decides to do something drastic."

He looked unconvinced. "If you had simply wanted to take the girls traveling, we could have gone to Paris or even Vienna. We've never been to Vienna."

She put down the brush and turned around, a look of resignation on her face. "That would not have done. It would have looked as if we were running away."

Now he was confused. "Why would anyone think Emily was running away?"

"All right. It would have looked as if Julia were running away."

He waited.

Lady Penworth sighed. "There has been talk about Julia's mother."

"Lady Doncaster? The Dowager Lady Doncaster, I should say." He smiled. "It did rather put her nose out of joint when she discovered that our Elinor had married Harry and is now the Countess of Doncaster. At any rate, I thought she was now living quietly, or at least distantly, in Naples."

"That creature could enter a nunnery and there would still be rumors about her. But it isn't so much what she's doing now." Lady Penworth wrinkled her nose in distaste. "It seems that Robby Sinclair has taken it upon himself to remind people—or at least any young men who seem inclined to pay court to Julia—of Lady Doncaster's past indiscretions and to suggest that Julia is likely to follow in her mother's footsteps."

Lord Penworth remained motionless for some moments. He finally broke the silence. "I take it that Doncaster was told nothing of this either?"

"Of course not."

"I believe I know something of the reason for this. I don't know the details, but there was a story going around last year that young Sinclair had done something less than honorable and Doncaster called him on it. There was no open scandal, but these days there's always a slight hesitation when Sinclair's name comes up."

"He was trying to get back at Harry through his sister? What a vile little wretch."

"No doubt. But this won't do, Anne. He can't be allowed to get away with that."

"Well…" Lady Penworth hesitated and a slight smile hovered.

Lord Penworth sighed. He knew his wife. "What did you do?"

"You know that Sinclair has been looking for a wealthy bride?"

He nodded. "I had heard that the Sinclair finances are not all that they should be."

"I was speaking with Mrs. Heath-Robinson. Sinclair frequently partnered her daughter. She commented that he was such a charming young man, just like his father. I reminded her that his father had been so charming that he gave his wife the disease that killed her and that left him a drooling idiot before he died himself, and, from all reports, it appears young Sinclair is indeed following in his father's charming footsteps."

He drew in a swift breath. "And is all of this true?"

"Oh yes. It's hardly the sort of thing I would make up. It's just that Sinclair's parents dropped out of society so long ago that people have begun to forget."

"But now they will remember."

"Assuredly," she said. "Sinclair is no longer invited to the Heath-Robinson house, and Mrs. Heath-Robinson is sure to tell everyone why."

He shook his head slowly. "Skewered with his own weapon."

"After all, if we had told you or Harry, you would have felt obliged to thrash him or do something equally violent. There would have been a scandal and that would only have made matters worse. Now we are all on this voyage because you could not leave me behind, and I could not leave Emily and Julia unchaperoned for the season. By next season, all anyone will talk about, if they say anything, is how brave and adventurous the girls are."

"Have I ever told you, my dear, how grateful I am to have you for my wife and not my enemy?"

"Don't be silly, Phillip. You would never do anything dishonorable to make an enemy of me. That's why I love you. Or at least, that is one of the many reasons."

෴

Nuran, the maid who had been assigned to Emily and Julia, had nearly finished. After helping them remove their gowns and corsets, she had folded the garments and put them into the huge wardrobe. Next she poured warm water over their hands for washing, took down their hair and brushed it thoroughly before plaiting it for the night, and finally laid out their night robes while glancing at the girls frequently to see if she was doing everything correctly. She seemed to speak very little English, if any, so they had rewarded her with smiles and nods of assurance.

When she finally left, Emily looked around the room and sighed. The brass bed looked almost identical to the one she shared with her younger sister. The dark walnut wardrobe with a looking glass between the two doors and the marble-topped washstand could be found in a thousand London houses. "How very familiar everything is. We've come all this distance, and the only exotic note is the head scarf Nuran wears."

Julia laughed softly. "Did you hear Lady Bulwer complaining? She managed to insist that all the servants wear Western clothes, but they were adamant about the head scarves. If she wanted female servants, they could work only in the women's rooms and they had to wear the head scarves."

"The scarf does look bizarre with crinolines, doesn't it? Why does Lady Bulwer bother, do you suppose?"

Julia shrugged. "I expect she is homesick. But Mr. Oliphant said that the sultan has been trying to modernize his empire and wants his subjects to wear Western clothes. Perhaps it's not what she wants so much as what her husband wants."

*Mr. Oliphant?* Had Julia pronounced that name in a tone that hinted at interest? Emily perked up. She was not certain, but she thought there had been slight hesitation that might signify something. She did hope so. Julia had been so sad—more than sad. She had been almost hopeless last fall, showing no interest in anyone or anything. She hid it well, however. A stranger looking at her would never have guessed that she was distressed. One had to know her well to guess that anything was wrong, and even so, Emily did not know precisely what the problem was.

Perhaps Mama had been right to insist on this trip. At least Mr. Oliphant seemed to bring a spark of interest to Julia's eyes.

"It seems we shall have a pair of young men

accompanying us on the way to Mosul. The Frenchman seems quite interesting." Emily curled up in the middle of the feather bed—made from English feathers, she would wager—and tried to look uninterested in Julia's response.

"Do you think so?" Julia frowned slightly. "You should be careful there. I suspect he may be an adventurer."

"Really? That would be exciting."

Julia frowned more sharply. "I'm sure this trip will be quite exciting enough without looking for additional dangers. Do not forget yourself and do something you will later regret."

"What I will regret will be returning to see the same dull people having the same dull conversations at the same dull parties and always doing precisely what is expected. Do you not tire of it all? Every young man I meet seems like every other young man I meet. They all do the same things, think the same thoughts, say the same things. They are so boring."

"Boring? I might not use that word, but yes. There is indeed a sameness in the way they all think."

Emily looked at her friend sharply. Julia seemed to mean more than she actually said. Emily decided to ignore that for the moment. "M. Chambertin," she said, "seems quite different. He doesn't even look English. Well, of course he doesn't." She laughed at herself. "He is French. But it is more than that. He may not be terribly good-looking, but he has a lively countenance and a ready smile. A very attractive smile. He seems to find everything amusing. Since he does not seem to be bored himself, he is unlikely to be boring. And I like the way he moves. He is rather catlike, prepared to pounce if necessary."

"Emily…"

"Now Mr. Oliphant," said Emily, ignoring Julia's frown, "is quite handsome. Indeed, he is almost excessively handsome. Do you not think so?"

"His manner is perfectly gentlemanly." Julia managed to sound slightly repressive, but there was a blush rising on her cheeks.

"Oh, perfectly gentlemanly! You mean he behaves just like a proper English gentleman. How perfectly boring! It would be a pity to come all this way and spend our time with people who are just like the ones we left behind in London." She eyed Julia cautiously.

Julia's head snapped up. "No. People here are not at all like those in London. There is one enormous difference. No one knows me here. And no one knows my mother."

"Oh, Julia, darling Julia!" Emily sat up, stricken. "You cannot be serious. You worry far too much about your mother. No one who knows you at all could possibly think you are anything like her."

Julia gave her a cynical look. "Robby Sinclair?"

She dismissed him with a wave. "You know he was just trying to retaliate on your brother. No one paid him any heed."

"People did, of course. As you said before, they all think the same thoughts. But that is not the problem." Julia's mouth tightened, and she looked away. "I don't know who my real father is."

"Poof. That's nothing. The same is true of half the members of society." Emily waved her hand airily.

"It's not as if your father—the late earl, I mean—was a devoted parent whom you loved dearly. As I have heard it, you rarely saw either him or your mother."

"You don't understand. I am not complaining about the lack of paternal—or maternal—love. I don't care a fig about that. I don't even care that my mother was a notorious whore. Not really. Now that my brother has married your sister and taken over as my guardian, I need never see her again. But because I don't know who might have fathered me, and because my mother claims that she does not know either, I cannot know who his other children may be."

Emily realized what the real problem was. Her hands turned icy. How had she failed to consider this? How could she have been so lacking in perception that she never saw Julia's real fear?

Julia turned to face her and gave a short, angry laugh. "You do see, don't you? Every time I meet a young man I wonder, 'Are you someone I could marry, or are you my brother?' How can I know? Should I ask him if his father knew my mother? That will simply remind him of the scandals. Shall I ask, 'By the by, do you happen to know where your father was in October 1838?' I cannot ask, so I can never know."

"Julia." Emily held out a hand, and Julia grasped it.

"I will never forgive my mother. Never."

# Two

THE SOUNDS OF THE GENTLEMEN RETURNING FROM their formal visit to the palace drifted into the salon where the ladies were having tea. Lady Bulwer, almost completely overwhelmed by her dress of purple and yellow plaid taffeta, tilted her head to listen, and then continued to pour from an elaborate silver tea service. Two handsome young footmen in livery—purple, laced with gold—passed trays of pastries.

Utterly delectable pastries of flaky pastry with some unusual nut, dripping with honey. Emily had to force herself to wipe her fingers on her napkin, when she really wanted to lick them clean. She felt as if she were six years old again, with her nurse insisting that a lady would never lick the crumbs of icing from the plate. Being a lady had many advantages, she knew, but looking greedily at the beads of honey on her plate, she recognized some disadvantages as well.

There were pastry crumbs all over her lap, she noticed, as well as a few more drops of honey. She tried dabbing them unobtrusively with her napkin, but only smeared them. Her mother and Julia were, as usual, immaculate. She did not know how they managed to keep their crumbs from falling all over the place. Did they know some secret to selecting only well-behaved pastries?

"Well, that went quite well, I think," declared Sir Henry, leading the way into the salon. "Abdülmecid was exceedingly gracious. He must have received good reports of you from his ambassador in London."

"I hope so. I fear that my command of French does not equal the sultan's." Lord Penworth shook his head ruefully. "I trust I did not commit any insulting solecisms."

"On the contrary," said Chambertin cheerfully. "You make it that the sultan feels superior. There is no flattery that could be so effective."

That produced a bark of laughter from Sir Henry. "And talk of a railway fits in nicely with his *Tanzimat*, the modernizing reforms he's been trying to bring about. He'd be pleased to see a railway connection to Baghdad and Basra, especially if someone else pays for it, eh?" He rubbed his hands. "Well, now that that's taken care of, I think we could all do with a cup of tea."

Eventually, everyone settled down with a cup of tea. To Emily's regret, Sir Henry dismissed the footmen with their trays of pastries. She consoled herself with the fact that M. Chambertin had immediately come to her side and requested permission to join her. Permission she gave, of course. How could she resist? He had a remarkably attractive smile. Mr. Oliphant, she noticed, did not sit beside Julia, but he did stand where he could look at her without appearing to stare. Clever.

After watching to make certain that the servants

closed the door, Sir Henry turned to Emily's father. "Shouldn't take too long now. The grand vizier will know you have the sultan's approval, and he'll send over the *firman* with no delay."

"Is a firman a who or a what?" asked Emily.

Sir Henry looked at her in annoyed surprise, which annoyed her in turn. Did he think she was unable to speak? Or simply too deaf to have heard him speak? She noticed M. Chambertin's mouth twitching to suppress a grin.

"Yes," said Lady Penworth. "What is a firman?"

Since he could not ignore Papa's wife, Sir Henry huffed, but resigned himself to being asked questions by women and adopted a tolerant tone. "It's an order issued by the sultan, or rather, by the grand vizier in the sultan's name. In this case it will give you permission to travel through Mesopotamia and will require all his subjects to give you any assistance you request."

"How very convenient," said Lady Penworth. "Does it actually work?"

Chambertin's grin could no longer be restrained. "It works quite well in theory. In practice…" He shrugged. "In practice, it depends on how far away the sultan's troops are."

"True enough," Sir Henry said. "That's why Oliphant here will be finding you a reliable *kavass*, an official courier, and he'll make sure he has some troopers with him. That's to make people pay attention to the firman."

"Are you truly determined to make this trip, Lady Penworth?" Lady Bulwer frowned and pursed her lips in distress. "We could make you quite comfortable here at the embassy, and you can avoid almost all contact with those nasty natives. One can go for weeks without seeing any of them. Except for the servants, of course."

"Thank you, but I have no desire to avoid the inhabitants of a country where I am a visitor."

Lady Bulwer did not seem to notice the icy tone of her guest's voice and continued. "The Turks are bad enough, but on your journey you will be forced to deal with Arabs. They are utter barbarians, all of them—dirty, filthy, and completely untrustworthy. You can never believe a word they say, even if you can find one who speaks English. And to expose innocent young ladies like your daughter and Lady Julia to such creatures—I can't believe you have truly considered how distressing it will be."

There was an awkward silence, broken when Mr. Oliphant carefully put down his cup. "You will excuse me," he said, and walked stiffly from the room.

The door had scarcely closed behind him when Sir Henry turned on his wife and burst out, "Blast it, Matilda, can you never learn to keep your fool mouth closed? He's a damned useful fellow, and we need him."

Shaken by this attack, she lifted a hand to her mouth. "I didn't mean… I forgot…"

The visitors all looked confused. Chambertin leaned over and murmured to Emily, "Oliphant's mother is an Arab. I must go to him."

❦

Oliphant was staring out the window when Lucien came into his room. It was a quintessentially English room, Lucien thought. Tortoiseshell brushes on the dressing table, Dickens novels on a shelf—*David Copperfield* and *Bleak House*—and *On the Origin of Species* beside the bed. Nothing out of place, everything in shades of brown, a hard chair by the writing table, and doubtless cold water in the pitcher of washing water. A typical room offered by the British embassy to its British employees and to visitors. Ugly and uncomfortable. He was grateful that he was staying at the French embassy, where one could expect a reasonable level of elegance.

*I will never understand the English. When discomfort cannot be avoided, one must bear it. But to deliberately seek it? Idiocy.*

"Enough, *mon ami*. There is no need to enact a tragedy. We all know that Lady Bulwer is a narrow-minded idiot. Even her husband knows this is so. No one pays her any heed."

"I am not ashamed of my parentage…" He swung around angrily at Lucien's snort of disbelief. "I am not! But I do not wish it to be sneered about by that old…"

Since Oliphant's voice had trailed off, Lucien completed the thought. "Witch? Beldam? Harridan? Hag? You English have so many names for such a creature. Do you have so many of them, then?"

Oliphant managed a laugh, but it sounded more bitter than amused. "We Arabs have even more names for them. Do you have so few of them in France?"

"Ah, no, we have our own surfeit. And some might say that our old men are even worse."

"And so you hide among the Turks and the Arabs?"

"Hide? No. I have no need to hide, and no more

do you. You have nothing to be ashamed of. Why pay attention to silly old fools like Sir Henry and his even more stupid wife? They are nothing. You are far superior to them and should treat them with the disdain they deserve."

"You can perhaps ignore them. I cannot. I must make my life among people like them." Oliphant turned around to face him. "I never attempt to make a secret of my birth. It is just that…" His voice trailed off again.

"It is just that you prefer to speak of it yourself, and not make it sound as if it is something shameful."

Oliphant said nothing.

Exasperated, Lucien wanted to shake his friend. "And you think Lord Penworth and his family think as Lady Bulwer does? If so, you are a fool. You ran off, but me, I saw them when she spoke. They despise her, not the people she speaks of. Not you."

"Fine. They are not the sort to kick the filthy Arab out of their path. They may even tolerate him at their table, and go out of their way to treat him kindly. Do you really think that sort of condescension is better than contempt?" Oliphant swung away and slammed his hand against the wall.

Lucien regarded him silently for a long moment. Finally he said, "I think it is you who treat them with contempt. I see them all. Lord and Lady Penworth look coldly on Lady Bulwer. And their daughter? What she felt was anger. Her hand clenched around her cup, and I thought for a moment that she would throw it at the old beldam."

Oliphant looked at him uncertainly.

Lucien smiled. "Yes. Lady Penworth had to put a hand on her to restrain her. I think you should not judge them too quickly."

"*I* judge them?"

"Is that not what you are doing? And on the basis of what? You assume that they will judge you, despise you, and so you judge them first so you can despise them. Is that not what you are doing?"

Oliphant turned away again. "You do not know what it is like. You have not spent your life among people who feel nothing but contempt for one half of your family or the other."

Lucien shrugged. "No, I have not that experience. But even if you know how the worst behave, why assume that these people are like the worst? Let us give them a chance."

"Ah, but she is so beautiful."

"Beautiful?" Ah, that might explain the depth of Oliphant's distress. It was not the reactions of the parents that concerned him, but the reaction of the daughter. He was surprised to discover that he felt a twinge of annoyance, almost as if Oliphant were poaching. That was nonsense, of course. Lady Emily was nothing to him. A mere acquaintance. Still, he would not have called her beautiful. She was something much better than that. She was attractive, full of life, full of interest. Beautiful was too boring a word for her.

"And the perfection of her demeanor, pale and beautiful as an alabaster carving."

Lucien wondered if there was something wrong with his friend's eyesight. Pale? Lady Emily? She was full of light and color, with hair like dark honey, trying to escape the pins of her coiffure, and eyes of a blue so brilliant he could not find words to describe it.

Oliphant continued softly, "She sits there in utter stillness, as if she is not touched by this world."

That was too much. Oliphant could not be serious. "Are you mad? She is never still, that one. Even when she is sitting there being polite with Lady Bulwer, you can see her toes fidgeting as if she cannot wait to run off on the next adventure."

Oliphant now looked at Lucien as if he had lost his mind. "Fidget? Lady Julia would never fidget."

"Lady Julia?" Lucien stared and then burst into laughter. Of course it was the very proper Lady Julia who would appeal to Oliphant. "*Eh bien*, now I understand. And it is well that it is so, is it not? You have eyes for only one lady, and I see only the other."

Oliphant slumped into dejection once more. "That is all very well and good, but it does not change the fact that Lady Julia is far above me."

"How so? She is a lady and you are a gentleman, is that not so?"

"That is not all, and you must know it. She is the daughter of an earl. Her brother married Lady Emily's sister, the daughter of one of England's most important noblemen. And me? I am the son of an English gentleman who was a minor diplomat, betrayed his family by marrying an Arab girl, and now is forced to live in exile in Cairo."

"And I am a Frenchman, wandering the globe like an adventurer, no? What does it matter? Friends do not concern themselves with each other's ancestors.

We all come together for a few weeks, or perhaps months, and then we will part. Let us enjoy the voyage while it lasts."

"That is easy enough for you to say," said Oliphant with a bitter smile. "No one sneers at your parentage."

"No?" The side of Lucien's mouth lifted in a cynical smile. "Perhaps not. But no one ever knows what problems there are with families, do they?"

That stopped Oliphant, and he took a long look at the other man. "That message that came for you from the French embassy. Was that concerning your family?"

Lucien shrugged. "It was from the *notaire*, the attorney. He is being importuned by some of my relatives, who say I must return and be a good little boy. I write to assure him that he can continue to ignore them."

"A good little boy?"

"That means someone who will obey my *grandpère*'s every order, cater to his every whim. Me, I cannot live that way. I will not." He shook off the thought and grinned at Oliphant. "Instead, we will have an adventure, no? We will cross the mountains in the company of two lovely ladies, and who knows what will happen?"

The next day, after leaving his letter to the notaire at the French embassy, Lucien strode through the streets, barely slowing his pace as he wound his way through the crowds. Amazing, the crowds in this part of the world, at least in the cities. Beyond the cities were vast empty spaces. He slowed his pace suddenly and laughed at himself. Did he think to escape the memory of France and his relatives by walking quickly? He had tried that years before. It did not work.

Enough. That was the past. He would think about what lay ahead, not what lay behind. This trip over the mountains, it promised to be amusing. Lady Emily thought herself prepared for the trip, did she? Her talk of carrying a revolver—he found himself smiling at the memory. If she could actually hold it and shoot it, he would be amazed.

She was not prepared, of course. None of them were, because ladies were never prepared for encounters with the real world. They would screech and squawk and have to be helped over every little bump in the road. It would slow them down immeasurably. But he had no reason to hurry back to Mosul, so he did not mind.

After all, Lady Emily was pretty and cheerful. It would be no hardship to help her over a few bumps. She even seemed reasonably intelligent. If her parents had brought her on this trip, perhaps she was not as ignorant as most of her kind. It might be amusing to talk with a woman whose conversation was not limited to fashion and gossip.

But thinking of fashion, he must speak to them about their clothes. David would be embarrassed to do so, and Lord Penworth would have no way to know—not when his guide to the region was Sir Henry, who knew nothing of this part of the world outside the court.

But those charming gowns the ladies wore would be impossible on the journey. Their skirts were wider than some of the trails they would travel.

They were going to need Turkish garments. He smiled to himself. He would have to make clear he was not talking about the flimsy harem costumes that were the stuff of European fantasies. In reality, the Turks were far more prudish than Europeans in terms of what the women wore. But they were going to need the kind of clothing that would make it possible for them to ride donkeys and horses and go on foot when necessary.

He would have to take them shopping himself. There was no one else to do it, and someone needed to be practical. The *maman* seemed to be a sensible sort of woman. Unlike that foolish Lady Bulwer, Lady Penworth was not affronted by the fact that she was in a foreign country. Lady Julia, however… He made a face. She was a beauty, *sans doute*, but one of those cold, very proper ladies. More beautiful than Lady Emily, perhaps, but it was Lady Emily who intrigued him. She had a bit of a devil in her.

He wondered how long they would manage before they turned back. Three days? A week? He hoped it would be at least a week. It would indeed be amusing to travel in Lady Emily's company.

# Three

THE MARE SHE HAD BEEN GIVEN PICKED HER WAY
carefully around the boulder that protruded into the
trail, never putting a hoof wrong. And wasn't that a
mercy, thought Emily. She was exceedingly grateful to
find herself on a horse who knew what she was doing.
At least today she was sitting on the horse. Yesterday
they had been higher up in the mountains on a trail
that was barely wide enough for someone on foot, and
they had all had to walk, leading the horses and mules.

Here they were, a week from Samsun, and,
according to Mr. Oliphant, they had covered barely a
hundred miles of the five hundred miles to Diyarbakir.
Perhaps she should not have been quite so scornful
when he spoke of the difficulties of the trip. The road
was rising again, and mist shrouded the top of the
mountain, making it impossible to even guess how
much higher they had to climb.

And, she thought ruefully, perhaps she should not
have been quite so scornful of Lady Bulwer's menu
choices. For the past two days, they had dined on
nothing but yogurt and eggs, with very chewy bread

and hard cheese for lunch. She pulled her dark cloak closer around her and shifted slightly to try to find a more comfortable seat on the unfamiliar Turkish saddle. As usual, she failed.

"Cold?" M. Chambertin guided his horse beside hers, smiling with his eyes, the only part of his face she could see. Like all of their party, he had a scarf wrapped over the lower part of his face, protecting against the bitter chill of the cloudy day.

"Not at all," she lied. After all, it wasn't as if anyone could change the temperature, so there was no use complaining about it.

Irmak, the Ottoman kavass who was in charge of this expedition, turned around and gave her a disbelieving look. It was also a disapproving look, but she was growing accustomed to that. Irmak seemed to be censuring everything about her all the time. She had found it intimidating at first, but she was growing accustomed to his enormous curving mustache and heavy brows, so she smiled back at him. He gave a snort of something that might have been laughter as he turned away. Perhaps he was not really so disapproving. It might be those eyebrows that made him look so fierce. That and the mustache.

Making an effort to be positive, she turned to M. Chambertin. "These garments are remarkably comfortable. It was sensible of you to insist that we acquire them." Indeed, the layers of garments that the Turkish women wore actually were comfortable, probably the most comfortable clothes she had ever worn, at least in public. However, she couldn't help feeling as if she had simply wrapped herself in the contents of the laundry basket. There seemed to be no effort made to ensure that the different parts of the outfit—she had no idea what they were called—matched or even harmonized. She doubted they were at all becoming. They might even look dowdy.

Except, of course, on Mama and Julia. They managed to look stylish, even elegant, in second-hand garments that made no pretense of fitting. But while her collection of whatever these things were called just hung about her like clothes on a line, theirs made them look as if they were swathed in exotic raiment. How did they do it?

The scarf across her face, though—she did like that. It was called a *yashmak*, she had learned, and left only her eyes uncovered, so it should make her look mysterious. She hoped it did. Mysterious would certainly be better than dowdy. She cast a sidelong glance at M. Chambertin.

He was laughing, drat him. And he managed to look quite dashing in his voluminous cape.

"Insist? You cannot be serious. You think I insisted to Lady Penworth? I doubt anyone ever does that. Fortunately, your mother is a woman of great good sense and can see reason."

"Yes. Mama is not one of those silly creatures who put propriety before safety and comfort. We could hardly travel over these mountains wearing corsets and riding sidesaddle."

"And her daughter is also a woman of good sense." His eyes suddenly looked serious. "It is not simply a matter of comfort as we ride. Robed as we all are, it is not immediately obvious that we are Europeans.

Anyone observing us cannot be certain that we are infidels. They must approach nearer, and by the time they can identify us, we can identify them. There are those in these mountains who would seize on any reason to attack strangers, but they prefer to attack those who will not fight back."

"But we have not seen a soul in all the time we've been riding except when we come to villages."

"That does not mean no one has seen us." He pulled down his scarf a bit to smile at her, unnecessarily. She could easily see his smile in his eyes. "I do not mean to frighten you, just to make you careful. Accompanied as we are by the kavass and his soldiers, there is little danger that anyone would attack us. But you must never wander off on your own."

She gave a snort of laughter and looked around. "I am in a wilderness of rocks and trees in a strange country where, I am told, wolves, bears, and wild boar abound. I have no idea where I am, and aside from the bitter cold, the sky looks as if there may be a storm at any time. Do you really think me the sort of fool to leave the protection of this company?"

"No, I do not think you a fool at all. But the warning is not only for this mountainside. Throughout this journey, whether we are in mountains or in villages or in cities, nowhere must you go alone."

"Nowhere?" She raised her brows skeptically.

"Nowhere," he said firmly. "Irmak is already distressed that I am speaking to you. Since you are the daughter of an important man, a bey if not a pasha, you and the other women should be guarded and kept from the sight of men. He is inclined to think that he should cut off my head for my impertinence in riding beside you, but your father does not seem to object. It confuses him."

She started to laugh, but the laughter faded when he did not join in. "You cannot be serious. You expect me to shut myself up in the women's quarters? The *hareem*?"

"No, no." He did smile now. "I would never suggest anything so foolish. I only ask that you be prudent. This world is very different from England." He smiled more broadly at the irritated noise she made. "Yes, I know. That is why you have come here, because it is different. But it is not always easy to recognize the ways in which it is different. One must step carefully to not give offense without intending it. And it is even harder for women. I do not ask you to shut yourself away. I only ask that you take care."

She felt irritated, more irritated than she should. It was sensible advice, no different, really, than the advice her mother had given her before her first diplomatic dinner. Did he think she was an idiot? She kept her eyes turned straight ahead and concentrated on the trail as it proceeded on its zigzag course through spruce trees and patches of snow. Snow in April. Well, that was different. "Are you giving the same advice to my mother and to Julia?"

"I would not presume. Lord Penworth is a wise man, and a well-traveled one, I think. He will know how to give your maman advice without ruffling her feathers as I have ruffled yours. Lady Julia seems to be possessed of a decent sense of caution, and in any case, Oliphant will watch out for her."

She nodded.

"You are not angry?"

She considered briefly, then made a face. "No. It's sensible advice. I was only annoyed that you thought I needed it."

"Ah, for that I apologize. I was not certain. You understand?"

That made sense, she supposed. He did not know her well enough to trust her common sense, so she said, "Fair enough."

"*Bon.* Good. We are friends then? *Copains?*" He offered a smile with the question.

"Copains. That means comrades, doesn't it? I like that. We're comrades." She put out a hand, and they shook on it. "And since we are copains, you may call me Emily."

His smile broadened. "I am honored. And my name is Lucien."

Copains. She liked that idea. She had never had a young man want to be her friend, not since she had been a child and she and her sisters had run free with their brothers' friends. Now that she was a young lady, she no longer had friends, at least not male friends. She had suitors, boring young men who flattered her in hopes of receiving her father's patronage. Foolish young men who patronized her, thinking she was as stupid as they seemed to think all women were. One day she would have to marry one of them, she supposed. What else was there for her to do?

But M. Chambertin—Lucien—was offering to be her friend. Friends were equals. Friendship was something truly special, something of extraordinary value. And she would value it. Oh yes, she would value it.

Besides, there was the fact that he was a very attractive young man. Not handsome, no. But definitely attractive, especially when he smiled. His smile was really quite dashing. It held the promise of excitement—of danger, even.

Best of all, she liked the idea of being friends with an adventurer. Someone who was not at all like the young men she had known all her life.

Ahead of them, Irmak and three of his men led the way. She glanced back. Julia was riding with Mr. Oliphant, both of them silent as usual. It was amazing how straight they both sat on their horses, no matter how long they had been riding. Straight and silent and unsmiling. She wanted to poke them.

Then came her parents. They brought up the rear not, she knew, through weariness, but simply so Papa could keep an eye on everyone. And they were not really the rear. Behind them were half a dozen more troopers and a string of mules carrying their luggage.

They looked a sorry lot. All of them were wrapped in dark cloaks, masking any hint of fashion. Even the troopers had gray capes with hoods covering those odd red hats they wore that looked like inverted flowerpots. Could anything be further from a carriage ride in a London park or a railway journey from Victoria Station? It was strange and foreign and so very different.

Precisely what she had wished for. Well, an adventurer's friendship was more than she had dared hope for, but as for the rest? She must remember to be a bit more careful with her wishes. A slightly higher level of comfort would be nice. That thought made her laugh at herself. In a few months, she would be back home, safe in her little cocoon, with all the comforts possible. This was her chance—probably her only chance—to see a bit of the world outside the confines of proper English society, to have a bit of adventure, to discover what she was capable of. She was determined to enjoy it, discomforts and all.

❦

Two weeks later, her feelings about this adventure had encountered a few ups and downs. That, it occurred to her, was a suitable phrase for this trip across the mountains. Twists and turns would do as well. Or highs and lows. What it had not been was boring, and she was rather pleased with herself. Throughout, she had behaved sensibly. Not only had she not complained, but she had coped. She had not humiliated herself by being a burden for the others and requiring assistance. She had been equal to every challenge the trip presented.

There had been times when they rode through sheets of blinding rain, with howling winds trying to hurl them to the ground. Then they would round a bend in the road—or trail—and find themselves in bright sunshine, so warm—no, so *hot*—that their cloaks dried in minutes. They traveled over barren sheets of rock, where a few tiny sprigs of green clung to life. They crossed a ridge and saw spread below them a broad cultivated valley, green with new crops in fields and orchards bright with blossoms. Through the valley ran a river with the town spread out on either side.

The contrasts along the route had been fascinating, but Emily could not deny that she was grateful for the power of the firman. Wherever they stopped, Irmak presented it to the mayor or governor or whoever was in charge, and they were immediately welcomed as guests into the best house in town. Everyone was bowing to her father and calling him *effendi*. She and, she suspected, all the others were especially grateful for this after the night when there was no town and they had been forced to take shelter in a deserted village. A blanket strung up between crumbled walls provided some privacy for the women, but they still had to sleep on the ground, wrapped in blankets that smelled of horses, using their saddles for pillows. And if the ground hadn't been hard enough in the first place, pebbles seemed to creep along and lodge themselves under her hips.

It had not been a bed she would ever choose, but she could not deny that the absence of a roof meant that the stars had been spectacular. Also, it was pleasant not to be shut away for a change. That was beginning to be tiresome.

In every town or village where they stayed, Emily, her mother, and Julia, along with their maids, Nuran and Safiye, were hustled into the women's quarters as soon as they entered the house where they were staying. It was disconcerting, and the first time it happened she had opened her mouth to protest. Lucien frowned at her, and she realized later that this was precisely what he had meant by his little lecture. Mama and Julia had obviously been given the same lecture, because they offered no objection. She fumed in silence, but saw the sense of it. As a guest in someone's house, it would be the height of rudeness to flout their customs. But it was frustrating.

Mama noted her annoyance at being shut away, and she pointed out that they could console themselves that they were being given a glimpse of Ottoman society that the men would never see. That was probably true, but an even greater consolation was the comfort of the women's quarters.

It wasn't just the comfort of soft cushions and warm braziers, welcome though those were after a day atop a horse. The rooms were fascinating. The first night they stopped in the village of Kavak and stayed in the house of someone who seemed to be the mayor or some such. It was a small village, and it was a small house. The mayor looked extremely nervous, but to be fair, she had seen that most people looked nervous when Irmak began barking orders at them. Especially when Irmak was backed by a troop of armed horsemen.

They entered a paved courtyard, and the women were immediately ushered up a staircase to a balcony looking down on the courtyard. A door opened for them, and a curtain was drawn aside so they could enter.

Emily had never seen a room like this. She gaped— she was sure of it. Julia, who could maintain perfect, impenetrable poise under all circumstances, sucked in an audible breath. Even Mama stumbled slightly.

In one sense the room was bare. There were no

chairs or tables placed around. The whole center of the room was bare. The far side of the room was a large bay window, but shuttered with a sort of carved lattice, letting in the last of the daylight but making it impossible to look out unless you were right up against it. And making it impossible for anyone to look in, as well. That was probably the point of it.

But the room was filled with color. Around three walls there was a sort of deep bench, covered with rugs and heaps of cushions—brightly patterned cushions in a rainbow of colors. Strong colors—deep reds, blues, greens. No delicate pastels here. A pair of brass lamps with panels of red glass hung from brackets on the walls, though they had not been lit yet, and an ornate brazier warmed the room.

Three women stood there, all dressed in loose tunics and wide trousers. The one in the middle seemed to be the lady of the house, since her blue tunic was elaborately embroidered in arabesques of green and yellow, and she wore a headdress from which gold coins dangled. The other two women were more simply dressed, also in tunics over loose trousers gathered at the ankles, but without embroidery and without jewelry.

They all smiled at each other uncertainly. Emily was feeling rather grubby after a day on horseback and felt as if she looked a lot worse than the servant girls. Their hostess seemed to be trying to assess the status of her visitors.

Safiye, as maid to Lady Penworth, took charge of communications. She was an older woman, of an age with Lady Penworth, with a small but round body. Her lack of height in no way detracted from her sense of importance as maid to the wife of an English pasha. None of them were quite sure what she said, but the word *pasha* appeared quite often in her introductory speech, and their hostess seemed to be suitably impressed.

Once they were out of their cloaks and scarves and boots, their hostess led Lady Penworth to the corner of the room and gestured for her to be seated on the bench. The other two women, who seemed to be servants, brought basins and pitchers of hot water that was poured over their hands. Small tables were set beside them, and coffee was brought in tiny cups.

Since Safiye and Nuran spoke very little English, and the English women had no language in common with their hostess, communications were limited to smiles and gestures. These were, on the whole, sufficient to create an atmosphere of friendly comfort, especially since Lady Penworth had taken care to include in her baggage small gifts for the women—lace scarves and mitts, tins of biscuits, and bars of Pears soap in tissue wrappings.

But it was frustrating, this inability to speak directly to anyone.

❧

Lucien checked the girth on his saddle as he did every morning before they rode out. It was the sort of precaution he was accustomed to take, living among strangers in strange lands. He had become accustomed to doing the same with Emily's saddle, though he did not care to examine his reasons for doing so too closely. She was, after all, a friend, and she probably would not have known to check the girth herself. It was not that he was mistrustful of their Turkish escort, but the servants had no particular reason to feel protective of the foreign women.

With a private smile, he noticed that Oliphant also checked his own and Lady Julia's saddles.

This morning, before even the troopers had mounted, Emily appeared, pulling Julia along with her to join Lucien and Oliphant. "Mr. Oliphant," she said then paused. "Really, this formality seems excessive on a journey like this one. Please allow us to address you as David, and in return you may call us Emily and Julia." Lucien stifled a smile. He could see Julia dart her friend a shocked look, but Emily looked as if such informality were entirely ordinary.

"I would be honored," the invariably punctilious Oliphant managed to say in a somewhat strangled voice, carefully not looking at Julia. Those two avoided each other's eyes so carefully that the attraction between them could not be more obvious. From the sparkle in Emily's eyes, she too knew which way the wind was blowing.

But she was as careful as he was not to comment. Instead, she said, "Now, we have a request to make of you gentlemen. We have found it somewhat embarrassing to be unable to converse with our hostesses, and, as I understand it, this situation is likely to continue. Could you teach us enough Turkish phrases so that we will be able to at least greet the people whose guests we are? And to thank them?"

He and Oliphant exchanged startled looks. Oliphant said carefully, "You wish to learn Turkish?"

"We will probably need Arabic as well, won't we?" Julia added. "That is what will be spoken once we reach Mosul. Or am I mistaken?"

"No, you are not mistaken." Oliphant looked at Julia with an odd expression. "But you do realize that Arabic and Turkish—these are not precisely fashionable. Most ladies do not learn such languages."

"Nor are they easy languages to master," added Lucien. "Most Europeans, not just ladies, do not see the need."

"We are not such fools that we think we can master the languages in a few short weeks," said Emily, frowning in irritation. "But surely it would be courteous of us to at least make an effort."

Irmak had come out and was frowning and moving about in an effort to get everyone mounted and on their way, rather like a particularly fierce sheepdog. Obediently, they all mounted up and followed where he led on a road, or rather a path, that led out of the riverside village before winding up another mountain.

When the path widened sufficiently to ride two abreast, Lucien joined Emily. "Your maman, she approves of this?"

"This? This trip, you mean?"

"No, no. That you should speak with the women of the house where you stay. That you should learn their language."

"Of course she approves." Emily looked at him in surprise. "Why would she not? It was her suggestion that we try to learn enough of their language to at least thank them for their hospitality."

Lucien shook his head in bemusement. These

English ladies were a constant surprise. Had the world changed so much in the years he had been away? Or was England so different from France? Perhaps it was his grandfather who was so different. "You know, do you not, that these women are not of your class? That they are peasants, or at best a step up from that?"

"All the more reason for courtesy," she said firmly. "We are being foisted on them willy-nilly. I doubt they would choose to have us for guests, but when Irmak rides in, waving the firman, would they dare refuse?"

That picture was worth a smile—anyone daring to ignore Irmak, but Lucien still felt uncertain. They rode in silence for a while before he said, "You are of the English nobility. My grandfather would say that these villagers—peasants, he would say—should be grateful for the opportunity to serve you."

"And my father would say that our wealth and position mean that we should never take advantage of those less fortunate," she snapped. "I do not wish to speak ill of your family, but I do not care for your grandfather's attitude."

"Me, I do not greatly care for it myself." In fact, he disliked it very much, and so had his father. It had been the cause of much stress in the house when he was young. "To be polite, I must remind myself that my grandfather is very old. He remembers the *ancien régime*. He is a boy still when the Revolution arrives, but old enough to see friends and family go to the guillotine during the Terror, and he does not forget. He does not forgive. But that was long ago, and the world has changed. He finds it hard to accept this."

He had not intended to talk about his family. He had not done so in years, but he felt a need to tell Emily about them. At least a small bit about them. So he said, "He and my father fought often. After my father died, I was not comfortable living in my grandfather's house."

"And your mother?"

He shrugged. "She died when I was young, ten years of age. That was not many years after we went to live with grandpère."

"Are you the only child?" She sounded surprised.

He felt surprised at the question. "Yes. You think that unusual?"

"Well, I suppose it seems so to me because there are six of us. I have two sisters and three brothers, and we did seem to fill up the house when we were children. It must be lonely to be the only one. Have you no other family?"

He did not want her pity, so he employed that useful shrug again. But he did answer. "There are cousins, a few aunts, an uncle. Unlike my father, they are all obedient to grandpère's wishes and, like him, they see me as disobedient, lacking in respect." He could remember those dinners, those interminable dinners, with all the family sitting stiffly at the long table, grandpère at the head of it, and all of them, even his little cousin Annette, staring at him in silent disapproval. Though grandpère's disapproval rarely remained silent for long. "The final explosion came when grandpère announced that he had arranged a marriage for me with Mademoiselle Fournier, the daughter of a neighboring family."

"You did not care for her?" Emily asked cautiously.

"There was nothing about her to care for or not care for." He shook his head. "She was…she was docility personified. If her papa said, 'Stand up,' she stood up. If he said, 'Sit down,' she sat down. Just like a dog, no? If I claimed that the sky was green, she would agree. If I said that the sun rose in the west, she would agree. She had no thoughts of her own. She simply embodied what was expected. It was as if she did not really exist.

"In short, she was precisely what my grandfather thought a wife should be, exactly like my grandmother and my aunts. They do what is proper and fashionable, they say what is proper and fashionable, and it is as if they have no desires or opinions of their own." He looked at Emily, riding beside him on a small mare, a sure-footed mount, yes, but not a beautiful one, not elegant. A sensible horse in these mountains, but not the sort of horse one would ride on parade in Paris. And Emily herself, sensibly bundled up in a shapeless cloak as cheerfully as if such a thing as fashion did not exist. He could not imagine Mlle. Fournier in such a situation. Or his aunts or cousins. The mere suggestion would doubtless have them in a swoon.

He offered a prayer of thanksgiving that he was here with Emily beside him and not at La Boulaye, where everything was dedicated to enhancing the importance of grandpère, and every penny that did not provide splendor for him went to restoring the chateau to its former glory.

Emily's voice broke in on his thoughts. "Were they unhappy marriages, your parents' and your grandparents'?"

Unhappy? He had never truly thought about it. But now that he looked back... "Not unhappy, no. No one complained, they did not fight, there was no shouting. But there was no happiness either. The husband was always polite to the wife, and the wife was always obedient to the husband. It was not like the marriage of your parents, but it was what they seemed to expect. It is what was planned for me."

"But it was not what you wanted for yourself, and so you refused the marriage. What about Mlle. Fournier? Was she dreadfully upset?"

Had she been upset? He had never given that aspect of the matter any thought. But no, she could not have been. Why would she be upset? She might not even have known about the plan. "Such a marriage would have been as cruel to her as it would have been to me," he said. "I would have been constantly demanding of her what she could not give, and I could never be the kind of husband she expected. That grandpère does not understand this, that goes without saying. He cares only that she brought a rich dowry. When I refuse, he says things, we both say things that should not have been said. Since my parents were both dead by then, there was nothing to hold me. And so, I departed."

"Goodness." She looked at him with sympathy.

"That was five years ago," he continued.

"Five years!" She sounded shocked now. "Five years without seeing your family?"

"To not see my family, this is no penance. They carry with them heavy chains, demands and obligations, nothing more." He looked at her, so sad and solemn. Her family seemed to be a very different proposition. Could she even imagine what it was like to live with all that fear and seething resentment as they all trembled before his grandfather?

"Do you not grow homesick?"

He gave an insouciant shrug. Did he? Perhaps. But only a little. "Not for my grandfather's house, not for La Boulaye. But sometimes when the desert is so very hot and dry and everything is brown, I think about the days when I was a small child, when we lived at Varennes, in the house of my mother. Or even later, when she would take me back there on visits from time to time. I remember sitting on the riverbank, under the shade of an oak tree, holding a fishing rod while she sat and watched me. But then I think to myself of all the places I have not yet seen. Samarkand. Is that not a wondrous name? It conjures up mystery and adventure, an unknown world. I think I must see Samarkand. And follow the ancient Silk Road to China through the Gates of Jade. Another wondrous name, is it not?"

He must not forget all the places he planned to see, all the wondrous, intriguing places in the world. That was what he wanted—to see for himself all those cities that were such fascinating names on the map.

It was dangerous, riding beside Emily, talking with her. More than dangerous. It was a distraction. She made him start to think about other things, the things he had given up, the places he had once known. He must not think about such things. They had been left behind when he made his decision years ago. Leaving them behind had not been a loss. He had chosen to free himself from their chains. He would not submit to the tyranny of his grandfather.

Just then they crossed a ridge, and the barren cliff along which they had been riding gave way to gentle hills dotted with herds of goats. On the south-facing slopes were orchards just coming into bloom. Peach trees. He could almost smell the blossoms. After the wild trail they had been following, it looked peaceful.

Emily pulled up her horse to look. "How beautiful," she whispered.

Yes, it was beautiful. It reminded him, somehow, of home. The spring sun bringing the orchards to life, just like the sun on the vineyards of Burgundy.

Ah, she was dangerous. He had not thought of his home in years. She made him remember the years of his childhood in Varennes. It had not been a bad childhood. In those years they had managed to keep their distance from grandpère. Or perhaps in those years grandpère had been less obstinate, less tyrannical. Or perhaps he himself had simply been too young to know about the battles.

It did not matter. For better or for worse, the past was past. He had made his choice. There was no going back.

# Four

THE LAST VILLAGE HAD BEEN UNEASY. NO ONE HAD
been unfriendly, but there had been none of the
innocent curiosity Emily was accustomed to. They
had been greeted with all the customary phrases and
gestures, but it was perfunctory, as if the villagers
were going through the motions while looking over
their shoulders for something. Even the village itself
looked uneasy. The market square was deserted long
before sunset, and there were no men gathered there
to talk and drink coffee. In the silence of the night,
she could hear soft voices calling to each other from
the rooftops.

The unease had infected their party as well. They
had mounted quickly that morning, with none of the
usual laughter and joking comments from Irmak's
troopers. They had been riding quietly for several
minutes before Emily noticed.

Whatever had upset their party in the village had
not been left behind. The unease was traveling with
them. Not only were they riding much closer to each
other than usual, with none of the troopers talking

cheerfully or suddenly darting off in search of game, but all the men—Lucien, David, even Papa—were riding with their rifles across their laps.

There had been no explanation offered, so one would have to be demanded. Emily spoke in an undertone to Lucien. "What is going on? What are you not telling us? What are we supposed to be afraid of?"

His mouth lifted in a half smile, but he continued to scan the rocks surrounding them. "We are not telling you anything so that you will not be frightened. Irmak insisted on it. Your papa and I did not think it would work."

"Well, now that I am frightened, will you please tell me why? Is it whatever frightened the villagers back there?"

"You noticed that too? Why am I not surprised?" He shot her a quick glance before he turned back to the rocks. "This is Kurdish territory, but those villagers back there, they are not Kurds." He stiffened, fixing his eyes on a crevice in the rocks, but there was no movement. He eased back. "One of the shepherds did not return yesterday evening. When they went out to look for him, they found his body. He had been murdered."

She was not going to panic, she told herself. She was not going to shriek. She was not going to show fear at all. She was going to remain calm. It took her a while to be reasonably certain she would not squeak when she tried to talk, but eventually she achieved that level of control. "What makes them think he was murdered?"

He snorted. "Believe me, they knew."

"But why blame the Kurds?"

"Have you not seen the Kurds? They bristle with weapons. They are warriors, always ready to fight. They do not like being ruled by the Ottomans. They do not like Turks. They tend to kill those they dislike."

"What has that to do with us? We are not Turks or Ottomans or anything except visitors to this part of the world."

"We are Infidels. The Kurds also dislike Infidels. And Arabs. They dislike Arabs. And when they run out of other people to dislike, they dislike other Kurds."

"That's ridiculous."

"You must remember to tell them so when they ask for your opinion," he said dryly.

She sniffed, but held her tongue. The tension was affecting her. She found herself scanning the cliffs above them. So intent was she that she did not realize at once that the riders in front had stopped. Fortunately the little mare noticed before she ran into anyone. Irmak and his men began to move again, slowly, and then halted once more. When they went around a curve she saw why.

Ahead was a fork in the road. Blocking one side were five horsemen. Kurds. She recognized the huge turbans wrapped around high hats that the Kurds all wore. The one in the middle wore a bright red tunic. All of them had curling black beards, and all of them were heavily armed with ancient rifles, at least two pistols apiece, powder horns, ramrods, cartridge cases, curved daggers resting in their sashes, and each one carried a spear at least ten feet long with a wicked-looking point and, incongruously, a bunch of feathers tied to it.

They did not smile.

Lucien was not smiling either. No one was smiling. That was more intimidating than the weapons. She had grown accustomed to smiles. All the villagers seemed to greet newcomers with smiles, though the ones directed at Irmak and his troopers were nervous smiles. And even though Irmak frequently scowled, his men spent much of their time laughing and joking.

David moved up to the head of their party and spoke to the Kurds, presumably in their language since it sounded unfamiliar. The man in the red tunic looked over the rest of their party before replying—rather curtly, it seemed to Emily. David spoke again, and a rapid exchange followed. David was the recipient of fierce glares from the Kurds, but he received them impassively. Eventually, Red Tunic made a guttural noise—half laugh, half sneer—and the Kurds wheeled and rode away.

No one moved until they were quite out of sight. When David finally relaxed in his saddle, the others all did as well. He rode back, followed by an approving look from Irmak and smiling remarks from the troopers.

"Thank you," said Papa, who rode up to greet him. "I see your diplomatic skills are even better than Sir Henry promised."

David flushed, but Emily thought it was a pleased flush. "The Kurds are not foolish. They could see that we are a strong enough force to defeat them. So I simply asked if this is the right road for Diyarbakir."

"Isn't it?" Mama asked curiously. "I didn't know there was any question about the route."

"There isn't." David smiled, beginning to relax. "I have been here before. But people are always pleased to give advice and directions. And in this case they added a few sneers about Turks who could not find their shoes on their feet."

The rest of that day's journey was quiet enough, but still tense. Even after they left the mountains and were crossing a high plain, no one was willing to relax completely. It was with an almost audible sigh of relief that they came within sight of Diyarbakir.

Not that Diyarbakir was a particularly welcoming sight at first. The city, encircled by high black walls studded with huge round towers, loomed up on a cliff at the edge of the desert with no sight of green. If this were a fairy tale, Emily thought, Diyarbakir would be the castle of the wicked ogre, but at least it looked powerful enough to keep threatening Kurds at bay.

As they drew closer, they could see that the cliff fell off down to the Tigris River, its banks edged with palm trees and the slopes covered with gardens full of blossoms and new leaves. This made the city seem a trifle less ominous. Once they were within the walls, the city was remarkably clean and bright, its streets unusually broad. While this was encouraging, Emily could not fail to notice that Kurds made up a large portion of the population, striding about the streets, each one with a hand on his rifle or dagger. Since no one else seemed to feel threatened by this, she decided to keep her misgivings to herself. Perhaps it was only habit that kept their hands so close to their weapons.

Their host for the next few days, until Irmak arranged transport down the river for them, was an Armenian merchant named Najarian. He had traveled sufficiently to be acquainted with European customs, so, for a change, the ladies were not kept so strictly in the women's quarters.

That did not mean there were no restrictions. The women dined in the same room as the men but were seated at the far end of the table. Too far for them to be able to take part in the conversation. Emily took some comfort in the discovery that she could at least listen to the men's discussion and did not have to wait for the next day when she could ask Lucien for an account.

Not that the conversation was precisely comforting. She had known, of course, that the Ottoman Empire contained a great many nationalities within its borders. She had not realized that even after all these centuries they were still so mistrustful of each other.

Mr. Najarian, for example, as a merchant, might be expected to welcome a railway to ease the difficulties of trade. However, he had decidedly mixed feelings on the subject. His first thought was that it would aid the movement of the sultan's troops in their efforts to keep the Kurds in check. That he considered a good thing. His second thought, however, was that a slight change in mood in the capital would mean that a railway would aid the movement of the sultan's troops should they decide to exterminate the Armenians. He did not seem to consider this a far-fetched notion.

This was a way of looking at things that had never occurred to her. She tended to assume that the world was a reasonably peaceful place, where one felt reasonably safe and secure. Even here. After all, the Ottoman Empire had been around for so many hundreds of years that she thought of it as more or less settled.

Mr. Najarian's remarks did not worry her, precisely, but she did notice that her father looked more thoughtful than usual.

After dinner they all sat in the courtyard. Although darkness had fallen, the air was not yet chilly. A few oil lamps were set about, casting flickering shadows but doing little to dispel the darkness. She was grateful when Lucien came to sit beside her. She had grown accustomed to his presence and felt warmed by his nearness. He had become someone she could talk to easily, so she mentioned her uneasiness to him.

He shook his head and smiled. "Is this part of the world peaceful and settled? No. Few things on this earth are ever settled. And while the Ottoman sultans may have ruled for many centuries, in much of their empire the rule is more fiction than fact. The local pashas pay little attention to the sultan's decrees. They obey if it is convenient. And if it is not..." He shrugged. "As for the Arab tribes, the Bedouins—they do not think that anyone rules them."

"None of that is particularly comforting."

His smile widened. "You need not have any fear. They may prey on each other, all these pashas and all these little tribes, but they do not harm Europeans. Partly it is because we have no part in their ancient feuds. We are irrelevant. But even more, I think, they consider the danger too great. Not only would the sultan be angry, but the European governments would be angry. And the European troops have much bigger guns than the local tribes do."

She raised her eyebrows. "In other words, they will not harm us because Queen Victoria might be annoyed?"

"They would not put it quite that way."

"No, I don't imagine they would. How many of them have even heard of Queen Victoria?"

"Now there you might be surprised. Stories travel swiftly, and a woman ruling over a great nation—there is a tale worthy of the Scheherazade."

"Unbelievable, you mean?"

"No, no, because there are many to assure them that it is true. And that in turn impresses them. A woman who is so powerful that men obey her? The very thought inspires fear!"

They laughed together, and Emily did feel reassured. So she told herself. But perhaps it was simply Lucien's nearness that comforted her.

She would think about that another time.

## Five

EMILY WASN'T QUITE SURE WHAT SORT OF CRAFT SHE had been expecting when David and Lucien announced that they had arranged transportation on the river for the five-day trip to Mosul. Nothing quite as large or elaborate as Papa's steam yacht, of course. That was big enough to carry them from London to Constantinople. Still, in her imagination she had pictured something like the pleasure boats people took on the Thames.

She had not expected this.

Floating placidly on the river in front of her were half a dozen rafts. Not boats. Rafts. Rough wooden platforms sitting atop some sort of balloons. Three of them were piled high with their baggage and two had tents covering half their area.

To make matters worse, Lucien was standing next to her, all too obviously enjoying her reaction.

She couldn't help it. The best she could manage was a question. "What are those?"

"They are called *keleks*," he said, as if that were an adequate explanation.

"They are keleks," she repeated. "I seem to have asked the wrong question. What I should have asked is, where is the boat to take us to Mosul?" There had to be a boat, didn't there? After all, Mama and Papa were standing there quite calmly, and so was Julia. Calmly, but not looking around for a boat.

There wasn't going to be a boat.

Lucien hadn't warned her because he had been looking forward to her confusion. That could not be allowed. She was not going to look like a timid little fool. She smiled with as much confidence as she could muster. "Rafts then. That should be exciting."

He threw his head back and laughed. "Well done, my lady."

She took a closer look at them. The tents were well supplied with cushions and a brazier. For heat, she supposed, but also perhaps for a bit of cooking. The braziers were adequate for making tea or coffee, she had learned, or even for cooking a meal of sorts. But what on earth were those balloon things the wooden platforms were sitting on? She asked.

"Inflated goat skins," he replied promptly.

She looked at him incredulously.

"No, no," he protested, "I do not make a joke. They truly are goat skins. And indeed, it is a most practical arrangement. There are some two hundred of them for each raft, so if one of them is torn by a rock, the journey can continue with no problem. And to find another goat skin for a replacement is never a difficulty."

"Inflated goat skins. How…clever."

"It is a most ancient way to travel on the river.

For thousands of years, rafts like this have been on the Tigris."

"Thousands of years." She tried to imbue her words with a semblance of enthusiasm. "Mama must be ecstatic."

He grinned. "So she says. And now your papa confers with our captain."

A tall cadaverous man with a bushy beard loomed over Papa, which was not easy to do. Papa was a tall man himself. The bearded man was wearing a sheep-skin coat and one of those high hats wrapped around with cloths to make an enormous turban.

Emily's eyes widened. "He's a Kurd."

"Indeed." Lucien nodded in agreement.

"But you have been telling us how dangerous the Kurds are."

"And that is why people hire them for the trip to Mosul. The river is by far the easiest way to travel, but it winds through territories the Kurds consider theirs. If we travel on rafts captained by Kurds, the other Kurds are more likely to leave us in peace." He took her hand and tucked it under his arm. "Do not distress yourself. We will keep you safe."

"I'm not frightened, just confused. You seem to keep telling me contradictory things."

"Yes, I fear that is the way of it here. Someone who is a friend today may be an enemy tomorrow. It is necessary to always take care."

Why was it, she wondered, that men always seemed to feel it incumbent on themselves to warn women of the dangers of the world? Did they think it made them look braver? Or did they think women were too foolish to recognize danger when they saw it? After all, when she encountered a scowling man brandishing a spear and carrying assorted weapons, she was hardly likely to think him meek and mild.

So it was that she boarded the raft with a mixture of irritation and nervousness. However, they were not long under way when she found herself entranced by this mode of travel. It was remarkably comfortable to sit on the heaps of cushions while gliding smoothly over the water. Each raft had two oarsmen, who did not so much propel the boat as guide it along the current while a captain directed them. It was a simple arrangement, but worked well. Obvious, she told herself. If it didn't work well, it would not have continued for thousands of years.

She was not the only one who found it enjoyable. Julia managed to unbend a bit from her perfectly upright posture, and Mama leaned back and sighed happily. They looked like a pair of Oriental princesses, reclining there. They had removed their cloaks, and their tunics and other garments draped gracefully over them. Emily looked down at herself. The fringe on her sash had gotten caught in the knot and there was a mysterious stain on her tunic. She couldn't imagine what she had spilled on herself.

"Such bliss," said Mama. "It is such bliss to not be on a horse, to sit on something soft."

Papa smiled at her. "No one would have known you were not enjoying every minute of it."

"Well, there was no point in complaining when there was nothing to be done about it, was there?" She reached up a hand to Papa and when he took it, pulled him down to sit beside her.

Lucien snatched up one of the cushions and tossed it on the ground so he could lounge at Emily's feet, looking completely at home. It occurred to her that he was rather like a cat in that way. He could manage to make himself at home in all circumstances. That was doubtless useful for an adventurer.

"They like each other, your maman and papa," he observed.

"Of course," she said. It seemed an odd comment.

"Ah, do not say 'of course' so easily. It is not so ordinary, you know."

"Well, it's hardly unusual."

He looked at her quizzically. "You think not? Consider the married people you know. Do they have this liking between them?"

She laughed. "Well, my sister Elinor and her husband—Julia's brother—certainly do. And my brother Pip and his wife."

"They learned, perhaps, from your parents. Me, I have known far more like Sir Henry and Lady Bulwer."

She made a face and he laughed.

"What of your own parents?" It was an intrusive question, but she couldn't help being curious.

He gave that Gallic shrug again. "When I was small, yes, perhaps, but I do not know truly. I do not remember them together. If I was with one of them, the other was not there. After a while we went to live with my grandfather, but my father and grandfather were always fighting. My grandmother was there too, but she was of no importance to my grandfather. She always obeyed him and always worried about what he might want, and grandpère, he accepted. This was what he expected, you see, that his wishes were all that mattered. My grandmother wanted my mother to make my father obey grandpère too, but I do not think my mother could have made my father do anything, even if she desired to attempt it. I think perhaps maman died when I was young just to get some peace."

"How sad. For them and for you." It was sad. More sad than she knew how to say.

"Ah, no, not for me." He grinned up at her. "Not sad at all. It means that I am free to explore the world, to go to all those places with the beautiful names."

"Samarkand. The Gates of Jade," she said. But she still thought it terribly sad. He was free to be an adventurer, but freedom of that sort meant not caring about others and having no one who cared about you. It was not a freedom she would choose. But perhaps he did not really have a choice.

For all that he sounded eager for adventure, she could hear a note of sorrow in his voice. Or was that only her imagination? Emily did not think so, and she longed to comfort him.

*❧*

They stopped to camp each evening, since the rocks and wind made it impossible to travel on the river in the dark. The servants gathered wood for a fire and cooked a dinner in a large pot—rice, with bits of mutton and vegetables seasoned with aromatic spices.

The Kurds were obviously startled when the English ladies not only ate with the men but were served first. Lucien heard the servants explaining that this was indeed the custom of the English pashas, and in their country the sultan was actually a woman with no one above her. The Kurds shook their heads in disbelief. He must remember to tell Emily about this. It would amuse her.

The ladies themselves made an effort to conform to local customs, washing their hands in the running water of the river and eating with the fingers of their right hands only. And they did not turn up their noses at the simple fare they were offered. Lady Penworth even brought out her newly learned Arabic phrases to praise the cook for his efforts.

"Can you imagine what Lady Bulwer would say to this?" Lucien asked Oliphant with a laugh.

But Oliphant did not share his amusement. "Lady Bulwer feels it necessary to maintain her position," he said, his voice holding more than a trace of bitterness. "These ladies are so assured of theirs that they have no need to assert it. They are so high up that the difference between a chimney sweep and a mere gentleman is indistinguishable."

"Oliphant…" Lucien shook his head in exasperation.

"No, it is true. They know who they are and are comfortable with it. There is no uncertainty." Oliphant paused and looked sharply at Lucien. "You too. You have that same assurance, that same comfort. Who are you, really?"

That was an uncomfortable question. Lucien shrugged it off. "*N'importe.*"

Oliphant's mouth twisted in a sour smile. "That's right. It isn't important—for you. But for some of us…" He left the circle around the fire and strode off into the darkness.

There was no point in following him. When he was in this black mood, wallowing in his unworthiness, there was no talking to him.

It was foolishness as well. From what he could see, Lady Julia was quite as taken with Oliphant as he was with her. Everyone in the Penworth party seemed to be aware of this, and no one seemed to think there was any problem. If he was not mistaken, Lady Emily had taken it upon herself to arrange the order of the march so that Oliphant and Julia regularly rode together, with no objections from Lady Penworth.

He smiled to himself. He had no objection to this arrangement either. Riding beside Emily had been nothing but pleasure.

Back in Constantinople, he had considered himself fortunate to be able to attach himself to Lord Penworth's party mainly as a matter of safety. He was willing to deal with danger when it presented itself—and it had presented itself often enough over the past few years—but he was not such a fool that he must seek it out. Traveling with an English nobleman would provide a measure of safety. Enough safety, he expected, to make the trip almost boring.

When they set out, he had assumed that he would be riding with Oliphant, and he had looked forward to the trip. Oliphant was, perhaps, a bit stiff and cautious, always careful to be proper. But once he relaxed, he was an intelligent companion. Conversation with him was usually interesting, and he was grateful to have such an amiable companion for the journey.

Lady Emily had been a surprise.

Oh, he had been pleased to encounter her at the

embassy. She was pretty enough and full of life. It was enjoyable to flirt with her. Even once he discovered that she would be one of the party going to Mosul, he had not expected anything beyond a mild flirtation. That was the most he had ever enjoyed with the ladies of his acquaintance in France, who were interested in no conversation more profound than the latest gossip. As for the women of the Ottoman Empire, they were no different from the ladies of France, too ignorant to converse on any topic. Were the English different, or only Emily?

From where he stood at the edge of the camp, he could see the three ladies. They did not sit on the ground, but the troopers had fashioned seats for them from the saddles and bundles of something or other. The firelight was dancing over Emily's face as she turned this way and that to make sure she did not miss anything. They all wore scarves over their heads, but he could see a few locks of Emily's hair peeking out as if impatient to be free.

He had never known someone like Emily. There were women with whom one could enjoy an interesting conversation in the salons of Paris, but these were artists or courtesans or married women of scandalous reputation. Emily was indubitably a lady, and an innocent young lady at that. She was something outside his experience. In France, someone like her would be so closely chaperoned that she would never be allowed to exchange more than a few platitudes with a man outside her family. They would try to turn her into Mlle. Fournier, and that would destroy her.

Did Emily even know any platitudes? He had

certainly never heard her converse about the weather
other than to laugh about it when a storm tried to
blow them off a mountainside. Nor had she fussed
about the damage the dust was doing to her wardrobe.
Come to think of it, he could not recall her ever
making a fuss about her clothes.

She had looked quite lovely in the gowns she wore
in Constantinople, gowns that were assuredly in the
height of fashion and without doubt the sort of thing
she was accustomed to wearing. A trifle mussed, to be
sure, with her hair trying to escape its pins, and never
quite so elegant as her maman and Lady Julia. But
attractive. Most attractive. Yet she had not hesitated to
don Turkish garb, and in that she looked quite adorable. As she did now, sitting by the fire.

He stared at her for a few minutes longer, watching her hands wave about as she recounted some tale
to her mother. He turned away and walked off into
the darkness along the riverbank. He felt restless. It
was doubtless the enforced inactivity on the raft. He
walked quickly, or as quickly as it was possible to walk
in the dark. Not really dark, not with the moon and
stars providing their light. There were cliffs on one
side, a wall of blackness, true, but on the other side was
the river, wide here, and rippling with moonbeams.

He stopped to watch the river. There was something fascinating about water. One could watch it
forever. A river was always changing, always new, full
of surprises.

Emily was like that.

When they first set out and he found himself riding
beside her, he had thought that he had been assigned

by her father to reassure her, help her over any difficult spots, and generally hold her hand. To his surprise, none of that had been necessary. What he needed to do was respond to a barrage of questions, some practical, some abstract, some about things that required thought, and some that he was unable to answer at all.

She was interested in everything—the scenery, the villages, the people, the sights, the sounds, the smells. She noticed everything, and her comments were sharp and perceptive and amusing. He found himself seeing things he thought were familiar in a new way.

In short, he enjoyed talking with her. He did not think he had ever enjoyed conversation with a woman before. They had become friends. It was a novel experience for him, being friends with a woman.

It was not that he did not notice how attractive she was, how nicely formed. He was not a blind man, after all. Even in the loose Turkish garments, when she removed the enveloping cloak, the sash circled a small waist, and it was clear that she was nicely rounded both above and below. And when he lifted her from her horse, she felt just right in his hands.

Yes, she was attractive, but he had found other women attractive, and he had found them often enough over the years. This was different. He liked Emily, and this liking was something new for him.

# Six

ON THE FOURTH DAY, THEY WERE FLYING ALONG ON A swift current beneath a brilliantly clear sky. Cliffs of broken yellow stone rose a hundred feet or more on either side of the blue river. The colors were so vibrant that the scene looked as if it had been painted by a child.

Emily had left the tent, and Lucien began to turn to her to share his thoughts on the scene when he saw a puff of smoke and a glint of metal by one of the boulders on the cliff. At that moment a bullet plowed into the deck beside him, and he heard the shot.

He flew across the feet separating them to knock Emily to the ground, covering her with his body. "Keep down," he ordered when she tried to raise her head. More bullets fell about them, most splashing into the river. He had his pistol in his hand, but he could not see a target on the cliff. The Turkish troopers on the next raft were firing away but not to any useful purpose that he could see.

Meanwhile, the oarsmen on their raft, who had first dropped their oars in a panic, were now working madly to keep them from being dashed against the rocks as the current swept them around a curve. The skipper joined them, shouting encouragement, until a bend in the river had them out of sight of their attackers. As the wild rocking of their craft ceased and they resumed their placid drift, Lucien became aware of his more immediate surroundings.

To be precise, he became aware of Emily lying beneath him. A warm, soft Emily lying beneath him, a situation his own body found most agreeable. Her breasts were pressed against his chest, and he was positioned between her thighs. She was so soft, such a perfect match for him. She did not appear to be distressed by their position, for she was making no effort to extricate herself. Did she understand what their position was? Could she tell just how agreeable his body found this position? Because his body was reacting most strongly to this juxtaposition.

She was looking up at him with an expression of dazed surprise. He wondered if he was looking at her with the same expression. Her hands were sitting on his shoulders, not pushing him away but not drawing him down. Just touching him. Her lips were parted ever so slightly. In surprise? In invitation? He was close enough to feel the damp warmth of her breath. He was overcome with longing and began to lower his mouth to hers.

An outburst of noise called him to himself. The captain of this fleet was roaring with laughter, and Oliphant was bellowing at him in fury. Lucien hastily pushed himself up and helped Emily to her feet.

"You are all right?" he asked. "You are not hurt?"

He wanted to check, to make sure she was not injured, but he hesitated to touch her. An hour ago, he would not have hesitated, but things were different now. Everything was different. He stood there, looking at her uncertainly.

"I am fine. I must thank you for protecting me." She was ignoring the shouting to the side of them and looking at him still with that dazed surprise.

A remarkably unruffled Lord Penworth came up to calm the shouting. "Mr. Oliphant, would you be so good as to tell me what is going on? Are we to expect more attacks of that sort?"

No, Lucien saw, his lordship was not unruffled. He was seething with cold fury.

Oliphant looked thoroughly ruffled and glared at the captain. "This buffoon says that was not a serious attack and we have no need to worry."

The captain was grinning and looked decidedly unworried. Lucien wanted to hit him.

Lord Penworth took a deep breath as if to control himself. "Not serious? You will forgive me if I find bullets flying inches from my family to be a matter of considerable seriousness." It was a sentiment with which Lucien heartily agreed.

There was another exchange in the Kurdish language between Oliphant and the captain. The captain's remarks were punctuated by roars of laughter which seemed to provoke Oliphant to bursts of fury. When Oliphant seemed on the verge of throttling the captain, the Kurd softened his laughter and made placating gestures.

Oliphant turned to Lord Penworth. "He claims that

it was not a serious attack because no one was injured. They fired on us only as a sort of warning because the Turkish troopers are with us."

That was the first time Lucien had ever seen Lord Penworth lose control. The marquess turned a look of fury on the captain and appeared ready to strike the man. "You were aware that the troopers were part of our party but never mentioned that they might be a source of danger. You assured us that with you and your men conducting us, we would be safe."

There was another exchange of translations, and Oliphant, tight-lipped with fury, bit out the reply. "He says that if he had not been here, if they had not seen that you were protected by Kurds, they would not have missed."

Lord Penworth spun about and stood motionless, his hands clenched, before stalking into the tent to join his wife. Lucien realized that he himself was trembling, whether with anger or relief he was not certain. It took a moment before he brought himself under control enough to lead Emily in her father's wake. He held out his arm, and she laid her hand on it, very lightly, very formally. They did not speak.

Within the tent, Lady Penworth was sitting composedly and greeted them with a brilliant smile. "Mr. Oliphant," she said, "I believe I owe you an apology."

"An apology? Whatever for?"

"When you said this trip would be difficult, I thought you were one of those tiresome gentlemen who think a woman exhausts herself on a stroll in the park. I had no idea it would be so exciting."

He flushed. "It is I who should apologize. I should

have made clear to Lord Penworth how difficult it would be. And how dangerous."

"I am to blame," said Penworth, taking his wife's hand. "I dismissed the warnings, relying on the assurances of the vizier, who said the mere presence of the troopers would ensure our safety. Had I listened to Mr. Oliphant, I would have made arrangements for you to return to England or at least remain safely in Constantinople."

"Nonsense, my dear," said Lady Penworth, patting her husband's hand. "I wouldn't have missed this for the world!"

"No more would I," said Emily, leaving Lucien's side to join her mother.

Lady Julia, whose cheeks were flushed becomingly, said, "Indeed, it is the most exciting thing I have ever experienced."

*These women were mad.*

Lucien turned away and went outside to seethe. Did they not realize what danger they had been in? Emily had been walking toward him. Had she been a step closer, that bullet would have plowed into her, not into the deck. And they were calling this *exciting*?

He walked to the front of the raft, where the wind might blow away some of the turmoil inside his head.

He did not understand what had happened to him. It was some sort of temporary madness—that had to be it. He never acted impulsively. Always he thought before he acted, even in danger. No, *especially* in danger. It was a cool head that had gotten him out of ticklish situations from Morocco to Persia.

If he had thought about it, even for a second,

he would have gone to the protection of the ladies. Naturally. There was no doubt about it. He was not a scoundrel, after all. He would have behaved just as the others—Oliphant and Lord Penworth—had. At least he assumed that was how they had behaved. He had not actually seen them.

No. He had not seen anyone. That was because the moment that bullet struck the raft, his only thought had been to protect Emily. It had not even been a thought. It had been pure instinct.

This was not permissible. He could not allow himself to be ensnared. He would not be tied down, chained by obligations and responsibilities.

No, that was unjust. She had made no effort to ensnare him. She had used no wiles. That was what was so dangerous. She was a pretty girl, yes, with that dark honey hair and that soft, luscious body... No. He had known pretty women before, beautiful women. None of them had caused him to stop thinking.

It was that she used no wiles. She did not even try to tempt. There were no little wiggles, no pouting lips, no sidelong glances or fluttering lids. She did not even tilt her body to display her lovely bosom. It was her directness and her honesty that were the danger.

She had offered friendship, and he had welcomed it. It had been a pleasure to ride beside her in friendly companionship. He had not seen any danger.

But of course! That was it! That was the explanation. She was a friend, and naturally, when danger threatened, he immediately sought to protect his friend. There was no need to think of this as romantic or sentimental or any of that sort of nonsense.

Assuredly she was an attractive woman, but that was beside the point. He noticed this because she was his friend. If he noticed that her eyes were a particularly vivid blue, sparkling with excitement at every new discovery, that was of no more significance than the fact that Oliphant had dark eyes. He thought for a moment. Oliphant did have dark eyes, didn't he? Yes, he was almost certain of it.

*N'importe.*

She was a friend. That was all there was to it. And as for that rather embarrassing way his body had reacted—that had nothing to do with Emily. It was just that she was a woman and he was a man. One's body had these reactions, after all. It was just nature. There was no need to think there was anything else to it.

He heaved a sigh of relief. She was a friend, and in a month or so, she and her family would depart, and he would be on his way to distant places. He would travel the ancient Silk Road. He would go to Samarkand, Tashkent, Kashgar, and on into China through the Pass of the Jade Gate. He would continue on his adventures.

But he did not return to the tent.

❧

Inside the tent, Emily joined her mother and Julia in making light of the attack. Poor Papa looked so upset that they could hardly do anything else. At least it provided a distraction, and she sorely desired a distraction.

What had happened earlier? Lucien was her friend. She liked him and enjoyed his company, but she didn't understand quite what had happened.

Well, of course she knew what had *happened*. Those ridiculous Kurds had fired shots at them, and Lucien had thrown her to the ground and thrown himself over her to protect her. It had been very brave and gallant.

But then something else had happened.

She should have been feeling bruised and crushed under him, but she didn't. She had liked the feel of his body lying on hers. She had liked it very much. She could not remember ever having liked anything quite that much, certainly not in quite that way. It felt *right* somehow. In fact, she had wanted to pull him closer.

His mouth had been just above hers. She could feel him breathe, and she could have sworn he was about to kiss her. Or she was about to kiss him. Perhaps both.

Then David had startled them into awareness by shouting at the captain. She did not know whether to bless him for that or curse him.

All she knew was that when Lucien sprang away so abruptly, she felt bereft. She had lost something she had not even known she wanted.

# Seven

SOMEONE MUST HAVE BEEN WATCHING FOR THEM,
because when they arrived in Mosul, Mr. Rassam,
the British consul, was at the dock to greet them. It
was one of the odder moments of their journey. Mr.
Rassam was a native Assyrian, an olive-skinned gentleman sporting the kind of fiercely exuberant black
mustaches Emily had seen on many of the Ottomans.
At the same time, he was dressed in perfectly proper
morning clothes, complete with a black frock coat and
a black silk hat.

He was the only one so properly dressed.

She and Mama and Julia were all still wearing
their Turkish garments and were enveloped in the
blue robes that seemed to cover all the women in
this part of the world. Those robes were beginning
to feel a bit stifling under the hot afternoon sun, but
Lucien had warned that the robes were necessary any
time they were out of doors, and that the black veils
would be a good idea as well. The men had left their
heavy cloaks behind with the cold in the mountains
and were wearing loose brown jackets, trousers,

and boots, along with low-crowned broad-brimmed brown hats to protect them from the sun. They looked thoroughly relaxed.

Nonetheless, Mr. Rassam greeted them with punctilious formality, and Lord and Lady Penworth responded in the same manner. It was amusing, really. Her parents might have been at a diplomatic reception at Buckingham Palace for all the attention they paid to their somewhat disreputable attire. Emily hoped that this did not mean that the restrictions of society were closing in once more and the adventures were over.

However, it was probably just as well that Mr. Rassam had come to meet them. Mosul was far larger than any of the other towns they had seen after leaving Constantinople, much too large for Irmak to simply wave his firman and expect everyone to jump. And David Oliphant had never been here before. Without Mr. Rassam present to meet them, they would have had to rely on Lucien to guide them, and Emily did not want to rely on him—or have her family rely on him—at present.

She was feeling decidedly ambivalent about Lucien at the moment. Ever since that—that what? That rescue? That half embrace? That almost-kiss? Ever since that whatever-it-should-be-called, he had been avoiding her. True, she had tried to avoid him at first, but by the time they stopped for the night, she had gathered together her courage and her manners and tried to thank him for protecting her. But he had brushed her thanks aside as if it embarrassed him.

Did he regret almost kissing her? And if so, why? If he regretted it because her father was a marquess and he was just an adventurer, well, that was foolish of him. Admirable, perhaps, but foolish.

If, on the other hand, he regretted it because he thought she was too forward and was trying to trap him, then she was thoroughly insulted. She was Lady Emily Tremaine and while she might not be the most beautiful young lady in English society, she had more than enough suitors already and certainly had no need to entrap anyone.

At the moment, what she wanted most of all was some privacy to think about all of this. She was uncertain about his feelings, but also about her own. She had never felt quite this way before, and she needed time to think about it all. One would think that desolate mountains and wild rivers would provide not just privacy but solitude, even isolation. But no, they had all been thrown together so completely on the journey thus far that a thought could not cross her mind without someone noticing and commenting.

"Are you not feeling well?" Papa was looking down at her in concern.

That was precisely what she meant. Could she not even ignore her surroundings for a moment without comment? She put on a cheerful smile. "I'm fine, Papa. Just a bit tired."

He patted her on the shoulder. "Well, there is no need for you to worry anymore. Mr. Rassam tells me that he has a house prepared for us, and we should be settled there in no time at all. All safe and sound. No need to worry anymore about Kurds."

Kurds were the least of her worries, but she probably should not say so to her father. She managed to smile again, and noticed that Lucien was helping David deal with their baggage. Keeping his distance, as he had ever since the shooting. Well, if he could keep his distance, so could she. Was he as confused as she was? She certainly hoped so. She disliked this uncertainty, especially this uncertainty about her own feelings.

Everything was somehow topsy-turvy. No one was behaving normally. She was keeping a tight rein on herself while Julia was relaxed and laughing, Mr. Rassam, who was an Assyrian, was dressed like an ever-so-proper Englishman while Papa looked almost like a ruffian in his slouch hat and loose coat. People were shouting all around her, and she could not understand a word.

Nothing seemed familiar. Even the faces of the servants who had been with them all through this journey—Nuran, Safiye, and Zeki, who was Papa's manservant—blended so well into the crowd that they seemed like strangers. Irmak was barking orders at his men as usual, but without his usual confidence. The troopers seemed to be swaggering, the way men do when they are unsure of themselves.

Emily felt unsure herself. She allowed herself to be bundled along, settled on a donkey, a rather odiferous donkey, and led through noisy squares where everyone seemed to be shouting and then down dark, narrow, silent streets—alleys, really. These were lined with buildings protected by heavy doors and with mere slits for windows. Nothing penetrated here, not the clamor of the squares, not the glare of the sun. An unwelcoming place, but then every town they had entered had looked unwelcoming, built to defend the residents rather than to greet newcomers.

She was tired. It had been no mere excuse when she told her father so. Last night she had found it difficult to sleep. No, not difficult. It had been impossible to sleep, and it had been equally impossible to get up and pace around to relieve her restlessness. That would have had her parents hovering over her in concern and asking questions she couldn't answer. So she had spent the night tossing and turning and reliving the attack. No, not the attack. She had to stop trying to hide from her own thoughts. What kept her awake was the memory of Lucien's body. And the memory of her own body, reacting in a way she didn't understand. What had happened to her?

She felt herself flushing every time the memory returned, and it kept returning. She didn't know what was wrong with her. It wasn't as if she had never been close to a man before. Well, not in that position, of course. Blast! She could feel that flush rising again, and she was grateful to be wrapped in the voluminous blue cloak that hid her face as well as her body.

Emily had been close to other men. Of course she had. When she danced, there had always been partners who pulled her too close. And there had been gentlemen who tried to embrace her—two gentlemen, anyway. One particularly vain peacock and one old friend who had decided it was time to settle down and thought they might suit, being old friends and all.

Those encounters had been tiresome and annoying. None of them had made her feel anything like the way she had felt with Lucien. She didn't even know quite how to describe the way she had felt. She was a practical, sensible young woman. She was not the sort to get swept away on a tide of passion like the heroine of a romantic novel.

Was it a tide of passion? She wasn't even sure. What was a tide of passion like? And why would it be called a tide if it was creating this heat, this fire inside her?

She came to herself abruptly and found herself no longer on the donkey. She was inside a house and her mother and Nuran were helping her out of her clothes. She tried to protest, but her mother shushed her as if she were a baby, and before she knew it, she had been washed, her hair had been plaited, and she had been inserted into a clean nightgown and tucked into bed even though it was not fully dark yet.

At least now she could think in privacy, she thought, just before she slipped into a deep, dream-less sleep.

❧

Lucien arrived at a house a few streets away and was admitted by Hamiz, who ran the household. He promptly took charge of Lucien's baggage, chattering a welcome and declaring the entire household ecstatic over his return. Too tired to respond with equal enthusiasm, Lucien asked for the whereabouts of M. Carnac. The information he brought was not what Carnac had hoped for, and he wanted to deliver it as soon as possible. What he would do then, he was not sure, and that uncertainty was vexatious. He was not accustomed to uncertainty.

"*Lucien! Vous êtes de retour!*" A young woman came flying down the staircase and threw herself on him.

He staggered slightly and laughed as he held her away from him. Speaking also in French, he said, "Yes, Mélisande, I am back, as you see."

"We did not expect you so soon. Did you go to Paris? What was it like there?" She hung on his arm and gazed up at him, her face shining with excitement.

"No, no, only to Constantinople." He patted her hand. "I will tell you all about it later, but run along now, little one. I must speak with your papa."

With a flash of temper, her face settled into its familiar little pout and her grip tightened on his arm.

"Now, now, none of that," he admonished, "or you will not have the journals I obtained for you."

"The journals—you found some? *Le Follet? La Mode Illustrée?*" The pout shifted into excited delight.

He nodded, extricating himself from her grip. "But first I must speak with your papa."

He crossed the courtyard and knocked on the door of the room Carnac used for an office but did not bother to wait for a reply. Carnac was always too immersed in his studies to notice anything as trivial as a knock on the door.

Sure enough, there he was, hunched over his desk, peering intently at a piece of clay. Light from the single window focused in on the desk in a narrow beam, leaving the rest of the room in obscurity. Tables large and small, cabinets and shelves all were covered with irregular heaps of what Lucien knew to be bits of clay tablets covered with cuneiform inscriptions. If Carnac had heard Lucien enter, the oblivious old man gave no indication. He sat immobile, his disordered hair and bristling beard so covered with dust that he seemed at one with his artifacts.

Although tempted to simply leave, Lucien forced himself to move forward until he could reach out and tap Carnac on the shoulder.

"Eh?" The old man lifted his head slowly, peering over his glasses. "What…? Ah, Chambertin, you are back. And so soon. That means good news, does it not? How much funding have they offered?" He smiled hopefully.

Lucien wished he had some way to soften the news. "I regret, the answer was no. There is no money."

The look of dismay on Carnac's face was everything Lucien had feared. "No money? They cannot mean that. You mean there is no money right away. There will be money later. That is it, no?"

Lucien shook his head. "I spoke with the ambassador several times. He regrets it, but there is nothing more he can do."

The old man shook his head in disbelief. "I will write more letters. I will write again to the director at the Louvre, to the emperor himself."

"The ambassador has written to them all himself, and he has had replies from them. The answer is always the same. There is no money to continue with the excavations here."

"But the emperor—surely he can see the glory for France…"

"The emperor least of all. He is too busy with Mexico, with Cochinchina, with all the rest of the world. He has little interest in the distant past. What money they have at the Louvre goes to Greece or to Egypt."

"Greece. Bah. Statues of pretty boys." Carnac had managed to get to his feet and had removed his apron. He looked around and eventually found his coat draped over a piece of bas-relief. He snatched it up and pushed himself into it as he stumbled from the room. Lucien reached out a helping hand, but Carnac shrugged it off in irritation. "No, no. I must think. We will talk later."

With a shake of his head, Lucien went off to his own rooms to collect some clean clothes. Then off to the baths, where he relaxed in the steam, had pitchers of water poured over him, drank coffee, gossiped with acquaintances, and tried to not think about Emily. He failed.

❧

Dinner at the Carnacs' no longer seemed bizarre to Lucien, any more than Mélisande's costume did. She had managed to create for herself a voluminous skirt that seemed to have been cobbled together from several different garments, and her blouse was covered by a vest she swore was just like one she had seen in *La Mode*. She looked very like a child playing dress-up, which, he supposed, she was.

They sat on chairs at a table, eating with forks and spoons that Mélisande had discovered in the market a few years ago. The room, opening onto the courtyard, held not only the table and chairs, but also two padded chairs and a European oil lamp. That was really too much furniture for the small room, but it was the only one on the ground floor that had not been taken over by clay tablets and broken statues. Mélisande claimed that it was a French parlor, and it was her pride and joy.

The food, though, was that of Mesopotamia—rice with some vegetables and an occasional bit of meat. This evening, the rice had almonds and raisins as well as onions and lentils and a bit of mutton, all seasoned with a good bit of cumin, cloves, and a dozen other spices. Emily would approve. He smiled at the thought. Odd that this meal should now seem ordinary, when it was so different from the wine-laced sauces and mustard-flavored dishes of Burgundy. He scarcely missed them, he told himself, though he did miss having wine to accompany his meals, and perhaps a brandy afterwards.

He especially missed the wine today.

Carnac brooded in silence at the head of the table, but Mélisande chattered away about the articles she had found in the journals Lucien had brought for her. There had been an account of a grand Parisian reception in *Le Follet*. "When I go to school in Paris, I shall see all these people when they promenade in their beautiful clothes in the parks and on the grand avenues." She smiled blissfully. "And one day I shall take my place among them. You will see."

Her father scowled at her and turned to Lucien. "Hamiz tells me that you traveled with an English party."

"Yes, that's right."

"English!" Carnac said it as if it were a curse, and perhaps for him it was. He had not forgiven the

Englishman Layard for the fame he had received, fame Carnac thought belonged rightfully to Botta and the French. Nor had he forgiven the English for the collection of Assyrian artifacts that Layard had sent to the British Museum, or for the ones Rassam's brother Hormuzd had sent there.

He perhaps had a point there, Lucien acknowledged, since Hormuzd Rassam's successful excavations had been conducted in the section allotted to the French. However, it seemed unbecoming for a man who claimed to be interested in nothing but scholarship to focus so much on fame. And also, Lucien had listened to far too many diatribes on that subject. They had already become boring months ago. He started to stand and excuse himself.

"Wait," Carnac commanded. "These English, they plan to excavate?"

"Not at all. Lord Penworth is here at the behest of his government to consider the possibility of building a railroad from Basra and Baghdad to Constantinople."

"He is not a scholar then?"

"No, though his wife is interested in antiquities."

While Carnac returned to brooding, Mélisande perked up. "An English lady? She is fashionable, perhaps?"

"Very elegant, I would say. And she brings with her two young ladies not too much older than you, her daughter and a friend." Why was he telling them this? Emily and her family—they were safe here now, and the adventure of their journey from Constantinople was over. There was no need for her to see him again. He had no right to intrude on them.

Mélisande's eyes widened, but before she could speak, her father raised a hand to silence her and demanded, "He is important, this English lord?"

"Important?"

Carnac waved a hand impatiently. "His government, men of that sort. They think him important?"

"Yes, I believe so. The ambassador in Constantinople seemed to think him important, and the sultan as well."

"And he is rich?"

"One of the richest men in England, I am told." Lucien regarded Carnac warily. He was not sure he liked the direction in which this seemed to be heading.

"Good." Carnac smiled in satisfaction. "You will call on him. I will go with you. And I will invite him to see the excavations. His wife will be impressed, and so he will be impressed, and then he will provide the moneys I need to continue."

"I am not sure…" Lucien began uncertainly.

Carnac held up a hand. "It is decided. Those fools in Paris, the Louvre, the emperor, they should have supported me. Now, so much the worse for them. The glory will go to England. We will go first thing in the morning." He stood and marched out of the room before Lucien could object.

Mélisande jumped up in excitement. "And I will go too. They will know all about fashion, the young ladies, and about balls and parties. And they will be able to tell me if it is true, what they write in the journals. Oh, Lucien, thank you!" She flung her arms around his neck and kissed him before snatching up her journals and running off.

There was less enthusiasm in Lucien's expression as

he remained at the table sipping his coffee. Mélisande was in many ways a delightful child, but she must be what, fourteen? Not really a child any longer. And her mother had died four years ago, or something like that. He had been told, though he had not paid much attention when he arrived last year. Still, she should not be here in Mosul. There was no life for her here. Carnac should have sent her back to France when her mother died, not kept her here to keep house for him. He could have sent her to his family or to her mother's family. There must be some family somewhere, and if not, he could at least have sent her to school as he kept promising he would.

Carnac's obsession with Nineveh had aroused Lucien's admiration when he first arrived. He thought it praiseworthy dedication. Now he was no longer so certain. When he ignored his daughter's needs, when he was not even aware that she had needs, this was not so much dedication as utter selfishness.

Was it a good idea to introduce her to Lord Penworth's household? He did not doubt that Emily, and Julia and Lady Penworth as well, would treat her kindly and try to put her at her ease. Emily, he was sure, would never mock the girl for her bizarre clothing and manners. But Mélisande was not a fool, for all her lack of education. She would see immediately the difference between the world she had grown up in and their world, the one she read about in the ladies' journals that were her only reading material. Differences that were greater than she realized.

Would Carnac too see the differences? Would he see the difference between the way a man like Lord

Penworth cared for his family and his own behavior? For Mélisande's sake he hoped so, but he doubted it. Carnac was not stupid, but he was obtuse and oblivious to everything outside his studies.

Lucien should, of course, call on Lord and Lady Penworth in any case. They had been kind enough to allow him to travel with them. The least he could do was make certain that they were well settled in and see what he could do to be of service to them. That also meant he would see Emily, but that was not his object in calling. Not at all.

# Eight

THE SUNLIGHT COMING THROUGH THE FRETWORK OF the shutters made an interesting filigree pattern on the tile floor of the sleeping chamber. It was the first thing Emily noticed, and it had worked its way into a dream in which it was the pattern of the magic carpet on which she was escaping from Lady Bulwer, who kept insisting she would never reach the Gate of Jade. Or something like that. It all tumbled into confusion as she blinked her eyes open.

She had obviously spent a restless night, since she was on her stomach with her legs tangled in a coverlet, her head and arm dangling over the side of the bed. That, no doubt, was how it had come about that the first thing she saw was the pattern of sunlight on the floor. She blinked some more, shook her head to get rid of the dream remnants, and focused on her surroundings.

They were extraordinary surroundings, similar to the apartments in homes where they had stayed, but far roomier and far more luxurious. Apart from the wooden shutters with their complicated curlicue cutouts, there were ottomans and cushions covered in glowing silks, a small table with what looked like mother of pearl inlays in an intricate, delicate pattern of geometric shapes, and an entire wall of cabinets, all of them decorated with more carvings and inlays. The bed itself had sheer silken draperies in a rosy shade suitable for a fairy-tale princess. And the air was filled with a sweet floral fragrance. Was it perfume?

She rose and went over to the window, moving quickly because the moment she stepped off the silky carpet, the tile floor was cold under her bare feet. The shutters were firmly fastened, and she soon gave up trying to open them. Peering through the cutouts, she could see a low balcony wall entwined with a vine covered with white blossoms. Jasmine. That was the source of the lovely scent. Beyond that she could see the tops of trees. The courtyard had made little impression when she arrived yesterday but must be grand indeed to have such large trees in it. The sun was just appearing over the flat roof of the building, so it must still be early.

Her stomach growled. Early or not, she was hungry. She had gone to bed—or been put to bed—so early yesterday that she had missed dinner, and she really wanted something to eat. But this was a strange house. She not only didn't know where things were, she didn't know who else was here. It probably would not be a good idea to go wandering around in her nightdress and wrapper. She eyed the cabinets optimistically.

It was as she hoped. While she slept, the elves—or more likely Nuran—had unpacked her baggage and put everything away. The poor girl must be exhausted, and Emily hoped she was having a good long sleep this morning.

Out came a chemise, petticoats, stockings, garters, her old half boots. Her hand hovered over a corset, the one she could fasten herself, and she took it out along with hoops. She dressed quickly, ending with a skirt and bodice in blue-and-white-checked muslin. The lightweight garments were in need of pressing, but that couldn't be helped. She brushed out her hair, twisted it into a neat chignon at the nape of her neck, pinned it into place, and examined herself in the long mirror that stood in a corner of the room.

The familiar sight of Lady Emily Tremaine looked back at her, the proper young lady who was the daughter of the Marquess and Marchioness of Penworth, the young lady who was perfectly at home in the parlors and ballrooms of London. The boring parlors and ballrooms... She suppressed that thought. She needed the familiarity of her usual appearance. The novelty and excitement of the journey had been exhilarating, and more novelty and excitement awaited, she was sure. But the encounter with Lucien—the very close encounter—had thrown her off balance. It was as if some stranger was inhabiting her body. She needed assurance that she was still herself while she tried to decide just what that encounter had meant and what she thought about it. Looking like herself might help.

But first she needed to find something to eat.

Sometime later, when Lady Penworth entered the

courtyard, her daughter was sitting on the side of the fountain in the dappled shade of an overhanging tree.

"Good morning, Mama." Emily waved at a tree. "The one in the corner over there is a lemon tree but this one and the others are all orange trees. And this is Shatha. She is the cook and makes the most delicious soft, flat bread." She smiled at the small woman dressed in multicolored garments who was bent over a brazier on which something sizzled with an appetizing meaty smell.

Lady Penworth smiled at the cook and nodded her head in greeting. "*As-salaam alaikum*," she said, pronouncing the Arabic greeting carefully.

Shatha beamed back and bowed. "*Wa alaikum assalaam*," she said. What followed was a spate of Arabic that sounded to be questions. When the only response was blank looks, she popped up and directed Lady Penworth to sit on a bench in the shade of the loggia that surrounded three sides of the courtyard. She placed a folding table beside her, which was in no time filled with bowls of yogurt and dried fruit, boiled eggs, and a plate of steaming bread.

"Have some bread and honey," Emily said. "The honey is incredibly delicious." She was trying to be her usual cheerful self, but given the peculiar look her mother was giving her, perhaps she was not entirely successful.

However, Lady Penworth did not make any comment. She did, however, beam with pleasure when Shatha produced a steaming pot of tea and some cups. "Would you care for some?" she asked, as she filled a cup.

"Yes, thank you." Emily accepted the cup gratefully and breathed in the aroma, the familiar aroma. She frowned in puzzlement. It was a *very* familiar aroma. She looked at her mother in surprise.

Her mother nodded. "You are quite right. I brought the tea from home, not knowing what might or might not be available, and saved it until we were settled in one place for a while. I gave it to Altan, the servant who appears to be in charge of the household here, last night. I find myself ready for something familiar." She took a sip of the tea and smiled contentedly. "They do know how to brew tea here. I am so very glad."

Mama was looking at her again and seemed about to say something, but Julia came in, followed almost immediately by Papa and Mr. Oliphant. Emily was grateful for the interruption, since any comment Mama made was likely to be an awkward one. It was not that Mama was the prying sort of mother, or the sort who was always scolding her children. It was simply that she noticed too much, and her remarks reflected that. Anything she said now was likely to be about their most recent adventure, and Emily was still trying to sort through her feelings.

Once her father and Mr. Oliphant arrived, however, concerns about feelings were irrelevant. Practicalities took over. The intention was that they would stay in Mosul for a month while Lord Penworth examined conditions here, so there were plans to be made, living arrangements to organize, servants to meet, and some sort of communications to establish. Mundane tasks, but all new and strange here in Mosul.

Lucien felt uncomfortable in his frock coat and trousers with a silk hat in his hand, hardly the garb that allowed him to pass unnoticed through the streets of Mosul, but Carnac had insisted on formality for this visit. It would, he insisted, be only proper, and it was necessary to impress the marquess. Lucien doubted that the marquess would be terribly impressed by Carnac's rusty coat and limp cravat, even more dated than Lucien's own, but he held his peace. How Mélisande was dressed he did not know, for she was enveloped in her blue robe, as anonymous as every woman in Mosul.

A servant admitted them and led them into the courtyard where Lady Penworth and the young women were seated. He noted his surroundings automatically—the elegant pillars surrounding the courtyard to support the balcony above, the carved octagonal fountain in the middle of the area, the elaborate pattern of tiles on the floor in brilliant shades of turquoise and yellow and blue. The part of his mind that was always aware of his surroundings noted all that, but what filled his sight was Lady Emily.

Dressed in something pale blue and filmy, with miles of skirt surrounding her, she sat on the bench built against the wall of the house amid the piles of pillows that cushioned it, along with her mother and Lady Julia. Now that he looked at all three of them, with Lady Penworth in the center, they looked like a queen and her court. They were beautifully turned out, dressed as they had been in Constantinople, in fine fabrics trimmed with ribbons and flounces. Not a wrinkle marred their costumes, not a hair was out of place. Well, the lace on Emily's collar was not quite straight, and a few locks of her hair had escaped their pins. A particularly charming lock was dangling down to caress her cheek. His finger itched to trace its path.

On the table in front of them was a tea set, an English tea set—teapot, sugar bowl, creamer, large English tea cups—and a plate of what looked like English biscuits. It looked utterly misplaced in the setting but also just right.

No one would believe that these delicate creatures had just spent three weeks on horseback crossing the Taurus Mountains, putting up with innumerable hardships, and had then ridden rafts down the Tigris and been shot at by reckless Kurds—all of that not simply without complaint but with positive enjoyment.

Here, within the traditional courtyard of an Arab house in Mosul, they should have looked ridiculously alien. Yet somehow, they looked completely at home. Like fairy creatures, conjured up by some genie. Had he been enchanted by some spell? He could not stop staring at her, willing her to look up and meet his gaze.

At last she did, and for the first time since he had met her, those blue eyes were filled with uncertainty. A faint blush tinted her cheeks, and she dropped her gaze. He was not the only one who had been disconcerted by their encounter on the raft. Good, he thought savagely. At least he was not the only one being tormented by that memory.

"M. Chambertin, how good of you to call," said Lady Penworth with obvious pleasure, her voice breaking into his thoughts.

He stepped up to her and bowed over the hand

she offered. "Lady Penworth, may I present M. Carnac, the gentleman who is working on the ruins of Nineveh, and his daughter, Mélisande."

"I am delighted to meet such a distinguished scholar. M. Chambertin has told us much about your work." Lady Penworth turned her charming smile on Carnac. "We are just having some tea. Won't you join us?" She glanced at one of the servants who immediately carried over a folding chair.

The old man did not seem charmed. He bowed stiffly and spoke abruptly. "I have no time for that. I had hoped to have a word with Lord Penworth. Where is he?"

Lady Penworth's smile did not falter, though her eyes narrowed slightly, and the hand that had been hovering over the teapot froze before returning to her lap. "I'm afraid he and Mr. Oliphant are not here at the moment."

Carnac grunted in displeasure. "When does he return?"

"My husband is here in Mosul on official business, you understand. He has a great many meetings to arrange and will have to do some traveling." Lady Penworth's smile was beginning to wear thin, and there was a decided edge to her voice.

That edge recalled Lucien to the reason he was here—his excuse for being here—and he decided he had better intervene before Carnac created a disaster. "M. Carnac was hoping to invite you all to see what is being done at the Nineveh excavations. At the Kouyunjik mound, he is uncovering a royal palace, and there are some marvels to be seen. I told him that

Lord Penworth had mentioned your interest in antiquities, and he thought you might enjoy seeing these." He was relieved to see Lady Penworth look less irritated, and he thought—hoped—that Emily looked at him with approval. For his tact, if nothing else.

"Indeed, we would all be interested in seeing the excavations," Lady Penworth said. "I fear we are still all at sixes and sevens today, but perhaps you and your daughter would care to dine with us tomorrow? And you too, of course, M. Chambertin."

This time Carnac's grunt was less offensive, accompanied as it was by a nod rather than a scowl. "Good. We will come."

As he was turning to leave, Emily chimed in. "Perhaps Mlle. Carnac would be willing to stay and visit with us for a while? Lady Julia and I would be very grateful if she could tell us something about life here." The smile she directed at Carnac was very like her mother's, perfectly courteous with no warmth in it. She did not look at Lucien at all.

The old man turned around and frowned at his daughter as if he had forgotten her presence, and he probably had. Mélisande had been so silent that Lucien had almost forgotten her as well. Now, when he turned and took a good look at her, he was stricken with guilt.

The child was almost in tears. She had done something bizarre to her hair, which poked out in stiff ringlets, and her dress was adorned with every flounce and flower she could make in imitation of her fashion journals.

Emily had come over and took her by the arm,

smiling kindly. "Please say that you will stay. It is always a bit lonely for newcomers like us in a strange place." She managed to sound as if Mélisande would be doing them a favor by remaining with them. That was his Emily, always aware of the feelings of others, always sympathetic.

He caught himself. What was he thinking? *His* Emily—where had that thought come from? He had no business thinking that way, no right. She was not his. He did not want to think of her as *his*.

Carnac shrugged. "Why not?" he said as he turned to leave. At Lucien's cough he paused long enough to say to Lady Penworth, "Until tomorrow."

Lucien suppressed an impatient sigh as he watched Carnac march off. "I will send a servant to wait for Mlle. Carnac and take her home," he told Lady Penworth. He stopped, uncertain of how much he should try to explain. He did not wish to embarrass Mélisande, but they needed to understand that she really did not know much—anything—of European manners and customs. He looked to Emily for help, but she was ignoring him. "It is not often that European ladies come to Mosul," he said to Julia, who was at least looking at him.

Julia seemed to understand. At least she smiled reassuringly at Mélisande. "I am sure we will have much to learn from each other."

Mélisande, on the other hand, looked both uncertain and resentful. He had thought this was what she wanted, but he might be wrong.

"My English, she is not good," she blurted out.

"Then we will speak in French," said Emily,

switching smoothly to that language. "And perhaps you will be able to help us with our Arabic. Come, Julia, let us go upstairs."

He watched with satisfaction mixed with frustration as the two English ladies swept Mélisande out of sight. He had known Emily would treat the child kindly. Throughout their journey she had always been curious about other people, concerned about their feelings, and he was pleased by the understanding of Mélisande's needs that she showed.

Still, he was annoyed that he had not even had a chance to speak to Emily, that she had not tried to speak to him. It bothered him that he was annoyed, but it also bothered him that he felt pride in seeing her kindness. There was something proprietary about the feeling, and that made him uneasy. He had no business having proprietary feelings about any woman, especially not Emily. Lady Emily. The journey was over. They were no longer comrades. It would be best if he began once more to think of her as Lady Emily.

Lady Penworth's voice broke in on his thoughts once more. "Please sit down and join me, M. Chambertin."

He accepted a cup of tea, not without trepidation. He was not sure what she wanted to discuss.

"You need not worry about Mlle. Carnac. We will take good care of her."

"She could not be in better hands, I know."

"M. Carnac does not seem to greatly concern himself with his daughter." The statement was really a question.

"He is much occupied with his work, you see." That was an explanation, he supposed, but judging from her raised brow, he doubted that Lady Penworth considered it an excuse. He did not consider it such himself.

"Dedication to one's work is doubtless to be admired," she said as if she did not believe a word of it.

"If I may say something…" He hesitated, but when she offered no objection, he plunged in. "The dinner you are planning, it might be best if you do not include Mr. and Mrs. Rassam."

"Why ever not? The Rassams are the only people we know here and have been very helpful to us."

"There has been much competition between the English and the French concerning the excavations here at Kouyunjik, the palace of Ashurbanipal, and at Dur-Sharrukin, the palace of Sargon. The mound of Kouyunjik was divided between them, and Hormuzd Rassam, the brother of this Mr. Rassam, was working on the English section. He grew impatient with his lack of success, and since the French were not, at the moment, working on the mound, he transferred his attentions to the French section."

"Ah," said Lady Penworth, "I am beginning to see. This Hormuzd had some success?"

"An entire room covered with bas-relief, in most excellent condition, and narrating a lengthy story of warfare. In addition, there were hundreds of clay tablets that promise much information."

"And where are these treasures now?"

Lucien raised his hands in a resigned gesture. "In the British Museum."

She laughed softly. "Oh dear. I gather that M. Carnac holds this against our Mr. Rassam?"

"He does not forgive what he sees as theft, stealing the glory that should belong to the French. It does not matter to him that this Mr. Rassam had nothing to do with his brother's activities and shows no interest in the excavations."

"In that case, I doubt either of them would enjoy dining together. I will refrain from putting the cat among the pigeons this time."

# Nine

As the time for the dinner neared, Lucien was plagued by conflicting emotions. He wanted a chance to speak with Emily, Lady Emily. Did he look forward to this too much? It could not be that he missed riding beside her, having her to talk with during the day, he told himself.

Ah, of course he missed it. Why deny it? But surely he could put that out of his mind. The journey was over. She would soon be returning to her life in England, and he would soon continue his travels. No, he wanted to speak with her to thank her for her attention to Mélisande. That was it.

That attention had obviously been to good effect. When it was time to leave for the dinner, he had scarcely recognized Mélisande. Today her brown hair, tied back from her face with a ribbon, fell straight down her back with no ringlets. She wore the same dress she had worn for their visit yesterday—at least he thought it was the same dress. It was the same color, but it seemed to have lost all its ornamentation and looked the better for it. She appeared before him looking uncertain, but beamed when he told her how charming she looked.

Carnac did not look charming, but then he never did. Annoyed, resentful, disgruntled—any of these usual expressions, but not charming. Lucien had been forced to spend a good half hour convincing the man that he should not begin by demanding that Lord Penworth finance his excavations.

"But he is rich, you said," Carnac protested. "Why should he not spend his money on something of value instead of on fripperies for his silly wife?"

"Do not, I pray you, insult his wife. She is not at all a silly woman, and Lord Penworth is most fond of her."

Carnac snorted in disgust. "Women are all foolish, and men who indulge them are fools as well."

It was pointless to argue with Carnac on this subject. Lucien concentrated on trying to persuade the man that the most effective tactic would be to invite Lord Penworth to see the excavations and to view the carvings that had been uncovered, just waiting for transport to France—or to England, if that should prove necessary. Then when Penworth expressed interest, a request for funding could be made. Lucien thought it prudent to suppress his doubt that any great interest would be shown, but he also doubted that Carnac would be able to make a request rather than a demand.

A grudging consent was the best Lucien could get, and he felt worn out by the time they departed. Carnac charged ahead, leaving Lucien to take care of Mélisande. The girl took his arm in ladylike fashion, and when he looked down to compliment her, she looked up at him through her lashes with a shy smile.

*Bon dieu!* Was she trying to flirt? This was not at all her normal behavior, and he could not believe that Emily had suggested such a thing. Emily did not flirt. Was it Lady Julia's suggestion? Mélisande was a child, much too young for that sort of behavior. He tugged her along in her father's wake, hurrying enough so they all arrived together.

❧

Emily felt shy. This was ridiculous, she knew. She never felt shy. Nonetheless, she had felt shy yesterday when Lucien—M. Chambertin—arrived, too shy to even speak with him, and she felt shy now as well, seeing him standing there in the courtyard with her parents. Everyone else was down there already, and she was not sure why she lingered up on the balcony, but linger she did.

What was it about him that made her feel this way? The moment she had heard his voice, her heart had started beating faster and she had run up here to try to recover herself before she had to speak to him. Half-hidden behind a pillar, she watched him as he greeted her parents with perfect courtesy, introducing M. Carnac and his daughter to Papa.

What was it about him? He was not terribly hand-some. Mr. Oliphant was far better looking. Even her brothers back home were handsomer—and taller as well. His hair was still too long, and his nose was still too long as well. He did not cut a heroic figure. He was no Hercules, although she had discovered that his slim figure was surprisingly well muscled. And his smile transformed his face. It did not make him handsome, but it made you want to share his excitement, his enjoyment of the world.

At the moment he seemed on edge, darting glances around the courtyard. Was he looking for her? He stilled suddenly, then turned and looked up, straight at her, almost as if he had felt her eyes on him. She could not move, as if trapped in his gaze, until finally he took a step toward her. That set her free, and she hurried downstairs to join them all.

She felt shy again when she reached them, and she stopped at her mother's side. He was still looking at her and smiled uncertainly. She managed to smile back the same way, but then his smile broadened, and so did hers, until they were both smiling broadly and happily, and it was as it had been on the journey across the mountains. He was Lucien, and they were friends again. Copains.

Except that there was an awareness that had not been there before, a physical awareness, and a desire to *touch* him. This was some sort of madness. She shook her head to clear it. She was not going to think about that. She must not think about the way his nearness made her feel. What she needed was a cooling drink, but there was none at hand.

Instead she tried to concentrate on the others. Julia and David were standing off to the side, engrossed in each other as usual. Had he said anything to Julia yet? Made any sort of declaration? It was odd, now that she thought about it. He was an extraordinarily handsome man, and in her experience, good-looking men tended to be all too arrogantly certain of their charms. Yet he seemed almost diffident.

Was it because his mother was an Arab? Really, that simply made him more interesting, exotic. Although now that she thought about it, there probably were some people back home who would be difficult. Stupid people, but they could be upsetting if you were sensitive, she supposed. But Julia certainly wouldn't care. She had her own uncertainties.

Did they need a further prod? She started to step toward them but decided this was not the best setting for a prod.

M. Carnac, on the other hand, was not diffident in the slightest. He was simply ignoring Mama completely and devoting all his attention to Papa. This was not endearing him to either of her parents.

"It is useless. I tried to tell him, but he does not listen." Lucien was standing beside Emily, looking down with a rueful smile.

"He seems determined enough. What is it that he wants so badly?"

"Money." Shock must have shown in her face, because he laughed softly before he continued. "No, he is not greedy, that one. He wants money for his excavations, for his studies. He concludes that since your Papa is here, he must be a wealthy man and must therefore be willing to contribute to the cause of scholarship."

"He is a very foolish man if he thinks that he can convince my father of anything by being rude to my mother."

"I am afraid my father, he says that women are of no importance." Mélisande had joined them.

The child was looking a bit woebegone, which was understandable if she had been ignored, so Emily smiled at her and switched to French. "You are look-ing very pretty this evening." And that was perfectly true. The girl had obviously taken Julia's strictures to heart and was dressed with a simplicity that suited her young years.

"Thank you. It was kind of you and Lady Julia to help me. I must learn how to dress so that I will not be ashamed when I go to school in Paris."

"Is that where you are from? Paris?"

"Not I myself, you know. I have been always here, since I was a small baby. But my mother, she was from Paris, and she told me much about it, how wonderful it is, how beautiful, and all the elegant people. Ah, I shall be so happy to be there at last." A look of blissful anticipation spread over Mélisande's face.

Emily could not help feeling doubtful that anything, even Paris, could live up to the girl's expectations, but she said, "Yes, it is a very beautiful city."

Lucien looked as if he was about to express doubts as well, but he was forestalled by a loud exclamation of pleasure from Carnac. He had extracted a promise from Lord Penworth to visit the excavation in three days' time.

"You will accompany Lord Penworth and show him the way, *non*, Lucien?" Carnac beamed satisfaction.

"And my family," added Lord Penworth dryly.

"Of course, of course." Carnac waved a dismis-sive hand.

"Do not worry. I will be there too," Mélisande whispered to Emily. "It is boring, but I can show you and Lady Julia where we can sit in comfort and drink mint tea."

On that note, the party moved into the dining room.

Whoever had arranged the furnishings of this house for them had judged things very well, Emily concluded. The house itself was an Arab house, with draperies and rugs and cushions everywhere, all creating an air of Oriental luxury. At the same time there were chairs to sit on and a table to eat off with plates and cutlery to conform with European habits and comfort. They had all eaten with their fingers from a common dish on their journey to this place, but Emily could not deny that she found it more comfortable to eat with a fork from her own plate and to sit in a chair, rather than cross-legged on a cushion.

The chef had apparently decided to impress them with his skills. Dinner began with a variety of pickled vegetables, tiny meatballs, and a salad that seemed to be composed of minced herbs. That was followed by a stew of lamb and vegetables served over rice, all of it seasoned with unfamiliar spices of wonderful fragrance. She savored each mouthful.

M. Carnac, on the other hand, seemed totally indifferent to the food, which he shoveled into his mouth almost unconsciously. Her parents kept trying to keep the conversation general, aided by David and Lucien, but M. Carnac kept trying to drag it back to his excavations. He did manage to bring total silence to the table with a remark about slavery.

The silence was so total that he even noticed it himself and paused with a forkful of rice suspended midair. "What is the matter?" he demanded.

"Ah, you mentioned slavery," said Lord Penworth. "But I was under the impression that the sultan was endeavoring to bring it to an end."

Carnac shrugged dismissively. "What the sultan wants may have importance in Constantinople. This far away, it signifies little. Oh, there may not be as many Greek or Circassian children as there once were in the slave markets, but there are plenty of Africans. Most buy their household servants that way."

Lady Penworth gasped and looked hastily around the room, as did Julia and Emily. Suddenly the meal did not seem quite so delicious, and the house itself lost charm.

"No, no, do not worry," Mr. Oliphant assured them. "Even if Mr. Rassam would tolerate it, he knew that you would not."

"My father does not employ slaves either," put in Mélisande.

While the English party looked relieved at this, Emily noticed that Lucien greeted that remark with a slightly cynical look.

"Indeed, no," said Carnac. "It is not worth it. There are seasons when it is impossible to dig, and it is better to have workers who can be dismissed when there is nothing for them to do. Slaves have to be fed and housed even when they are useless." He returned to his meal, oblivious to the shocked looks directed at him.

By the time the Carnac party left—and Emily had the impression that Lucien had done his best to hurry them out—everyone was feeling exhausted.

Lady Penworth heaved a sigh. "I must say that I find M. Carnac's conversation a bit difficult to sustain."

"We need not visit his excavations, my dear, if you would prefer to avoid him. I will make our excuses." Lord Penworth looked at his wife with concern.

"Nonsense," she said. "Do you think I have traveled all this way, and crossed those dreadful mountains, to finally reach one of the most remarkable sites on earth, only to be put off by one disagreeable old crosspatch?" She reached up to pat her husband on the cheek. "Besides, I feel certain that M. Carnac will wish to speak only to you, so the suffering will be all yours. The rest of us can be guided by M. Chambertin. He may not be as knowledgeable as M. Carnac, but we are none of us scholars, so that will not matter."

"We will need Mr. Oliphant's company as well, will we not?" Emily asked innocently, with an eye on Julia.

"Of course," said Lady Penworth. "One never knows when one will need to have a puzzling communication translated."

∽

Rather to the Penworths' surprise, Lucien and Mélisande appeared the next day with a note from M. Carnac putting off the visit to the excavation for a week. Asked about it, Mélisande shrugged indifferently and went to seek out Lady Julia. It was left to Lucien to explain that M. Carnac had uncovered something that he considered extraordinary and wanted to be able to display it to them properly.

That was not much of an explanation. Lucien acknowledged as much. However, since Lady Penworth was curious but far from desperate to see the excavation, and no one else displayed more than tepid interest, the explanation sufficed. Lord Penworth had more than enough to occupy him, interviewing merchants and officials and examining records, with Oliphant beside him to translate. Lady Penworth decided to explore the bazaars and enlisted Lucien's aid in this endeavor.

Mélisande attached herself to Julia and Emily, rather like a leech, Emily thought. She peppered them with questions about fashion and etiquette, and had quickly decided to take Julia for her model rather than Emily. Emily was startled at first—she was not accustomed to being snubbed—but after a moment's thought she was relieved. Mélisande's every utterance began with, "When I am in Paris…" The girl's lack of interest in anything that did not affect her was childish and irritating.

After four days of this, when Mélisande had finally departed without the invitation to dine that she had been angling for, Emily and Julia retreated to the roof. The sun was low enough so that the day had begun to cool off, and there was a pleasant breeze up on the roof.

Emily sat on one of the benches and leaned back against the parapet, closing her eyes. "I like this time of day, when the sun is warm but not hot."

Julia, who was sewing a narrow band of lace onto the collar of a blouse, smiled. "It is the same early in the morning, you know."

"Yes, but I rose early every morning on the journey here. I feel entitled to be lazy for a few days now." She opened her eyes and looked at Julia's needlework with a slight frown. "Are you making that for Mélisande?"

"Yes. The child does long for trimmings on her clothes and she goes much too far when she does it herself."

"Such a fuss about clothing."

Julia put down her sewing and glared. "That is grossly unfair. You have never had to worry about clothing because you have always been properly dressed. You grew up with someone to guide you. I know just how Mélisande feels. Until my brother married Elinor, and she and your mother took me in hand, I was as ignorant as poor Mélisande and as badly dressed."

Emily was immediately contrite and made apologetic noises.

Julia ignored her and continued. "You have no idea what it is like to always feel uncertain, to always be afraid that you don't know the right thing to do or the right thing to wear. It's dreadful and humiliating."

"Surely you do not still feel that way."

Julia picked up the blouse and resumed her sewing. "I am not sure one ever stops feeling that uncertainty."

*And that,* thought Emily, *is why you are always so careful to be proper*. But she did not speak her thought aloud. Instead she turned and looked out over the rooftops going down toward the river. People had come out to sit on some of them, and, on a few, women had made a small cooking fire to prepare the evening meal. The smoke drifted past, the smell mingled with the odor of roasting coffee beans. A pleasant smell, but foreign. Nothing like London.

*If I found myself living here, I would feel that same uncertainty. I would always wonder if I was doing the right thing.*

"I do not know precisely what my difficulty is with Mélisande," Emily said. "She wants to know how to behave, but it is difficult to know what to tell her. She dreams of balls, but is she ever likely to attend one, even if she goes to France? We could teach her how to curtsy when presented at court, but I doubt that is likely to occur. Should we be telling her how to run a household of a hundred servants? Or how to manage with a single maid of all work?"

Julia laughed. "And does either of us know how to do that?"

"No," said Emily, shaking her head ruefully. "But you know what I mean."

"Yes, but perhaps the person to ask is Lucien. He knows the family better than we do." Julia snuck a quick glance at her friend.

Emily was frowning. "It is difficult to ask him anything when he never comes near us." And that was, she knew, the reason for her unsettled mood. She stood up and walked over to the other side, where she could see the hills rising to mountains to the north. She stared at the scene for a few minutes while she considered her feelings. She didn't want to think about Lucien, so she concentrated on Mélisande. Then she turned back to Julia. "There is something about Mélisande that I do not like. I think it is that she does not like us. She simply wants to drain us of information that will be useful for her."

"You may be right. She is not a particularly likeable

child. Still, I cannot help but feel sorry for her. She has no parents, no family to look out for her and her future. If she is selfish, she has cause. She must fend for herself." Julia smiled sadly. "That could easily have been my fate."

Emily shook her head. "No, it could not. You have a kind and generous heart. She—I do not think she cares two pins for anyone else."

# Ten

MARSHES EDGED THE EAST BANK OF THE RIVER, GIVING way to the inevitable palm trees and, beyond that, a grassy plain, dotted with some sort of yellow daisy, and groves of almond and mulberry trees that were in full bloom. Once the party heading for Kouyunjik had ridden away from the river and the cries of the boatmen, the occasional chirpings and buzzings of insects were the only sounds around them. The path was wide enough for them to ride two or three abreast. Conversation would have been easy, but the novelty of the scenery kept them silent.

Lucien was their guide today, but Irmak insisted on riding in front, with two of his men bringing up the rear, even though the scene seemed utterly peaceful. Emily was unable to decide if he was extremely conscientious or if the consequences would be so dire were anything to happen to Lord Penworth. He and his men wore those brimless red flowerpot hats. They seemed rather impractical. Her father, David, and Lucien all wore low-crowned tan hats with broad brims, which seemed to offer much better protection against the sun. She, her mother, and Julia wore similar hats, though in more attractive colors, and with colorful ribbons for decoration.

Lucien seemed to be clothed in no color at all. Now that they had left the grassy plain behind and were nearing the hill that he said was Kouyunjik, the hill that had once been Nineveh, he seemed to blend right into the landscape. His hat, his jacket, his trousers, even his horse were all a pale yellowish tan almost indistinguishable from the sands of the desert around them. It was so striking Emily felt obliged to comment on it. And she could comment on it, since today he was accompanying her instead of her mother.

He grinned at her. Sometimes she thought he considered everything deserving of a grin.

"I do not doubt it. I am sure that both my horse and I have been covered with sand and dust so many times that we have decided it is best to surrender. And there are times when it is as well to be able to be inconspicuous." He waved a hand at her. "You too are beginning to fade from sight."

She looked down to discover that her lovely green habit was indeed turning dun-colored. Brushing at it succeeded only in raising a small cloud of dust which promptly settled on her once more, but not before making her sneeze.

When she recovered, she said, "Should anyone planning a trip here ask me for advice, I will be sure to recommend a wardrobe in tawny shades."

Lucien continued to look amused. That look was as much a part of him as the clothes that made him fade into the background. Not that he was always dressed in sand-colored garments, but—now that she thought about it—he was almost always dressed in a way that made him inconspicuous. An amused observer of the scene, rather than a participant. A member of the audience, not an actor on the stage.

She suspected that she had just noticed something important about Lucien. Something important, and a bit disturbing. Why would he choose to do that? There was more to him than she had realized.

They rode along in silence. It was a companionable silence, but then it always had been. At least, she thought it had been. She had been comfortable with him all through the weeks of their journey through the mountains. He had seemed comfortable with her as well. After all, he was the one who said they were copains. Had he changed? Had he withdrawn since the incident on the raft?

Incident. What a ridiculous word for it. The word might be used for the shooting, which probably could be considered an incident. She could just imagine a world-weary traveler at a dinner party saying, "An interesting incident occurred on our trip down the Tigris…" She laughed—just slightly, but enough to make him look at her. She shook her head to assure him that it had been nothing of significance.

But what had happened on the boat had most definitely been of significance to her. Not the Kurds shooting at them—that had been over so quickly that she hadn't even had time to be frightened. It had not even been the fact that he had thrown himself over her to protect her, that he had risked his life to protect her. No, what mattered, what she was still struggling to understand, was the reaction of her body to the sensation of his body lying over her, pressed against her. That extraordinary nearness had made her aware of him in a whole new way, aware of his—she still did not know how to put it—his *maleness*, perhaps. And her own *femaleness*? Is that what she ought to call it?

Whatever it was, her reaction to the experience was unlike anything she had known before. That was disconcerting enough. What was even more confusing was the undeniable fact that she longed to repeat that experience—and the growing conviction that it was only the beginning, that there was far more for her to discover.

She had to stop thinking this way. She was Lady Emily Tremaine, and she had no business thinking this way about a French adventurer, someone she had met purely by chance because he happened to be in Constantinople when they arrived there.

Was it fate?

No. This was ridiculous. She could not let an encounter that had lasted no more than a few seconds, or possibly minutes, disrupt her feelings this way.

Still, she could not keep from wondering if that encounter had affected him in the same way. She thought perhaps it had. And if not precisely in the same way, she was certain it had been of significance to him. Reasonably certain, at any rate. That would explain the way he had been keeping his distance of late, annoying though that was.

There had been a change in the way he looked at her, a certain uncertainty. She shook her head to clear it. All this uncertainty was fogging her mind. But that protective shell around him, that way he had of using good humor to keep his distance—was that new, or had it always been there?

It had always been there, she decided. She had simply failed to notice it. She had been too willing to accept him at face value. She thought that grin and the frequent smiles meant only good humor. She had not thought of them as a mask.

She could pretend she did not realize it was a mask, of course. That would be the easiest thing to do. It would also be cowardly. There would be no risk, but she thought it was quite possible that there might be a great deal to gain if she was willing to take the risk and probe beneath the surface. More to gain than she had ever realized.

Life had become complicated.

By now they were nearing the hill. It was really more of a mound, she thought, a flat-topped mound all alone on the plain. At the base was a well with a few palm trees providing grossly inadequate shade. The road leading to the top was really a ramp, quite straight and wide, and long enough to rise gently.

"It had to be built this way to make it possible to transport the large sculptures," said Lucien.

"That makes sense," she said, ignoring the fact that he seemed to have read her mind. At the moment she wanted to ignore him, period. She needed to think, but she could not think now, not with him right beside her. Nor could she avoid him, not without having everyone—her mother—wondering what was the matter.

What she needed to do was concentrate on what

she was here to see. That should not be difficult. After all, they had come thousands of miles to see this place, the ruins of Nineveh. The least she could do was give it her undivided attention.

Unfortunately, when she looked around, the site was not promising. It looked no different from the plain they had just ridden through. There were rocks everywhere, a few sheds built of mud bricks, heaps of things covered with tarpaulins, and another ramp, this one leading down, but what it led to was also covered with tarpaulins. A dozen or so Arabs stood about in scattered groups, their white robes dingy with dust.

It looked arid, barren, and hot.

They dismounted, and she could not see that the other members of their party looked any more enthusiastic than she felt.

Irmak and his men remained mounted. He made a brief circuit of the site, peering disdainfully at the workmen. Then he raised his hand to signal to his men and led them back down the ramp to wait.

At the edge of one shed was an awning providing some shade, and cushions had been arranged on some rocks to provide seats. Mlle. Carnac had been waiting there and rose to greet them. Before she could say more than "*Bonjour*," one of the groups of Arabs parted to reveal M. Carnac, who hurried to them, beaming proudly and almost bouncing with delight.

Lady Penworth watched him coming and murmured to her husband, "He seems to have misplaced his churlishness."

"Ah, my lord, you will not believe what it is I have

to show to you." Carnac opened his arms in welcome. "You will, all of you, be struck with amazement. Even you, Lucien," he added, looking over at the young Frenchman. "We began to uncover this while you were in Constantinople, so you have not seen it. Come, come, all of you."

Taking hold of Lord Penworth's arm to lead him along, Carnac said, "You must understand, I did not speak of this when I dined with you because I was not yet certain. I hoped, of course I hoped, but I could not be certain, and I did not wish to speak too soon. *Ça va sans dire*. That goes without saying, does it not? But you will see, you will see."

The rest of the party followed, all of them looking both surprised and confused by this display of enthusiasm. Emily looked at Lucien in inquiry, but he only shrugged.

"I do not know," he said. "I have not been here since my return."

What Carnac led them to was a large pit, more or less rectangular, with tarpaulins covering three sides of it. The uncovered side was what looked like a heap of stones, but when Carnac ran down them easily, they revealed themselves to be arranged into a crude staircase.

Mélisande, displaying far less enthusiasm than her father, sighed. "I will wait for you in the shade and will have some tea prepared. You will find it all very dusty."

The rest of them began the descent a bit more cautiously than Carnac. Lord Penworth, as always, helped his lady carefully over the rocks, and David insisted on lifting Julia over the more difficult places as if she were too fragile to manage by herself.

Lucien glanced over at Emily a few times but seemed to assume that she was capable of walking on her own two feet. She was not sure if she felt insulted or pleased. Pleased, she decided, since she had no difficulty negotiating the descent and even leaped down at the end to land beside him. Quite gracefully, she thought. However, all that won for her was a friendly grin, as usual. What else did she expect?

Carnac fussed about, getting them to stand in just the right places, with Lord and Lady Penworth at the front of the group at one corner of the pit. The Arab workmen were lined up above them, smiling and looking almost as excited as M. Carnac. At his signal they pulled up the tarpaulin, revealing an entire wall of carvings. And then they uncovered the second wall and the third.

Emily was not sure how to react, since she did not know what she was looking at. Lucien, however, gasped in amazement. "*Mon Dieu.*" He stepped closer to the wall, moving very slowly, as if he could not believe what he was seeing. "*Mais, c'est incroyable!* This is incredible!" He turned to Carnac momentarily with a look of awe before returning to look at the carvings.

"We are standing in a room of the palace of Ashurbanipal, King of Assyria, known to the Greeks as Sardanapalus," declaimed Carnac, "a palace that has been hidden for more than two thousand years. These bas-reliefs celebrate, with incredible artistry, the prowess of the king in a lion hunt." He waved an arm with a flourish. "Come, look, see what no one has seen for all these centuries."

He was a bit theatrical, but no one could fail to be impressed. Her parents stepped closer to the wall, leaning in to see, as if afraid to touch. Emily and the others followed suit, looking in silence. Now that she had some idea what it was, she could see the figures, warriors with spears, and lions running. The lions were quite nice, she thought. They really looked as if they were leaping along.

Lady Penworth turned around and looked at M. Carnac with startled respect. "This is indeed remarkable. I have seen the bas-reliefs from Nimrod that Mr. Layard brought back to England and, of course, the enormous winged lions, but these are very different. Far more natural, created with far more artistry. Quite extraordinary."

"Quite impressive." Lord Penworth nodded. "Could you explain a bit more about them?"

"But of course." Carnac seemed to expand under their admiration. "These bas-reliefs, they tell a story. It begins here, where the lions are released from their cages. You can see how they leap at the chance for freedom. And here, the people climb the hill to watch as their king kills the lions."

As her parents followed Carnac, listening and looking intently, Emily remained at Lucien's side. He was engrossed in his examination of the carvings. The way he studied them, intent on every detail, impressed her. He had immediately seen that these carvings were something special. She had assumed that he was helping M. Carnac simply for the fun of it, as an adventure, but apparently she had been mistaken. There was more intellectual seriousness to Lucien than she had realized. He was something of a scholar himself, though he hid it for some reason.

She kept finding herself surprised by him. She was obviously less perceptive than she had thought. Or perhaps it was that people were always more complicated than they appeared at first. The more you saw of them, the more layers were uncovered.

Since she hesitated to interrupt him, she studied the carvings herself. The figures were stiff, rather like the Egyptian things she had seen, and the warriors in rows were all identical to each other. The king himself—she assumed he was the king, since he rode in a chariot and didn't look like the other figures—had a conical hat and an enormous beard. His stiff clothes were all decorated, with embroidery presumably.

"It's odd that the lions look more alive than the people," she said. "Do you think the artist's sympathies were with the lions?"

Lucien looked up at her and flashed a smile. "It is possible. After all, the artist was no doubt at the king's mercy just as the lions were."

"Oh! The poor lion!" The exclamation burst out when she spotted a panel in which a lion, pierced with arrows, writhed in agony. "Why do they always have to be so cruel?"

"Do you not think the people would prefer that the king kill the lion instead of having the lion kill them?"

"But why must killing and destruction be what they celebrate? Why not something pleasant?"

He shrugged. "In an age of violence, better to have

a strong, powerful king who can protect you either from lions or from armies. If the king is weak, the people will be conquered, and that is far worse for them, I think."

He stopped to examine a panel showing the king triumphant in his chariot and shook his head. "A strong king, but trapped even so. Look at him. Those embroidered garments, they might as well be chains. The people think the king is all-powerful, but what power does he have, after all? The chains of duty and obligation drag him down. The people think he is free because he rules them, but there is no freedom for him, only the responsibility. He must fulfill his role. He must always go out and kill the lion to protect them, whether he wishes to or not. He is trapped, just as surely as the lowest slave is trapped."

She shook her head, seeing his point but wanting to object.

"It is always so," he said. "It is the history of the world. Strong nations always seek to conquer weak nations. If you do not wish to be conquered, you must be strong enough to defend yourself. Or else you must be strong enough to break free. One way or the other, you are caught in the struggle. It is inescapable."

She seemed to hear an underlying note of bitterness in his voice, and he was not smiling. "Are you speaking of nations or of people?"

His grin returned swiftly, as if to deny that he might have been speaking of anything important, anything personal. "It is true of both, is it not? If one wishes to survive, one must conquer or flee."

She shook her head again, not wanting to think that

way. She would have argued, but he had returned to
his study of the carvings.

# Eleven

AT THE END OF THE FOURTH DAY SPENT TRYING TO arrange for the shipment of Carnac's discoveries to Europe, Oliphant followed Lord Penworth into the room they had established as an office. The marquess seated himself with a groan and glared at the steaming cup of mint tea that had been set on his desk. "You know, Oliphant," he said, "much as I recognize the need to accommodate the sensibilities of our hosts and their ban on alcoholic beverages, I'd give a great deal for a whiskey right now."

Oliphant was inclined to feel the same. Over the weeks of their association, he had developed a liking for the marquess, as well as considerable admiration for his tact and patience. Too many of the so-called diplomats he had dealt with over the years considered it their duty to bully the world into acceptance of British attitudes and beliefs. Not that the same arrogance could not be found in the French, as exemplified by Carnac. Had the Frenchman tried to arrange for the shipment of his artifacts, they would have remained in the ground, covered over with sand, for another millennium.

However, tact and patience exacted a toll, and the negotiations had been both frustrating and exhausting. Refusing the tea Penworth offered, he said, "I am amazed that you have been this successful. What with the Imam convinced that the excavations are desecrating the tombs of the faithful, the Cadi convinced that you and Carnac are conspiring to smuggle out vast quantities of gold, and the boatmen fearing that the tablets contain ancient curses that will bring demons down on them, I did not think you would make any headway at all."

"Well, now we wait for our letters to reach Namik Pasha in Baghdad, and for his letters to reach the Cadi here. To tell you the truth, I shall be glad for a few days free of obligations. I look forward to seeing something of this city with Lady Penworth and the girls. You are welcome to join us, of course, but need feel no obligation to do so."

"As a matter of fact..." Oliphant began, then stopped to fiddle nervously with some of the papers on the desk, neatening them into squared-off piles. "As it happens, my grandfather is nearby at the moment."

"Your grandfather?"

Oliphant held his head up stiffly. "Sheik Rashad. He is the chief of a tribe that spends the spring near here each year. I must visit him, and I wondered if I might invite Lady Emily and Lady Julia to accompany me. M. Chambertin has said that he will also join us. I assure you that the ladies would be perfectly safe."

"Your grandfather. Yes, of course. I had forgotten." Lord Penworth rubbed his hand across the back of his neck in a weary gesture. "Certainly you may invite them. They will no doubt be delighted."

That proved to be true. Lady Emily was all eager-ness, so much so that Oliphant suspected she had been bored of late, forced to remain in the house with the other women while he and Lucien were both too busy to act as escort. She would probably have welcomed an invitation to muck out the stables. Now she pep-pered him with questions until he finally told her to wait and see for herself what it was like.

Lady Julia was more restrained, but she smiled slightly as she looked at him. It was an understanding smile, he thought. She must know the reason for the invitation even without his explaining it. But then, she seemed to understand his every thought, and she must know how much he admired her. No, he did not admire her. He adored her. She filled his thoughts every moment of the day.

But he dared not say anything to her. Not yet. First she had to understand about his family. There was no way he could tell her about them or describe them and their life. She would have to see for herself. He could not possibly say anything to her until she had seen.

Of course, Lady Julia seeing his family for herself would almost certainly mean the end of anything between them. Not that there had actually been anything between them. Anything other than his own dreams, that is. No, it would be the end of any pos-sibility for something between them.

Could he bear that? Would it have been better to just leave everything unknown and unspoken? He could at least have kept his dreams of what might be. Wouldn't that have been enough?

No, that was beyond stupid. He could never make

himself believe that was enough. He had to know, one way or the other. If she saw his mother's family, if she met them and turned away in disgust—well, so be it. It would not be the first time that he saw disgust in the faces of those he thought were his friends when they entered an Arab camp.

She had not shied away once from the people they had encountered on their journey thus far. She had never treated them with anything but courtesy and respect. That much was true. But then, they were only curiosities for her, not people with whom she would be asked to ally herself. How would she react when the son of an Arab woman asked for her hand in marriage? Could she bear the thought that her children would carry the blood of uncouth barbarians, desert nomads who still lived in tents?

Was he mad to even think of her? She was so perfect, so untouchable, as if nothing could disturb her. Beautiful, yes, with a pale oval face and lustrous hair in sleek curves of mahogany around her face. Her eyes were the dark eyes of a gazelle, entrancing him. Yet those eyes always bore a hint of sadness. How he longed to banish all trace of sadness from her.

If only she would allow it.

❧

They set out on horseback early the next morning, riding west. Julia loved the early morning, full of possibilities. Her favorite time of day. Soon they had left the cultivated gardens surrounding the city behind, and the rising sun sent long shadows streaking ahead of them. With the gardens, they had left all color behind as well, it seemed. The short, dusty grass of the plain gave way in the distance to low dun-colored hills. Beyond them, to the northwest, the hills rose into low mountains with higher, snow-topped peaks beyond.

At David's request, Julia and Emily wore their proper English riding habits, brushed clean after their visit to the Nineveh excavations. Not that they would remain clean for long, Julia thought. At least her habit was brown to begin with, though the velvet trim had been a poor choice. They would have been more comfortable wrapped in blue cloaks like the servants, but that would not have marked them clearly as foreigners. It seemed that David wished to emphasize their difference.

In another reminder of the difference between Arab and European customs, David and Lucien rode in front of the two women, not beside them as they had in all their earlier journeys. The only sound to be heard was the rhythmic trot of the horses. There did not appear to be a road, yet Julia did not doubt that David was quite certain of the way. He knew precisely where he was going.

She understood the reason for this visit, the reason for the stiff tension in his bearing. She had walked into countless ballrooms, innumerable drawing rooms with that same stiff posture, a shield against the contempt and disdain of others. Even before she had learned of his Arab mother, she had recognized that protective barrier around him. Had he recognized the same in her? Was that the reason they had been immediately drawn to one another?

More likely, it was the reason they had approached

each other so cautiously, even though the attraction between them was unmistakable. She had recognized it at once, novel though it was. It was as if lightning crackled in the atmosphere when he came near her. Whenever he touched her, even just to help her dismount from her horse, she wanted to throw herself into his arms, and she was certain that he felt much the same way. She could see the heat in his eyes. Yet they both held back for, she thought, the same reason. They were both afraid.

It would not change anything if she told David that his Arab blood mattered not at all to her. He would not believe it, not until she had actually met his family and seen them for herself. He was too honest to misrepresent himself, and he apparently believed she was honest enough not to hide her reaction.

Unfortunately, Julia had more to hide than he knew. The time was coming when she would have to be honest herself. She dreaded that moment, yet she found herself also looking forward to it. It would be so liberating to tell the truth about herself. Even if he turned away from her. That would break her heart, but at least she would know that for her, love was an impossible dream. She would stop hoping.

She looked around at the harsh landscape. The pitiless sun glared down on every rock. There was nowhere to hide. There were no secrets here, no polite fictions. This was a place that demanded honesty.

Beside her, Emily let out a small sigh. "What a barren, inhospitable place," she said. "It intimidates me."

"Truly?" Julia was startled, and not only because

Emily was hard to intimidate. "I like it. It may be harsh, but it makes no pretense of being otherwise. It does not wear a mask. After living my life in English society, I find the honesty admirable."

Emily looked around, frowning. "Honest it may be, but it is also lifeless. We have not seen a living soul, not even an animal, since we left the town." Raising her voice, she called out to Lucien and David, "Do any creatures live here, or do only stones inhabit this place?"

David turned with a short laugh. "Oh, there are people. They just do not care to be seen yet."

Emily opened her mouth to express some doubt about that when one of the hills erupted in a crowd of horsemen, who came racing toward them, waving spears and emitting a loud unearthly cry. David lifted a hand to signal that they should stop, so they waited, grouped together, while the horsemen rode about them in circles.

Since David was sitting calmly on his horse, watching the riders with a small smile, Julia assumed there was no danger and relaxed herself. The riders were impressive horsemen, moving as if one with their horses, white robes flying about them. The steeds were impressive as well. They were not large—mostly mares, she thought—but nimble and graceful, wheeling about easily in a tightening circle. At length one of the riders flung his spear into the ground just in front of David and pulled his horse up to a rearing halt. David sat on his own horse, both of them perfectly calm.

The newcomer followed his spear with a spate

of Arabic. It was all too rapid for Julia to be able to understand any of it, but she followed David's example and sat imperturbably on her own mare. The only movement she had made since they halted was to pat the horse soothingly.

David replied to the Arab with an equally rapid spate of words, then turned to them with a smile. "May I present my cousin, Abdul? Please excuse his dramatics, but he fancies himself a horseman."

Abdul flashed a brilliant smile at them, greeted them with a florid flourish of his arm and spoke in heavily accented English. "Da'ud, you have brought the fairest of flowers to grace our humble tents. Our grandfather has sent me to offer them greetings and beseech them to take refreshment with us." With his hand over his heart he bowed his head, but any hint of humility implied by his words was vanquished by the laughter dancing in his eyes.

His resemblance to David was amazing, though the deviltry was his own.

"Da'ud?" she murmured to David.

"The Arab version of David," he murmured in reply. He fell back to ride beside Julia while his cousin and Lucien flanked Emily up ahead. It struck Julia as odd that now David wanted them to ride in a more European arrangement. Or perhaps it was not odd at all.

They traveled north and followed a path that wound between the hills, rising gradually. Riding beside David revived something of the easy friendship of their trek over the mountains. Julia relaxed into the familiar comfort of his presence beside her.

Abdul was concentrating all his efforts on Emily, and florid bits of flattery floated back to Julia and David as they rode along. Julia could not repress a choked laugh when she heard, "Your beauty is as spring rain to the parched desert of my heart."

David looked worried. "Lady Emily will not be offended, will she?"

"Heavens, no. She must be thoroughly enjoying it. M. Chambertin does not seem so amused, however." In fact, Lucien had lost his easy smile and was scowling at Abdul, who looked highly amused.

A sardonic smile twitched briefly at the corner of David's lips, and he muttered something that sounded like, "Serves him right."

Julia did not have time to examine that notion because their party had just come around a curve in the path. She could not restrain a gasp and pulled her horse to a halt so she could drink in the scene. Spread out before them was a valley, with brilliant wildflowers turning the grass into a glorious carpet and a stream running through it. Horses grazed on one hillside, sheep and goats on the others. When David had spoken of a camp, she had thought of perhaps half a dozen small tents. This was not a camp. This was a city, a movable city. Along the stream were rows of long black tents—dozens and dozens of them. People moved casually among the tents, and the breeze carried snatches of cheerful conversation.

David, who had seemed comfortable riding beside her only minutes before, had stiffened again. She doubted that he would believe her if she told him there was no need to worry. She didn't believe it herself. He thought his family was on trial here. She knew that she was the one being examined.

They arrived at the largest of the tents, and when they had dismounted, the entrance was drawn apart to allow an older man—the sheik, presumably—to make his appearance. He was an impressive figure, even taller than David, with an enormous black beard barely flecked with gray. He wore a richly embroidered red coat over the long white shirt that all the men wore and the striped kerchief on his head was held in place by multicolored tasseled cords.

Whether he was welcoming or not, she could not tell. He remained impassive while David greeted him and they exchanged formal greetings. Although she could not understand what was said, it was clear that David was introducing them—Lucien before the women, she was amused to note. However, she and Emily curtsied politely and received a penetrating stare followed by a brief nod and a glance at Abdul.

David flushed. "My grandfather, Sheik Rashad, invites you to retire to the women's tent, where he believes you will be more comfortable."

"Please thank him for his concern for our pleasure." Julia sent David a smile of understanding and was rewarded by his look of relief.

Abdul led them away to the women's tent, his lamentations at being deprived of their company belied by the laughter in his eyes. At least his nonsense kept Emily from being too irritated at being shut away.

The women's tent was almost as large as the sheik's tent had been. Easily a dozen poles held up the black roof. The high-pitched chatter ceased almost immediately on their entrance, and the women stepped aside, leaving a clear view of them for the elderly woman standing in the precise center of the tent, presumably the sheik's wife. She was dressed in a variety of colorful garments and wore a great deal of gold jewelry—bracelets, earrings, necklaces, even anklets. She stood very erect and examined the visitors carefully as Nuran stepped forward to introduce them.

By now, Julia had realized that Nuran's introductions were in a mixture of Arabic and Turkish and never entirely comprehensible to anyone. Once again Julia could recognize the word *pasha,* but little else. The sheik's wife replied, and Julia thought she heard the name Da'ud. When the woman fixed a stare on her, Julia thought she had probably heard correctly. She stared right back, keeping a pleasant smile on her face. This was probably David's grandmother, so she wished to be courteous though she refused to be cowed. "*As-salaam alaikum,*" she said.

The woman looked surprised, but smiled back. "*Wa alaikum assalaam.*" Then she gestured at herself. "Amsha." Taking Julia's arm, she led her and Emily to a rug piled high with cushions and waved for them to be seated.

Mutual incomprehension meant that conversation was largely nonexistent, though there were giggles aplenty. Most of the stares were friendly, although one of the younger women seemed inclined to sneer dismissively at Julia's minimal Arabic. The expression on her face looked very much like jealousy. Had she perhaps had hopes of David? Julia was surprised to find herself feeling a twinge of jealousy and lifted her head to stare the woman down. However, she and Emily had learned enough to express thanks and praise for the sugar water and sweetmeats they were offered, and most of the women seemed pleased by the effort.

More importantly, David's grandmother seemed friendly. She leaned over several times to pat Julia's hand and when the time came to leave she sent Julia off with an embrace. David also received an embrace from his grandfather before they departed, as well as one from Abdul that was accompanied by a remark that sent the men gathered around into gales of laughter.

Emily leaned over to Julia. "This was to introduce you to David's family, wasn't it? And they like you, they do. Oh, Julia, I'm so happy for you. Has he proposed yet?"

Julia shook her head. "I have been a coward. I have not told him about my family, about my mother. Now I must. It is bizarre, is it not? He knows his family and fears that I might not honor them as he obviously does. That seems so trivial compared with my fear that he might be unable to accept a family where none of us know who our father might be."

# *Twelve*

LUCIEN STRODE THROUGH THE STREETS TO THE Carnacs' house in a foul mood. He could not imagine what had possessed Emily to behave in such a way. She certainly could not have taken that flowery nonsense seriously. She was much too sensible and levelheaded for that. Why had she behaved like a flirtatious ninny with Abdul?

Yes, he supposed the fellow was handsome enough. Women seemed to think Oliphant was handsome, and his cousin certainly looked like him. Except for that silly mustache, of course. However, he would not have thought Emily that superficial. A child like Mélisande might carry on about a man's looks, just as a child could be attracted by a colorful toy. But not Emily. She was better than that.

Was it the novelty? Women liked flattery, he supposed, and that Abdul was certainly flattering her, pouring it on as if she was the most beautiful creature to have ever graced this planet, and she was lapping it up, blushing prettily and looking up at him through those long lashes of hers.

At least he had been the one to lift her from her horse, the one to put his hands around her waist, the one to hold her. Not that there had been anything important about that. It did not signify anything that she had been right there with his hands holding her close to him. Almost touching him.

Emily was pretty, of course. More than pretty. He couldn't deny it. Why should he? She must know it herself. There were those beautiful eyes, a lovely clear blue that hid nothing. And her hair, soft and shining now that it was no longer hidden under all those draperies, was full of all the shades of honey when the sun struck it. Did she expect him to tell her so?

No. He should not do anything of the sort. A man said things like that to a woman he was courting, not to a friend.

Emily was his friend. They were copains. He was not courting her. The memory seized him again, the memory of that moment on the raft when he had flung himself on her. It had been only to protect her, certainly. But he remembered the feel of her body beneath him, her long leg stretched out beside him, the softness of her under him, her mouth with lips parted just inches—a mere inch—from his own. He could feel the heat pool in his groin.

No. He must not think that way. She was here on a visit only, and soon she would be returning to her life in England. That was her real life. Her family was a family of importance, and she would marry some boring English gentleman and take her place among other families of importance. She was not some vaga-bond who could go wandering around the world.

He too was here only temporarily. Soon he would be on his way again, on to the next adventure. The ancient Silk Road, he reminded himself. He was going to travel that fabulous route all the way to China, then who knew where after that. There was a world of wonders to explore. Perhaps he could sail to the South Seas. Or he could visit Thailand, Ceylon, or India.

Then again, he could go north, seek the cold instead of the heat. Russia, the land of the tsars, where one could fly over the snow in a troika, wrapped up in furs. Yes, he would have to go to Russia one day.

He had a sudden vision of Emily wrapped in an ermine cloak, laughing as the snow swirled around her. Yes, she would laugh, and he would pull her to him and warm her…

No. He shook his head and blinked it away. That was nonsense. No woman, not even Emily, had any place in his future.

He stepped into the Carnac house and was assailed by the familiar stale scent of dust. Was this place never cleaned? The house where Emily was staying always smelled of flowers. This place smelled of decay. It was high time he left.

Before he could even lay his hat aside, Mélisande came running toward him. "Lucien, you must do something. You must talk to him."

"What is it? What is the matter?" he asked impatiently. She was crying, half-hysterical, and he really did not want to deal with childish tantrums at the moment.

"He says I am not to go to school, to Paris. He says there is no money for that. I must stay here. You must talk to him. You must make him see." The words were choked out between sobs.

"Calm yourself, Mélisande," he said irritably. "You know he says that at least once a month, and then he forgets all about it."

"But this is different. It is all the fault of those English. They praise his silly bits of clay and now he is convinced that he will be famous. He will do nothing but dig and dig and dig while I shrivel away here with no life, no hope. He cares nothing for me." She wailed dramatically.

Lucien could feel the headache building behind his eyes and rubbed his forehead. "Enough of this, Mélisande. You know your father cares for you." He tried to sound soothing, but it was difficult. He was not at all sure that Carnac cared two pins for his daughter or anything other than his excavations. If he were honest, he would acknowledge this, but he was not in the mood for temperaments. Certainly not for the temperaments of a demanding, whining child.

"You will talk to him, no? You will tell him that I must go to Paris. He will listen to you. You know he will." She was hanging on his arm, clutching at him as if he could solve her problems. She was being foolish. She had to know that her father paid no heed to anyone. Besides, it was not as if a year at a school in Paris would make any real difference to her life. She would just come back here at the end of it to keep house for her father.

Why was she doing this? He could not solve her problems. He had never been able to solve anyone's problems. Why did she expect him to?

Her carrying on must have disturbed her father,

because he flung open the door of his office and stepped into the courtyard. "Cease this infernal racket," he snapped at her. "How can I work with you screeching like a sick cat?" Then he noticed Lucien. "Ah, there you are, Chambertin. Where have you been all day?"

Before Lucien could snap out a rude retort, Carnac continued, "The French consul had one of his lackeys here pestering me. He wants to see you right away. There are letters or some such. You can't expect me to act as your secretary. You will have to deal with your affairs yourself."

The office door slammed shut again.

More letters. He had sent his replies from Constantinople. He had replied to Bouchard, at least. Had he not been clear enough? He did not wish to be bothered. Would they never cease badgering him?

Mélisande was tugging at his sleeve. More badgering.

He disengaged her hands. "You must excuse me. It appears that there is business I must attend to." At least the consul's message provided him with an excuse to leave.

❧

He had left? Mélisande stared after him openmouthed. He had left when she had asked him for his help? How could he? How *dare* he? Did he not see her distress? Was he blind, that he did not see her tears?

She stamped her foot in fury. *Bien.* Very well, then. If he was going to be such a stupid oaf that he could not understand her distress, she would have to confront her father herself.

She hammered on the study door. Her papa ignored her, of course, so she flung the door open and marched in.

A piece of paper fluttered on his desk and he snatched at it, turning to face her, frowning in annoyance. "Stupid girl, what are you doing? You know you are not to interrupt me when I am working."

"Since you are always working, how can I talk to you if I do not interrupt you?"

"If this is another of your complaints about the servants, I swear I will dismiss them all and you can do the work yourself. I do not care."

"That you do not care is understood," she snapped. "Fine. You do not care about me, and I do not care about your stupid work. What I do care about is my return to France."

Carnac snorted. "Return? What return? You have never been to France. One cannot return to a place where one has never been."

She ignored his quibbles. "You promised that I should go to Paris, to the school my maman attended when she was young. You said I must wait until I am fourteen and then I shall go. Very well. Now I am fourteen. It is time for me to go."

He turned back to his desk. "Do not bother me with this nonsense now, you foolish child. Do you not understand how important these new discoveries are? I have uncovered buildings, records, and carvings that no one has seen for more than two thousand years. I shall be the most famous Orientalist in all of Europe."

He turned his back on her. He always turned his back on her. She would no longer allow it!

Looking around wildly, she saw one of the clay tablets covered with the Assyrians' bizarre markings. Chicken scratches. She picked it up and smashed it on the ground.

That drew her father's attention. He spun around and stared at the fragments and then looked at her wildly. "What have you done? Are you mad? Do you have any idea what you have done?"

"I don't care," she shouted, quite as wildly. "All you care about is your stupid bits of clay. I am your daughter. You are supposed to care about me."

He bent over and began to carefully pick up the bits and pieces of the clay tablet, crooning softly. "Yes, yes, it can be saved. It is not so badly broken as all that. It can be saved."

"But what of me?" She began to sob. "How can I be saved? If I do not go to France, what will become of me? How will I ever be able to find a husband?"

Carnac whirled on his daughter, seizing her by the shoulder and dragging her to the door. "Get out of here. Get out of this room and do not ever come in here again, you viper. Be grateful that you are able to serve the cause of knowledge by taking charge of the house for me."

She sobbed harder. "But how can I ever marry?"

"Marry? *Bon dieu!* There are men all over this city. If you want to marry, go find one. Just leave me in peace!" He pushed her out of the room and slammed the door behind her.

Mélisande collapsed on the ground, sobbing. How could she ever find a husband if she was condemned to stay here in Mesopotamia? Did her father think she could marry an Arab? A Turk? No Frenchmen even came to Mosul. The only one she had ever seen was Lucien.

Of course. Her sobs faded. She sat up and began to think. Lucien. He was not planning to stay here forever. If she married him, he could take her to France. He would have to return there sooner or later, after all. He had family in France. Those letters the consul had sent the message about—no doubt they were from his relatives in France seeking his return.

That was the answer to all her problems. Why had she not realized it earlier?

She would marry Lucien.

❦

Some hours later, Lucien sat in a coffeehouse near the bazaar. It was late, and sensible, respectable citizens were safe at home, their doors and windows barred against the sort of riff-raff who gathered here. Although for riff-raff they were remarkably sedate. One group in the far corner grew excited from time to time over some gambling game, but most of the customers sipped their coffee and shared their hookahs in drowsy indifference.

At least they left him alone to stare at the letters. Three of them. They sat there on the low table beside the coffee. As if coffee could suffice to deal with such letters. He needed a bottle of wine. Several bottles of good, rich burgundy. The wine of La Boulaye. He could almost taste it still, spicy and earthy, strong enough to enable a man to deal with these letters.

At least they were not bordered in black. The old man still lived.

The one from his grandmother was no different from all the others she had sent, full of whining reproaches for his failure to return and do his grandfather's bidding. How could he turn his back on a dying old man? As if nothing on earth mattered except grandpère's wishes. Since "the last wishes of a dying old man" had been the excuse for the old man's tyranny since Lucien's childhood, he had no difficulty discounting her letter.

The one from his uncle was only slightly different. It too was filled with whining reproaches, only in this case the reproaches were for his failure to return and restrain his grandfather. Presumably, old age had addled grandpère's brain still further, and he was failing to support his family in adequate fashion. Uncle Pierre could do nothing, in small part because he was not an uncle at all, merely the husband of a cousin, but in large part because he was a fool and always had been.

Lucien had been receiving—and ignoring—such letters for years now. They had all said much the same thing: he was an insolent and disobedient boy and should return at once to live under his grandfather's roof and his grandfather's commands. He was twenty-seven years of age and still they called him a boy, just as his father had been called a boy till the day of his death. All because his grandfather possessed the title of Comte de la Boulaye. Since Lucien never replied, his relatives could tell themselves that he never received the letters. That was surely less insulting than the replies he would send, were he to reply.

The third letter, however, was more of a problem. M. Bouchard, the notaire who handled all his legal business, had rarely written before. He had usually been perfectly capable of handling both grandpère and the estate on his own. Unfortunately, there was now a new problem. It seems that the old man had somehow discovered the school in the village of Varennes, and the plans for the hospital, and was in a fury. He was insisting that if there was money from the estate of Varennes, it should go to La Boulaye. His son's marriage had made Varennes part of the La Boulaye estate.

The comte was insisting that the rents from Varennes, the profits from the vineyards, should go to him and, Bouchard warned, the bankers in Autun were weak. They were intimidated by the comte. Possibly intimidated enough to give him what he wanted.

That was nonsense. It had all happened before. Any obligation was all in grandpère's head. Lucien had inherited Varennes from his mother. Bouchard wrote that he had, of course, told the bankers that the grandfather had no legal or even moral claim on the grandson's income, since the grandfather was hardly penniless himself. Logic made no impact, however. Lucien could have told him that.

It was worse this time though. Grandpère was dropping hints that Lucien was dead. It was preposterous, of course, but grandpère was threatening to go to court. He would doubtless be able to bully some poor attorney into handling the case. The problem was that Lucien might have to return to testify on his own behalf.

Why did he have to be the sacrifice? Surely

Bouchard could find some way out of this mess. He was a canny lawyer. The notaire must be able to find a way for Lucien to escape the chains of La Boulaye.

# Thirteen

JULIA SAT ON THE SIDE OF THE FOUNTAIN, WATCHING the ripples caused as the water from the upper basin trickled down into the lower pool. Letting her fingers float just on the surface of the water, she could feel the movement, barely disturbing it. The rhythmic sound of the constant splash was soothing, not quite obliterating the sounds of the servants moving about at their tasks, but softening them.

The marble of the fountain was cool, even through her petticoats, and the leaves of the orange tree filtered the sun. A fragment of poetry drifted into her head— "*Annihilating all that's made / To a green thought in a green shade.*"

She drifted too, not into but away from thought. Sounds, sensations, sights—she allowed them to make thought fade away. So much so that when David appeared beside her she was startled enough to create a small splash.

He quirked a smile at her. "Did you not expect me?" he asked.

She could not speak for a moment. He was dressed

very formally, in a black frock coat, gray trousers, and a subdued vest—the perfect clothing for the perfect gentleman. The perfectly handsome gentleman. Not just handsome. Beautiful. She could not imagine greater perfection in a man. If only she could look at him forever.

He almost looked assured, but she could see that he clutched the brim of his top hat so tightly that he was crushing it. That gave her courage.

"Please sit down." She waved him to the cushions strewn on the bench against the wall of the courtyard.

He ignored her gesture. "Lady Julia, I…"

"No," she interrupted. "Before you say any more, there is something I must tell you."

He staggered back as if she had struck him. She could see the color drain from his face. "My family— you—" He could barely speak.

Horrified, she lifted her hand. "No. You misunderstand. Your family is admirable. You love and honor them, and they are entirely worthy of that respect. Any woman—anyone—would be honored to be asked to be part of such a family."

He was beside her in a moment, raising her hands to his face. "Julia—"

She pulled her hands away and turned her face. "No, please, you must let me speak." After a moment, he stepped back, and she could feel the loss of the warmth his nearness had given.

She took a deep breath, then another. "Do you know anything of my family?"

He seemed startled. "I know that your father is dead, and the current Earl of Doncaster is your brother.

I know that he is married to Lord Penworth's oldest daughter. I realize that my birth is far below yours…"

A bitter laugh escaped her. "Then you know nothing of the Degraded de Vaux. My brother, my sister, and I share a mother, of that much we can be certain. But who fathered us? Not even our mother will—or can—say. It seems she was not simply unfaithful to her husband, she was unfaithful to her lovers as well." She looked at him then. "You have told me that your parents live in Cairo, that they have always lived in this part of the world."

He was looking more than a bit taken aback, but still managed to nod. "Except when I was at Oxford. They visited me there once, that must be ten years ago."

"Then you are not my brother. Do you realize how unusual it is for me to be able to say that?"

"Julia!" He stared at her, appalled. "My dear, sweet girl. Have you had to think about such dreadful things?"

"Everyone I have ever known is well aware of such things. It is my cowardice that has kept me from telling you about my family."

He took her hands in his and pulled her to her feet, his expression ineffably tender. "Well, you may stop worrying about them, now and for all time. I can assure you I care nothing about your family."

"You should. Were you to marry me, you would forever be encountering people who do know my family or who know about my family. English society is full of people who cast knowing looks in my direction, and it is full of men who think I am bound to follow in my mother's footsteps."

"The more fools they."

"No," she cried out impatiently. "You must listen. You have a career to make in the diplomatic service. Sir Henry spoke highly of you, and Lord Penworth also thinks highly of you. But what will happen if you appear with a scandalous wife?"

"What nonsense, Julia. You hear Lady Bulwer talk about filthy Arabs. Do you think that was the first time I ever heard such remarks? Do you have any idea how often I hear comments about 'a touch of the tar brush'? If that doesn't bother you, how can you think I would care about your mother's misbehavior? Do you really think the Ottoman pashas care two pins for the scandals of London society?" He laughed, which only served to anger her.

"The Ottoman pashas may not care, but I assure you that there are many in the Foreign Office in London who will care."

He laughed again, a gentle chuckle, and pulled her into his embrace. "My dear, I know more about this part of the world, I know more people in this part of the world, than any dozen men in Whitehall. They need me, I do not need them to make my way. Marry me, and forget that gossip. If you like, we can live out our lives without ever setting foot in London."

Melting into the safety of his arms, she leaned into his embrace until she called herself to reality and started to pull away. "No. You must think about this."

He pulled her back. "What is there to think about? I love you, and you love me. Can you deny it?"

She opened her mouth, but no words came out.

"Well then..." he said.

"No. I insist. You must consider what I have said. Three days." She backed away. "You must think about this for three days."

With an exasperated sigh, he shook his head. "You cannot possibly think that will make a difference."

"Three days," she insisted. "You must consider the damage my family could do to your career. Do not come near me for three days while you think on it." She turned and fled.

∽

Emily found her mother sitting in the inner courtyard at a table that had been set up in the loggia. She had her watercolors out and was making a sketch of the fragrant flowering plants arrayed in pots by the fountain. It was an idyllic scene, completely unsuited to Emily's mood.

"Hello, dear. Are you feeling at loose ends?" asked Lady Penworth. "I know your father and Mr. Oliphant are off somewhere trying to make arrangements with boatmen. Those carvings of M. Carnac are occupying an excessive amount of everyone's attention. I almost wish we had never seen them."

Emily made a noise that could have been construed as indicating agreement, and it drew a sharp glance from her mother. It did not, however, draw a question.

That was one of the more annoying things about her mother. She rarely asked questions. Emily's friends were always complaining about how their mothers quizzed them about every little thing—where they had been, who they had seen, what everyone had been wearing, what everyone had said. And those were the impersonal questions.

Lady Penworth never asked about such things. She never asked why you were upset. She waited until you told her, and she seemed to always know whether you told her or not. It was quite infuriating.

"Julia has told Mr. Oliphant about her mother and insisted that he think about it for three days before he comes to see her again," Emily said abruptly.

Lady Penworth nodded. "I see. Are you surprised?"

"Well, yes. She's utterly miserable with worrying, and, as far as I can tell, it's completely unnecessary. Anyone can see that he's mad for her."

"Mmmm." Lady Penworth frowned at her sketch, washed off her brush, and tried another color. "Why do you suppose Mr. Oliphant took you all out into the desert to meet his mother's family?"

Emily blinked. Was that a change of subject? She considered. No. It wasn't. "Julia—none of us, really—had ever met any of the desert Arabs. He wanted to be sure Julia knew what they were like. Is that it?"

Lady Penworth smiled slightly as she concentrated on her sketch.

"But that's ridiculous," said Emily. "No one would judge him on his family."

Lady Penworth turned a skeptical look on her daughter. "Really? Aside from Lady Bulwer, I can think of at least half a dozen families in London that would hesitate to let him through their doors."

Emily flushed. "Well, all right. I do know that. But Julia isn't like that. How could he think she is?"

"I am not, of course, privy to Mr. Oliphant's thoughts. However, I imagine that he wants Julia to know precisely what his situation is before she commits herself, recognizing that she would be too honorable to cry off afterward. Hence the visit to his Arab relatives."

"Well, yes, but…"

"Julia, in turn, wishes to be completely honest about her own situation. They are both far too honorable to mislead someone they care about. It is that very sense of honor that doubtless drew them to each other in the first place."

Emily slumped back in her seat. "You're probably right. But I still think he should say something to her. How can she be expected to know what he thinks if he doesn't say anything? Why are men so hesitant to say how they feel?"

"You are speaking of Mr. Oliphant?"

"Yes, of course." Emily could feel herself blushing. Of course she was speaking of Mr. Oliphant. She certainly wasn't talking about Lucien. Was she? She snuck a sideways glance at her mother, who was looking quite uninterested. At least she wasn't smiling.

Without missing a beat, Lady Penworth redirected the conversation. "What is Julia doing now?"

"She is going over fashion plates with Mélisande, trying to convince her that what is suitable for the Empress Eugénie and her ladies is not suitable for a schoolgirl."

"That should provide Julia with a distraction. I hadn't realized Mélisande was visiting us again. She seems to be here quite frequently." Lady Penworth was frowning, probably at her sketch.

"Yes, M. Chambertin brought her over a while ago."

"Ah, M. Chambertin. Is he here as well?"

"No, he left almost at once." Emily tossed her head with an air of indifference. "He seemed to be suffering from a fit of the sulks as well." Why that should bother her, she could not imagine. Lucien, M. Chambertin, had not had any private conversation—had not even made any effort to have any private conversation—with her since their visit to the Nineveh excavations. Not that she cared, of course. He was an adventurer, not at all the sort of person she should be thinking about. Not the kind of man who should be making her think the kind of thoughts she should not be thinking. She took a deep breath and let it out slowly.

Lady Penworth raised a brow at her daughter. "You cannot order other people's lives for them, no matter if you think you can do a better job of it than they are doing themselves." Ignoring Emily's look of outrage, she returned to the contemplation of her sketch. "Something is seriously wrong with this."

With an irritated sigh, Emily got up to look. "You've drawn the pots a bit lopsided," she said, "and you made the front one much too big. In your picture it's taller than the fountain."

"You're right. My draughtsmanship leaves much to be desired. Oh well, it will suffice as an *aide-mémoire* when I look back over our visit here." She began to collect her paints and brushes. "And Mélisande, is she at least cheerful?"

"Hardly. She is distraught because her father has said she will not be going to school in Paris because he will need all his money for his excavations."

"Pshaw." Lady Penworth shook her head in disgust. "I do not know which is more tiresome, the daughter with her histrionics or the father with his myopic selfishness. If that find of his were not so truly extraordinary, I would never let your father have anything to do with him."

Her mother's departure left Emily alone with her thoughts. They turned to Lucien. Her thoughts turned to Lucien whenever she was alone and in an uncomfortable fashion. She didn't want to think about him, at least not this way. It would be fine if she just thought of him as she did of any friend. That was all he was. Soon they would all be leaving Mosul. She would continue on the journey with her parents, on to Baghdad and then Cairo. He would go off to Samarkand or wherever.

This unfamiliar heat that flooded her body whenever she thought of him—it should not be happening. She should not feel this longing. This yearning sensation should not keep overpowering her. She should not let it happen, but she did not seem to have any control over it.

She must keep reminding herself that soon they would all leave and she would never see him again.

Why did that thought hurt so much?

❧

Lucien had spent the best part of the day—or the worst part, given the increasing heat—pacing about the town, downing innumerable cups of coffee, and visiting the waterfront where the rafts were being collected to transport Carnac's finds down the river to the port at Basra. Usually he enjoyed watching people go about their business, chatting with them, listening to their conversations. Today he simply felt like a stranger, an outsider.

Well, that was what he was, wasn't it? That was what he wanted to be, the outsider who observed but was never drawn in to the point where he had any obligations in a place. If that meant that he never belonged anywhere, that there was no place that he could call home, well, that had been his choice, had it not?

He had made friends in many places. Not friends, perhaps, because friendship carried with it obligations that could not be fulfilled by someone who would soon be leaving for another place. But if he had not made friends, he had at least made friendly acquaintances.

This place was different. Perhaps he had been here too long. Down along the waterfront the boatmen and captains had kept hailing him and asking him questions. Expecting him to know the answers. How soon did Carnac expect to be finished? What did Penworth think of the arrangements? Was Oliphant pleased with the packing? Would he be sailing with them?

No. He had nothing to do with this. He had started to suggest a better, more balanced arrangement of crates on one of the rafts before he caught himself. It was not his place to make suggestions or approve arrangements. None of it was his responsibility.

He fled the heat of the waterfront for the shadowy coolness of his favorite cafe. Everyone knew of his connection to Carnac and to Lord Penworth, so he found himself bombarded by questions about the shipment. One group of men wanted to know if it was true that the crates were filled with gold and precious jewels. He scoffed at that notion, but someone else insisted that it was true.

"The Cadi himself saw the gold," said one fellow, "and insisted on his share before he would allow the crates to be packed."

"Not just gold, but precious gems—rubies and emeralds," said another.

But there were others who dismissed such talk as fantasy. Lucien was about to agree when one of them said that it was not gold but demons that filled the crates.

Lucien laughed incredulously.

"No, no," insisted an old man. "There are ancient genies and afreets that inhabit the stones. Their cries and curses have been heard at night."

When he laughed at that, several of the men in the cafe assured him that there was great danger in removing such things from the place where they had been buried. "The demons, they have been let loose now," one man insisted. "There will be great danger for those who travel with them."

The bazaars and the coffee houses were filled with talk of Carnac's shipment, and the town seemed divided between those who believed the tale of gold and jewels and those who were convinced by the warnings of demons and afreets.

Neither logic nor scorn made any impression. Finally Lucien could take no more of such nonsense and stalked away. He wandered around for a while, but the heat of the day had been absorbed by the stone walls and the narrow streets seemed airless, suffocating. It was time for him to leave this place.

He should decide where he wanted to go next. Did he really want to travel the Silk Road? Perhaps he had enough of arid deserts and bare mountains. He could go to… He could go to any place on earth, but he was finding it difficult to think of a place he wanted to be.

That accursed letter from Bouchard. No matter how much he tried to ignore it, it kept returning to his mind. Was it not enough that La Boulaye had killed his father? It had been a succubus, draining him first of hope and then of life. Was he to be its victim too? He had escaped once. To return would be insanity. Nothing could be done so long as his grandfather ruled there, and his grandfather was inexorably draining the estate, feeding his vanity. Perhaps the old man was weakening now, perhaps he was dying.

And perhaps he would rally the instant Lucien appeared and trap him there forever to serve the glory of La Boulaye.

He did not want to think about it. Besides, it was doubtless time for him to collect Mélisande. Another who wanted to be a responsibility, and another situation where he was powerless to help. At least he could see her safely through the streets.

Perhaps he would see Emily. He had not had an opportunity to talk with her since the visit to Oliphant's relatives. No, that was not true. He had been avoiding her. Why had he been avoiding her?

Because she had become a problem, he thought, disgusted with himself. He was afraid to see her, afraid to face her. She was his friend, and he had liked being with her. All through their journey it had made him happy to be with her. But something had changed.

Not Emily. She was still forthright, honest. She made no demands.

No, that was not quite right. She never told him lies. That was it. Not even polite lies. Was there anyone else who never lied to him? Anyone else he could trust this way?

But there was more than that. She had begun to haunt his dreams. He would awaken in the middle of the night, tangled in a sheet, thinking she was there beside him, naked and welcoming. Even now, walking down the street, he could close his eyes and see that dark honey hair spread out across a pillow.

He burned for her. He wanted to sink his hands in that hair, drown in those blue, blue eyes, bury himself in her.

He stopped and slammed his hand against a wall. An Arab who had been coming in the opposite direction looked warily at him and crossed to the other side of the street.

What was he going to do?

# Fourteen

THE VIEW WAS SPECTACULAR. AS THE SUN SANK behind the mountains, the sky turned to gold and the mountains themselves deepened into purple. From her seat under the awning on the rooftop, Emily feasted her eyes on the magnificent sight. It was more glorious than anything she could have hoped for, infinitely more dramatic than any sunset she had ever seen at home.

On a nearby rooftop, someone was singing, one of those chants that sounded full of mournful longing. A girl longing for her lover? More likely a woman preparing the evening meal. But still, the music seemed full of meaning.

She tried to give herself over to the enjoyment of the moment, to empty herself of all thought and simply lose herself in sensation.

It wasn't working.

Admiring the scenery was no more useful than worrying about Julia's romance with David. No matter what she tried to think about, she always ended up thinking about Lucien. Blast the man. It wasn't as if thinking about him clarified anything. Her thoughts kept ending up in utter confusion.

She had enjoyed his company on their trip to Mosul, more than she had ever enjoyed the company of a young man. That much she could safely acknowledge. She could even understand it. He had talked with her as an equal, never assuming she was a helpless ninny. If he asked her a question, he listened to her answer, as if he were interested in her thoughts. And if she asked him a question, he answered her. He did not pat her on the head and tell her she need not worry about such things.

He had not been cautious, as if fearing to offend the daughter of the powerful Marquess of Penworth, or obsequious, hoping for some benefit from the acquaintance. He had not been deliberately charming or flirtatious, assuming that a few compliments would dazzle her, enabling him to get his hands on her dowry.

In short, he had treated her like a friend, rather the way her brothers treated her, although they were apt to be more patronizing than he was.

Had she been thinking of him as a brother? Was that why she had not been aware of him as a man at first? She knew he was a man, of course. She wasn't a complete idiot. But that knowledge had been submerged somehow.

Perhaps it was because she had not considered him as a potential suitor.

He wasn't, of course. She knew that. She could hardly marry a penniless adventurer. Her parents would never allow it. More importantly, and, humiliating as it was to admit, he had never behaved like a suitor. He had never given the slightest indication that he was looking for a wife. Well, of course he hadn't, because he wasn't. An adventurer went off adventuring. He didn't settle down with a wife.

He never even gave any indication that he thought of her as a woman. For that matter, she hadn't felt much like a woman while she was wrapped up in all those Turkish garments, completely enveloped in one of those ubiquitous blue capes.

Now she was dressed in her own clothes, so naturally she felt like herself again, like a woman. Only not quite like herself. The memory of a hard body pressed against her, the memory of his leg between hers had changed the way she saw herself. Her own reactions surprised her. She was noticing things about herself, about her body, that she had never realized. She was feeling things in places she had never thought about before.

It was more than those few minutes, seared into her memory though they were. Ever since then, her awareness of Lucien had changed as well. On the way to the excavations, she realized how well he rode, almost as one with his horse. When he lifted her from her horse, she realized how surprisingly strong he was. When he dined with her family, she could see the lively intelligence in his face. She knew that he was not particularly handsome. She was not blind. That did not matter. He seemed so vital, as if he were more alive than anyone else in the room, and that was far more attractive than mere handsomeness could ever be.

Most important, she felt a thrill run through her body whenever he touched her. Just the memory of his touch brought the thrill to her.

It was indisputable. She could not deny that she was attracted to him physically as well as mentally. But the crux of the problem remained. Was he attracted to her as well?

When he had landed on top of her on the raft, he had seemed as surprised as she was, and not simply by the collision. That stunned look on his face had come after they had caught their breath. Ever since, there had been a constraint in his behavior. The freedom of their journey was missing.

At the same time, there was heat in his eyes now when he looked at her. She was almost certain of it.

She stood up abruptly and began pacing across the roof. This was ridiculous. She knew she was pretty. Not a beauty like Julia, but quite pretty enough so that young men had frequently found her attractive. But she had always known when it happened. She hadn't cared, but she had known. Why was she so unsure of Lucien's feelings about her?

Was it because she was attracted to him?

That had never happened to her before, and it was thoroughly muddling her thinking.

But the muddle was not enough to hide certain facts from her. Facts that her sensible self could not ignore.

Lucien was an adventurer. He was wandering from place to place. He had cut his ties to his home in France and he had no interest in establishing new ones. He wanted no chains, no responsibilities.

She, on the other hand, had a family, and that

family was not just important to her but a vital part of her. She could not imagine turning her back on her family, cutting herself off from them forever. When she had dreamed about her future, she had dreamed of a new family, true, but still a family like her own in a safe, stable home.

How could she be thinking about a man who had no interest in a home or family, whose dream was to travel toward ever-vanishing horizons, with no ties that might hold him back?

This attraction could lead to nothing permanent. But that knowledge didn't prevent this infernal longing that possessed her. She wrapped her arms around herself in an effort to force it down. An unsuccessful effort.

If marriage was out of the question, could she have an affair? A month ago she would have said that she would never consider such a thing, but now the thought was there. It had appeared, tempting her.

No! She could never shame her family that way. They would not cease to love her, but they would be disappointed in her. They would pity her.

It would be too humiliating.

But still, there was this longing, this *hunger*.

She leaned against the parapet at the rear of the roof and stared down into the garden as it was slowly swallowed up by the lengthening shadows.

∽

She was silhouetted against the light, a glorious halo turning her into a goddess, a creature from another world in that instant flare before the sun finished its descent and darkness fell. Lucien stood there motionless, stunned by the powerful mixture of unfamiliar emotions that flooded through him.

It was as if he had never seen her before. She was—not beautiful, but more than beautiful. She was full of light and life. She was joy.

How had he not realized that before?

In that instant, all the lies he had been telling himself shriveled up and dropped away. He saw the truth. They were not copains. She was his woman. He did not want her as a friendly companion. He wanted her in his arms, in his bed, clothed in that dark honey hair and nothing else. He wanted her, desperately, hungrily, and he had to have her.

He must have made some sort of sound because she turned to face him, but then she too remained motionless, her expression hidden by the darkness.

As if in a trance, he prowled across the rooftop until he stood before her. His arms wrapped around her, and her hands lifted until they touched his shoulders. They did not push him away, nor did they embrace him. They simply fluttered briefly, like butterflies, and then settled. He smiled.

Carefully he lowered his face to hers, slowly and deliberately, until his lips brushed hers once, twice, and a third time before they came to rest. It was his intention, if he could be said to have anything as clear as an intention, to be gentle. He was not certain of her reaction and he wondered if he might frighten her. Then her lips softened beneath his, and all his conscious thoughts vanished. An irrational, insatiable hunger roared through him. Could he have devoured her, he would have done so.

He pressed her back against the parapet and slipped his leg between hers. His hand cupped her buttocks and pulled her up against him. Despite the layers of petticoats, she had to be able to feel his desire. His mouth slipped across her cheek and down to her neck. Her skin was so soft, so soft. He pushed her bodice aside, down over her shoulder, until he could reach her breast. He breathed in the scent of her, jasmine and woman mingled together. His tongue teased her nipple until she moaned softly and arched against him.

He smiled in satisfaction before he returned to her mouth. She opened to him, offering all her sweetness, and reached her arms around him to pull closer.

Yes, this was what he wanted. This was what he had been longing for. This. This.

He pulled her still tighter against him, seeking to unite them into one being. Without ending the kiss, he began lifting her skirts, those ridiculous miles and miles of skirts, until at last he reached the soft silk of her calf, her knee, her thigh.

A door slammed, the reverberations penetrating into his consciousness. Into Emily's as well, for she froze in his arms. He could feel her draw away, not only physically, and he wanted to cry out in protest at the loss.

"What do you want?" Her words were a hoarse whisper, as if they pained her. He could feel her breath, coming in gasps against his chest.

"You know what I want. I want you." His voice was rough, almost angry. "You want me too. Do not deny it." He tried to pull her back to him, but this time she resisted.

"No." She turned her face away. "No, I will not be your...your diversion. Your pleasant interlude in Mosul."

"No! No, that is not what I want." *How could she say such a thing? Did she think him a man of no honor?*

"What else can you mean? You will soon be off to Samarkand, to the Gates of Jade, to somewhere else. You know you will."

"And you will come with me." *Yes, of course. That was what he wanted.* "You must come. We belong together. We can find Samarkand together." His voice softened, and he caressed her cheek gently with his fingertips. With a smile, he bent to kiss her again.

But she did not smile in response. She pushed him away and shook her head. "No."

*No? She could not mean no. He would not believe it.*

"You cannot be afraid. Do not tell me you are afraid." He tried to make his voice teasing. "I will not believe it."

But she was still shaking her head, still not smiling. More than not smiling. She was looking sadly disappointed. "I am not afraid of the journey. But I would be a tie, an obligation. You do not want any obligations, remember? You do not want any ties to hold you back. Perhaps you do want a companion on your journey, a temporary companion. But I will not be that temporary companion. I want more than that. I must have more than that."

She pushed him away and ran across the rooftop, disappearing down the staircase.

His cry of protest died on his lips, and he realized that he was still holding out his hands to where she had

been. Slowly he dropped them and stood there, alone
and bereft in the darkness.

⁓

Emily managed to get to her room without meeting anyone and without collapsing. The room was
both dark and empty, exactly what she wanted. She
straightened her bodice and lay down on the bed,
hoping that no one would come looking for her.

Thank goodness she had not encountered her
mother or Julia. Either one would have wanted to
know what the matter was, and she did not want to
have to explain. Or they would have known, one look
at her and they would have known exactly what had
happened, and she did not want to talk about it. She
couldn't explain what she did not understand herself.
If she had been confused before, it was nothing to
the turmoil she was experiencing now. It was all
too shattering.

What on earth had she just done? Had she lost her
mind? What was wrong with her? How could she
have been so incredibly stupid?

Lucien had been kissing her with more passion
than she had ever dared imagine. He had awakened
longings she had not even known existed. She had
been swept along in a whirlwind of sensation, carried
toward a destination she did not know but a destination she knew was the one she sought. Every nerve in
her body had been crying *Yes! Yes!*

And then that damned door had slammed. Before
she realized what she was doing, the blasted interruption jarred her into being sensible.

*Sensible. Practical.* After all, she was sensible, practical Emily Tremaine. She knew what was expected of her. She had done what had to be done.

No. She hadn't been sensible or practical. She had simply been stupid.

This was the man she loved—she could not deny that. Not anymore. She had fallen in love with Lucien. The man she loved had swept her into a passionate embrace. His desire had been unmistakable, and she had responded with equal fervor. They were on the verge of—she wasn't sure exactly what they were on the verge of, but she knew it was what she wanted. It was what she had been wanting for ages, even if she hadn't realized it.

And what had she done? Had she been brave and courageous? Had she charged ahead fearlessly? Had she even stepped ahead nervously?

No. She had been *sensible*. She ran away. Because he had not promised a future filled with certainty. But who could ever promise that? The future was always uncertain.

The man she loved offered her passion and adventure, and she ran away.

She was the stupidest woman in all creation.

❧

Mélisande was unable to believe her eyes. She had gone up to the roof to find Lucien. He had come to escort her home, of course, though why he had thought to find her on the roof, she could not imagine.

She had been about to call out to him when she

realized what she was seeing. He was kissing Lady Emily. *Lady Emily!*

No! That was all wrong! He was not interested in Lady Emily. He was going to marry her, Mélisande Carnac, and he was going to take her to France.

She had it all planned.

It was absolutely necessary.

In a mixture of fury and despair, she fled, slamming the door behind her. She ran, and kept running, down to the courtyard, past the doorkeeper, out into the street. She had not even wrapped her blue cloak about her, so that her head and face were uncovered. People frowned at her as she ran past, and some of them shouted, but she did not care. She ran and ran until she was back in her father's house. She hesitated for a moment, but the cook looked up and seemed about to ask her something. With a shake of her head she dove into one of the store rooms. There, behind a crate of pottery shards, she curled up and sobbed.

When she was all cried out, she began to think.

It was not fair for Lady Emily to have Lucien. She already had everything any woman could possibly want. She was rich and safe, and she had all the clothes and jewels she wanted. She had even been to Paris and could go there again any time she chose.

Lady Emily did not need Lucien, but Mélisande did. Without him, she would be trapped here in Mosul forever. She would grow old and ugly and be buried under the dust of all these stupid broken bits of worthless pots. She swung her arm at the crate, but it was too heavy. Not only did she not knock it over, but she bruised her hand.

Tears of anger came now, and she stood up to pace back and forth across the narrow space. Her hand hurt, and she sucked at the bruise. The space was dark and dusty and small, like her life. She wanted to run, but there was nowhere to run.

Slowly her thoughts began to tumble into some sort of order. Lady Emily was at the center of her difficulties. She did not need Lucien. She was an English lady who already had everything. She had no business trying to steal Lucien.

She would be leaving soon, but it might not be soon enough. She might not be gone before Lucien was planning to leave, and he still did not know that he needed to go to France, not to Samarkand or whatever foolishness was still in his mind. Lady Emily was distracting Lucien, and so long as she did that, he would not realize that he needed to marry her, Mélisande, and take her to France.

The distraction had to stop.

Lady Emily must be removed.

# Fifteen

ALTHOUGH SHE WAS WELL COVERED BY HER BLUE cloak, and her face was hidden by the black veil, Mélisande did not deceive herself. These two knew who she was, but that did not really matter. They worked as diggers for her father from time to time, the most casual of the casual laborers. No one would trust them with any but the most menial tasks, for they were both lazy and dishonest. Everyone knew it.

They were perfect for her purpose.

She had found them sitting, half-asleep, behind the crates they were supposed to be loading onto the rafts, and their first reaction had been to excuse themselves. She waited. Eventually their fanciful tales of weariness and exhaustion on behalf of the French lord who employed them, accompanied by sly glances at the woman they obviously knew to be his daughter, wound down.

Then she told them what she wanted them to do.

They looked uneasily at each other, then at her, then back at each other. Truly they were ugly men. Dirty, scrawny, with ragged beards. The taller one, Hadad, had teeth that stuck out, making him even uglier.

It was the shorter one, Karif, the one who was missing the tip of a finger on his left hand, who spoke first. "A foreign woman? But is she not the daughter of the visiting pasha? The one who is a friend of the sultan himself?"

"What is it to you who her father is? She can vanish as easily as the daughter of the Greek merchant who vanished last year."

They shared a look again, and Karif said, a bit regretfully, "We had nothing to do with that."

Hadad added, "Twenty pieces of gold was the reward offered for her return." In response to Mélisande's frown, he shrugged apologetically. "Such things are known. Many people searched for her."

She made an impatient noise. "This one need not return, so there is no need to hide her."

Karif looked at her through narrowed eyes. "It is not a question of hiding her or not hiding her. Her father is a man of great importance. He has soldiers from the sultan at his command. There will be a great search, and many questions will be asked. No one will worry about how the questions are asked of poor men like us."

She narrowed her eyes in return. She was not accustomed to negotiating with such creatures. They were servants, and she had always given them orders. This situation was different, however. That she could see. They were as lazy and greedy as she had thought, and as lacking in scruples. But perhaps they were not as stupid as she had thought. Not when their own safety was in question. It would be necessary to negotiate. Just like buying melons, she thought bitterly. Her life was spent haggling with peasants.

"How much?" she asked.

Hadad shrugged—he seemed much given to shrugs—and lifted his hands. "A man who would do such a thing, who would make the daughter of an important foreign pasha disappear, he would have to disappear himself."

"Indeed," said Karif, nodding in agreement, "it is a dreadful thing to contemplate. A man would have to flee the city, leave his home and his friends."

"That would indeed be dreadful for a man who had a home, who had friends. But for men who have neither?" Mélisande allowed scorn to tinge her voice. "For such men, a change of city would be no hardship. And a change with gold to ease the way…?"

"One hundred pieces of gold," said Hadad.

She laughed in scorn.

Offers and counteroffers went back and forth. Truly, it was no different from buying melons. The sums were higher. That was all.

They refused to act with no gold in their hands, not trusting her to pay once she had what she wanted. She refused to pay in advance, not trusting them to fulfill their part of the bargain. Finally a payment of fifty gold pieces was agreed upon, ten to be paid in advance, the rest once Lady Emily had disappeared.

It was as well they had agreed to that price. Ten gold pieces was as much as she could lay her hands on. As for the rest, well, once they had stolen Lady Emily away, they would be in no position to come about demanding payment, would they?

The problem was finding a way for them to get close enough to Lady Emily to capture her. She never wandered about alone. She was always surrounded by family, friends, servants—people who would protect her.

It would be up to Mélisande to lure her away, to get her close to the wharves along the river. It should not be difficult. Lady Emily was a trusting and curious fool. She would soon learn the price of folly.

❧

Irmak walked along the river with two of his men, returning to their quarters after a rather lengthy night. The morning mist hovered over the water, drifting up to sneak ashore and find its way into the alleys, much as the morning fog did in Constantinople. At the wharves, the rafts were loaded, ready to begin the journey downstream. Once they were gone, perhaps this Lord Penworth would be willing to depart from this dismal city and continue his journey to Baghdad.

Baghdad would be the end of the journey for Irmak and his men. They could then return to Constantinople, and perhaps be sent someplace where they could see some action. Irmak had no complaint to make about Lord Penworth and his family. They made no unreasonable demands, they caused no difficulties. They even behaved sensibly.

He had been worried at the start of the journey. It was a difficult trek for civilians, and not one normally made by wealthy, pampered ladies. He had expected complaints, demands that would be impossible to

meet, tantrums, and tempests. He had been pleasantly surprised.

Admittedly, the women rode and spoke with the
men in outrageously bold fashion, but it appeared
to be their custom, and it did not create any of the
difficulties he had feared. In addition, the women had
won his admiration by their coolness under fire when
those lunatic Kurds had fired on them.

Still, they had been here in Mosul far longer than
expected. Lord Penworth had apologized for the
delay, but a delay it was. Supervising a clutch of peasants while they loaded crates of stones onto rafts was
hardly work for soldiers. His men were getting bored
and restless. Irmak was bored and restless himself.

He frowned. Two women had appeared up ahead
and were walking along the waterfront, where women
had no business being. One of them, he was certain,
was Lord Penworth's daughter. He could tell by the
way she walked—tall, not huddled, walking as if she
owned the earth. The other looked like the daughter
of that bad-tempered Frenchman. He stopped and
looked after them for a moment. He shook his head
to clear it. The effendi's daughter here, down by the
docks? She should not be here. Something was wrong.

He signaled to his men and followed her.

～～

Emily trailed along behind Mélisande, trying to
pretend some interest in whatever it was that had
the girl so excited. For her part, what mattered was
that there had been no word, no message of any sort,
from Lucien all day yesterday. No one had seen him.

She knew that, because she had asked. No one knew where he was. He had simply vanished.

Shouldn't he have something to say after the way they had parted? Even if it was just, "Yes, you are right. We must part." Or something. Something that would give her a chance to say, "Wait. Let us not be too hasty." Maybe she should just say, "Samarkand. Yes, I would like to go to Samarkand." Did it matter what came after that?

Well, of course it mattered. But did it matter enough to mean she would never see him again? No. She had to see him again. She had to tell him that she would go with him anywhere he wanted. Nothing would matter if she could be with him.

"Come along," said Mélisande, tugging on her arm impatiently.

Emily shook free and looked around. She had never been on this part of the waterfront before. In other places there were gardens running down to the water, some with vegetables, others with trees and flowers. Not here. They were walking along an unpaved street lined with buildings that looked decrepit even by Mosul standards. Admittedly all the buildings in this town looked gloomy, with their heavy doors and almost no windows, but here the walls were cracked and the alleys were too narrow to allow any light. And there were no people at all.

Warehouses, she thought, since this seemed to be a businesslike stretch of the river. A number of heavily laden keleks bobbed in the water alongside the wharves. They were probably part of the flotilla her father and David had collected to carry M. Carnac's finds down the river.

Was that what Mélisande wanted to show her? Something from the excavation?

She heard footsteps behind her and turned in time to see two men converging on her, one holding a cloth that he tried to drop over her. She twisted aside enough to escape most of its bulk, but not fast enough to escape the grasp of the other man. She screamed and struggled, trying to pull away, but he caught hold and pulled her back against him.

Trying not to panic, she slowed down, trying to think, and dropped her chin down to her chest. Then she flung her head back, hearing a satisfactory cry as she hit something boney and her captor released his hold enough for her to pull a hand free and reach back to claw at his face while she kicked out at cloth man coming toward her from the front.

They were shouting, whether at her or each other she had no idea since she didn't understand a word they were saying. All she could do was keep struggling. She did manage one satisfying kick on cloth man's shin, and she saw him stumble. And she was pretty sure her nails had made some inroads into the other fellow's face. But, good lord, they stank. How could they bear it?

Then all of a sudden, it was over. Her captor threw her to the ground, and when she lifted her head, she saw them running away, pursued by men in tan uniforms with red hats. Irmak's Turkish troopers. One of the troopers stopped to help her up, smiled when he saw she was not injured, and ran off to join the pursuit.

She stood, or at least leaned, against the building

while she caught her breath and waited for her heart to slow to a reasonable pace. Moving gingerly, she checked her limbs. Nothing seemed to be broken, though she was bruised in a number of places. Then she realized that Mélisande was standing there looking distraught. The poor child must have been terrified.

"It's all right, Mélisande. They are gone, and I am not seriously hurt." She wasn't really finished being frightened herself, but she tried to sound confident for the girl's sake and managed a weak smile.

Mélisande turned on her in a fury. "Those stupid Turks. They have ruined everything."

Emily wondered if she had hit her head. She felt decidedly confused and couldn't even manage a question. All she could do was look at Mélisande blankly. Then she asked, "The Turks? They were Turks who tried to grab me?"

"No, of course not. The Turkish soldiers are to blame."

"To blame? But they rescued me from those two men." Emily was growing more, not less, confused as Mélisande spoke.

"They were supposed to make you disappear, those two, and now the Turks have frightened them and they have run away. Where will I find another pair? And it will not matter if I do, because now everyone will know about it, so you cannot just disappear." Mélisande was swinging about, waving her hands rather the way an angry cat swishes her tail.

"They were supposed...? You wanted them to...?" Emily shook her head. Was it her French that was at fault? Was she misunderstanding what Mélisande was saying? "I don't understand. What are you talking about?"

Mélisande spun about to face her. "Lucien is mine! You don't need him, and I do. He must marry me so he can take me away from here, back to France. You cannot take him away from me."

Emily backed up a step, away from the building and the alley. "Really, this is absurd. What are you talking about? I am not taking Lucien away from you."

"Do not deny it. I saw you kiss him, there on the rooftop. You want him for yourself, but he is mine! He has to be mine!"

As Mélisande kept coming toward her, Emily kept backing away. She was getting nervous. What on earth had possessed the girl? She was talking like a lunatic. "This is ridiculous. Lucien does not belong to you. You are just a child."

That was obviously the wrong thing to say, because Mélisande shrieked in fury and flew at Emily, who held up her arms to fend off the girl's claws. Suddenly she was falling through the air. She screamed in fear. A stab of pain went through her head.

Then there was nothing.

# Sixteen

PERHAPS IT WAS THE CLARITY OF THE DESERT AIR THAT did it. Or perhaps it was the sheer discomfort of trying to sleep on stony ground, wrapped only in a blanket in the cold desert night.

Whatever it was, it had cleared his head. Lucien rode through the early morning toward the city of Mosul feeling far happier than he had felt in…in years, it seemed. To tell the truth, he could not remember ever feeling this happy. He threw back his head and laughed out loud.

Everything had been backwards in his mind. He saw it now. The only mystery was how it had taken him so long to come to his senses. How could he have been so blind for so long?

It was not the chains of La Boulaye that had turned his grandfather into a bitter and miserable man. It was the memories of a lost world, a world he was powerless to resurrect. The more he had struggled to return to that lost past, the more angry he became at his failure, and the more he took out his anger and frustration on those around him.

It was not the chains of marriage that had made his parents miserable. It was marriage to the wrong person. They had been trapped together in a house— never a home—as strangers to each other, strangers who had no desire to become better acquainted.

Marriage to Emily would be nothing like that. She was not a burden or obligation, not at all. Instead, she was liberation. She had set him free of the chains of the past and shown him the infinite possibilities for happiness—happiness with her.

It was love that made the difference, he had finally realized. Love did not chain you. It set you free. It opened the cage that set you apart from all others. Love opened the door to happiness.

And he loved Emily.

He pulled up his horse so he could concentrate on that thought. He turned the word over in his mind and smiled again. Love. Why had he never thought of that? It was so simple. Such a little word and it explained so much.

He nudged the horse into a brisk walk and continued toward Mosul.

As for La Boulaye, it was simply a place. Those who lived there might be happy or miserable. It was not the place itself that determined their feelings. Nor did he have to live at La Boulaye, under his grandfather's thumb. What had even made him think that was his only choice? His father had returned there for whatever reason, but that did not mean that Lucien had to.

The estate of Varennes was his own, his inheritance from his mother, the gift she had given him. It was a modest estate, nothing like La Boulaye, but it could support a family in more than decent comfort. It was probably nothing like the estates of the wealthy Marquess of Penworth either, but he did not think that would weigh too heavily with Emily. Varennes was a good estate. It had its own beauties. She would be able to see them.

He wanted to run straight to Emily, tell her of his realizations, and beg her to marry him. A grin took over his face. That was not precisely true. What he really wanted was to toss her over his shoulder, take her someplace private, and do all the things he had been fantasizing about. However, he was determined to do this properly.

First there must be permission from her father, and before he could ask permission to court the marquess's daughter, he must show himself to be respectable. He could not present himself in all his dirt, dusty and unshaven. He might not be a man of great wealth, but he was a man of property and of family with a noble heritage, and he knew very well what was proper. A nobody could not aspire to court Lady Emily Tremaine, but the grandson and heir of the Comte de la Boulaye could so aspire. Now he needed to transform himself into that man.

As he rode, he considered what he would need to do. A trip to the baths, certainly. He rubbed a hand over his the rough bristles on his chin. He must look like a vagabond. That would hardly do. And while he was getting clean, he must have Hamiz brush and press his frock coat. It had been stuffed back into his baggage somewhere.

Irmak scowled at the empty space by the waterfront. The two pieces of scum had escaped into the alleys, and now when he and his men returned to the place of the attack, Lady Emily and her friend had also disappeared. Where could she have gone? She had not appeared to be seriously injured, but surely she had enough sense to wait for an escort before she made her way home. He had never thought her a particularly stupid creature, and she had just seen for herself how dangerous the streets could be for a woman.

Where could she have gone?

His men prodded a few beggars and questioned a pair of workmen heading for the docks, but no one had seen anything. Or so they said. Irmak barked an order and his men fell in behind him as they marched to the house of Lord Penworth.

Their hammering on the door caused considerable confusion. The servants were up and about, of course, but the effendi—Lord Penworth—and his ladies were another matter. It was early, the bread had not been baked yet, and the coffee beans were still unground. Should they be disturbed when the household was not yet ready to serve them?

At first, it was only the doorkeeper who expressed his uncertainty, but then the woman bringing fruit from the market joined in, and soon everyone in the house had gathered in the courtyard. Everyone had an opinion, and all opinions were voiced repeatedly. The boys who served the lord and his aide, the women who served the lady and her daughters, all had something to say. The cook and those who cared for the house and those who ran errands were equally vociferous.

No one, however, had anything to say about the whereabouts of Lady Emily.

Finally, in exasperation, Irmak roared for silence. He received it. All eyes turned to him as a hush settled over the courtyard. He looked around, glaring at each one in turn, and then pointed at a man who was neither the youngest nor the oldest of the servants. "You. Go to Lord Penworth. Wake him if need be. Inform him that I am here to inquire about the safety of his daughter."

A collective gasp was heard. All turned to look at their neighbors, but when no explanation was seen there, they turned back to Irmak. The servant he had chosen bobbed his head in obedience and scurried off to do as he was bid. The rest watched Irmak, and Irmak in turn examined them. He noted which ones looked worried, which ones looked curious, which ones were storing up an item to be discussed in the bazaar, and which ones were enjoying a drama that caused them no pain.

He also noted one boy, a thin boy, the sort who raced all over the city carrying messages for a coin or just a bit of bread. The boy looked frightened. A look at one of his men ensured that the boy had no clear path to the door should he choose to run.

Lord Penworth descended the stairs rapidly, with Oliphant on his heels. Irmak approved the English lord's intent look, the look of a soldier, prepared and not about to descend into emotion. He gave his report as a good soldier should, terse but leaving out nothing. Oliphant translated quickly, and both of them obviously understood the seriousness of the situation at once.

By now the English lady had come down as well, along with the one who was not her daughter. The voices had risen, and a hum of interest rose from the servants, but they were not losing their heads. Oliphant turned to him to report that Lady Emily was not in her room and did not appear to be in the house at all. Had she been alone on the street?

No, he told them. She had been with the French girl.

The women were sounding confused and uncertain, the men as well. He had thought it odd himself, but they were foreigners and their customs were odd. He waved at his man to bring over the frightened boy, who turned out to be the one charged with opening the door.

Between Irmak's questioning and Oliphant's reassurances, the story came out. The French girl had appeared this morning, very early. The bread had not even been baked yet. It was much earlier than visitors would come, but they were foreigners, after all, and their ways were strange. When he peered out the door, she gave him a note to take to the young lady, the effendi's daughter. He was not sure he should disturb her, it was so early after all, but the French girl had often come to the house. It was not as if she was a stranger.

The door boy looked around for assurances and while all were looking very serious, no one seemed about to beat him or even blame him.

Then, the boy said, the young lady came down. Yes, she was dressed, though simply. Not in the great dresses the English ladies wear. He gestured with his arms to show the impressive size of the English hoop skirts and the comparative narrowness of the hoopless skirt. The young lady spoke to the French girl, and they went out together. It was odd, yes, but it was not his place to stop her. And besides, the ways of foreigners are strange.

The English spoke hurriedly among themselves and then gathered more clothing about themselves. They were going to the house of the Frenchman. Perhaps Lady Emily was there. If not, they needed to find out what the French girl could tell them. Would Irmak accompany them, in case they needed his help in searching for Lady Emily?

Of course. It was his duty to protect them.

❧

When Lucien arrived at Carnac's house, it was a scene of chaos. Lord Penworth's entire household appeared to have invaded. Irmak and his men were attempting to intervene between the servants of the two households, who seemed intent on starting a small war. Carnac himself was absent, off at the excavation as usual, but Mélisande was most definitely present, screeching and sobbing. Lord and Lady Penworth were trying to get at her, shouting to make themselves heard above the hubbub.

He had to force his way into the center, pushing aside servants and strangers who seemed to have come in off the street along with everyone else.

When he got to the center of the commotion, Lady Penworth seized his arm. "Lucien, you must make her tell us what has happened to Emily."

"Emily?" His heart stopped. "Something has happened to Emily?"

Lord Penworth, his voice tight with anger, said, "A

pair of villains attempted to kidnap Emily. Irmak and his men drove them off, but now Emily is nowhere to be found. Mélisande was with her when this happened but has gone off into hysterics rather than tell us what happened."

Lucien grabbed Mélisande by the shoulders, giving her a hard shake. "Stop this nonsense and tell us what happened. Where is Emily?"

"Oh, Lucien, thank goodness you are here." Mélisande hiccuped a sob. "Make them stop shouting at me. Protect me."

"Protect you from what? All anyone wants to know is what happened to Emily. Tell us, for God's sake." He shook her again.

All that produced was more wailing at an even higher pitch. He wanted to strangle the girl. Why wouldn't she speak?

Lady Penworth pushed him aside, seized hold of Mélisande with one hand and gave her a resounding smack with the other. Its echo reverberated in the sudden silence, and Mélisande's wailing ceased abruptly. Lady Penworth tightened her fingers on the girl's shoulders, pulled her close, and spoke in a low, furious tone. "Now you listen to me, you stupid child. We are talking about my daughter's life. Her *life*. Do you understand? You will tell me right now what happened to her or I will pluck your eyes out. I will carve your pretty face into mincemeat. Do you understand?"

No one doubted that she meant every syllable.

Mélisande tried to pull back. "It was not my fault. It was all an accident."

"What was an accident?" Lady Penworth demanded,

not loosening her grip in the slightest, but giving the girl a brief shake.

"Those men, they were supposed to take her…" Her eyes widened as her words produced a gasp in her listeners, and she realized what she had said. "I mean, they tried to take her. Only they failed, and we quarreled. She fell. That is all I know."

"What do you mean, *she fell*? Where did she fall? She was gone from the place where Irmak saw her, and so were you." Lady Penworth shook her again.

Mélisande twisted around. "Lucien," she pleaded, "it was not my fault. It was all an accident."

"Just tell us where Emily is. That's all we want to know." He tried to keep his voice calm when he longed to throttle the little brat.

She looked around but could find no sympathetic face anywhere. "She fell. She fell onto the raft. It was an accident, that's all."

Lady Penworth gave another shake. "And then? What happened then?"

"I was frightened. I ran away."

Lord Penworth intervened before his wife struck another blow. "We must find the spot. Irmak knows where he saw them. We will bring the girl along to make certain we are in the right place."

Lucien followed Irmak as the Turk marched toward the river. He could not bear to even look at Mélisande though he had her firmly by the arm and dragged her along. How could she have behaved so callously? He had to find Emily. She had to be all right. He could not bear it if she was hurt, or if…

He could not even think that.

# Seventeen

IRMAK STOPPED ABRUPTLY IN THE SPACE BY THE wharves where the attack had taken place. It was as deserted as it had been earlier. Even more deserted. There were still no people about, and now the keleks were gone as well.

Mélisande tried to pull loose, but Lucien held her arm in too firm a grip for her to be able to escape. She still gave out the occasional sob.

He turned her to face the waterfront. "Here? Is this where it happened?"

She sniffled and nodded.

"Damn you!" He pushed her away with such force that she would have fallen had one of the soldiers not caught her. "There are no rafts here. There is nothing. Do you mean you pushed her into the river and left her to drown?" Lucien turned and stood at the river's edge, looking down into its muddy depths in despair.

"No, wait." Oliphant caught his arm. "There would have been rafts here this morning, some of the ones we hired. The loading was finished yesterday, and they were to set out today. If she did fall onto one of them…"

Lucien straightened up and his eyes flashed with hope. "Yes, if…" He turned back to Mélisande and demanded, "Well? Were you telling the truth? Did she fall onto the raft?"

Again she nodded.

"But then where is she?" Lady Penworth looked around wildly. "If she fell on the raft, was she injured? Why didn't she simply get up?"

They all looked at Mélisande, who looked at the ground. "She might have hit her head when she fell," she whispered.

"Even so," said Lady Penworth, "someone should have seen her when the crews came to take the rafts." She stopped suddenly and advanced slowly on Mélisande with narrowed eyes. "Would they have seen her? No lies now."

Mélisande shrank back but there was no place for her to go. All eyes were fixed on her, and none of them were friendly. She licked her lips. "Perhaps… maybe…"

Lady Penworth looked at her with a mixture of anguish and despair. "What happened?"

"All right," Mélisande cried. "She fell between two of the crates and one of the tarpaulins fell down to cover her."

A moment of disbelieving silence descended.

Then Lucien took charge. "To the south the river is full of twists and turns. If I ride straight along the cliffs, I should be able to intercept them. At the worst, I will catch up to them when they stop for the night. If you come along the road with a carriage…?" He turned to Lord Penworth, who seemed startled to be taking orders but nodded. A carriage might be needed.

Then Lucien turned back to Mélisande. "Describe the raft. What was on it?"

She shook her head. "I don't know."

"Think, you little fool!"

She stepped back, cringing. "There were some crates."

"How many?"

"Three, no, four. Two on each side."

"That helps," said Oliphant. "There are only two rafts like that. They have the clay tablets, and the crates are about four feet square."

Lucien nodded. "You will need to stay here, so there will be someone who understands if, if there are any messages, or anything."

Oliphant nodded.

Once Lucien had left at a run, the others began to sort themselves out as he had ordered.

"I will need to pack some medical supplies, just in case," said Lady Penworth, setting out to return to the house. Suddenly, she stopped and began to sway. Her husband caught her, and she clung to him. "Oh, Phillip, she will be all right, won't she?"

"Yes, I'm sure of it. Lucien is a very sensible young man."

She nodded, but continued to cling to him as they made their way along, looking far older than they had been the day before.

Emily awoke to a rocking movement. It was a familiar sensation, the gentle motion of a kelek on the river. Pleasant. Soothing. She started to raise her head, but it hurt, it hurt badly. She groaned in pain but did not open her eyes. Why did her head hurt so badly? Perhaps if she did not move her head, the pain would go away. She sighed and let the gentle motion rock her back to sleep.

❦

The small square by the river was almost deserted. The Penworths and their household, along with Irmak and his troops, were all preparing to pursue Lady Emily. David Oliphant was preparing to organize a command station to receive any information.

Peering around a corner, the little door boy saw Lady Julia, still in the square. He had failed in his duty, he knew, when he had let the other young lady leave the house without anyone to protect her. He would try to make up for his failure by watching over this one and making sure she returned safely. So he watched and waited.

Lady Julia was about to return to the house with the others, hoping to be of assistance to Mr. Oliphant, when she saw that Mélisande had been left in a heap in one corner of the square. She found it difficult to call up much sympathy for the girl, but she couldn't be left here. She sighed and went over to the girl.

"Do get up, Mélisande. You can't stay here."

The response was a wailing moan. Or a moaning wail. Julia wasn't sure what it should be called, but it was an unpleasant sound, and quite useless if it was intended to garner sympathy.

"Stop this nonsense and get up," she said impatiently.

Mélisande lifted up her head. "It has all gone wrong. It wasn't supposed to happen this way. Now Lucien is very angry with me."

"Well, of course he is, and so is everyone else. What did you expect? What on earth were you thinking?"

"But that was not what I had planned. I just wanted her to go away."

"You wanted Lady Emily to go away? But why? Why have you suddenly turned on Lady Emily, who has never been anything but kind to you?"

"I saw them, Lucien and her. They were embracing. I saw them."

"Oh. Well." Julia felt slightly flustered, remembering how very young Mélisande was. And living here in isolation, perhaps she really had been that sheltered. "Well, there is really no need to be upset. That sort of thing does happen, you know, when men and women are attracted to each other. You must not consider it distressing."

"But of course I must be distressed." Mélisande rounded on her angrily. "Lucien is to marry me. It cannot be permitted that he should be kissing Lady Emily."

"Marry you?" Julia stared at the girl. "You cannot be serious. You are much too young to be thinking of marriage."

"But of course I must think of it," the girl insisted. "How else am I to escape from this place?"

Julia folded her arms like a stern governess and looked at the girl. "Do you seriously expect me to believe that you and M. Chambertin are betrothed?"

Mélisande made an expressive little moue. "It is understood, you see."

"Understood by whom?" Julia frowned. "Has M. Chambertin actually proposed to you?"

"No, no, he has always been most proper. That is understood. But he is also most sympathetic, so I know. A woman always knows, does she not?"

Julia threw up her hands in disgust. "Of all the dim-witted, simple-minded idiots! Do you have any conception of the harm you have done? Lady Emily's life is in danger because of you. For all we know, she could be dead. We have no way of knowing how badly you may have injured her. And all because a stupid little girl decides to spin romantic fantasies for herself!"

"I am not stupid! It is all of you who do not understand." Mélisande stamped her foot and sniffled.

"I wash my hands of you." Julia turned to depart. "Come along or stay here. I really do not care."

⌘

Concealed around the corner, Hadad and Karif had listened to the quarrel. They could not understand what was being said, but the woman with the Frenchman's daughter was clearly a foreigner, and here she was where M. Carnac's daughter had promised to bring her.

Hadad frowned. "Is this the same one? She does not look quite the same as she looked this morning, but I cannot tell the foreigners apart."

"She must be. Hear how they quarrel. And she is here where we were supposed to seize her."

"But that was supposed to happen this morning early."

Karif shrugged. "The soldiers interrupted then, so she brings her back so we can try again."

Hadad shook his head dubiously.

"Look! Here she comes, right toward us." Karif smiled in delight. "I will hit her with the stone, and you pick her up."

It did not work out quite that neatly.

Karif and Hadad had positioned themselves neatly in doorways on opposite sides of the street, but they were not so well concealed that Julia did not notice them as soon as she rounded the corner. Men trying to hide in doorways are rarely well-intentioned. Not being a fool, Julia turned to run.

Unfortunately, the ubiquitous blue cloak was designed for concealment, not ease of motion. Julia tripped and went sprawling almost immediately. Before she could rise again, Karif had swung his rock. She moved quickly enough to avoid the worst of it and receive most of the blow on her shoulder, but it was enough to make her cry out in pain.

The little door boy came shrieking to her rescue, and Karif swung around with a snarl to use the rock on him. They dodged back and forth, with Karif never getting quite close enough to land a blow.

Hadad hovered between Julia and the boy, not certain where to intervene. The boy had picked up a rock of his own to throw at the attackers. Karif swung wildly and called down curses on the boy. Then Julia began to get to her feet, berating Karif for picking on a child, and Hadad finally acted. He threw the heavy cloth over Julia—the cloth he had been carrying around since early morning. It muffled her cries and tangled her arms sufficiently for him to be able to toss her over his shoulder.

Calling to Karif to come along, he hurried down the alley. Karif landed a solid blow on the boy's back and followed. The door boy staggered, but pulled himself together and followed the kidnappers.

Left alone in the square, Mélisande stared after them in horror. No! This was not what was supposed to happen. Nothing should happen to Lady Julia. She did not know what to do. She took a step to follow them, but hesitated. Should she follow them? Should she go for help? She didn't know what to do. Would they blame her? But she had never meant anything to happen to Lady Julia. It wasn't her fault! It wasn't! They would blame her, and it wasn't her fault!

She ran blindly through the streets.

❧

It was several hours later that the bedraggled door boy finally reached home. Quiet had settled over the house like a pall. The absence of Lord Penworth and his family was not enough to account for the silence. The remaining servants moved about softly, speaking in whispers when speech was needed. It rarely was. Altan, who ruled over the household, did not even bother to scold Yusef for his absence.

He managed to locate Shatha, and discovered from her that Mr. Oliphant was the only one of the foreigners in the house. It was well that he was here, because Yusef doubted he could make any of the others understand what he had to say. At least he hoped it was well. He did not look forward to admitting more failure. This was twice that he had failed to protect one of the women of the house. Moreover, they all knew that Mr. Oliphant languished for love of Lady Julia. He would be very angry when he heard what Yusef had to tell him.

Two minutes later, Yusef knew his fears had been justified, but misdirected. Mr. Oliphant did not blame him. He blamed himself.

"She was left in the square all alone?"

"No, no, effendi, not alone," Yusef assured him. "The French lady was with her."

"I assumed she was with Lady Penworth." Oliphant closed his eyes. "Great God in Heaven, what have I done? How could I leave her?"

Yusef did not attempt to answer unanswerable questions.

"You said Mélisande, the French girl, was with her. What did she do?"

"They quarrel, effendi, and then the Lady Julia turns to leave and the evil men capture her. The French girl, she watches."

"Watches." The word came out as a whisper, but his fists were clenched so tightly the knuckles were white. "Could you see where they went?"

"I follow for a while, but I lose them as they near the walls." Yusef was apologetic. "But I did hear them. They argue, and the short one says they should not stay to collect the money from the French girl. They can get more if they sell her in the slave market in Damascus. The one with teeth that stick out says the trip is too dangerous and they should just take the fifty gold pieces they were promised. Then the short one says there is a slave caravan to the north. They can join that and travel safely. Then they go through a door and I cannot follow."

There was a moment of absolute stillness when Yusef finished speaking. It was so quiet that the boy thought Mr. Oliphant might even have stopped breathing. Then the storm broke. Mr. Oliphant slammed out of the room, shouting for Altan. Yusef was not sure where he went, but when he reappeared, his coat was gone, a gun was strapped to his leg, one dagger was in his belt and another in his boot, and he carried a rifle.

"Send to Mr. Rassam," he told Altan, "and explain to him what has happened. If there is any news about Lady Emily, send a messenger after Lord Penworth. And tell the servants to stay calm."

"Yes, effendi, yes. I will do as you say. And when will you return?"

"When I have Lady Julia."

# *Eighteen*

THE ROOM WAS ROCKING, NOT MUCH, BUT ENOUGH TO make Emily's stomach unhappy. She turned on her side, but the movement made her head hurt even more. Something was covering her, a heavy blanket that made it hard to breathe. She clawed at it—it didn't feel like one of her blankets—until she finally pushed it away and could breathe.

That was a bit better, but the room was still rocking. She was going to have to open her eyes if she wanted to know why.

Opening her eyes a slit, she saw the wall right in front of her, not a foot from her nose. Only it wasn't a wall at all. It was dark canvas, not just dark but dirty canvas, covering—what? She opened her eyes a bit more and turned her head to look up. It was covering some sort of box or crate. When she looked a bit higher, she saw sky, not ceiling.

Her eyes opened much wider, and she took a deep breath. Then she swallowed. All right. She wasn't in her room. She wasn't even in a building.

Where on earth was she?

She started to push herself up almost to a sitting position, leaning on one arm, but quickly discovered that was a mistake. Her stomach heaved, and her head screamed in agony. She moaned and closed her eyes again, leaning against the crate and waiting for her stomach to subside. At least the crate provided solid support.

After a few minutes, or maybe quite a bit longer, it seemed safe to open her eyes again. The light was bright enough to hurt them, but she could see that there were two crates, one on each side of her, and they were providing some shade so that she wasn't actually in the sun. That was up ahead of her, dancing on the water. Glaringly bright sun dancing on the water.

Water?

She blinked and looked again. Yes, it was water. She edged up a bit until she could look around the corner of the crate and see land, the gardens and palm trees that edged the Tigris everywhere she had seen. She took another deep breath. All right, she was on the river. In a boat? No, it had no sides. She was on a raft, a kelek. What on earth was she doing on a kelek and how had she gotten here?

Her legs were still tangled in the cloth that had been covering her, a piece of filthy canvas like the stuff that was covering the boxes. Disgusting. She pushed it away and pulled herself up to stand more or less vertical. That much exertion left her trembling, and she leaned against the crate until she felt steadier. The boxes were higher than her head, so she was still in some shade. That was a mercy, since the light she

could see was painfully bright. Even so, there was
more than enough light for her to see that her dress
was filthy. Lavender muslin was obviously a poor
choice of costume for whatever she was doing here.
She tried to brush it off, but her hands were as filthy
as her skirts.

It felt as if half of her hair was falling over her
face, and when she tried to push it back, her hand
came away sticky. Blood. Filthy as her hand was, she
could still see that it now had blood on it. Her blood,
coming from the painful place on her head. Her stomach turned at the sight.

What had happened to her?

Whatever had happened, all she wanted now was
to go home, and this raft wasn't likely to be taking her
there. Rafts leaving Mosul only traveled downriver to
Baghdad. They could not travel back upriver against
the current. She had learned that much in her time
here. Whoever was in charge of this craft was going
to have to at least put her ashore. Surely once she was
ashore, someone would help her get home. Surely.
Once she explained who her father was…if she could
manage to explain anything to people who would not
understand a word she said and who would have no
idea who her father was.

She swallowed down the panic. Panic was not
going to help.

She could hear soft voices chanting one of those sad
Arab melodies. At least that didn't sound intimidating.
A few steps brought her to the end of the boxes. She
winced as the bright sun hit her eyes, but she could
see two men lazily plying the oars while a third, the

captain, held the steering pole. They did not notice her, so she coughed gently.

The result was electrifying. The oarsmen stared at her wide-eyed and openmouthed while the captain dropped his pole and began a high, piercing cry.

She winced as the sound sent stabs of pain through her head.

"Please," she said, holding on to the crate to remain upright, "please, I need to go ashore." She gestured toward the river bank.

The captain raised his hands and looked at the sky as he uttered wailing sounds. She thought she heard the word "Allah" a number of times. Was he praying? She reached a hand out toward him and said, "Please…"

That didn't seem to help. The man closest to her leaped to his feet and began shouting and waving his arms as if trying to drive her away. She gestured at him to stop, but he only shrieked more loudly and the others joined in.

She took a step toward them and tried to make herself heard over their shrieks. That was obviously the wrong thing to do, because all three of them turned and dove into the water, leaving her alone on the raft.

She sank to her knees. What on earth was she supposed to do now?

❧

Lucien tried to work out the time, but he couldn't be certain. It had been past noon when he rode out of the city, close to one o'clock, he thought. And Mélisande had lured Emily down to the waterfront early, but that could not have been before sunrise. That was early, around five at this time of year, but it was unlikely to be earlier than six when they went to the waterfront. Time had to be allowed for the kidnapping attempt, time for Irmak's intervention, then Mélisande's attack. Who would have thought the child was such a vicious little beast? If anything had happened to Emily, he would...

No. He would not consider such thoughts. He must work out the time. The attack on Emily would have taken place at seven o'clock perhaps. That would put him six hours behind her.

No, not that long. The crews for the rafts had not arrived when Emily was attacked. So the rafts would probably not have set off until close to eight. That would put him five hours behind them. Perhaps only four. And then the rafts were heavy and unwieldy under their loads of stone. They would have to travel slowly to navigate the curves in the river, and all the islands—that would slow them down even more. On horseback he could go much faster.

Surely he could catch up to them.

He had to catch up to them, and it had to be soon.

His stallion thundered over the plateau above the river. The river curved out of sight from time to time, but never for long. Certainly not long enough for the entire fleet of rafts to be out of sight. Frustratingly, the only crafts to be seen were a few fishing boats.

Lucien forced himself to slow the horse to a trot. He would accomplish nothing by killing the beast, and his route was much shorter than the twists and turns of the river. At the worst, even if he missed them on the river, even if he rode past while they were hidden behind a bend, he would reach the place where they would stop for the night before the rafts reached it. That would be the sensible goal. At that point he could rescue Emily from whatever raft she was on easily and safely.

If she was still safe.

If she was not too badly injured.

If she had not already been discovered and...

No. He was not going to think about those possibilities. He would find her, and she would be safe and well. She would never be in danger again. He would make sure of that. He swore it.

The horse eased into a canter.

Time passed, but he had no sense of it. Nor could he say how far he had come. There was only the sound of the horse's hooves—a trot, then a canter, a trot, then a canter, the rhythm repeating over and over. And every now and then a halt when the river came into view and he paused to scan it, longing for a glimpse of the rafts.

His rounded an outcropping of rocks and discovered that his route was near the river once more, and this time—Yes!

Looking down the slope, he could see rafts, a dozen of them, maybe more, all transporting cargoes of crates covered with tarpaulins. One of the numerous islands in the river—a long one, this time—was forcing them into a narrow column. He started to urge the horse into a downhill race to intercept them before they could spread out again, but pulled up abruptly.

He saw her. It had to be her. He was much too far off to be able to discern features, but a figure in what looked like European skirts had emerged from behind the crates on one of the last rafts. Someone in a lavender dress. Someone who was standing and moving. It had to be Emily, Emily alive and well.

He gave a shout. She could not hear him, not at this distance, but he could not hold in his joy and relief.

He had just started to alter his course when he saw the crew of her raft stand up and jump overboard. What the devil was going on? He kicked the horse into a gallop and they flew down the incline and across the fields to the river's edge.

Emily's raft was drifting rather than traveling. The other rafts were leaving it behind. She was standing up and seemed to be trying to guide her raft to the bank with the steering pole, but with no one to man the oars, it was frequently spun about by eddies in the river. By some miracle, it had not crashed into any rocks, but it was traveling in circles. He was close enough to see her clearly now, having arrived at the bank downstream from the raft, but she did not seem to hear his shouts.

Muttering curses, he flung himself off the horse and had the presence of mind to tie it to a tree before he kicked off his boots and dove into the water. With powerful strokes that made nothing of the current, he headed directly for the raft, adjusting to its erratic course with barely conscious effort. Once he reached it, he hoisted himself aboard, only noticing the effort his swim had required when he had to lie still to catch his breath. He stood to see Emily, her face shadowed, her eyes wide with astonishment.

"Lucien," she breathed. "Lucien, it is really you. Thank God!"

He reached out a hand to her, and she flew into his arms.

Unable to speak, he held her so tightly she seemed a part of him. She was a part of him, though he did not know how to tell her this. He dropped kisses on her hair and face between murmured endearments. She clung to him in turn, whispering his name over and over.

A sudden jolt as the raft bounced off a rock almost knocked them from their feet, and they came apart enough to look at each other. His first clear sight of her stopped his breath. Those shadows on her face were streaks of blood. He reached out trembling fingers to touch her face.

"Ah, *chérie*, what happened?" He could barely get the words out.

"I don't know. I don't even know where I am, except that this seems to be a raft like the ones we came on. All I know is that I woke up with a terrible headache, feeling sick, and I was all tangled up in a piece of cloth. Filthy cloth," she said, with a bit of resentment creeping into her voice.

Although he was glad to see irritation begin to replace the fear that had been in her eyes when he first reached the raft, his own fears remained. "You are ill?"

"The nausea is better, but my head still hurts a bit."

He smiled slightly. "I do not doubt it. You must have been unconscious for hours. You've been traveling down the river for quite a while."

"Hours?" She looked around in bewilderment. "But what is this raft? And how did I get here?"

He did not want to deal with the second question,

not yet, but the first was easy enough. "This is one of the rafts your papa hired to carry the carvings from Nineveh down to Baghdad. There are many of them." He pointed up ahead, where a dozen other rafts were nearing the end of the island that had narrowed their passage. "But what happened to the crew of this raft? I saw men leaping into the river."

"I don't know that either. I don't understand it. It took me an age to untangle myself from that horrid cloth. When I finally worked myself free of it, I managed to drag myself up, holding onto those boxes, crates, whatever they are. I could hear voices, and I thought they could tell me where I was and how to get home. I tried to ask, but they didn't seem to understand. At first they just stared at me, but then one of them pointed at me and shrieked something that sounded like *afraid*. Then they were all shrieking, and they dived off the raft, leaving me here by myself. Why on earth should they be afraid of me?"

He frowned, puzzled, and then laughed aloud when he suddenly realized what had happened. "Not *afraid*," he said. "*Afreet*. An evil spirit. They thought you were an afreet."

"Well that's hardly flattering." She sounded affronted. "All I did was ask for help. I realize they probably didn't understand, but I did try waving at the shore."

He kept smiling, whether from amusement or relief he was not sure. "Many of the workmen are convinced that these carvings are haunted by the spirits of the ancients. Well, not haunted, precisely, but they fear the spirits are angry at being disturbed. I know it was most difficult for Oliphant to find men willing to ferry the crates down to Baghdad. There was much fear. Once men believe in the presence of evil spirits, it is impossible to convince them otherwise. And then you appear like, well, to tell the truth, like a ghost with your face pale and streaked with blood, and your hair also."

"Oh! Blood? On my face?" Her hands flew up and she looked appalled as she felt the matted tangle of her hair and the streaks on her face. "Blood all over me. Oh dear, I must look dreadful. Horrible. Why didn't you say something?"

Ah, but she looked adorable, so worried about her appearance. He pulled her to him. "All that matters is that you are alive and well. You are the most beautiful sight I ever saw." He cupped her head with one hand, tilting it so that he could kiss her properly. And he did.

He sipped at her lips, tasted, drank deeply. He molded her to him—she fit so perfectly against him—and caressed her. Holding her felt so right. It was as if chains that had bound him, chains he had not realized were there, suddenly melted away, and at last he was free.

"You are mine," he whispered to her. "Mine. We belong together. I will never let you go."

"Yes," she whispered back, her arms wrapped around his neck. "Together, wherever you wish to go—Samarkand, the Gate of Jade, wherever."

He smiled against her cheek. "No, not to Samarkand. We..."

She sighed and pushed away. "But first we have to get ashore. I hope you know how to steer this thing, because I was not managing very well."

His practical Emily had reasserted herself. Much as he regretted having to loosen his hold on her, he had to admit that she had a point. Unfortunately, although her hope was sensible, the truth was that he had no idea how to guide the kelek to shore. But before he could admit his ignorance, the sound of gunfire interrupted.

Their kelek, which had been turning erratically, was now trailing well behind the others, but those others were under attack. Dozens of small boats were pouring into the narrow passage, swarming around the rafts, and in between the gunshots came cries and shouts, cries that were too often cut off abruptly. Lucien cursed and threw Emily into the river before any stray bullets headed in their direction.

She came up sputtering. "Oh, that's *cold*! What...?" A bullet splashed in the water near them. "The noise—gunfire? We're being shot at?" She sounded quite outraged. "For goodness' sake, not again!"

He would laugh at her annoyance if this were not so dangerous. "Yes, again. But unfortunately, this is not Kurds playing their games with us." He looked around quickly. They were not too far from the shore. "Over there. We need to get out of sight and into those reeds. Can you swim?" Another bullet whizzed past them. This was not amusing. "Keep down!"

She nodded and disappeared beneath the surface.

"Emily!" What the devil was she doing? He hadn't meant that far down. Was she drowning? Before he could dive after her, she resurfaced. "What the devil are you doing?"

She tossed her head to shake off the water. "I can

swim, but not wrapped in yards of fabric. I had to get rid of my petticoats. They would drown me."

He opened his mouth to speak, but no words came out. She had terrified him, but what she had done, it was not just sensible but necessary. He should have thought of it himself, but he just wanted to get her down, off the raft, so she would not be a target. There was nothing rational for him to say, so he waved her toward the shore.

# Nineteen

THE WATER WAS FREEZING, AND SHE HAD NOT BEEN swimming since she was a child, swimming in the shallow coves of Dorset near Penworth Castle. The shore had not looked terribly far away from the raft, but the current was far stronger than she had expected. That had been stupid of her. It was the current, after all, that was carrying the rafts downstream. Of course it was strong.

She concentrated on swimming. Lucien was beside her, guiding her, helping her. Finally they were within reach of the shore. She kicked down and felt solid earth—well, semi-solid mud—under her. She gave a strangled laugh of relief and started to stand, only to have Lucien pull her down.

"Keep yourself down," he said in a low voice. "We do not wish to be seen."

He ushered her through the marshy edge of the shore, always keeping low, beneath the waving tops of the reeds. She dragged herself along the path he made through the tangle. The reeds seemed malevolent, the way they kept snatching at her. She had to pull

herself free with every step, if you could call it a step
when she was on her knees more often than on her
feet. Even when she was on her feet, she had to keep
bent over.

At least the water here wasn't as cold here as it
had been deeper in the river. That didn't mean it
was warm. She kept shivering, which did not help
her balance.

It may not have been only the cold that made her
shiver. Lucien had a grim look on his face. She had
never seen him look that way. More than the gunshots
exploding behind them, his expression convinced her
that there was danger.

They finally reached solid ground, of a sort. There
was a bank, only a foot or two high, but there was
grass growing on it, not reeds. It was scrabbly and
scratchy, not like soft English grass, but it was dry. She
collapsed on it with a sigh of relief and rolled over,
letting the sun warm her.

Lucien gave her a quick smile, probably meant to be
reassuring, and then turned back to peer through the
reeds. The gunfire had slowed a bit, but there were
shouts and shrieks, along with splashes. She crawled up
beside him and tried to see what was happening. There
seemed to be a great many people in the water. Many
of them were not swimming, just floating. Face down.

She shivered. "This is not Kurds trying to frighten
people as a joke, is it?"

He shook his head without turning to her. "No,
not Kurds."

"What, then?"

He pushed her head down abruptly. "Do not look."

But she had already seen. "They are shooting the people in the water," she said in a small voice.

"I am very much afraid it is pirates. And they are not very pleasant people."

She sat up. "Pirates? That's ridiculous."

He pushed her down again. "Do not let yourself be seen! Yes, pirates."

"That's ridiculous. There are no pirates in this day and age. Besides, this is a river, not an ocean." She was frightened. Even with Lucien beside her, she was frightened, and she did not like it. If only things would make sense, but this was not making sense.

At least her idiotic remark won a lopsided grin from him. "You will be more happy if I call them brigands on boats? That is what pirates are, no?"

"But why would pirates want to steal crates of ancient carvings? It's not as if they are valuable except to scholars."

"Ah well, it is the stories, you see." He stretched out beside her, keeping an arm over her. It was probably just to keep her from popping up and being seen, but it felt comforting. He gently brushed a lock of her hair off her face. That felt even more comforting. His voice was as gentle as his hand when he spoke. "I told you that many of the workmen thought that there were evil spirits haunting the carvings?"

She nodded.

"That was one of the stories being told in the bazaar. The other was that all those carvings and clay tablets were only a ruse. Hidden in those crates was a fortune in gold and jewels, the treasure of the ancients. That is obviously the story that the pirates believed."

"How ridiculous."

He shrugged. "They would call it ridiculous to make a fuss over a little bit of clay with marks like hen scratchings on them, things of no use to anyone."

The gunfire had subsided to nothing more than an occasional shot and had been replaced by thuds and cracks and loud splashes. Motioning her to keep down, Lucien peered through the reeds again. "It seems they have discovered their mistake. They are taking out their frustrations on the crates."

"On the crates?"

"That noise they are making—they are breaking open the crates and then, I fear, when they find no gold or jewels, they are throwing the contents into the river."

That halted her. "Oh dear. All those lovely carvings. M. Carnac will be so upset."

"Yes, he will. But I am out of sympathy with the Carnacs just now, and me, I prefer that the pirates take out their anger on the carvings and not on us. It is best that we keep out of sight here, no?"

A sudden burst of gunfire, with a few bullets reaching the reeds, had them both ducking their heads. A few shore birds flew up in noisy panic, drawing additional gunfire. When Lucien raised himself up to look, he muttered in disgust. "Idiots. They discover they have been foolish, so they fire their guns at anything. We had best keep still a while longer."

Emily was perfectly willing to do that. She huddled beside him, grateful for his encircling arms and taking comfort from his nearness. As the crashes and splashes grew fainter and the gunshots became more and more sporadic, the tension in her body eased.

Eventually, the noise faded away completely. When she felt Lucien lift himself up to look, she raised her head. "Are they gone?"

He turned and smiled down at her, the first real smile she had seen from him today. "Yes. They are gone. We are safe." Then his smile faded, and something new appeared in his eyes.

"What is the matter?"

"Your, your clothes. What happened to your clothes?" His voice sounded oddly hoarse.

She looked down and a flood of embarrassment washed over her. She was wearing nothing below the waist but a single stocking and her drawers, and they were so wetly plastered against her that they might as well be nonexistent. "I told you I couldn't swim in my petticoats." That came out sounding resentful rather than sensible, but she couldn't help it. She tried to lift the fabric of her drawers loose from her hip, but that only pulled it tighter elsewhere.

"Emily. My brave Emily." His voice was a soft caress. He trailed a finger down the side of her face. "The blood has all been washed away."

"Oh." She looked up at him, wasn't certain what to say. She tried, "That's good, isn't it?"

"Very good." His smile seemed to wrap around her, and then his arm did, turning her gently to lie half beside him, half beneath him. She could feel the coarse grass of the river bank tickling her legs. Lucien's face was above her. The heat in his eyes kindled a flame in her.

"Emily?" he asked.

"Yes," she said. "Yes." She knew what he was asking. Did he truly not know her answer?

His kiss was demanding, voracious. She welcomed it and wrapped her arms around his shoulders, pulling him down to make demands of her own. This time there would be no slamming doors to interrupt them. This time she would not turn coward and flee.

What remained of her bodice and shift soon disappeared as his fingers nimbly dispensed with buttons and ties. His hands, his clever hands, slipped over her, caressing her and introducing her to sensations she had never even suspected.

Her hands were busy too, slipping under what remained of his shirt, exploring the hard muscles of his chest beneath the soft curls of hair.

Then her drawers were gone too, and his hand slipped between her thighs to caress her there, moving higher and higher. He was touching her there, and she gasped in shocked surprise and then only in surprise and then in astonished pleasure. She had not known she could feel such sensations. Her body arched up to meet his hand, and she heard herself crying out. And all throughout, Lucien kept murmuring, "Yes, yes, my love, *ah chérie, comme ça.*"

He kissed her again, swallowing her final cry. But when he began to undo his trousers, he suddenly stopped.

She reached to help him, but he grasped her wrist to hold her hand still. His voice was strained, as if he was in pain. "Emily, we will marry, no? That is understood, is it not?"

"Yes, of course." Did he fear she might say no? Did he think she would say no to anything he asked?

His trousers were gone, and he settled himself

between her thighs. In a fleeting moment of rational thought she considered how odd it was that such an unfamiliar position should feel so natural, so right. Then he pushed into her, and she cried out again, this time in pain.

It hurt. It really hurt.

She looked up at him in astonishment.

He looked as if he too were in pain. "I am sorry, chérie. *Je regrette. Mais ça sera mieux.* It will be better."

Even as he spoke, the pain eased a bit, as if her body were getting used to him.

He began to move in her, pulling back and then pushing in. The pain did ease, and it was no longer actually unpleasant. He began to move faster and faster. "Not long," he gasped, and then cried, as if now he was in pain.

He held himself over her, propped up on his elbows with his head bowed, breathing heavily, as if after a race. When his breathing eased, he rolled to the side, one arm over his eyes, the other pulling her close to his side. It had sounded as if he were in great pain before, but now he was smiling.

"Are you all right?" she asked.

He huffed a laugh. "Chérie, it would not be possible to be better." He turned to kiss her lightly. "But you, I am sorry there was pain for you. It happens so, the first time, for many women. But no more. I promise you that there will be no more pain the next time or any other time. Only pleasure."

She wanted to believe him. He would not lie to her, she was sure of that. But how could he know? Oh well, the early part had been wonderful. There would always be that. And right now, lying here on his shoulder, tucked under his arm, this was lovely too. So warm and peaceful.

The next thing she knew, Lucien was shaking her to wake her up.

# Twenty

HER HEAD RESTED ON HIS CHEST AS SHE DOZED. HE tilted his head just a bit so that her dark honey hair brushed across his nose. It was almost dry now though it still smelled of the river. Never would he have believed that he would consider that a delightful smell, but mingled with the scent of Emily, it was the most marvelous of perfumes.

He had never felt such peace, such joy, all mixed together. He had known pleasure before, many sorts of pleasure, but he did not think he had ever felt this total contentment before. His arm tightened around her, holding her safe against him. *She had been so brave. Was there another woman with such courage? She will always be safe now. I will keep her safe. She is mine. My magnificent Emily.*

Unhappily, they could not remain here. They had to return to Mosul, to her family, and, sooner or later, to his. He gave her a little shake to awaken her and called her name.

Still dozing, she made a little sound of pleasure—if she were a cat, he would have called it a purr—and nuzzled his chest. He dropped a kiss on the top of her head and then stood up, reaching a hand down to lift her to her feet. "Come, we must depart. Your parents are greatly worried about you, and they cannot be far behind. We must go to meet them. And we must not encounter them with you looking as if you have just been ravished." He had buttoned his trousers and began replacing what clothes she had.

She tilted her head back and smiled wickedly. "Ravished." The smile gave way to a confused frown. "Worried about me why? And why was I on that raft in the first place? How did you come to find me? What is going on?"

"You do not know?" That had not occurred to him. She had not said anything. But then, there had not been much time for conversation. Or rather, the time they had was not wasted on conversation.

She shook her head. "Mélisande came to the house very early. There was something she wanted to show me down by the river, something secret." She wrinkled her nose. "That girl is much given to dramatics, you know. At any rate, I went with her. I was feeling a bit uncertain, you know. You had vanished without saying anything, without any message." She paused and looked at him uncertainly.

He pulled her to his side. "Forgive me, my love. I was being stupid."

Her look remained uncertain, and this time she did not melt against him, but she nodded as if she agreed about the stupidity and continued. "There were two men who attacked me—I remember that. I remember struggling with them, but then I thought I saw Irmak and his men come to chase them away. Did they come back?"

"No, it was not those men. Irmak did run them off. I am afraid it was Mélisande. She pushed you, she said, and you hit your head. Or it may be that she hit it for you. But you landed on the kelek, and she hid you behind the crates."

She stared at him round-eyed. "Mélisande? But why on earth would she do such a thing?"

"I do not know, but I fear it may somehow be my fault." A wave of guilt swept over him. "I fear I do not pay much attention to her distress when her father says he will not send her to school in Paris. I do not take her seriously."

Emily waved her hand dismissively. "Of course you didn't. She is always carrying on about one thing or another, seeing herself as the heroine of her tragic tales. But I assure you, I will have a few things to say to that little miss when we get back."

He was able to smile now. "And me, I will speak to your father as soon as we return. We can be married in Baghdad easily enough, I think. There are officials there, and even priests, if you prefer. And then we can leave."

She lifted her head to give him a dubious look. "I have no objection to being married soon, but I may need a bit of time to prepare for the journey. I have no idea what I will need in Samarkand. What is it like there?"

"Samarkand?" He was momentarily puzzled, but then smiled. "No, we do not go to Samarkand. We go to France. We can stop in Paris if there are things you need, and then we will go to my home, to Varennes."

"What?" She had her hands on her hips and was staring at him. "What are you talking about?"

He could not stop smiling. "How adorable you look." He tucked a tumbled curl behind her ear. "Do not distress yourself. Are you not pleased? I thought you had no great longing for Samarkand."

"I don't. But I thought that was where you wanted to go." She stepped back and regarded him doubtfully. "And what is this about Varennes? Is that where your grandfather lives? I thought you did not like living with him."

"No, no, he is not there. He remains at La Boulaye. We need not have anything to do with him." He paused, considering, then shrugged. "Well, we need not have much to do with him. Varennes is my own estate, from my mother. You will like it, I hope. It is not enormous, but there is a pretty house, and the vineyards that surround it produce good wine. We can be comfortable there, you will see."

"Yes, but I don't see. I don't see at all. What about Samarkand and the Gate of Jade? What about all the places you want to see?" She waved her hands about, frowning. "What about all those chains you want to escape, those obligations, those…"

He pulled her to him and silenced her with a kiss.

"I made a discovery," he said. "With you, there are no chains. You set me free. I love you, and you are everything I have been seeking."

Her expression softened. "That's lovely. Because I really don't want to be an obligation, you see."

He kissed her again, and she seemed to enjoy it almost as much as he. This time she softened in his arms at once, molding herself to him. He began a leisurely exploration of her mouth and almost purred himself as she ran her fingers through his hair.

Then her fingers tightened on his hair, and she pulled his head up. "Wait," she said. "You said you have an estate of your own? What do you mean?"

He winced and reached up to loosen her fingers. "The estate of Varennes is mine from my mother, so you need not worry. We will not be dependent on my grandfather."

She held him back with a hand on his chest and narrowed her eyes at him. "Do you mean to tell me that you are not an adventurer? You're…you're what? A farmer? A man of property? You're just *ordinary*?" Her voice rose in outrage. "You have been misleading me all this time?"

"An adventurer? Certainly not. Whatever gave you that idea?" He felt affronted. "My family has been established in the ancient nobility of Burgundy for centuries. Whatever made you think that I was an adventurer?"

She laughed at that, and it was not an understanding laugh. She looked quite annoyed. More than annoyed. She looked furious. Why should she be upset that he was a man of family? This made no sense.

Sensibly or not, she continued to glare at him. "What gave me that idea? Oh, perhaps it was the fact that you were wandering about the globe with no particular purpose. Or the fact that you claimed to be estranged from any family you might have and had no ties to anyplace, at least none that you considered important enough to mention. Or perhaps that you spoke only of the many places you wanted to visit. And look at you!" She waved her hand at him.

He glanced down at himself. He did have his trousers on, and the remains of his shirt, but that was all. "You are wearing even less," he pointed out.

"But I was attacked. And you, half the time you are unshaven, you need a haircut, and you wear those dun-colored clothes all the time."

"But that is just practical," he protested. "I never said I was an adventurer."

"No, but you never said that you weren't. And don't tell me that you weren't aware of what everyone thought."

His lower lip stuck out in a pout briefly before it retreated to a rueful grin. "It is possible, just possible, mind you, that your misapprehension might be considered reasonable."

"After all this, it turns out that you are just a perfectly ordinary gentleman. Just like every other man I have ever known." She folded her arms and turned away from him.

Her annoyance began to irritate him. "But this is ridiculous, is it not? You were willing to marry a rootless adventurer and travel the world with him, but now you turn away from me because I am...what? Someone your parents might approve?"

"Well, yes."

"Emily, this is ridiculous. And besides, I am not an ordinary gentleman."

She looked at him uncertainly. "What do you mean, you are not an ordinary gentleman?"

"I am Lucien August Gilbert de Chambertin, and

my grandfather is the Comte de la Boulaye. I am his heir, so you will one day be a comtesse. I am sorry if this offends you."

"Your grandfather is a *count*?" She continued to glare at him, but eventually a corner of her mouth twitched in the beginning of a smile. "I am being ridiculous, aren't I? But I had screwed up my courage, you see. I was ready to run off with you to Samarkand or wherever, and you have quite cut the ground from under me."

The smile turned into a self-mocking laugh. "You have ruined my opportunity to be a heroine worthy of romance, one who gave up wealth, luxury, her position in the social whirl, all to follow her own true love. And not only must I give up all those dreams of drama, but I suppose you plan to put an end to encounters with kidnappers and pirates and demented children who want to kill me. I will dwindle into a wife in a marriage of dull respectability with a perfectly acceptable gentleman who is even a nobleman. Alas!" With her fist to her forehead, she struck a dramatic pose.

"I see that it will be difficult for you to give up the excitement of pirate attacks and such, but I do promise to try to keep you from being too bored." He pulled her back into his arms.

"Mmmm." She nestled against his chest. "You promise I will not be bored?"

"A man can only do his best."

Some minutes later, he pulled away again. "We must get you into your clothes, or at least what remains of them. Then we try to find my horse. Your parents are following, and I think they will be happier with me if we present ourselves to them as boring and respectable."

"Ah yes," she sighed. "Papa does tend to worry."

"And how do you suppose I felt when you disappeared?" He pulled her against him once more and held her tightly before taking a deep breath. "But I hope we get to the horse before they do. Then at least I will be able to wrap you in a blanket for respectability."

∽

The trip to the horse, wherever he had left it, was not the most comfortable of strolls. Emily began to think that she would not mind seeing the end of this particular adventure. They did manage to find a path of beaten dirt along the fields that edged the river, but the sun was high and the path was hot—hot enough to feel as if it were burning the soles of her feet.

When Lucien noticed her limping, he tried to fashion shoes from leaves that he wrapped around her feet, fastening them in place with ties of twisted grass. For a nobleman, he was quite good at improvising solutions and would make a very good adventurer, she told him.

He kept worrying that the walk was too difficult for her, so she had to keep up a brave front. It wasn't as if there was actually any alternative to walking. She tried to take her mind off her sore feet by looking around her, but rows and rows of unfamiliar vegetables did not provide much of an interesting diversion. It seemed miles before they reached the trees where the horse waited, and it may have been.

The horse snorted impatiently and pawed the dirt when they appeared.

"He is not happy with me," Lucien said sadly.

Emily limped to a hummock and sat down. "I expect he's thirsty, waiting here where he can hear the river but too far away for him to reach it." She licked her dry lips, thirsty herself.

"Most annoying for him." Lucien untied the horse and led him to the river, where he did indeed drink deeply while Lucien filled the canteen hanging from the saddle and soaked the remains of his shirt in the water. When they returned, he tied up the horse once more and knelt down beside Emily. Once they had both drunk their fill, he began to gently wash her feet.

"Oh, that feels so wonderfully cold."

"I hope it does not sting too much. Your poor feet are all cut and bruised. Your maman will doubtless have some ointment for them, but when we return you will spend the next days sitting still with your feet on a cushion."

"That sounds appealingly luxurious." It would be even better if he were beside her. From the look in his eyes, he shared that longing, but they both knew that her parents would never permit it.

Lucien was most efficient and competent. It was no wonder she had thought of him as an adventurer, although those qualities would doubtless be useful in running his estate or anything else he chose to do. She had never realized how important competence was—and, now that she thought about it, how unusual it was.

Once he had put on his own boots, he fed her some bread and dried apricots that he had in his saddle bags, and some more water. The simple meal was surprisingly delicious, possibly because she had not eaten since last night's dinner. Next he wrapped her up in a blanket, like a baby in swaddling clothes, and set her before him on the saddle.

He kept one arm wrapped tightly around her as they rode at a gentle walk, and she rested against him. She felt cherished and protected, with no desire to move from the circle of his arm. She would have laughed at herself were she not so happy. Independence and self-reliance were desirable qualities. That could not be denied, and she expected them of herself. But sometimes—now—it was very nice to be taken care of.

As they rode, he told her bits and pieces about his home in France—the gray stone house with the long windows; the little balcony outside his bedroom window when he was a small boy, from which he could reach the branch of an oak tree; the long table in the kitchen where the cook had fed him bread and jam. Out of doors, there had been the rows and rows of grapes, where old Louis taught him how to prune the vines. Around the bend in the road was the village where his friend Henri lived.

"You miss it," she said after a silence.

Another silence followed before he said, "Yes, I suppose I do. It has been so long. My mother would take me there sometimes to visit, to stay for a few days, a week, but I have not truly lived there since I was a boy of six." Looking down he saw her look of surprise and explained, "That was when we went to live with my grandfather at La Boulaye."

"And that was not good."

"No, that was not good. My mother was accustomed to her own household, but my grandmother was mistress of La Boulaye. My father was accustomed to running his own life, making his own decisions. My grandfather expected total obedience. My father thought improvements should be made to the estate, new vineyards planted, more modern methods used. My grandfather would spend only on display, on carriages, on grand parties, on presentations at court. And so they fought all the time, and my aunts and uncles stood by and whispered and my grandmother wailed. It was not a happy house."

"Then it is just as well that we will not need to live there. We shall live in your house of gray stone with the oak tree outside the window, and it will be a happy house. I insist upon it."

He hugged her to him even more tightly and dropped a kiss on her head. They rode along contentedly.

After perhaps an hour, the rescue party appeared. Her father and Irmak rode in front, followed by a carriage—an exceedingly impressive carriage, high and square, painted bright yellow with red wheels and a red roof fringed with silver. Irmak's troopers rode in a column on either side, and red pennants flew from their lances.

Her father's shout when he saw her brought her mother half out the carriage window, and Lord Penworth spurred his horse into a gallop. Lucien brought his horse to a halt and tightened his grip on Emily as they waited. She was glad to see them. Of course she was. But she could not help but regret the end of this interlude with Lucien. She did not want to leave the circle of his arms. And the way his arm tightened around her, he did not want to let her go either.

The next few minutes were a chaotic mix of cries and questions and assurances as Emily tried to convince first her father and then her mother that she was indeed safe and well. Even Irmak was hovering over her, trying to see that she truly was uninjured.

It was their distress that brought home to her how serious her situation had been on the raft. Lucien had appeared so soon after she recovered consciousness that she had not had time to be properly frightened. Well, she had been frightened by the pirates, but by then she had Lucien with her. And once he was there, her attention had been so completely focused on him that nothing else, not even the pirates, had seemed of much importance.

Now, she was horrified to see tears running down her mother's cheeks. They were tears of relief, but still, her unflappable mother, who did not turn a hair at an attack by lunatic Kurds, her mother in tears? That resigned her to leaving the circle of Lucien's arms, though he seemed loath to let her go. His arm tightened around her when her father first reached up for her, but he too looked at her mother's face and bowed to necessity.

Her father lifted her down gently, as if she were still a small child, carried her to the carriage, and settled her carefully inside. She tried to point out that she was really quite all right, but no one seemed to be paying any attention. Her mother and father were both thanking Lucien, with hugs from her mother and claps on the back from her father and not quite coherent

speeches from both of them. Lucien kept leaning over
to look at her, so she looked out the window to smile
at him. That seemed to reassure him somewhat, and
when her mother climbed into the coach, he joined
the other men on horseback. At a signal from Irmak,
the whole party turned to head back toward Mosul.

As the ungainly carriage made its awkward turn,
Emily, still cocooned in her blanket, found herself
bouncing from side to side. She had to laugh at her
awkward state as she tried to unwrap herself without falling.

"My dear, are you all right?" Lady Penworth caught
her daughter to keep her from tumbling off the seat.

"Quite all right. I just hadn't realized how thoroughly Lucien had bundled me up."

"But you are not injured?" Not waiting for an
answer, her mother unwrapped Emily's arms and lifted
them to make sure there were no-broken bones.

"No, really, the only thing that hurts is my feet."

Pulling the blanket from Emily's legs produced
silence in the carriage. Finally, Lady Penworth said,
"You are almost naked."

Emily looked down. She was wearing her drawers,
and while they were a bit dirty, they were intact.
More or less. But she was barefoot, and barelegged
from the knees down. "We had to swim," she said.

"Swim?"

Emily nodded. This was going to be awkward.
She didn't want to make her mother even more
distressed than she already was, but she had to explain
her near-nakedness. And there was a perfectly reasonable explanation. She just needed to make it sound

reasonable. "You see, the crew on the raft thought I was a ghost because of the blood on my face, so they jumped overboard. But I didn't know how to steer it. Then Lucien came, and he swam out to the raft, but the pirates attacked, so we had to jump back into the river. I couldn't swim to shore in my skirt, so I had to take it off." She looked at her mother with wide, innocent eyes. "You do see, don't you?"

Lady Penworth took a deep breath and let it out slowly. "Blood on your face?"

"From the cut on my head. But it all washed off when we swam to shore. So really, there's nothing to worry about."

A sound halfway between a gasp and a laugh escaped from Lady Penworth. "Oh, my dear child, you seem to have escaped from your ordeal with far less stress than the rest of us."

Emily considered that. "I expect that's because I was unconscious for much of it, and then there wasn't really time to think."

# Twenty-one

IT HAD NOT BEEN DIFFICULT FOR DAVID TO FIND information about Hadad and Karif. They were well known in the poorest quarter of Mosul, where they were neither liked nor trusted. Useful information was something else. No one sought to protect them, but even a few coins brought little information of use.

They had tried to hire a pair of camels or, failing that, a pair of horses, but to no avail. They lacked the money in hand, and those who possessed such beasts simply laughed at their promise of future payment. All knew them well enough to be certain that should they ever come into the vast sums they claimed they would soon possess, none of that wealth would ever be used to pay their debts.

However, a pair of donkeys had disappeared. They were elderly beasts, possessed of very little strength, but they had an owner, a peddler of even greater age and less strength. The peddler had taken a nap, certain that his donkeys would never expend the energy to stray. Alas, when he awakened, his donkeys had not only gone but managed to unburden themselves of the peddler's packs. This added insult to the theft. An honorable thief would have at least pretended to covet the peddler's goods.

The general opinion was that only Hadad and Karif were foolish enough to steal such worthless beasts. Unfortunately, no one had noticed them taking or, more importantly, departing with the donkeys. Many offered theories about where they might have gone, but none had any knowledge.

As for the location of a slave caravan, all claimed they knew nothing of any such thing, and neither persuasion nor bribes nor threats could bring forth any information. Aside from the fears engendered by the slave traders themselves, there was the fear of the sultan's wrath. All knew that the Europeans were urging the sultan to end the slave trade. Not only was Oliphant a European, but he had arrived in Mosul accompanied by the sultan's troopers. These were matters in which a sensible man did not involve himself.

There was more than one route across the desert to Damascus, and no way to know which one had been chosen by the slavers. David needed to find information quickly. There was only one place he could go for help, one person he could turn to.

It was still early afternoon when he pulled up his horse before the tent of Sheik Rashad. Within, the sheik, robed in pure white, was seated on a glorious carpet in rich tones of blue and red. Along the sides of the tent, the sheik's followers sat in less elegant comfort. They were far enough away to allow the sheik to conduct conversations in private, but every gesture and expression would be observed. Forcing himself to act calmly, while every muscle in his body was coiled to spring, David observed the necessary formalities. He managed, just barely, to restrain himself as coffee was offered and accepted, but, even so, it did not take long for him to pour out his tale once his grandfather had indicated his willingness to listen.

The sheik sat silent for several minutes, his eye on his grandson. David remained immobile under the scrutiny, never flinching. To show distress would be unmanly. He forced himself to be stoic.

"This woman," said Rashad finally, "she is the one you brought here?"

"She is."

"Why did you bring her? Did you wish my approval or hers?"

"Both. I would wish for you to respect and honor my wife, as I would wish my wife to respect and honor my family."

The sheik dipped his head in a brief nod that might have indicated approval of David's answer. After a pause he said, "Your grandmother and aunts found her pleasing and respectful."

David's brief nod might have indicated that their approval was welcome.

The sheik paused once more to observe his grandson. "And if we do not find her?"

"I will find her," David said. There was no question in his mind.

The sheik nodded. "If you do not find her before she has been disposed of in Damascus?"

"I will find her," David repeated, his voice cold. "It

is for her sake that I wish to find her quickly, to spare her pain and humiliation."

The sheik raised his brows at that, but did not argue. He glanced over at one of the men at the side of the tent who immediately leaped to his feet and hurried to bend an ear to the sheik's quiet instructions. Once he had left, David and his grandfather sat in silence, sipping their coffee. Only the tight line of his jaw and the stiffness of his shoulders betrayed David's tension.

Abdul entered in a flurry of draperies and with a beaming smile. "You are in luck, cousin. We have had watchers keeping an eye on the slavers, just in case they cast an eye on our horses, so we know precisely where they are. If your villains plan to join them, it will not be difficult to find them."

David could not manage a smile, but he stood to clasp Abdul's arm. "Thank you, cousin." He was grateful for the information and assurances, but even more for the understanding he saw in Abdul's face.

⁓

Rashad, with David and Abdul on either side of him, rode at the head of the small troop of half a dozen men. All were dressed in dark blue robes and rode dark horses, making them almost invisible now that the sun had set. A scout had met them and pinpointed the location of the kidnappers.

The sheik held up a hand to halt the riders at the edge of a small ridge. He beckoned David to follow him, and they proceeded to the edge of the ridge on foot until they could peer over the edge. The kidnappers had made their camp beside a small stream, and Julia and the donkeys were tied to a lone palm tree. The donkeys were drooping with weariness, but Julia was standing straight, imperious as a queen.

The shorter of the two men—Karif, from the description David had been given—came over to her and said something in a voice too low to be heard on the ridge. Julia's response, however, was perfectly clear, pronounced slowly in execrably accented Arabic: "Thy mother committed adultery with a monkey. Thou art a creature as low and dirty as a shoe, thou wretched grandson of a plucked vulture, great-grandson of a stinking jackal!"

It was not clear whose gasp was loudest, David's or his grandfather's, but the choked laughter was the sheik's. Had Karif not reacted with such fury, he would certainly have heard them. David was about to charge to the rescue, when the kidnapper was stopped by his colleague. "Don't be a fool," the second kidnapper—Hadad—said, seizing a handful of ragged robe to drag Karif back from striking Julia. "You know her value is in her beauty. Striking her will leave scars and bruises." When Karif stopped struggling, Hadad continued in soothing tones, as if to a fractious child. "We will give her no food for a few days. That will punish her for her insolence and perhaps make her more docile when we get to the slave market."

Throughout this exchange, Julia had never flinched. She regarded her captors with a contemptuous sneer that seemed to cause Karif's hand to twitch as if he longed to strike her anyway. Greed conquered pride, enforced by the pull of his partner's hand, and he turned away and left her.

David realized that his grandfather was still chuckling.

"She has the courage of a lion, that one," the old man said.

David smiled. "And the eyes of a gazelle."

"Admirable in a queen, no doubt. But for a wife, should not a man seek a submissive, obedient woman?" Rashad asked.

"That is not what I seek."

Rashad nodded, in what seemed to David to be approval. "So be it. She will give you fine, brave sons." He then waved his followers to circle around to the other side of the camp.

It was over almost instantly. Ludicrously simple, after the anguish that had gone before.

Hadad and Karif were sitting beside a small fire, intent on their meal. A slight sound made Hadad glance up and freeze, the bread halfway to his mouth. Karif noticed Hadad's immobility first, and then the reason for it.

Half a dozen figures, barely visible in the darkness, surrounded them. Their silence made them no less terrifying, for while their faces were almost covered by the folds of their head scarves, the firelight glinted ominously on the rifles and scimitars that they carried. Abdul stepped forward.

That was enough to loosen Karif's tongue, and he began to babble. "Take the woman, oh master of the desert. Take her as our gift. She will be worth hundreds in the slave market in Damascus. Or keep her for yourself. Take her and spare your miserable servants." He bowed his head to the ground, and Hadad did the same.

Abdul put his foot on Karif's head to grind his face into the dirt and rested the point of his scimitar on Hadad's neck. The others shared in his laughter.

Meanwhile, David used his dagger to slash through the rope binding Julia to the tree. She stood in silent terror, looking wide-eyed about her at the dark figures who had taken over the small camp. It wasn't until she looked into David's eyes that she recognized him and, with a cry, fainted into his arms.

He held her gently, caressing her tenderly. All the while he murmured soft endearments in a mixture of Arabic and English, "*Habibi*, my love, you are safe, my heart, you are my life."

When she came to her senses, she still could not speak, but clung to him, trembling, in the circle of his arms.

Abdul swaggered up, grinning broadly. "A dramatic rescue, cousin. Now it only remains to determine what should be done with these curs. It will be as you decide. Shall we chop off their heads or merely their hands?"

David's hand clenched. He would like nothing more than to chop them to bits himself, but then Julia raised her head and looked at Abdul in confusion. Despite her recent efforts, she spoke far too little Arabic to understand what he had said, fortunately. David was torn. He had no intention of exposing her to more violence—she was still white with terror—but these vermin could not be allowed to go unpunished.

He thought for a moment, and then smiled. "They wished to deprive my lady of food and drink. Very well. Take them out to the desert and leave them there, with no food or water, to make their way back to Mosul, or anyplace they prefer, as best they can."

A disappointed look crossed Abdul's face, but he said, "As you will."

Sheik Rashad, on the other hand, gave an approving grunt. "We will return to the camp where your grandmother and aunts can care for her. Bloodshed would have been inauspicious before the wedding."

*Wedding?* David had no objection to a prompt wedding, but he suspected that Julia might prefer to have some say about it. He looked down. Her eyes were shadowed and face was drawn. She was in no condition to speak, no less make decisions. He needed to get her away from here to a place of safety. Tomorrow would be time enough for talk.

# Twenty-two

THE SUN WAS ALREADY LOW ON THE HORIZON WHEN the Penworths' small caravan began the return trip. Irmak declared that it was far too late for the party to reach Mosul that night. Much though Lord Penworth wanted to have his wife and daughter safely beneath his own roof, he had to agree, especially since Irmak assured him accommodations that were both safe and suitable were at hand.

The kavass had been, as always, alive to his surroundings. Scorning the two closest villages, he led them to a town that boasted not only a small sheik who was overjoyed to have the opportunity to honor the sultan's firman, but also baths for both the gentlemen and the ladies.

Lady Penworth offered no objection and was in fact delighted to have both the opportunity to see to it that her daughter's scrapes and bruises were cared for and the opportunity to hear the tale of her adventures without having to cope with her husband's reaction—to say nothing of having the opportunity to acquire garments to provide decent covering for the girl before her father saw her.

When she had heard Emily out, over a meal of mutton and rice, she chewed in silence for a moment, giving herself a chance to digest both the meal and the information. After considering both what had been said and what had not been said, she heaved a sigh. "You will allow me to explain all this to your father."

"Of course," said Emily.

Lady Penworth was not entirely happy.

Lord Penworth was having an even more difficult time of it.

When he finally managed to have a private word with his wife, the first thing he said was, "Chambertin wants to marry Emily."

"Yes," his wife said. "Emily said as much."

"But..." He was having difficulty finding the right words. "I thought he was an adventurer. An intelligent adventurer and a pleasant enough fellow, but still, just someone who was passing through. And now he claims to be the heir of the Comte de la Boulaye. Says his name is really *de* Chambertin. He seemed rather offended that I expressed some doubts about that."

"Well," said his wife, "he never precisely announced it, but one could surmise something of the sort. He was hardly diffident in his manner. He has the sort of arrogance that comes of being born to wealth and power."

He looked at her with more than a bit of annoyance. "You knew this?"

"Well, not the precise title, of course," she said with an air of surprise.

"And may I ask how you happened to know this?" He sounded a trifle annoyed.

"I asked Lady Bulwer, of course, while we were at the embassy. She is the sort of woman who would never allow a gentleman into her drawing room without being reasonably certain of his pedigree. We were about to set off on a lengthy and difficult journey, during which the young people would inevitably be thrown together. She assured me that the French ambassador's wife had assured her that he was from an ancient and noble family."

He looked at her with disbelief. "Do you expect me to believe that you considered him suitable for our daughter because his grandfather was a French count?"

"Of course not." She made a face at him. "You know me better than that. Lady Bulwer knew nothing about his actual position, only that it was high enough to make him welcome at the French embassy, and you know how particular the French can be. I suppose it's because since the Revolution there has been all that confusion, what with the émigrés and the restoration and the new titles. They must find it difficult to know who is who, so to speak.

"I simply wished to be certain that, should things develop between them, he could support her. Emily can cope with all sorts of eventualities—including pirates, it seems—but I do not think she has any notion how to cope with penury. It is a skill I would prefer that she have no need to learn. I know the French aristocracy has lost most of its political power, but Lady Bulwer seemed to think he was quite well off. His evening clothes were quite good for a Frenchman.

As for any possible failings of character, I consider Emily quite capable of discovering those for herself."

He sighed in resignation. "You might have told me. I felt rather a fool when Chambertin felt obliged to explain that he was not an adventurer. And he did appear, after all, to be a fairly competent one."

"I am sorry, my love." Lady Penworth looked contrite. "It never occurred to me that you did not know. I was certain that Sir Henry would have told you."

"He doubtless would have, had he not been such a fool."

"There is that," his wife conceded.

"But I do not like it. He is not the sort of man I would have chosen for Emily. There is a dishonesty about all this playacting that I cannot approve, and I told him so."

"Playacting? Just because he did not trade on his family's position?"

"No, that isn't the problem." He frowned. "There seem to be problems that he left behind, problems that should be of concern to him. And rather than face them and deal with them, he ran away. That seems to me to be a failure of character."

"How did you leave things with him?"

"I told him I would have to think about it."

Lady Penworth tilted her head and smiled approvingly. "Excellent. A bit of uncertainty will be good for both of them."

꧁꧂

The party returned to Mosul in apparent harmony but with some unease below the surface. While

Lord Penworth was enormously relieved to have his daughter recovered safe and sound, he was not assured that her suitor was all that one could have wished. Chambertin may have been a scion of the French nobility, but his failure to present himself as such did not sit well. The marquess was accustomed to dealing with men he could not trust—the political world was full of them—but he did not want to give his daughter to such a man. Then also, there seemed to be a degree of selfishness in Lucien's willingness to consider only his own convenience in ordering his life. If he objected to his grandfather's treatment of people on his estate, why was he wandering about the globe instead of protecting them?

Lady Penworth was fairly certain that her daughter had not been entirely forthcoming about what had transpired down river. On the other hand, she suspected that her daughter's discretion was all to the good. Relations with one's children were often easier when parents remained ignorant of facts it would be uncomfortable to know. But she did not like the notion that Lucien had acted in a way that made Emily's discretion necessary. And she did not like to think that she might have relied overmuch on her daughter's good sense.

Emily was feeling frustrated by being cooped up in the carriage. For all its glittering decoration, it was not very comfortable and jolted badly over the roads, which were sadly maintained in any case. She would far rather have been riding with Lucien, in his arms as she had been yesterday. In addition, her father seemed concerned about something and her mother was distracted when they should have been happy and relieved to have her back. She did not know what was bothering them, which bothered her. Surely they could have no objection to Lucien. They had always seemed to like him. And since he was the grandson of a count rather than an adventurer, she did not see how there could be any objection.

Lucien was churning with a mixture of insult and panic. It had never occurred to him that his suit might be unacceptable to Emily's father. Had he inherited something of his grandfather's pride and arrogance that made him assume he would be welcome? It bothered him to think this might be true. He had thought that by omitting any mention of his family, he was refusing to trade on his heritage, but Lord Penworth seemed to think he was making a mockery of those he met by pretending to be someone he was not. Resentment flared at that recollection. Never had he mocked his inferiors. Well, at least he had not done so very often. Only when they had been fools.

Was it possible that Lord Penworth would refuse to let him marry Emily? That was unacceptable. He had to find a way to prove himself worthy to her parents.

All these worries dwindled into insignificance as soon as they arrived at the house in Mosul.

They were greeted by an utterly distraught Mr. Rassam. His large dark eyes brimmed with tears, and his fierce mustache had drooped into despair as he raced to the side of Lord Penworth.

"My lord, my lord, I have not known what to do. There has been no word from Mr. Oliphant, no word at all!"

After a startled moment, Lord Penworth swung down from his horse. "What do you mean, no word from him? Is he not here? He was to remain in case additional information about my daughter's disappearance came in."

"But that, my lord, was before the other young lady disappeared."

"What do you mean, disappeared?" Lady Penworth had stuck her head out of the carriage and addressed Rassam. "And which young lady? Mademoiselle Carnac?" She added, in an undertone, "That would be no great loss."

"No, no, Mlle. Carnac is still present. It is the Lady Julia who is gone."

Lucien tried to push his way through the crowd of observers who filled the street. They had probably been drawn in the first place by the carriage—a scarlet roof, gilded doors and embroidered curtains created a sight rarely seen in the narrow streets of Mosul. He had to pluck a pair of boys out of the way to enable him to get near the carriage and its passengers.

If the carriage had drawn the crowd in the first place, the drama was keeping them here. It didn't matter that few if any could understand what was being said. Eyes darted back and forth from Rassam's dramatic gestures to Penworth's horrified reaction to the carriage where Emily and her mother were trying to get out. Lucien struggled to get close enough to help them.

The scene might have played itself out in public had an urchin not inserted himself between Rassam and Lord Penworth, staring up to observe their expressions.

Lord Penworth looked down at the small intruder and, with an oath quite foreign to his usual courtesy, he seized the boy by the shoulder and moved him out of the way. Irmak and his troopers held back the crowd while Lucien and Lord Penworth ushered the women into the house. The door boy closed the door firmly on the disappointed crowd, but not before he saw the urchin's father cuff his ear for spoiling the show for everyone.

Once inside the room Lord Penworth used for an office, Rassam produced the hastily scribbled letter that Oliphant had left, outlining what he had learned about Julia's kidnapping.

"Slavers!" Lady Penworth clutched her husband's arm. "Oh no, Phillip. No."

Lord Penworth had turned as pale as his wife, but made an effort to sound reassuring. "We will find her," he said. But the words sounded hollow.

Lucien cursed long and fluently in French. He felt sick. This was, at least in part, his fault. He was the one who had introduced Carnac and his daughter to the Penworths. To think that he had felt sorry for Mélisande. How had he failed to see what a viper she was?

As if reading his mind, Emily said, "Where is Mélisande? She is the one who has caused all of this. Perhaps she knows something that will help us find Julia."

"I will bring her here, her and her father." With a fierce scowl, Lucien was prepared to drag them bodily and indeed might have preferred some resistance. At a signal from Irmak, two of the troopers followed him.

His mood had not improved by the time they burst into Carnac's residence. The servants took one look and tried to scuttle out of the way, but Lucien caught hold of one. "Where is Mlle. Carnac?" he demanded.

She was soon discovered, sitting in the inner courtyard. When she first saw that Lucien had come, she began to smile, but her look faded to panic when she saw his expression, to say nothing of the two troopers following him. "I didn't do anything," she said, her voice high and thin. "It wasn't my fault."

He waved the Turks to seize her and turned to lead the way back. "Tell Carnac to come at once to Lord Penworth's house," he snapped at one of the servants peering at them from behind doorways. "I have no time to explain matters to him."

When they returned, they found Lord Penworth pacing back and forth in the courtyard, with Rassam trotting beside him. One man would begin a thought, then shake his head to discard it as useless. Then the other man would do the same. Lady Penworth was holding her daughter possessively, and Emily chewed her lip, as if frantically searching for some idea that would enable them to find Julia.

Lucien pushed Mélisande forward, and she stumbled to a halt in front of Lady Penworth. "But I didn't do anything," the girl protested, sobbing. "I never did anything to Lady Julia."

Lady Penworth straightened up and seemed to grow taller. "You were there. You were seen. You saw what happened, and you did nothing to help." Her voice was implacable. There was no taint of pity.

"No!" Mélisande shook her head wildly. "I never

meant anything to happen to Lady Julia. They weren't supposed to take her."

"But they did take her," said Emily. She stared at the girl incredulously. "You saw it happen, and you did nothing. You did not even tell anyone. Why? Julia was always a friend to you. Why did you not at least go for help?"

"I was afraid. You would have blamed me. You already blamed me. I didn't mean anything to happen to Lady Julia, but you would have said it was my fault." She turned to clutch at Lucien's arm. "Lucien, tell them I am innocent. It was not my fault."

"Of course it is your fault," he snapped. "How can you deny it? Now you must tell us who those men are and where they will have taken her."

"How am I to know where they will take her?" Mélisande pushed away and glared at him. "They are stupid Arabs who work sometimes for my father. Very stupid. I tell them to take Lady Emily and make her disappear, and they take Lady Julia instead. It is all a mistake. They are so stupid."

It was all he could do to keep from throttling her. His hand was half raised to strike her before he caught himself. He might have done so if Emily had not stepped in front of him.

"Make me disappear? But why? Why do you want to harm me?" Emily looked both confused and horrified.

"It is all your fault." Mélisande turned on her. "You are stealing Lucien from me. You must know that he is to marry me and take me to France. How else am I to escape this place?"

"Marry you? Are you mad?" Lucien stepped back, aghast. "Whatever gave you that lunatic notion?" He turned to Emily. "I swear to you, never did I say to her a word to make her think such a thing."

Emily waved a hand dismissively. "Of course you didn't. Good heavens, I am quite certain you do not go around seducing schoolgirls. But this little viper..." She advanced on Mélisande. "What did you tell them to do? What will they do to Julia?"

"I don't know! I don't know! They do not tell me their plans." Mélisande threw up her hands. "Why do you keep asking me?"

Just then, Carnac arrived in a flurry, clothing tossed on carelessly and beard matted, to seize Lord Penworth by the lapels. "What is the matter? Has something happened to the shipment?"

The marquess—and it was suddenly a marquess who stood there in full possession of his unquestionable power—looked down frostily and removed Carnac's hands. "The shipment is of no importance. What matters now is that your daughter has caused Lady Julia to be kidnapped, possibly by slave traders. Every power at my command, every power at my government's command, and every bit of knowledge at your command, is to be devoted to rescuing Lady Julia. Nothing else matters."

"Kidnapped? Lady Julia? What nonsense is this? Why would she want to do such a thing?" Carnac shook his shaggy head in disbelief.

"Tell them I didn't mean it, Papa. Tell them I never meant to harm Lady Julia." Mélisande hung on her father's arm, her face blotchy with tears.

"You see," Carnac began, recovering himself a bit. "My innocent daughter would not…"

"Your daughter is anything but innocent." Lucien took hold of Carnac's shoulder and swung him around to glare fiercely at the old man. "Her plans misfired, and the fate she intended for Lady Emily befell Lady Julia instead."

"And you are to blame, you stupid little man," said Lady Penworth, swinging him around in turn and shaking a finger in his face. "Had you paid any heed to your daughter, taken even the slightest care of her, none of this would have happened."

"Easy, my love, there will be time for that later." Lord Penworth gathered his wife to him. "First we must find Julia."

"Oh, Phillip, what are we to do?" She looked up at him, her face crumpling.

Still cold but now calm, Lord Penworth looked at Carnac. "Two men who sometimes work for you…" He picked up Oliphant's letter and looked at it again. "Hadad and Karif. Where can we find them?"

"Worked for me?"

"On the excavation." The thread of Lord Penworth's patience was snapping.

"Bah. How would I know? I do not know their names, these workmen. They are all useless fellows anyway." Carnac shook his head dismissively.

Lucien lost patience completely and seized the old man by the shoulders again, giving him a shake. "Think, you old fool. They have Lady Julia and we must find them. Where do they live?"

Fear was beginning to dawn in Carnac's face as the

distress and anger of those about him finally registered. He licked his lips as if he realized they would not allow him to dissociate himself from the situation and glanced at the faces about him, all unfriendly. "I don't know, I… Perhaps my headman would know."

"And he is where?" Lucien gave him another shake.

Carnac winced. "Near the warehouse. He lives near the warehouse."

They dragged Carnac along to the warehouse area, and eventually managed to locate the house of the headman. He was not at home—that would have been too easy, thought Lucien bitterly. Carnac was pulled along as they began a search of nearby coffee houses, not because he was wanted but because the others would not recognize the headman.

When they finally located him in a nearby coffee-house, he was cooperative. He was horrified to hear what had occurred and was willing, even eager, to be of assistance. It was only that—Hadad and Karif? Where did they live? He raised his hands in a helpless gesture. Perhaps here, perhaps there. Did they even have a home?

Lucien would gladly have strangled the fellow, but that would hardly have helped. They trudged back to the house, having discarded Carnac somewhere along the way, and gathered with Irmak around a map, trying to decide on the most likely places to search.

Of course, thought Lucien, David was not a fool. He would already have searched the most likely places, wouldn't he? But would they all think of the same places? He closed his eyes and tried to think of something sensible to do. If he could not think of some useful action, could he at least think of something to say to Lady Penworth and Emily? They sat huddled in a corner of the courtyard, and he could almost see the cloud of worry around them.

"Effendi, effendi! A message!" Little Yusef came running in.

Penworth snatched the paper from him and tore it open. The distress on his face changed into amazement, and he sagged against the wall in relief. "She's safe! Oliphant has her and she's safe!" He looked around at the others joyfully before he returned to the note. "He wants to know if Emily is also safe—we must send news at once. He says he has taken Julia to his grandfather's camp, and if Emily has returned safely, they will remain there until they are…married." He blinked at that and paused to read it again. "Yes, that's what it says. If all is well here, they will be married and will return the day after tomorrow." He looked at his wife uncertainly.

She looked as startled as he, but recovered more quickly. "Well, no one can say it is a complete surprise. It's not a bad match for her, and they seem fond of each other. There will have to be another wedding of course. Getting married in an Arab camp is hardly suitable for an earl's sister."

Emily gave a choked little laugh and collapsed against Lucien, who was too relieved to say anything. He just held her.

# Twenty-three

NIGHT HAD FALLEN BY THE TIME LUCIEN WAS ABLE TO escape the discussions in the courtyard. It had been something of a revelation. He had not been aware of how much the marquess—and his wife, as well—knew about the servants here and the ones who had accompanied them from Constantinople, to say nothing of Irmak and the Ottoman troopers.

Perhaps he should not be surprised that his own efforts for Varennes, taken from afar with no personal involvement, should be viewed as inadequate. He had prided himself on being unlike his grandfather, but perhaps he had been measuring himself against the wrong yardstick.

But before any of that had happened, there had been the excruciating hysteria on the part of Carnac when he learned that the fleet of rafts had been attacked and most, if not all, of the shipment was at the bottom of the river. He had come racing to the house to demand that Lord Penworth take action immediately to deal with this tragedy. The boatmen who had been slaughtered he dismissed with a shrug.

It took a while before he could be made to understand that when Lord Penworth spoke of what needed to be done, he was talking about providing for the families of the men who had been killed or injured.

"But we must send an expedition at once to recover the shipment," Carnac protested. "The stone, it is soft and will be damaged by the water, by the currents."

Mélisande, who had trailed along behind her father, seemed to find this amusing. Emily had taken one look at the smile on her face and departed.

Eventually, the Carnacs departed, dismissed rather forcefully, and followed by Lord Penworth's look of scorn.

"What ought we to do about them?" asked Lady Penworth, tilting her head.

Her husband shook his head. "The temptation is to simply leave them here to rot, but Julia and Oliphant are entitled to have a say. And Emily as well." He looked around and frowned when he did not see his daughter.

"She went upstairs," said Lady Penworth in a reassuring tone. "She is quite safe."

"Yes, well…" Lord Penworth rubbed the back of his neck and managed a smile. "That's all right, then. Chambertin, I wondered if I might impose on you for a bit. Since Oliphant isn't here, I find myself in need of a translator."

"Of course, sir. I will do my best." What else could he say? His future father-in-law was not enthusiastic about his suit—he had heard himself described as a "frivolous ne'er-do-well"—so he needed to provide some evidence of his seriousness. He could hardly say, "Please excuse me. I wish to go make love to your daughter."

Afternoon stretched into evening as recent events were pieced together. Servants were thanked individually with words and with coins for their efforts. For his courageous attempt to help Julia, the little door boy was rewarded with a gold ring from Lord Penworth and a kiss from Lady Penworth.

Lucien was then enlisted to draft an account of the numerous ways in which Irmak and his men had displayed courage and gallantry, though the final letters to the vizier and the sultan would have to wait for Oliphant to put them in proper form, to say nothing of the correct Ottoman Turkish of the court. Lucien had had enough difficulty translating the spoken Arabic of the servants for Lord Penworth—the written language of the Ottoman court was beyond him.

They were seated in the office—Lord and Lady Penworth and Lucien—with both the door and shutters open. The breeze entering the room felt pleasantly cool, and the sound of the fountain underlined the quiet of the courtyard. Lucien blotted the final sheet of his notes and carefully closed the ink bottle and wiped the pens, hoping he would now be free to seek out Emily.

Lord Penworth leaned back, rolling his shoulders with a slight groan.

Lady Penworth, still sitting perfectly erect and managing to look neat and unwrinkled in the dress she had put on the day before when she set out in search of her daughter, tilted her head thoughtfully. "I believe we have done all that we can at present."

"Yes," agreed her husband. He looked over at

Lucien with an expression best described as rueful approval. "I must thank you, Chambertin. You have been a great help."

Lucien shrugged. "What I have done today is nothing. I still cannot comprehend how Mélisande could have behaved so, that she could have thought… I swear to you that I never gave her reason."

Lady Penworth held up her hand. "Do not try to understand. You are a personable young man, possibly the only one she has ever met. Given her situation, one can see how she would have woven you into her fantasies."

Lord Penworth straightened up abruptly. "My dear, you cannot mean to excuse…"

"Not at all. Whoever said 'To understand all is to forgive all' was talking nonsense. I can understand a great many things I consider unforgivable. I was simply telling M. de Chambertin that he need not feel responsible for the girl's behavior."

The use of the *de* with his name brought a flush to Lucien's cheeks, and he began to apologize once more for misleading them, but she waved his words away.

"At least no real harm was done by your deception," she said. "But there does remain a problem. You have been staying with the Carnacs, and I cannot think that you will find it comfortable to return to their roof. I think you must stay here. You can send someone to fetch clean clothes for you, and we have more than sufficient rooms in the men's quarters."

"Good heavens, I hadn't even thought about that," said Lord Penworth. "Of course you must stay here. It would be far too awkward for you."

"You are most kind, and I am most appreciative of your invitation." Lucien gave a bow of gratitude to Lady Penworth, but gratitude tinged with frustration. It was indeed most kind of Lady Penworth—and most inconvenient. Under her parents' roof, he would be required to behave with great circumspection. Were he living elsewhere—well, obviously not in the Carnacs' house—ah, it would make no difference. Emily would never be permitted to visit him, and even if she could, no rooms he could rent would provide any real privacy.

He was mad, that was all, quite mad. Mad with desire for Emily. All he could hope for was that her parents would agree to a wedding soon. Would a few days be possible?

He set out in search of Emily.

He found her on the roof, bathed in moonlight and looking impossibly ethereal. No, not ethereal. But bewitching. Against the inky sky, she was frosted with starlight, as enchanting as the moonbeams that caressed her. A magical creature, not an afreet but a genie, and he was under her spell.

When he came up behind her, she turned into his arms as if she had been waiting for him, as if she belonged there. No, she was not ethereal. She was real, all softness and smelling of jasmine. He rested his cheek on her hair, a silky cushion, and breathed in the sweetness of her. She was dressed in all her skirts and petticoats again. The fabric was silky soft, but there were layers and layers of it. Even so, his hand running down her back, pressing her to him, remembered the shape of her body, the curve of her buttocks.

He pressed a kiss on her temple, then on her cheek, and she turned her face to welcome his kiss, drawing him into her sweetness. The kiss began tenderly, but then heat flamed between them and hunger called forth more hunger.

His lips explored her cheeks, the sensitive spot behind her ear, the lovely line of her neck. She made little noises of pleasure while her fingers threaded through his hair to hold him close. The row of buttons running down the front of her bodice had started to part, and his hand slid into the lace-lined passage toward her breast only to find itself tangled in the ribbons of her chemise.

That was enough to make him pause and recall him to his sense of duty. He lifted his head and straightened his back, holding her face against his chest as he tried to ease his breathing. Her heart beat against him as rapidly as his own. "Forgive me," he said hoarsely. "I want you so, I have been longing for you, but I must not...not here in your parents' house."

For a moment, the only sound was the sound of their breathing, then she sighed. "That is one of those masculine rules, is it not?"

He choked on a laugh. "Yes, I suppose it is. And I fear it is a rule that your papa would consider of the highest importance. Since I wish to persuade him to agree to our marriage, and to agree that it must take place as soon as possible, it would be a great foolishness to anger him."

"Not Papa. Mama."

"Mama?"

"Yes. The great foolishness would be in angering

Mama. She would probably like to arrange a grand wedding in London, and it could take a year for her to arrange that to her satisfaction. If we wish to marry soon—and I wish that too—we must persuade her to agree."

Lucien looked dubious. "I do not think she dislikes me, but I do not know how to persuade her."

"Of course not. That is my task. She will wish to make her approval uncertain to begin with, because she doesn't think we appreciate things we get too easily, but I understand her." She smiled ruefully. "And she understands me."

"I think perhaps your maman frightens me even more than your papa. They are a formidable pair, those two."

"Nonsense."

"But yes. You do not see it perhaps because you have always known them. Your father is a most powerful man."

"Well, I suppose he is. After all, he is a marquess."

Lucien shook his head. "That is not what I mean. It is part of it, perhaps. His title, his position—they set him above many. But it is more than that. For example, it is his word that will determine whether or not there is to be a railroad here, is it not? That is not because he is a marquess but because he is respected and trusted by those who sent him. They know that he will give them an honest answer, not colored by his own self-interest. And then, when we were in Constantinople, I could see that the sultan was pleased by his visit. His name was known. And even those who would not know his name—Irmak is pleased to serve him because he considers you father a man of honor."

"Goodness, you make him sound quite dreadfully pompous." She was half laughing, half puzzled.

Lucien stared down at the floor with a frown. "I am not sure how to make it so that you understand." He looked up and faced her. "My grandfather is also a nobleman. He insists on every gesture, every word of respect that he considers owed to him. He is alive to every slight. He will punish any man who does not bow low enough before him, who does not remove his hat quickly enough. He once ordered the mayor of the village to have a man whipped for not removing his hat in my grandfather's presence."

"But, but how utterly ridiculous in this day and age."

The side of his mouth quirked up in an ironic half smile. "Ridiculous, yes. And fortunately the mayor did not obey, much to my grandfather's fury. But that is what my grandfather is like. That is how he deals with the world. Your father does not need to insist on the gestures because he already receives the respect they imply. Tell me, do many on your father's estates go hungry?"

"Oh no. Papa would never permit that. He is always informed of any problems, whenever anyone is injured or ill. The tenants, the people in the villages— they are our responsibility, after all."

"Responsibility, yes." Lucien nodded thoughtfully. "That is why he thinks ill of me. He thinks I have failed to live up to my responsibilities, and he has reason. I have done some things for Varennes, but many problems I will not hear about, not when I am so far away. And I have not taken care to arrange things so that the problems will be addressed even in my absence."

"Well, that can be taken care of as soon as we reach Varennes."

# Twenty-four

Two days later, they gathered at the city gate to welcome David and Julia. The newly married pair were accompanied by a dozen men, presumably his cousins, since all of them resembled David to a remarkable degree. In addition to providing a protective circle around the bride and groom, they led a pair of magnificent horses, inky black, a stallion and a mare. Onlookers, who had gathered to see what was happening, smiled on the bride and groom, but viewed the horses with gasps of admiration.

The cousins acknowledged the admiration with smiles of pride. They could not, however, match the happiness in David's smile when he looked at his bride. Her smile was hidden by a veil but her eyes shone brilliantly and rested on her husband more often than not.

In fact, Emily thought, they seemed to be contained in a sort of bubble of happiness. David smiled and joked with his cousins, but it was obvious that his thoughts were only for Julia. Even when they were not actually touching, they leaned toward each other, as if on the verge of an embrace.

Emily was happy for her friends. Extremely happy.
Really, she was. It was just that she could not prevent
the twinge of jealousy twisting inside her. David and
Julia did not have to stand six feet apart, as she and
Lucien were standing, with her parents in between
them. They were right beside each other, and after he
lifted her from her horse, David kept his arm around
her, a gesture both possessive and protective.

When Julia reached her, the veil pushed aside as she
threw her arms around Emily in an utterly uninhibited
embrace, those twinges of jealousy vanished, washed
away by the waves of Julia's joy. Emily realized that for
the first time since she had known her, there was no
wall of reserve around Julia. For the first time, Julia's
face bore no trace of fear, and she did not carry herself
tensed as if to ward off scorn and insult.

Tears welled up in her eyes, mixed with the
laughter of happiness, and Emily saw that her mother
was sharing the same emotions. All the way back to
the house, tucked away in the carriage, the women
laughed and cried and hugged and communicated
perfectly without a single coherent sentence.

Once they had arrived at the house, Lady Penworth
and Emily, with Nuran and Safiye fluttering behind,
escorted Julia to the two rooms that were now to be
hers and David's. Her hands lifted to cover her mouth,
Julia stood in the middle of the room and turned
slowly, drinking it in.

"Do you like it?" asked Lady Penworth, sounding
unusually uncertain. "We had not much time, but
Nuran and Safiye helped us decorate it."

Emily lifted the silk hangings around the bed and let

them float back into place. "I love this golden shade. It always looks beautiful on you. And you have to walk barefoot on the rug. It feels marvelous underfoot."

"I do love you," Julia half laughed, half sobbed as she flung her arms around Emily. "And you too, Lady Penworth. You are my real family."

"Of course we are, my dear." Lady Penworth seemed to be having a bit of difficulty with her voice and was obliged to use her handkerchief to dab at her eyes.

In this flurry of emotion, Julia's outer robe had fallen to the floor.

"Julia! Your dress!" exclaimed Emily. "Or robe. Whatever it is, it's gorgeous!"

Julia smiled shyly. "It is, isn't it?" She held out her arms as she twirled around to better display the elaborate gold embroidery that covered the front, sleeves, and hem of the loose white robe in wide bands of arabesques. "It was a gift from David's grandmother and aunts."

"Your hands!" Lady Penworth gasped. "Surely you haven't been tattooed?"

Julia smiled and held her hands up. The backs were covered in more arabesques, in red this time. "No. It's henna, and it will fade. The ladies did this for me, before the wedding. The designs are supposed to bring good luck."

"How lovely." Emily held Julia's hand to examine the design. "It looks like lace. Does it hurt?"

"Goodness, no. It's just painted on. And it was fun, really. I didn't understand most of what was said, but all the women were laughing and joking while they painted my hands and we ate fruits and sweets and drank mint tea and…" Suddenly her eyes filled with tears. "And they made me feel welcomed. Part of a family. Just as you do."

The women dissolved into another wave of tears and laughter and embraces.

❧

Lady Penworth had not known what to expect, but the servants had known. Altan had assured her that there was no need for her to worry. Everything would be done as it should be for the pride of the house. One could not have Mr. Oliphant's cousins return to Sheik Rashad complaining of the poor hospitality of the bride's family.

An entire lamb had been roasted for the occasion. There were platters of fragrant rice and vegetables, bowls of dried fruit and nuts, sweets dripping with honey, and cups of cold sherbet and hot mint tea. The Arab guests were seated on carpets spread out in the courtyard, while the Europeans sat on chairs or benches, but they all shared laughter as well as food.

Lucien sat down beside David on the bench in the courtyard. The cousins had stopped teasing him, and had subsided into joking among themselves. The teasing had obviously bothered David not at all, and he leaned back against the wall looking utterly relaxed and utterly happy. He was watching Julia, who was in turn stealing glances at him—and sharing smiles—as she sat with Emily and Lady Penworth.

"Well then, my friend, you have your happy ending." Lucien clapped David on the shoulder.

"Indeed." It took a while for David to tear his eyes from his wife and look at his friend. "And you too, you rescued Lady Emily and brought her safely home. All is well there?"

Lucien shrugged. "A tale for another day. But tell me, those horses you brought with you—you do not plan to ride off into the desert with your bride?"

"Ah, no. They are for Julia's brother. Her bride price." He grinned at the look on Lucien's face. "And there is a story here. The stallion is descended from the stallion my father offered as my mother's bride price, a stallion he received as a gift from the sultan's own stable. And the mare is the pride of my grandfather's own breeding. Will Julia's brother understand what he is being given?"

"My God, if he doesn't, he is ten thousand times a fool! I can name you a dozen Frenchmen who would give a king's ransom for such horses. And Julia does not speak of her brother as if he is a fool."

David smiled, almost to himself. "I did not think so. But I have something to say to you. When you were teaching the ladies Arabic, you seem to have gone a bit beyond polite phrases."

"I do not think…" Then he remembered a day when they had been riding over a barren mountainside that seemed to go on forever. David had been in conference with Lord and Lady Penworth, and he and the young women had been a bit bored. The memory made him flush slightly. "I told them how colorful some of the Arabic insults could be. It was only a joke. Surely she would not have said anything like that to your family."

"No," agreed David. "She would never do that. Instead she flung those insults at her captors, much to my grandfather's delight. Her courage won him over." Then David's smile faded. "She said that you had told them never to say such things, that insults like that could get them killed." He looked straight at Lucien. "Not much of a joke, eh? Especially when that is why she said them. My grandfather underestimated her courage. She wanted to provoke her captors to kill her. She would rather have died than be a slave."

Lucien said nothing. What could he say?

David looked back at his bride. "I could not deal with her captors as I would have liked because she would have seen. But if anyone endangers her again, I will kill him. I will keep her safe. I swear it."

It had been amusing to teach the proper English ladies insulting Arab curses. At least, it had seemed amusing at the time, a little joke. Perhaps it had not been a very good joke though, not if it had actually endangered Lady Julia. He had never considered that possibility.

Now all Lucien could think of was the hours when he was searching for Emily, not knowing where she was, if she was alive or dead. And then when the pirates had been shooting... Yes, he knew precisely what David meant. He looked over to where Emily sat with her mother and Julia. She was the most beautiful woman in the world. Not as elegant as her mother, perhaps, and not as porcelain perfect as Lady Julia, but beautiful with all the joy of life in her. Yes, he would protect her with his life.

"...so our children will know where they come from."

Lucien realized David had been speaking while he had not been listening. "Forgive me. My thoughts were wandering."

David smiled tolerantly. "I was saying that we may settle in England. Lord Penworth thinks there will be employment for me in the foreign office, and he tells me that with the backing of Lady Penworth and that of Julia's brother, it should not be too difficult socially. But we will visit here often, I think. My family approves of Julia, the women like her, and she likes my family. And it is important, I think, for our children to know all aspects of their heritage."

"I wish that Lord Penworth approved of me." Lucien could hear the resentful note in his voice, but he had been unable to prevent it. When he saw the startled look on David's face, he managed a twisted grin and a shrug.

"He does not approve of you? But why? Surely your birth is high enough. After all, he did not disapprove of me as a husband for Lady Julia."

"It is a matter of my birth only insofar as he thinks I have been evading my responsibilities." Lucien shrugged again. "And perhaps I have. It must be confessed that I never conceived of having responsibilities as Lord Penworth does."

There was a flutter of draperies and flounces on the other side of the room where the women were preparing to leave.

"Excuse me," said David, springing to his feet, "but it is time for me to withdraw." He flashed a grin at Lucien and ignored the tide of laughter and joking remarks rose from the cousins. Julia was barely through the door when he followed after her. The other women were also leaving.

Lucien watched Emily disappear through the door to the women's quarters and felt very much alone.

# Twenty-five

THEY WERE NOT GOING TO REMAIN IN MESOPOTAMIA one minute longer than necessary, Lord Penworth announced the next morning at breakfast. Lady Penworth, who was the only one present to hear him, nodded agreeably. Her husband scowled.

"I mean it, Anne," he said. "There is nothing in this godforsaken desert that is of the slightest interest to England, and I have no intention of putting my family at further risk because Colonel Chesney has a bee in his bonnet about running a railway through here. Telegrams are making the mails irrelevant for urgent messages. And as for moving troops in a hurry, which I suspect is the real concern, it makes far more sense, and will be far cheaper, to put a decent steamship on the Red Sea to travel to and from Suez. They are building a canal there, and even if they weren't, there's a railway from Suez to Alexandria, and that's all that's needed."

"I entirely agree, my dear. And I know you thought so before we ever left England, and you would not have made this trip if I had not urged it on you. It is very good of you to be so accommodating." She took a sip from the small cup of strong Turkish coffee and grimaced. "You know, I have tried to develop a taste for Turkish coffee, but I greatly prefer the bowl of milky coffee that the French serve for breakfast. I look forward to having it again, with one of those nice buttery croissants." She put the cup aside. "Now what were we talking about? Oh yes, our departure."

"Yes, my dear, our *imminent* departure. Now, how long do you think it will take you to have everything packed?"

"Oh, not long, not long at all. A matter of days, I imagine. However, there are a few things that must be considered."

He sighed. "What sort of things?"

"First of all, I assume Julia and David will be traveling with us."

"Naturally. Married or not, I have an obligation to see Julia safely home. Doncaster would hardly thank me for abandoning his sister in a place where women get kidnapped."

"Well, there is the matter of Julia's wedding. I'm sure she and David are married in the eyes of God and all that, but I am not at all sure that an Arab wedding in the desert is considered a legal wedding in England. And I am quite certain it will not be considered a proper wedding by English society. Certainly not a proper wedding for the sister of an earl."

Lord Penworth looked glum. "Can't they just have another wedding when we get home?" he asked, suspecting that there was some reason his wife would consider this perfectly reasonable solution unacceptable.

"Really, dear." She shook her head pityingly at him. "It will take us easily a month to get home, and more time than that to arrange a London wedding. What if their first child is born eight months after that? They will have enough problems without the added gossip. And Doncaster will hardly thank us for providing his sister with more difficulties."

"Surely people would not be so…" His voice trailed off at the look on his wife's face. Apparently people would. "Well then, what do you propose?"

"Well, David has said that his parents live in Cairo. There is a good-sized English community there, so I am certain we will be able to arrange a wedding with sufficient pomp. David must notify his parents immediately, and I will write as well, so preparations can begin even before we arrive. We must also send a telegram to Elinor and Doncaster giving them the news. Letters will arrive in London long before we do, so we can prepare the ground for the newlyweds, so to speak, and there will be time for Elinor and Doncaster to arrange a celebratory ball for them."

Penworth felt relieved. This was far less complicated than he had feared.

However, his wife had not finished. "Then there is M. de Chambertin," she said.

That deserved a renewed scowl. "What about him?"

"I expect that he will wish to travel with us. Don't you think so?"

He grunted dismissively. "He's been traveling about

by himself for years, it seems. I can't imagine why he would suddenly need us to protect him."

"It is not that he needs protection," she said patiently. "It is that he wishes to marry our daughter, and I do not think they intend to be parted unnecessarily. If you attempt to play the cruel father, he is enough of a romantic to take it into his head to carry Emily off. And while she may be a very practical girl, she is also sufficiently in love to agree."

"What utter rot." He scowled at the bowl of yogurt in front of him and thought that he would be quite happy to never see yogurt on his breakfast table again. "Damn. Very well, he can come with us."

Lady Penworth smiled her approval and ate a spoonful of her yogurt. "You know, I think he is not quite so irresponsible as you seem to think. After all, he worked very well with us the other day, and you cannot deny that he quickly saw the best way to rescue Emily. You might talk to him about his grandfather."

❧

Emily and Lucien were on the roof once more, this time in the early morning. Mist was still floating over the river but above it the air was clear. Should they have chosen to look to the east, they could have seen sun rising over the hill of Kouyunjik, silhouetting the huts in which the finds from the excavation were stored. They did not look that way. They looked only at each other.

There had not been any explicit arrangement to meet here, but neither was surprised to see the other. This was, after all, the one spot in the house where privacy could be found, at least occasionally, and they were delighted to take advantage of it. After several minutes, or perhaps longer—it is to be confessed that neither was paying attention to a clock—Lucien sighed as he nuzzled her neck. He drew back and said, "I am going to go mad, you know."

She gave a small displeased sigh of her own. "Don't stop."

"I must stop now if I am to stop at all. It is, as I told you, a rule about your father's roof."

But his arms were still around her, and she held fistfuls of his shirt. "I could point out that we are not under my father's roof. We are on top of it."

"Ah, you are a creature most dangerous," he said with a strangled laugh. He stepped back and detached her hands from his shirt. "I must convince your father of my virtues so that he decides I am a man of responsibility."

She tilted her head and looked at him consideringly. "We could elope."

"Run off and ask the grandfather of David to arrange an Arab wedding for us as well? No, no, you would not like that. It would cause your parents great pain, and one does not do that to those one loves. And me, I would feel shamed to fulfill your papa's worst fears about me, for he is a man I greatly admire. No, I must convince him that I can live up to his expectations."

"Very well. If you insist, we will go down and join my parents for breakfast and I will be a dutiful and obedient daughter, and you can be a proper aspiring suitor." She started for the staircase, then looked back with a wicked grin. "But perhaps you should tuck your shirt back into your trousers first."

❦

Lady Penworth looked up at their entrance and smiled. "There you are, children. Do join us. We are discussing plans for our return. M. de Chambertin, may I assume that you will wish to accompany us?"

Lucien, who had appeared nervous despite the neatness of his attire, now looked relieved, but it was Emily who said, "Naturally."

Lord Penworth's side-whiskers seemed to quiver disgruntledly, but his growled greeting was almost neutral.

As she carefully chose a date from the dish before her, Lady Penworth remarked, "We will have to decide what to do about the Carnacs"—her husband growled less neutrally—"but that discussion should include the Oliphants."

The mention of the Carnacs brought a flush of shame to Lucien's face, but Lady Penworth leaned over to pat his hand. "You must not blame yourself, Lucien—may I call you Lucien?"

"But of course," he stammered.

She smiled kindly. "You must not blame yourself. I'm sure you had no idea that Mélisande had become infatuated with you. Young men pay very little attention to the fantasies of young girls, and I doubt that you needed to do anything other than exist to make you the hero of her daydreams. After all, you are probably the first attractive young man she has ever met, and then you are French as well." She waved her hand. "But that will be dealt with later. Just now, Phillip, why don't you take Lucien with you and decide how we should travel and all that sort of thing. Emily and I have some plans to make as well." She bestowed a brilliant smile on her husband.

Lord Penworth chuckled as he rose. "Come along, Chambertin. We are being managed. You had best grow accustomed to it."

As she watched them disappear in the direction of Lord Penworth's office, Emily wondered what plans, precisely, her mother had in mind. She took a deep breath and turned to face whatever it was.

The first thing she was faced with was a sheaf of paper along with writing implements. "We need to make lists, or we are sure to overlook something," said Lady Penworth.

*Ha!* thought Emily. When was the last time her mother had overlooked anything she did not choose to overlook?

Ignoring her daughter's sniff, she walked back and forth under the loggia. "First, we need to prepare for Julia's wedding. David should, I think, send a telegram as well as write to his parents. Julia must write to them as well, of course, and I will write suggesting that we have the wedding there."

Emily looked up. "But they are already married."

Lady Penworth gave her daughter an appropriately *silly child* look. "A desert wedding will make an excellently romantic tale to tell their children. It will hardly suffice for the sister of an earl and a man with a career to make in the foreign office. Since Cairo is where his parents live, it is a perfectly acceptable venue for their wedding. His parents will know who should be invited, and I will write to the consul-general as well to discover if there are any visitors of importance at the moment. Do you know who holds that post at present? Never mind, your father will know."

Emily noted down *Write to Oliphants, consul-general.*

"We must write to Elinor about the guest list for the ball to celebrate Julia's wedding. I wonder if it would be best held in London or at Doncaster Abbey?" Lady Penworth frowned in consideration, tapping her cheek. "London will be better for the foreign office people, but people may have left London by the time we return."

"Perhaps you could let Elinor decide. She is quite good at being a society hostess."

Lady Penworth shook her head. "Elinor may not know all the people it will be important to invite. The queen and Prince Albert will decline, of course, but the Princess Royal and Frederick may come if they are in England. She has always been friendly to Elinor. And then I will write to friends, letting them know so they can in turn rally support."

"Really, Mama, you are talking as if this is a military campaign." Emily huffed a little laugh.

Her mother did not smile. Instead she frowned. "That is precisely what it is. David is an outsider, and Julia has had problems. It will require effort to make them accepted in society."

"But you don't even know if they *want* to be accepted by society—by the stuffy kind of society that cares about things like whether or not the Princess Royal attends a party."

Lady Penworth paused in her pacing and looked steadily at her daughter. "You know better than that. No matter what you may think of the people who make up society—and I will readily agree that many of them are fools—their acceptance is important to both David and Julia, and it will matter to their children. If he chooses to make a career in the foreign office, he will need to be accepted as one of them. And Julia—you know how much her mother's scandal has weighed on her. If they later decide to withdraw from society, that is one thing. To be excluded is something else entirely."

Emily's doubt obviously showed on her face, because her mother exclaimed impatiently, "Think, child. You have always been protected by the power of your father's position. Not only is he a marquess, but he is respected because he has always behaved honorably. People want his support, and if not that, at least they do not want to offend him. You are no longer a child. You are going to be plunged into French society by virtue of Lucien's position, and you will need to help him establish himself. Do not delude yourself that it will be easy."

*It cannot possibly be as difficult as Mama is making it sound. There must be an easier way to handle this.* Then Emily smiled innocently at her mother. "But we have a wonderfully romantic tale to tell, don't we? Like something out of the *Thousand and One Nights*. Handsome sheiks, horses galloping over the desert sands, bazaars full of silks and spices, the sun rising over the ruins of ancient civilizations."

"Yes," said her mother with a touch of acid in

her tone. "We will not need to mention the dirt, the insects, the Kurds who find it amusing to shoot at strangers, and the ease with which a child can hire murderers."

"But surely the tale of dramatic rescue will only add to the romance." Emily's eyes were now dancing with glee. "And think how much more impressive it will be if it is *two* rescues and *two* weddings."

"No." Lady Penworth spoke with finality. "There will be no accounts of rescues. I am sure all the young ladies of London delight in such stories between the covers of a book. I do not intend for my daughters to be the focus of such tales when they are whispered over the tea cups. Then it is no longer a tale, it is simply salacious gossip. I am quite serious, Emily. This is not to be discussed outside the family. You will have to save the tale of your romantic rescue for your grandchildren."

"Mama, you are ignoring what I said about *two* weddings."

Suddenly her mother looked very tired, slumping slightly—her mother's posture was *always* perfect—and rubbing the space between her eyes. "Whatever possessed me to urge your father to bring us here?" Her voice was so soft she might have been talking to herself. "You could have been killed. Both of you could have been killed, and all because of that stupid, selfish, little brat. Who would have expected her to be so foolish, so desperate?" She tilted her head back, eyes closed, and bit down on her lower lip.

Emily did not know what to do. Her mother did not get upset. That was one of the givens in the universe. Whatever happened, Mama dealt with it with aplomb. Whatever the problem, Mama made it go away. She reached out a hand to touch her mother's arm. "Mama?" she asked tentatively.

With a deep sigh, Lady Penworth straightened up, patted her daughter's hand, and managed a tight smile. "Yes, I heard you. Two weddings, you said. Absolutely not."

"Mama! Why not?"

"For one thing, you must not overshadow Julia's wedding, and you would most assuredly do that were you to marry at the same time. For another, the French are quite as punctilious as the English, and Louis-Napoléon is even more so, given his uncertain support now that he has made himself emperor. A hasty wedding in some obscure foreign city will not do."

"Mama!"

"My dear, I know this has all been very dramatic, and it is highly romantic to be rescued by a dashing young adventurer…"

"But he isn't an adventurer. His grandfather is a French count."

"Yes, but you didn't know that, did you?" Lady Penworth's shrewd, all-seeing eye was in evidence again.

Since her mother was quite right about that, Emily couldn't meet her eye and said nothing.

"And I assume you do not know anything about his family."

"Oh, but I do." Emily lifted her head up. "Lucien has talked quite a bit about them, or about his grandfather at least. He seems to be an unpleasant man, but

Lucien says that he has his own estate so there is no need for us to live with the count. Besides, he must be very old."

"Old!" Lady Penworth smiled tolerantly. "Yes, I suppose he is. Well into his eighties by now. But still a man of some power and influence, and none of it benign. I have heard of him from friends in France. He was one of the moving forces behind the White Terror after the restoration of the Bourbon king, Louis XVIII, and he is still one of the ultra-royalists. He persists in behaving as if the Revolution never happened. He would be a comic figure if he did not have so many followers."

"Well, that needn't worry us. I don't think Lucien is terribly interested in politics, and that was all a long time ago."

"A long time ago? Perhaps it seems so to you, but people have long memories. And in France, everything is political—the books you read, the music you hear, everything. The estate Lucien has inherited from his mother is near his grandfather's estate, your father tells me. That means that his grandfather can create serious problems for you with neighboring families."

"Oh, Mama, please don't make difficulties!" A moment ago marriage to Lucien had been almost within her grasp. She had known it. Yes, Papa was raising objections, but she knew he would never deny her what she truly wanted. Mama, though—she had not expected Mama to be a problem.

"I am not trying to be difficult, child, but I do not think you have any idea what you are facing. You have known M. de Chambertin only a short while—yes, I know the circumstances have been unusual, but still, a foreign country, a difficult family…" She shook her head ruefully. "There are always problems in life. Must you seek out more?"

"I am not seeking difficulties, Mama, but if these difficulties exist, I will not avoid them. I cannot. Together, Lucien and I can face anything. And without him…without him I do not know if I can face anything at all."

Lady Penworth regarded her daughter long and thoughtfully. At length she gave a resigned huff. "Well, I am sure you can cope if you must. But I do not see why my children must marry into such difficult families. And I do not see what objection they can possibly have to being married from their home."

Emily threw her arms around her mother with a crow of delight. "You know I love Penworth Castle, and I promise we will visit often, but we would have to wait months and months to marry there. I could not possibly wait!"

"People do, you now," said Lady Penworth, a trifle acidly. "Indeed, there are many who consider a year to be a reasonable length for an engagement."

"And how very sorry I feel for such insipid couples," said Emily, laughing. She wanted to shout with happiness, but did not want to try her mother's temper too much.

"But if the wedding is not to be at our home, it will have to take place in France. Yes, France," said Lady Penworth when Emily exclaimed in protest. "As you have pointed out, he is the grandson of a French count, and he is marrying the daughter of an English marquess. It is inconceivable that the wedding should be some hasty, hole-and-corner affair. The assumption would be that there was some embarrassing reason for the secrecy." At that point, Lady Penworth fixed her daughter with a gimlet eye. "I trust there is no such reason and that you would tell me immediately should such a reason be forthcoming."

Emily felt herself shrinking in her seat. She blushed furiously and whispered, "Yes, Mama."

# Twenty-six

THEY TOOK SHELTER UNDER THE AWNING ON THE ROOF. It was not simply a matter of privacy. The rooftops were all deserted in the middle of the day, when the awning was needed to provide relief from the blistering sun.

"She is right, your maman." Lucien leaned against the parapet with Emily in his arms, resting against him while he caressed her back in an effort to soothe her. "It will be better if all is done as it should be."

"As it should be! That is so sensible, and I am so tired of being sensible. I have been sensible all my life," she grumbled, twisting her fingers into his shirt. "Do you realize that by the time we get back to England, and all the balls and receptions to honor David and Julia take place, and we go down to the castle, it will be at least December, and more likely January or February, before we can be married?"

He pulled her close and buried his face in her hair, her soft honey hair. She even smelled sweet, and a little spicy. "I could not wait so long. It drives me mad, being so close to you, and not being able to have you. Ah, I should have been a better man. Then perhaps this would not be so difficult."

"Are you regretting what we did?" She sounded half-frightened, half-outraged.

He could only smile, but the smile was tinged with rue. "One does not regret the fulfillment of one's dreams. One can only be grateful. But when the world intrudes, it brings with it fear. You will tell me, will you not, if there are any…complications? Because then I will carry you off at once, and we will be married at the nearest consul's office. It must be arranged that your parents blame me, and not you."

"Oh, is that what is bothering you?" She turned scarlet and hid her face against him. "You need not worry. Yesterday…well, never mind. Just, there is nothing to worry about."

"You are certain?"

"Yes." Her voice was muffled against him. "I have an older sister, and when she was enceinte…well, she talked a lot about it. And how you know."

He tightened his hold on her and pressed his mouth to her temple. "I should, I know, be pleased that I have not made difficulties for you, that I have not given your father reason to despise me. But there is a part of me—not the most honorable part, I fear—a part of me that wishes I had a reason, an excuse to carry you off at once."

"And I wish that too." She sighed. "Almost a year to wait. I do not think I can bear it."

"As to that…" Lucien stepped back with a grin and tilted up her head with his fingers so he could look into her face. "As to that, I have an idea. My uncle, the brother of my mother, lives near Avignon. His family estate, the chateau, it is there."

"I thought you said you had no family, or very little family."

"I was speaking then of my father's family in Burgundy. But most of my mother's family is in the Vaucluse. My grandparents died long ago, but my uncle remains, and there are many cousins. It was to this uncle that I went when I first left my grandfather's house. He is not fond of my grandfather, you see, nor does my grandfather approve of him. So if I marry from his house, it is most proper, most fitting that only my mother's relatives be in attendance."

A delighted smile crossed Emily's face. "And how soon could we be in Avignon?"

"We go to Baghdad, Basra, then we stop in Cairo for the wedding of David and Lady Julia—a month? Six weeks at most before we can marry."

She fell into his arms and they spun around, laughing in delight.

❧

Emily and Lucien were still smiling—and sitting side by side, hand in hand—as Lucien explained his plan to Lord and Lady Penworth. They were in the room Lord Penworth used as an office. He sat behind the broad wooden expanse of a European-style desk in a stiff leather chair, with Lady Penworth in the armchair upholstered in a sensible brown twill and the young couple on a pair of uncomfortable and unadorned wooden chairs.

Lucien's plan sounded wonderfully reasonable to

Emily, but she could not fail to notice that although her parents listened attentively, they were not smiling. They were not actually scowling, but they regarded Lucien with less than unbridled enthusiasm.

"I do not wish to pry into matters which are none of my concern," said Lady Penworth, obviously considering this most definitely her concern, "but could you tell me the reason for the animosity between the two sides of your family?"

"In part it is political," said Lucien, waving a hand in that French gesture that dismisses things as unimportant. "My mother's family, none of them are strong monarchists. Not revolutionaries. They have no desire to see heads roll, you understand, but they would be happy to see no more of the Bourbons."

"In that case, I wonder that your grandfather wished his son to marry into that family," said Lord Penworth. "I understood you to say that he is a strong monarchist."

"Indeed he is," said Lucien, "one of the ultras. But he covets the estate of Varennes, which lies alongside his lands and was my mother's inheritance. Since she is a woman, he assumes she has no thoughts, no opinions that must be considered."

Lucien correctly interpreted the strangled noise that came from Lady Penworth to signify that she considered such a belief to be beyond idiocy and anyone who held such a thought to be a fool. He smiled in agreement and said, "That is the other reason for my uncle's dislike. My mother was his older sister, and he was most fond of her. It angered him greatly that her husband's family made her unhappy."

Lord Penworth's fingers were beating a tattoo on the arm of his chair, something he did only when he was not happy with the course of events. Emily eyed him nervously. "Perhaps," he said, "you could tell us a bit more about your uncle."

"But yes." Lucien fidgeted beside her. He sounded less confident that he had been at first. "He is Baron Antoine de Marbot, and he serves as a deputy in the assembly, though not a passionate one. It is mostly to protect his family and its interests that he involves himself. In his part of the Vaucluse, in Provence, the family is of considerable importance socially, and they are far from poor. My uncle did much to advise me about my affairs, and I have benefited from his advice."

"Will this not put him in an awkward position in regard to your grandfather? No one needs enemies, and your grandfather, as I understand it, is still a man of some influence. Will it not seem that your uncle is encouraging you to defy your grandfather, whose heir you are?"

Lucien nodded. "That is why he will be most happy to help me. Not only will it displease my grandfather, but it will also be of help to my uncle to be seen to have me in his camp, so to speak. Others—including the emperor—will be pleased to think that at least one family will no longer pine for a restoration."

While Lord Penworth mulled this over, Lady Penworth asked, "Is your uncle married?"

"But yes," said Lucien, "and I have four young cousins there."

"In that case, the feelings of your aunt might be a matter to consider," she said. "After all, it is on her shoulders that the burden of arranging the wedding will fall, and that is no small burden."

Emily felt a twinge of guilt. This would not have occurred to Lucien, but she should have thought of it. She had seen the preparations for other weddings, and it was no small task. Especially if it was to be the kind of socially prominent wedding that Mama clearly considered necessary.

Lucien's surprise and confusion were obvious, and Lord Penworth also looked startled. Lady Penworth and Emily exchanged looks of understanding.

"Lucien, you will send a telegram to your uncle immediately, to be followed by a letter explaining all in detail. I will write to your aunt—you will give me her direction—and we will endeavor to work out a manageable schedule. Phillip, you will need to send a telegram to your secretary. He may need to travel to Avignon to arrange places for us all to stay, and he must discover if anyone we need to invite is staying in that part of the world. Come along, Emily. We have a great deal to do."

With that, Lady Penworth swept from the room. Emily sighed, but followed dutifully behind her.

⤜❧

In the cool of the evening, they all gathered in the courtyard to consider the remaining problem. The household had settled back into its usual rhythm. The chatter of the servants, punctuated by occasional bursts of laughter, made a distant hum. The ubiquitous perfume of coffee mingled with the scent of the jasmine vine, an odd commingling that would always mean Mosul to Emily. Most of them sat or reclined on the colorful cushions that softened the benches in the loggia, but Lucien sat at Emily's feet, resting his head against her leg. She held her hand where she could tangle her fingers ever so slightly in his hair without her mother seeing what she was doing. Perhaps Mama just pretended not to see. It didn't matter. His hair was delightfully soft and silky.

Julia looked different. It was nothing spectacular. Her hair was dressed in its usual neat chignon, she was wearing a familiar dress of yellow-and-white-striped India muslin, and she was sitting with her usual perfect posture, her hands folded in her lap. Only perhaps her posture wasn't quite as perfectly erect as usual. The set of her shoulders wasn't quite as rigid as usual. And the expression on her face wasn't quite as impassive as usual.

Everything about her was just a bit softer than usual. Not a great deal, but enough to be noticeable. The hint of a smile hovered around her mouth. And even when she was not looking at him, she seemed to be in tune with David. It was as if they breathed in unison. Then they looked at each other and smiled. Tiny little private smiles inside the bubble of happiness that protected them from the rest of the universe.

Emily could feel the tears prickling at her eyes. This was why people wept at weddings. The happiness was too extraordinary. It demanded a response.

Lord Penworth cleared his throat, and the bubble shattered. A sigh of regret washed almost audibly over them as they turned to look at him.

"I know you are all fully occupied with plans for

the future, but we must clear away the detritus left by recent events. We cannot condone Mlle. Carnac's actions, nor can we absolve her father of all responsibility." He gave a short, angry laugh. "Although M. Carnac seems to think that is the case. I have received two letters from him so far, asking—no, demanding—that we begin efforts to rescue his crates from the river."

Lady Penworth shook her head in disbelief.

Lucien also shook his head. "He has only one idea in his head, that one. He sees nothing else. That I should have brought him and his daughter into your acquaintance, I cannot begin to tell you how much I regret it."

"You cannot claim all the blame for yourself. There was no need for me to involve myself in his project," said Lord Penworth.

"What is done is done," said Lady Penworth. "There is no point in berating ourselves for actions that were taken from the best of intentions. What remains is the task of deciding what to do now. I assume it is up to us and not to the local authorities?"

"Er, yes," said David. "Much though I would like to recommend official... Despite the sultan's efforts..." He threw up his hands in a gesture of surrender. "If we involve the authorities, it will be a mess. It will be a diplomatic embarrassment for all the countries, and we could be trapped here forever."

Lord Penworth nodded. "That is what I feared. But I don't like the idea that Mlle. Carnac will escape punishment."

Lady Penworth closed her eyes for a moment

before speaking. "When I think what could have happened... She wanted Emily killed. It doesn't matter that she was not going to do it herself. That is what she wanted. And then Julia—Julia, who had gone out of her way to be kind to the girl. They were going to sell Julia into slavery and that, that *creature* never even raised an alarm." She looked down at her hands, which were trembling on her lap. Clenching them, she said, "I am sorry. When I think of what she put us through, what might have happened, I could chop her up into little pieces."

Julia gnawed at her lip and decided to speak. "But nothing did happen. In the end, I mean. In the end, everything turned out all right."

"Really, Julia!" Emily sat up straight. "It's all very well and good to be charitable and forgiving, but that little monster was perfectly willing to have us killed. That does not leave me feeling in the least charitable."

"Not charitable, precisely, but I keep thinking... She's really just a child, still. And she has had no education to speak of. Her mother taught her to read and write, but she's terribly ignorant." Julia looked around at the others as if asking them to understand. "And desperate. Really desperate."

Emily shook her head in exasperation. "How you can sympathize with her..."

But Lady Penworth held up a hand to interrupt and spoke slowly. "No, Emily, Julia is right. Mélisande is just a child. A foolish, selfish child, but that may be because she has never been taught any better. She has no one to take care of her, so she tries to take care of herself. With potentially disastrous consequences this time, but…" Her voice trailed off, and she frowned in thought.

Emily looked thoughtful as well. "It must have been dreadful for her, growing up here with no one but that horrid father of hers."

Lord Penworth looked at his wife with a dubious expression. "My dear, you are not going to start managing the Carnacs' lives too, are you?"

Lady Penworth nodded decisively. "Well, someone must take charge of that girl, and her father is obviously not up to the task. If she is left here, there is no future for her. None at all. She must be taken in hand. At the very least, she needs an education."

"*Tiens!*" Lucien exploded. "You will reward her by sending her to Paris? A fine lesson that will be."

"No, Lucien, not Paris. I was thinking…" She turned to David. "Are there any schools in Cairo, do you know?"

He blinked in surprise and thought for a moment. "There is a convent of French nuns," he said slowly, "the Sisters of the Good Shepherd. They take in girls, I think."

"Perfect. A convent school would be just the thing. Then, if she behaves herself and does well, in a couple of years we can think about a school in France. But I will make it clear to her that this depends entirely on her behavior. Are we all agreed?" Lady Penworth looked around at the others.

They looked at her in stunned silence, but no one offered any objections.

Faced with Lord and Lady Penworth, in full aristocratic arrogance, Carnac offered no objections to his daughter's departure either. Indeed, he accepted the news that Lady Penworth was about to appropriate his daughter with indifference. He did, however, continue to voice strenuous objections to Lord Penworth's refusal to make any effort to rescue the drowned artifacts, but no one paid him any heed.

Mélisande came before the Penworths in trepidation. Accustomed as she was to being berated for things beyond her control, like a poorly cooked dinner or an out-of-season sandstorm, she had been envisioning far more extreme punishments than a scolding this time. Would she spend decades in a Turkish dungeon? Did the Turks still torture prisoners? Would they cut off her head and stick it up on the wall? She might not have intended the disasters that befell, but she was honest enough to admit to herself that she was the one who set them in train.

When Lady Penworth announced sternly, as if pronouncing sentence, that she was to be sent to a convent school in Cairo, Mélisande just stared at her. She could not quite believe what she heard. "A convent school?" she whispered at length.

"Yes," said Lady Penworth, "in Cairo. What happens after that will depend entirely upon you. If we have good reports of you from the sisters, if you are diligent in your studies and obedient in your behavior, it may be possible for you to continue your schooling in France. We shall see."

"I will be able to leave here? To leave Mosul? I do not have to stay here forever?" Hope began to blossom.

"You do need an education," said Lady Penworth. Her face was still stern, though her voice had softened.

"You will take me away from here? Oh, thank you!" Mélisande threw herself to her knees and clutched Lady Penworth's gown. "You will save me!"

"Good heavens, child, get up," said Lady Penworth, looking thoroughly embarrassed. "One of the things you will need to learn is to eschew these dramatics."

And so, with no further ado, Mélisande was packed up with the rest of the Penworths' baggage for the trip to Cairo. She was very quiet on the journey, keeping out of sight as much as possible, but until the convent doors closed behind her, she observed Lady Penworth carefully and imitated, as best she could, that lady's bearing and gestures. For Lady Penworth was, after all, a woman to whose orders men paid attention.

# Twenty-seven

THEIR ARRIVAL IN BAGHDAD FELT LIKE THE END OF THE journey. It wasn't, of course. They were still a thousand miles from home, and Baghdad looked very much like Mosul—narrow streets with dun-colored buildings and tiny windows, throngs of people in exotic costumes speaking mysterious languages. At least they were still exotic and mysterious to Emily. It was all doubtless perfectly ordinary to the people who lived here.

If it wasn't the end of the journey, it was the first step back into the familiar world. They had arrived here traveling on keleks, with Irmak and his troopers bristling with arms to discourage any river pirates. The next stage of their travels would be on a steam ship, first down the remainder of the river to Basra, then across to the Red Sea and up to Suez. They were leaving the ancient world for the modern.

They were also bidding farewell to Irmak, who was now free to return with his troopers to Constantinople. Nuran and Safiye went with him, and that leave-taking was surprisingly difficult. The women all shed a few tears, or more than a few, and embraced before the two maids departed, bearing with them thanks and good wishes as well as more tangible gifts.

"This is a part of traveling that I never considered—saying good-bye to people you have liked and will never see again," said Emily, staring at the door that closed behind them.

"Yes, but the only way to avoid that is to never meet new people, or if you meet them, to never like them. And that would be dreadful," said her mother.

Changes.

She had been so eager for change when they arrived in Constantinople, and there had been changes aplenty once they left the embassy house. For almost two months now she had been living in a world that was very different from her own, and she had grown accustomed to it. When she returned, would everything that had once been familiar seem strange?

In Baghdad they stayed at the consulate, a newish edifice, built like a European house with corridors and at least some plumbing, though the business offices still opened onto a central courtyard. The consul-general was Colonel Kemball, a British officer whose unaffected manner put everyone at ease. The members of his staff were also soldiers, and just the presence of so many Englishmen seemed to put a distance between her family and the surrounding world.

There was one serious problem with the consul's residence in Baghdad. As far as she had been able to discover, there was no access to the roof. And even if there had been, Lucien was not staying with them.

For Lucien, the trouble began when he left them to settle in and presented himself at the French consulate, explaining his need to stay for a few days before continuing on to Cairo. Instead of offering him the usual welcome, the underling sent to greet the visitor stared at him as if he were some dangerous intruder, muttered a half-incomprehensible excuse, and vanished into an inner room.

Moments later a small man wearing a black frock coat and a furious expression burst out of the inner office. Accompanying him were a pair of soldiers who hurried to seize Lucien by the arms.

"Such impudence!" The little man was stuttering with anger. "How dare you seek to impose yourself upon me using a dead man's name? We will give you a place to stay—in prison!"

For a moment Lucien was too startled to react. Then one of the soldiers tightened his grip, and Lucien threw him off in fury.

"Take your hands off me, you *canaille*!" He pulled himself free and turned on the sputtering creature before him. "And how dare you speak to me in such a tone? Who do you think you are?"

The little man drew himself up. "I am Jean-Marie Beauclerc, the French consul at Baghdad and, as such, the representative of the government of France and of the emperor, Napoléon III. And I am not to be imposed upon by some charlatan who claims to be the grandson of the Comte de la Boulaye, when the comte himself tells us that said grandson is dead."

"What?" Lucien was stunned for a moment. "But…

but that is preposterous. As you can see for yourself, I am most certainly not dead."

"I see someone before me who is not dead." Beauclerc gave a sniff. "But the identity of this not-dead man I do not know."

Lucien had been keeping a tight rein on himself for what seemed like ages. He had behaved himself in Mosul. He had behaved himself on the journey to Baghdad. He had done nothing with Emily that could not have been seen by her parents—well, almost nothing. At least, he had done none of the things he wanted to do. But this was insupportable.

He exploded.

He shouted. He raged. He demanded. He threatened. Indeed, when he finally calmed down and saw Beauclerc and the soldiers standing ashen and trembling before him, he realized that he had behaved exactly as his grandfather would have behaved. The realization sobered him. Not completely, but enough to enable him to take part in a rational discussion.

Lucien produced his identity papers. Beauclerc agreed that they were in order, but pointed out that they could have been stolen from a dead man. Lucien wanted to know what made the consul think Lucien de Chambertin was dead. The consul produced a letter from the comte's man of business saying that the comte's grandson was dead and wishing to know if he had any effects, any possessions in Baghdad.

That produced another explosion. Was that vicious old man trying to impoverish him? How could he marry Emily if he had no way to support her? He raged until Beauclerc assured him that nothing had been sent to the comte—indeed, nothing had been found. That calmed Lucien momentarily until the consul asked if he had any way to actually prove his identity.

Lucien felt as if he had tumbled into a nightmare.

"Of course there are people who know me," he said. "I have just come from Mosul in the company of Lord Penworth and his family. And David Oliphant of the English foreign service."

Beauclerc pounced. "But how long have they known you? The comte's man writes that your grandfather has not had any word from you for five years." He leaned back with an air of triumph.

"They have most certainly had…" Lucien stopped abruptly. All those letters to which he had never replied. Could they honestly believe him to be dead? He had written only to… "Of course," he said triumphantly. "I have written frequently to the notaire. M. Bouchard knows I am alive and well."

And that meant that his grandfather and other relatives also knew he was alive and well. Bouchard would have told them so. This had to be some ploy to force his return, unless it was simply theft.

Mention of a notaire gave the consul pause, but he remained uncertain. The notaire was in France. They were in Baghdad. Letters took weeks to cover the distance.

"The telegraph," said Lucien, smiling in satisfaction. The sultan's passion for modernizing had brought this into existence only recently, and while the telegraph wires did not cover the entire empire, the line from Baghdad to Istanbul was reliable, and from there France was easily reached.

Faced with the young man's assurance, and considering that his behavior accorded only too well with what might be expected from the Comte de la Boulaye's grandson, the consul was no longer inclined to toss his visitor into the nearest prison. Neither was he happy to welcome Lucien. His offer of hospitality—a room at the consulate—was a trifle begrudging. He consoled himself with the thought that if his visitor proved to be an impostor, he would be easily apprehended.

It was late the following afternoon when Lucien arrived at the British consulate, to call not on Lady Emily but on her father, Lord Penworth. To speak with the marquess in private, he said.

The young man was pacing in agitation when Lord Penworth arrived at the small room Colonel Kemball had offered. "Is something amiss, Chambertin?"

Lucien ran a hand through his hair, opened his mouth, then closed it and turned aside to take a deep breath. Facing Lord Penworth again, he spoke rapidly, his accent more marked than usual. "It is my grandfather. He decides that I am dead. In any case, he persuades the bankers at Autun—that is the town near us—he persuades them that I am dead, and takes the money I have on deposit there."

"What!" Lord Penworth stepped back, shocked. "But…but that's impossible. He cannot do such a thing."

Lucien's mouth twisted in a bitter smile. "No? But it seems that he has done precisely that."

"This cannot be allowed. We must write—no, we must telegraph to the authorities."

The marquess's outrage had a calming effect on

Lucien. "We have done so, the consul and I. Many telegrams, back and forth. M. Bouchard—he is, you know, the notaire who handles my affairs—he has kept Varennes out of the comte's hands. And the bank, they now know, but it seems that the money has disappeared."

"What are you going to do?" Penworth sounded curious as well as concerned.

"What can I do? I cannot demand that my own grandfather be sent to prison. It is as well I am thousands of miles away or I might try to throttle him, but prison? No. The shame, the scandal..." He shook his head.

Penworth nodded. "How bad is it?"

Lucien endeavored to outline the situation. "It is bad, but it is not total devastation. I have money elsewhere, other investments. There is some here in Baghdad, some in Cairo, and more in Avignon. It is just—this was the money I had set aside for Varennes, for improvements on the estate, for the house. It will require a few years before it will be what I want for Emily."

"Other investments?"

Lucien flushed slightly. "As I travel, I sometimes make small arrangements, send things back to France to be sold. Rugs, a few antiquities. I partner with a few men here in Baghdad, in Constantinople."

"So you are something of a businessman."

Although it was not said in a condemnatory tone, Lucien stiffened. "A man would be a fool not to be," he said, "especially when I desired to be independent of my grandfather."

"I tend to agree." Penworth was staring at him, assessing him. Lucien had to make a deliberate effort not to squirm under the scrutiny.

"Are you asking my daughter to live in poverty?"

"No, it is not that bad. It is only that, for a few years, we may need to be careful. And the bankers—they are frightened now. Some of the money may be recovered."

"Careful," repeated Penworth slowly. "Do you expect me to allow my daughter to marry into a situation where she will have to pinch pennies?"

"I think the decision must be Emily's," Lucien said stiffly. "I will not disguise the situation from her, but neither will I give her up. I do not think she will send me away." She would not turn away from him. He was certain of that. He *was*. Why this sudden terror? Why did he feel as if iron bands were tightening around his chest?

❧

He need not have feared. Emily greeted the news with distress, but not over the prospect of pinching pennies. She was reasonably sure she could manage that, though her mother expressed some uncertainty. What upset her was the behavior of Lucien's grandfather. Unable to sit calmly, she paced back and forth in the sitting room where she and her mother had retired. "I cannot believe such *perfidy*!" she exclaimed.

Lady Penworth blinked at her daughter. "Perfidy?"

Emily blushed slightly. "I like the word, and I do not often have an opportunity to use it." She collapsed into a chair next to her mother. "Am I being foolish?

It is just so infuriating for his own grandfather to treat Lucien so."

"I know," said Lady Penworth with a smile. She reached over to pat Emily's hand. "We may be able to shrug off injuries done to ourselves, but not injuries done to those we love."

Emily heaved a sigh. "I want to do something to help. I want to fix it, and I don't know how."

Her mother shook her head. "Even if there were something you could do, you should not do it. Lucien would not thank you. It is humiliating enough for him to have to admit his grandfather's..." She tilted her head, considering. "Actually, perfidy is a good word for it."

"Thank you."

"But nonetheless, you must not try to interfere," Lady Penworth continued. "This is one of those things men must work out for themselves. You will have enough to do dealing with the social problems that will be present when you get to Burgundy."

At that, Emily sat up and frowned. "Social problems?"

"Of course. I doubt Lucien will wish to actually prosecute his grandfather—that would create an appalling scandal. So those relatives who are dependent on the old comte may try to make life uncomfortable for you and Lucien. It will be your task to remind them, ever so tactfully, that it is in Lucien's power to create that scandal and humiliate them all. There will be others in the neighborhood as well. You can use your charm on them, but you may need to point out, again tactfully, that the comte is old and in the not-too-distant future, Lucien will replace him."

"Oh dear." Worry replaced Emily's anger. "You are much better at that sort of thing than I am. And so is Elinor."

⤮

Lucien spent little time with them over the next few days. He explained that he had business to attend to, and that was true enough. There were various enterprises that he needed to settle before he returned to France, investments that he was forced to liquidate, thanks to grandpère. More importantly, there was a purchase he needed to make.

It took longer than he had expected. By the time he arrived at the dock, the baggage had all been loaded on the steamer, all the other passengers were aboard, and the sailors had begun clearing away the ropes.

Lucien sprinted up the gangway, to the relief of the officer on deck. By the time he reached the cabins, the rhythm of the engine had changed, and he was vaguely aware of the shouts of the sailors as the ship cast off. He skidded to a halt when he realized that the package he was holding was wrapped in a piece of cloth that was more rag than anything else and tied with a grimy string. Not a romantic appearance. He tried to untie it, but in frustration resorted to the knife in his boot. Tossing the wrappings aside, he opened the small box within. Yes, it was exactly what he had wanted. Would it also be something Emily wanted? Sudden doubt assailed him, but it was too late. He stepped forward, trying to remember which of the doors was hers. The captain had told him, but…yes, it was the third one on the right. He knocked rapidly, three times.

The door opened immediately, as if she had been standing right beside it. Perhaps she had. She had her hat on, a wide-brimmed straw, and gloves, as if she was about to go out. Or perhaps she had just come in.

His mind was dithering, and he hadn't even opened his mouth yet. "Emily." He managed to get that far but stood there staring at her. He wasn't sure precisely why. She looked no different than usual, but her usual was so precisely what he wanted. Everything he wanted. "Emily," he repeated, "I may enter?"

She stepped back to let him in, an uncertain expression on her face. It was a tiny little cabin, with a bunk and room for nothing more than her trunk. There was a small window, but it was too crusted with salt for anything outside to be visible. He gestured for her to sit down on the bed, and she did so, still looking uncertain. That uncertainty was increasing his nervousness.

It was time. He took a deep breath and went down on one knee. "Lady Emily, you must know by now that I love you deeply and completely, and wish above all to be with you, to have you always beside me. Will you marry me and accept this ring as a pledge of my devotion?"

She looked at him in confusion. Ah, she was adorable when she was confused, but please God, not uncertain. She must not be uncertain. Would she not take the ring?

"But you already…" She took a deep breath and smiled a glorious smile. "You didn't come aboard with us. I was afraid that you might have changed your mind, that you had decided to simply forget about your grandfather, that the call of Samarkand was too strong."

"Why would you think such a thing?" He felt half-relieved, half-offended that she should doubt him. "When you opened the door, you looked uncertain. I thought perhaps you were annoyed that I had not fulfilled all the formalities."

"And so the proposal on bended knee?"

She was smiling at him. Happiness bubbled up to escape in laughter. "All honor is due to my lady."

She looked down at the ring he held out to her, seeing it fully, and gasped. "It is incredible."

"That is why I was always busy," he said, slipping it on her finger. "For you I wanted the Roxelana ring, an emerald surrounded by diamonds. The design is that of the ring the famed Sultan Suleiman the Magnificent made for his beloved wife. I sent messages to the jeweler from Mosul, but it took time for him to find the right stones and then to make it, and I was afraid it would not be ready before we sailed. I fear I have been driving him mad, hanging over his shoulder."

"It is so beautiful," she said softly, holding her hand out to admire it. Then she swung around to look at him in concern. "But your troubles, all the money your grandfather stole—you cannot afford such a ring."

He closed his hand over hers and rested his forehead on hers. "Yes I can. I wanted this ring for you. There will be other jewels in the future, I promise you, though you may have to wait for them. But this ring—it will remind you—it will remind us—of our adventures here. When the snows pile up at Varennes and the wind blows against the windows, when you have to face my relatives at Boulaye, you will touch this ring and it will keep you warm."

# Twenty-eight

James Oliphant, David's father, had the tall, rangy build and chiseled features of a Scot, traits his son had inherited. He also had the sandy hair and fair skin of a Scot, skin that was reddened by the inescapable glare of the Egyptian sun. From his mother, Anmar, David had inherited his coloring—olive complexion, dark hair and eyes. While both his parents were good-looking individuals, Emily decided, neither one could approach David's extraordinary handsomeness.

Any consideration of their appearances vanished in the warmth of their welcome. The Oliphants were clearly delighted that their son had found a bride and were disposed to agree with him in viewing her as the epitome of all goodness and beauty. That in turn made the Tremaines, who were all protective of Julia, disposed to think highly of the Oliphants' intelligence and good nature.

Mr. Oliphant and his wife, whom he called Annie, insisted that the entire party stay at their home, a large villa on the banks of the Nile. Like most of the buildings they had seen in this part of the world, the exterior was plain. This one had thick white walls and shuttered windows. Inside, it was an oasis of luxury, combining the cushioned softness of European chairs with the rich textures of Oriental fabrics and the brilliant colors of the tiles.

The villa was set in a large garden reaching down to the river. Trees shaded the buildings and a canal flowed through the garden between banks of turquoise tiles. Unfamiliar blossoms in brilliant hues filled the beds lining the pathways. A high wall surrounding the garden shut out the shouts and clamor of the city, but it was so disguised by vines and shrubs that it seemed as if the garden was endless, a world in itself.

"The ancient Persians called a garden like this a paradise," said Lucien, looking about him, "and it is not difficult to agree. Shall we make a walled garden at Varennes, with a canal like this running through it?"

Emily's smile mirrored his. "And so we will live in paradise?"

"Of course."

They began to lean toward each other, but Lady Penworth called before they could explore the possibilities of paradise. Emily scowled with frustration but dutifully followed her mother into the guest quarters. Once inside, her sigh turned to one of sheer pleasure, echoing her mother's. It was not that the house was beautiful. It was, in the Arabic way of bright colors, intricate designs, and open space. But what enchanted them was that the rooms were cool.

When they had first arrived in Constantinople, the bright sunlight had delighted Emily, and after the bitter cold they had encountered in the mountains, the warmth of Mosul was welcome. However, as the weeks progressed, the warmth had turned to heat. Now, in the middle of May, Emily knew why travelers called the sun merciless, and she understood why the inhabitants of the region built their houses with thick walls and small windows to keep it out.

"I do not think I will ever again complain about the cold drafts at Penworth Castle," said Lady Penworth. "A roaring fire can banish the chill, but with the heat, one can do nothing but cower in the shade and wait for the sun to set. And it is still early in the year. How can people bear to live here?"

"Lucien says that one gets used to it," said Emily.

"Lucien says?" Lady Penworth raised her brows. "How very wifely that sounds."

Emily felt herself blush.

"I hope you don't plan to dwindle into one of those fools who can only parrot their husbands' words and have no thoughts of their own," her mother continued.

At that Emily laughed.

After a moment's thought, Lady Penworth laughed as well. "No, I don't imagine you will."

As the days passed, Emily found that even had she wished to parrot Lucien's words, she would not have been able to do so because she heard very few of them. The gentlemen appeared only at dinner and not always then. It was a bit frustrating. By the third day, even Mama was beginning to look irritated.

Immediately after dinner, the gentlemen had withdrawn to Mr. Oliphant's office once again. That left the ladies only themselves to talk to as they sat in the garden beside the canal.

Lady Penworth finally gave in to her curiosity. "What on earth are they up to?"

Mrs. Oliphant made a helpless gesture with her hand. "My husband says it will be a surprise. All I know is that it is some scheme of M. Chambertin's."

"Lucien?" Lady Penworth looked sharply at her daughter, who lifted her shoulders and shook her head, denying any notion about what was going on. "He hasn't decided to plan a trip to the North Pole or some such, has he?"

"No," said Mrs. Oliphant, frowning slightly. "I do not think it has anything to do with travel. I think it is business of some sort. Trade, perhaps."

Trade? How odd. Emily was certain that her father had been quite dismissive of the potential for trade with Mesopotamia.

The ladies looked at each other, shrugged, and turned to a discussion of wedding plans. It was turning into quite a grand celebration, with an ever increasing number of guests. Since wintering in Egypt had become quite fashionable, there was still a crowd of visitors to Shepheard's Hotel, and many of them were friends or acquaintances of the Penworths or of the Doncasters. Then there were the English residents and the diplomatic corps in Cairo and Alexandria.

Mrs. Oliphant was delighted at the number of people who would be attending her son's wedding. "They would not have come had you not been here," she told Lady Penworth, "and had the bride not been the sister of the Earl of Doncaster."

"The more fools they." Lady Penworth dismissed them with a toss of her head. "This menu you have designed provides a fascinating mixture of European and Arabic dishes. Don't you agree, Julia?" Julia opened her mouth, but before she could speak, Lady Penworth had turned back to Mrs. Oliphant. "You are providing your guests with just enough of the exotic to make them remember this wedding, and enough of the familiar to make them comfortable. Brilliant." Emily and Julia looked at each other, laughed softly, and let the older women go over their plans again and again.

The next day, the gentlemen returned to the house so early that the ladies had to be roused from their afternoon naps. Once they were properly laced up and groomed, they arrived in the salon to find the men in a smugly satisfied mood.

"It was all M. de Chambertin's idea," said Mr. Oliphant.

"Your betrothed is a very clever young man," Lord Penworth told his daughter, who smiled prettily and did not say that she was quite aware of that. Nor did she say that she had not thought that the cleverness he had shown her was something of which her father would approve. She did, however, turn to Lucien with a question in her eyes.

Lucien gave that French shrug. "It is a bit uncomfortable, for we are taking advantage of the troubles of others, but the troubles are there whatever we do. That we cannot change."

Lady Penworth had little patience with such indirection. "Precisely what are you talking about?"

"You know they have begun fighting in America," said her husband. When they all nodded, he continued,

"It seems likely that this is turning into a civil war that will not be over quickly. The southern states will not give up their slaves willingly. That means that the supply of cotton to the English and French mills will be disrupted."

"Lucien noticed the boats carrying cotton on the Nile," said David, clapping Lucien on the back. "He investigated and realized that Egyptian cotton could replace the American cotton."

"It is of excellent quality," said his father, "far better than Indian cotton. Indeed, it is of better quality than the American cotton."

"In short," said Lord Penworth, "we have formed a company to import Egyptian cotton to France and England. Mr. Oliphant can handle things at the Egyptian end, Lucien knows the people in France, and David and I can take care of things in England."

"Goodness," said Lady Penworth. "Lucien, it appears that you have hidden depths."

He lifted his chin defensively. "I realize that it is a war that makes me think of this, but to encourage cotton here in Egypt is not a bad thing. Indeed, the quality of the cotton here seems to be so high that there should always be a market for it, especially for the finer goods."

"That is brilliant of you." Emily stepped to his side and took his arm.

Lady Penworth smiled at them. "I agree completely. I meant no insult to you, Lucien. On the contrary. I had feared that you might be like your grandfather, content to live off the labor of others with no thought beyond your own convenience and well-being."

"That world is gone," he said, shaking his head dismissively. "France has no need of aristocrats who do nothing but preen themselves at court while the peasants toil in the fields. If we are to survive, we must see to the improvement of the peasants and lead them into the modern world."

"You are an idealist, M. de Chambertin?" asked Mrs. Oliphant.

The corner of his mouth lifted in a half smile. "Nothing so noble. Merely a pragmatist. If the family of the Comte de la Boulaye—my family—is to flourish, things cannot stay the same. They must change, and it is better to choose the way to change than to be swept aside by change."

Mr. Oliphant rubbed his hands. "Well, this particular change seems likely to benefit us all. I must say I am grateful that my son brought you here."

Later that evening Emily and Lucien managed to step aside for a brief embrace in a dark corner of the garden—all too brief.

"I had no idea you were so clever in business," said Emily, holding tightly to his arm as they walked toward the others.

"You do not mind?"

"Why ever should I mind?"

He shrugged. "Sometimes the English, they seem to think that one is not a gentleman if he concerns himself with matters of business."

"I cannot believe Papa suggested such a thing."

"No." A smile tugged at his lips. "I believe that he was relieved to think I had found a way to pay your bills from Mr. Worth."

Laughter gurgled up in her. "And I am relieved as well. Feel free to concoct other schemes if you like."

He pulled her to him for another quick kiss. At least it had started as a quick kiss, but somehow it lengthened. He finally pulled away and rested his forehead on hers. "The business schemes, as you call them, at least serve as a distraction. Otherwise I think only of you and fear I will go mad with longing."

～～

The day of the wedding dawned bright and sunny, and not quite as hot as the preceding few days had been. Not that the bride and groom would have noticed, any more than their families did. A dozen Cairo seamstresses had created a magical dress from the silk Lady Penworth had brought from Baghdad. An overskirt of sheer white silk shot through with threads of gold was looped over a creamy underskirt. Petals of silk formed the sleeves and trimmed the hem. The bride's veil was of a silk so transparent as to be almost invisible save for the golden flowers embroidered along the edge.

It was a gown in the height of Parisian fashion with just enough of the exotic to turn Julia into some magical, otherworldly creature. Beside her, David glowed with an equally otherworldly happiness as they greeted all the guests and gracefully accepted their good wishes.

Leaning over to speak softly to Lady Penworth, Mrs. Oliphant said, "I cannot remember when I last saw David so relaxed, so assured. I bless the day you brought Julia to my son."

Lady Penworth, watching the young couple, said,

"And I have never seen Julia so alive, so vivid. Your son has torn down the wall she built around herself. It is as if together they are more themselves than they had ever dared to be before."

They clasped hands and shared smiles—and brought out handkerchiefs to blot the happy tears.

# Twenty-nine

OVER THE PAST FIVE YEARS, LUCIEN HAD BEEN THROUGH many dangers. He had survived shipwreck, desert sandstorms, brawls in taverns too disreputable to have a name, attacks by brigands—all manner of perils. Never had he been afraid. Not until he met Emily, and even then his fear had been for her.

Now, as the carriages taking them from Avignon neared the Marbot estate, he felt…not fear. Not really. But worry. Uncertainty. This was not an accustomed sensation for him.

What if Emily did not like his family? They were a boisterous crowd, his Marbot cousins. She was not stiff-necked, he knew, but they might put her off.

And her parents, how would they react? The Marbot clan was not at all elegant, as he remembered them. Would Lord and Lady Penworth find them too insignificant for an alliance with their family?

The chateau. He had loved the chateau from the first time he saw it. It had been warm and welcoming, a refuge from the chill perfection of La Boulaye. But while it was a large building, it rambled about in no special order and was far from fashionable.

If they scorned his family, would they also scorn him? He was not worried about the comte, not his father's family—the Tremaines were welcome to scorn them. He did himself. But he had great affection for his Marbot family, not just gratitude for the assistance they had given him. He knew too that Emily loved her family. What would happen if the two families disliked each other? It would not be a disaster, perhaps, but it would not be comfortable. And so he worried.

He sat across from Emily in the carriage with her parents. She was nervous herself. This he knew because she held herself very still, the way a rabbit remains motionless when the hawk is hunting. Even her hair seemed confined, all of it sitting smoothly under the foolish little straw hat perched on the front of her head. A rosy plume curled around and seemed likely to tickle her cheek if a breeze caught it, but there was no breeze in the closed carriage.

She was sitting half-turned so that she could look out the window, and he knew the moment she first saw the chateau. Her eyes widened and she drew in a sharp breath before asking, "Is that it?"

He turned to look out, just to make sure nothing had changed, and nodded. "Yes, Château Marbot."

"Oh," she breathed out, tossing him a look of utter delight before she returned to examining the château. "It's lovely. Enchanting."

The worry eased slightly. The château was hidden from view by some woodland for a few minutes, then they turned into the gates, and the long straight drive led up to the entrance. Large old trees shaded the house from the afternoon sun, making a dappled pattern on the cream stone and the dark red tiles of the roof. Pale blue shutters flanked the long windows, and pots with small lemon trees stood sentry at the double doors of the entrance.

The doors were flung open as the carriage drew to a halt, and his aunt and uncle stepped out to greet them. They were standing stiffly and dressed more formally than usual. Uncle Antoine was wearing a black frock coat with tan trousers and waistcoat and a stickpin in his black tie. Much the same thing that he was wearing himself, Lucien thought, with a self-conscious glance down. And Tante Marie was wearing a silk dress in a bright magenta, nothing like her usual subdued appearance, with a lacy cap on her gray hair.

His cousins were nowhere in sight.

Once they were all out of the carriage and approaching each other, he realized that he was not the only one who was on edge. Everyone seemed to be not so much worried as wary. Lucien performed the introductions—"Baron de Marbot and his wife… the Marquess of Penworth and his wife…my fiancée, Lady Emily Tremaine"—and everyone made the appropriate responses, bows and curtsies. Everyone was very polite. Excruciatingly polite.

As the women were led to their rooms by Tante Marie, Lucien and Emily exchanged glances of, of what? Worry? Uncertainty? Despair? Some mixture of all these emotions? He did not know anymore. Then she ducked her head docilely and hurried up the stairs. Docile? What was wrong with her? He watched her disappear into the corridor at the top of the stairs, and when he turned around, his uncle and Lord Penworth had disappeared as well.

Muttering assorted imprecations, he pulled off his coat, tossing it on a chair in the hall, and strode out the door, loosening his cravat as he went. Maybe a long walk would calm him down.

What the others were feeling, he did not know. How they would deal with each other was out of his hands. What he himself was feeling was frustration at the uncertainty, at the endless waiting.

He wanted Emily. He wanted her in every way—in his arms, in his bed, walking beside him. He wanted to make love to her. He wanted to touch her. He wanted to talk with her. But all the time, she was kept just out of his reach, surrounded by other people. Even if all went well, there was still a week to wait before there would be a wedding.

He was going to run mad.

❧

By the time he returned, there had been an invasion. The world was overrun by strangers and the noise was enough to drown a man. Young girls were shrieking, young men were shouting, and everyone was laughing. Pandemonium.

After a moment—and a few deep breaths—he realized that not all of these vociferous creatures were strangers. Half of them were his cousins, a few years older and proportionally louder than he had last seen them.

The others? Ah, from the way they were dancing

around Emily, they must be her brothers and sisters. He narrowed his eyes. Yes, there was a resemblance among them all. Off to the side, Tante Marie and Lady Penworth were standing arm in arm, smiling at the melee. One couple stood beside them, a man whose stiffness reminded him of David and a lovely blonde woman who was animated enough for both of them.

Lady Penworth saw Lucien and beckoned him over to introduce him to her son Phillip, Lord Rycote, and his wife, Lissandra. She then returned to her conversation with Tante Marie. They seemed to be sharing tales of the trials and tribulations of motherhood. This was not a conversation for him.

Turning away from them, he found himself face to face with Rycote, who was regarding Lucien with some distrust. For his part, Lucien thought that Rycote looked far too pompous to be Emily's brother. Also, he disliked the fact that Rycote was several inches taller than he.

"This is all a bit hasty, isn't it?" Rycote drawled.

Lucien stiffened. "I do not find it so."

Lady Rycote sighed and batted her husband on the arm with her fan. "Do not be an old man, Pip," she said in delightful Italian accent. "It took me only a few days to know we would be married, even if you did not realize it so quickly."

*Pip? This pompous fellow is called Pip?* Lucien grinned at them, but said nothing. There was no need. He could see Rycote's stiffness melting away in the warmth of his wife's smile.

"I suppose I should welcome you to the family."

Rycote stuck out a hand. "Or warn you about it. It's chaos out there."

Lucien took the hand and they shook with equal firmness. "A stranger would find it difficult to tell your family from mine, when it comes to chaos." There was no need to mention his father's family.

"This is the easy part," said Rycote darkly. "Doncaster and my sister Elinor are still in Avignon, examining the fellow his sister Julia married."

"David Oliphant? A truly good man, most honorable. And my friend."

"That won't stop Elinor. She and Doncaster are very protective of his sisters."

"As a man should be."

Rycote grinned then. "Just a warning. They'll be arriving tomorrow, and then Elinor will start on you."

He was not truly worried about that, but even if he had been, the worry evaporated when Emily appeared at his side. She took his arm, and all was well.

❧

Two days later, a cricket game was in progress. It was France versus England. The English visitors had attempted to explain the game, but the French hosts had had waved away the need for any but the most basic description of the game. To be precise, Lucien's cousin Henri had done the waving. An athletic but swaggering young man of about twenty, Henri assumed that he could play—and win—any game. Lucien himself was not so certain.

Henri was also highly amused to discover that the English allowed the girls to play.

"They'd have our heads on a platter if we tried to stop them," muttered Rycote.

With a laugh, Henri agreed that his sisters should play as well, but he stationed them well away from the pitch to field. "If they must play, at least they can do no harm there."

Emily seemed to be about to speak, but her older sister, the one married to Doncaster—Elinor, that was her name—shook her head and stepped up to bat.

"I will throw you a gentle one, yes?"

Elinor smiled. Lucien shook his head. If Henri hoped to survive to old age, he would learn to be very careful around smiles like that.

Henri ran up and tossed the ball, just as Rycote had demonstrated. His form was excellent.

Elinor stepped forward and hit the ball in a screaming drive that just missed taking off Henri's head and eventually disappeared among the trees at the edge of the field.

Two of Henri's sisters were hugging each other and squealing with delight. Henri was staring at Elinor in disbelief. Elinor's smile had turned decidedly smug.

"Only four runs," called her husband. "It bounced before it went out."

She shrugged nonchalantly and lifted the bat to await the next pitch.

Henri narrowed his eyes and nodded. The game began its descent into chaos and laughter. The French girls began trying to prove they were as good as the boys, and the English girls were more interested in helping them do so than in winning. Emily turned out to be a most unusual bowler. She could get the male batters out with no difficulty, but the women, especially the youngest ones, scored run after run.

Lucien could feel the joy bubble up in him. It was all so idyllic.

What would his life have been like, he wondered, if he had grown up here, with his mother's ebullient family, instead of in the gloom of La Boulaye?

He had not even met the Marbot family until after he walked out, leaving his grandfather and his grandfather's plans behind him. He had come here angry and uncertain, knowing nothing of this half of his family except that his grandfather despised them, and being half-afraid that they would despise him in turn.

Instead, they had welcomed him, and spoken endlessly of his mother and her joyous, loving nature. How had she been able to bear it, going from this life of laughter to the cold pride that shadowed everything in his grandfather's chateau?

Was it the sunshine that made the difference? He considered that. No. Emily's family were all as full of joy as his cousins, and England was hardly known for its warmth and sun. It was not the place. It was the people. It was his grandfather who had drained the joy from La Boulaye. He could not allow that to happen to Emily. They would stay well away from the comte.

But this, they could have this, could they not? They could make a home where children laughed and played, unafraid, unintimidated. Emily would know how to do this. She had grown up in a family where happiness was permitted, where laughter was not frowned upon.

As they all walked back to the house after the game

had ended, with a score as chaotic and uncertain as the play had been, Lucien managed to draw Emily off the path and into the trees. A moment later she had her arms around his neck and was kissing him enthusiastically. Naturally, as a gentleman, he had to respond in kind.

When they eventually stopped to breathe, only slightly more disheveled than they had been from the cricket match, Lucien rested against a tree and Emily rested against him. He breathed in the scent of her, slightly sweaty, still sweet.

"This is what I want," he said.

"Me?"

He huffed a laugh into her hair. "Always you. But I meant a home like this, where people laugh."

She tilted her head back to look up at him. Her smile showed him that she understood precisely what he meant. "Of course. And our children will run and shout and drive you mad with the noise they make. We will be happy." She gave him her promise with that smile.

She was his happiness. She was what he had been seeking all this time.

# *Thirty*

SHORTLY AFTER BREAKFAST, THREE WAGONS ARRIVED from the station in Avignon. Each carried four large boxes and at least a dozen smaller ones. Madame de Marbot took one look at the labels on the boxes, smiled, and told her husband to take the gentlemen out shooting or riding or something. Anything that would keep them occupied and out of the way for the day.

Lady Penworth heaved a sigh of relief as the servants carried everything upstairs. "I did not think Mr. Worth would fail us, but one never knows."

Worth? The magical name captured the attention of all the women from the oldest to the youngest. It sent the men scurrying from the room to obey Madame's orders.

"Since Mr. Worth had your measurements from our visit at the start of our trip, I sent a telegram asking him to make a wedding dress for you," Lady Penworth told her daughter as she led her into the dressing room. "And I ordered a few other gowns as well, all to be sent here. And, of course, the little things you would need for your trousseau—undergarments, shoes, hats." She waved a hand at the tidal wave of tissue paper, silk, lace, feathers, and flowers that was spilling out of the boxes in a floral-scented torrent as eager hands uncovered the treasures.

Emily stared at it all, feeling overwhelmed. Panicked. She was going to drown in silk. It was enough to make her wish she were back on that dreadful raft on the Tigris. At least when she had been trying to steer it, she had felt some control over her life. Now, it was her own family that was sweeping her along, just as Lucien's family was sweeping him along. Always keeping him out of reach. And now she was expected to go into spasms of delight over clothes?

"Emily." Lady Penworth took her daughter's chin and turned her to face her. "I know you do not share Elinor's fascination with fashion, or even mine and Julia's. However, you are about to marry the grandson of a French nobleman. You will have to face not only his family but also his peers, those in Burgundy and those in Paris, and you will have to face the French court, which is, thanks to Empress Eugénie, exceedingly fashionable. You will have only one chance to make a first impression, and it must be a good one."

Emily opened her mouth to speak, but her mother ignored her and continued. "How good an impression you make will also affect the way Lucien is treated, so resign yourself to it. For the next few months, you will be an elegant and fashionable lady. Eugénie also patronizes Mr. Worth, so when you are invited to visit the court, she will recognize and approve your choices."

Emily wanted to either run away or dig in her heels. Instead, she was being dragged along by her mother. "What makes you think we will ever go to court? Lucien has not said anything about wanting to do that."

Lady Penworth looked at her daughter with a mixture of pity and exasperation. "Child, I repeat. You are marrying a member of the French nobility. In addition, you are the daughter of an important English peer. Of course the emperor will invite you to court. He would be delighted to win the support of the heir of the Comte de la Boulaye, especially since he cannot hope for the support of the grandfather. I am sure that your father and M. de Marbot have been giving Lucien advice on how to avoid committing himself without giving offense."

"But…" This was not what Emily wanted her life to be like, and she was quite sure it was not what Lucien wanted either.

Her mother smiled sympathetically. "Don't look so appalled. In all probability, it will only have to be done once. All you will need to do is admire the empress. That is not difficult—she is quite charming and attractive—but it is important. She craves admiration. As for the emperor, try to keep away from him if you do not have Lucien by your side. Louis-Napoléon fancies himself a ladies' man and can be rather a nuisance."

"The prospect is not at all attractive." Emily pressed her lips together to keep from saying precisely how unattractive she found it.

Her mother ignored her. "After that, you can go

to Varennes and never worry about the court again, if that is what you wish. But that first visit must be made, and these garments"—she waved her hand at the rainbow of silks and satins, muslins and velvets— "are your armaments."

A bit of ribbed red silk caught Emily's eye, and she reached over to pull it out for a better look. It was a Zouave jacket, trimmed with black embroidery, and was paired with a red dress of heavy silk, trimmed with the same embroidery. It was really quite, well, quite dashing. She couldn't restrain a smile. Much more dashing than her clothes usually were.

Her sister Elinor lifted out a white tulle ball gown, trimmed with blue flounces, with a long *duchesse* sash. "You will look absolutely beautiful in this," she said with a delighted gasp.

"Tomorrow, for the ball, you must wear it," said Mme. de Marbot, clasping her hands in pleasure.

Emily looked at it dubiously. It was lovely, but looked so innocent. Not at all dashing, like the red silk dress.

"The red dress is for after you are married," said Lady Penworth dryly. "The white tulle before."

*After I am married.* She looked down at the red silk and loosened the fingers holding it so that she wouldn't crush it. *Oh yes. The white dress for the old Emily, the red dress for the new.*

~

The day of the wedding dawned bright and clear. Emily could not help feeling pleased, considering it an auspicious omen, even though every day for the past two months had dawned bright and clear. But one never knew.

As usual, she awakened before her sister and crept as silently as she could over to the window to watch the sunrise. Susan, her younger sister, was sharing the room with her now that the Marbot estate had been inundated with guests—de Marbot relatives of all ages. It was ludicrous, really, that Lucien could have said that he had no family. He just hadn't met them all, or perhaps even known about them.

She pushed the casement open, allowing the sweet-spicy scent of wisteria to flood into the room. Clusters of the pale purple blossoms dangled above her head. It must be a truly ancient vine to have spread over the entire wall of this wing of the house. Reaching over to the side, she pulled off one of the foot-long panicles and turned to look at the sleeper.

Her whole family had come for her wedding. Even the Doncaster family that Elinor had married into, such as it was. She had not realized how much it would matter to her to have them all here as she set off on the next stage of her life. Would she ever be able to tell them all how much she loved them? How important to her they were and always would be?

She carried the wisteria over to tickle Susan on the cheek. Her sister wrinkled her nose and batted her hand at the annoyance for a good minute before finally opening her eyes and sputtering a few words.

"You aren't supposed to know words like that," said Emily. "Now wake up thoroughly, slugabed. It's my wedding day, and I can't enjoy it properly if I have to tiptoe around to avoid waking you up."

Susan's scowl eased into a smile. "I love you too."

From then on, the day passed in a blur for Emily. She discovered that she could not actually swallow any of the breakfast that was brought to her room, though she did manage a few sips of coffee—milky French *café au lait*, not the inky Turkish brew. After that, she was taken in hand by her mother and Elinor.

It began with the new undergarments that had arrived with the gowns from Mr. Worth—a chemise and drawers in linen so fine it felt like silk and trimmed with lace so beautiful it seemed almost criminal to cover it up. Even the corset was pretty, embroidered with small pink roses. She sat down at the dressing table while Mme. de Marbot's maid went to work on her hair. It seemed to take hours while braids and ringlets were arranged in a concoction that was topped with a wreath of orange blossoms and the antique lace veil that Elinor had worn at her own wedding.

"So that you will be as happy in your marriage as I am in mine," said Elinor softly.

The sisters looked at each other tremulously.

"No tears," commanded Lady Penworth. "Not yet." She brought out the gown Mr. Worth had created.

Not even Emily could look at it without a sigh of pleasure. Of cream-colored satin, the bodice was trimmed with a deep fall of lace that continued around to form the sleeves. An overskirt edged with more lace was pulled back by a pair of satin bows and four more bows formed a line down the front of the skirt.

It was a beautiful dress, but when she looked at herself in the long cheval mirror, she seemed to be looking from a long distance off. It was as if the girl in the mirror were someone she had known a long time ago. Someone she remembered but no longer knew well. She had become someone else over the past months, and she was only masquerading as this sheltered innocent in the cream satin gown.

This odd feeling of being two people at once continued. It was the daughter and sister—the old Emily—who was led downstairs and placed in the carriage beside Papa, who smiled at her, but it was a sad smile, as if he knew. It was the old Emily who walked into the mayor's office for the civil ceremony that was required in France. There was a stiffly proper young man watching her nervously as Papa led her in. His hair was darkened by the oil that held it stiffly in place. His cheeks were shaved so closely that they seemed paler than the rest of his face. His black coat fit snugly, and his stiff collar forced his head up.

He looked like a stranger until she stood beside him. Then he took her hand and grinned at her, and she grinned back. He was Lucien, her adventurer, and they were about to set off on a grand journey together.

# Thirty-one

MUCH AS SHE LOVED HER FAMILY, HAPPY AS SHE HAD been to meet Lucien's relatives, Emily was exceedingly grateful to be spending her wedding night away from them. Their rooms in the Hôtel d'Europe were lovely—the building had, after all, started out life as a marquess's palace. They were also quiet, looking out over a courtyard.

Extremely quiet.

After all the tumult of the day, the embraces and the noisy good wishes that had followed them down the drive as they left, she should enjoy the quiet. There was, after all, no need for her to feel nervous. They had done this before. It had been... She knew... There was no need for her to be nervous.

The lamp had been turned down, so there was a soft glow in the room. She tried to settle herself in the huge bed. Should she lie down or sit up? She had neglected to ask Elinor about that particular point of etiquette. There were so many pillows, she could just lean back against them, and she would be half-sitting, half-reclining.

She was still piling up pillows when he came in, and she stopped in mid-pile. She just stopped. He was wearing a robe, a quite gorgeous robe of heavy, dark green silk. That wasn't what had stopped her, though.

The robe stopped halfway down his calves and his legs and feet were bare. In the opening at the neck, she could see a vee of skin and a few dark curls of hair.

She couldn't stop staring at those curls. They meant that he wasn't wearing anything under the robe. She swallowed and made herself look up at his face. He was smiling a little, looking uncertain, almost as uncertain as she felt.

He sat down on the edge of the bed beside her and began playing with her fingers.

"You aren't wearing anything under that robe," she blurted out.

"No," he agreed. "Does that bother you?"

She examined her feelings. "No. But does that mean... Am I overdressed?"

That made him smile. He switched to playing with the lace edging the neckline of her nightgown. Her new nightgown of silky, almost sheer, linen.

"It is a very pretty nightgown, but perhaps we should remove it. I would not want to damage it," he said, still smiling.

He stood up and drew her to her feet beside him. A lift of his arm, a lift of her arms, and *poof!* the nightgown was gone. Seconds later, his robe had also fallen aside.

In the soft lamplight, he looked almost golden. Beautiful. She reached out a hand to touch him and ran her fingers hesitantly over the hard muscles of his shoulder and arm.

"Emily." He sighed her name as he pulled her gently, tenderly against him and buried his face in her hair. "Chérie, I know there was pain for you before, but this time it will be better. I will make it good for you, I promise."

His hands moved gently, deliciously down her back, and he brushed kisses over her eyelids, her cheeks and—oh, behind her ear. She gave a little gasp, and could feel his smile as his mouth moved lower.

Then she was on the bed, and his hands were moving over her, gently, then more intently, everywhere, and there were all these sensations, strange, marvelous, until she could no longer think. She could only feel as she flew through the universe.

Later, much later, she drowsily opened her eyes to see sunlight sneaking between the curtains. She lay spooned against her husband—her *husband*—with his arm wrapped around her. Protectively? Possessively? Perhaps both, but cozy and comforting in any case.

He had been right. It was much better the second time. She would have to tell him. With a sigh of contentment, she went back to sleep.

❧

It was another three weeks before they reached Burgundy. Her parents had been right. The emperor wanted to see them—an invitation arrived the day after the wedding—so they had spent a week at Fontainebleau. Lucien had been charming, gracious, and noncommittal. Emily had been charming, gracious, and admiring. She had to admit that her mother had also been right. The Worth gowns pleased the empress. What pleased her even more was that they were not quite as dramatic as the empress's own gowns. Nor were Emily's jewels terribly impressive. This was also pleasing. Emily's most dramatic piece of jewelry was the Roxelana ring, but this carried with it an aura of romance from the exotic East. Emily was therefore forgiven for its magnificence and established as an acceptable bride for a future comte.

Best of all, they had been given a delightful room at the palace with a view of the *Jardin de Diane*, with its fountain topped by a statue of Diana. The blue flowered wallpaper and matching bed linen and upholstery were, they discovered to their amusement, used in any number of the guest apartments. Whether this was a matter of economy, with a good price given for quantity, or simply a paucity of imagination, Emily could not decide.

More importantly, the room had a large and comfortable bed of which they made good use. Fontainebleau was so enormous, with more than a thousand rooms, that it was impossible to keep track of visitors. They needed to appear only when specifically invited. The rest of the time, they indulged themselves in a privacy of the sort they had never before enjoyed, and came to know each other in new and delightful ways.

When the time came, they left the court with the good wishes of the emperor and empress—and their own unspoken hope that they would never need to return.

By the time they reached Burgundy, it was already late June. When their carriage turned in at the gates of Varennes, Emily had her first view of her new home. It was not an ancient building, perhaps little more than a century old, three stories high of smooth gray stone, topped with a mansard roof. Black shutters flanked the long windows, and a simple stone porch covered the entrance. It might have looked austere were it not for the glossy paint on the door and shutters and the sunlight sparkling on the windows.

She pulled her head back into the carriage and turned to see Lucien watching her nervously. "Don't be foolish," she said. "It's beautiful."

"Ah, but you have not seen inside. You must remember that no one has lived here in many years. Everything will be old, faded."

"Good. That will make it easy for us to turn it into our own home." She was growing accustomed to speaking French all the time. Perhaps she would soon start thinking in French. She leaned over to give Lucien a quick kiss, which turned into a much longer, more thorough embrace that ended abruptly when the carriage pulled to a halt.

The door of the house opened to let out an elderly man whose gray mustache drooped but whose eyes were sharp. His dark coat and trousers betokened respectability rather than fashion.

"M. Bouchard." Lucien bounded up the steps eagerly, pulling Emily behind him.

"M. de Chambertin." The elderly gentleman bowed politely, and there seemed to be a smile under that mustache, though it was difficult to be certain.

"Emily, this gentleman is M. Bouchard, who has cared for Varennes in my absence and who has made all the preparations for our return." Lucien looked at Bouchard with real affection, somewhat to Emily's surprise. This was the first person in France—aside from his relatives at Marbot—toward whom her husband had shown real warmth, not a somewhat distant courtesy.

"*Enchanté, madame.*" Another polite bow, but definitely no smile this time.

Emily refused to be put off by the notaire's stiffness. After all, she was now wearing the red silk gown with the Zouave jacket. So she smiled her honest smile and held out her hand. "I am very glad to meet you, M. Bouchard. My husband has told me how much he owes to you for all your help over the years. And I must add my appreciation. The house positively sparkles with welcome."

The smile was apparently honest enough to win a response, as M. Bouchard blushed slightly and rewarded her with a shy smile of his own as he bent over her hand. "I fear that all I could arrange was cleanliness. The house has been kept in good repair, of course, but all is sadly out of date."

Wearying quickly of the formalities, Lucien was tugging her into the house. "Come, I want you to see inside."

With an apologetic look at the notaire, she entered the hall, floored with large grayish-blue tiles. A wide oak staircase with a heavy wooden balustrade rose up to a landing that circled three sides of the entrance. Light poured in from the two windows flanking the door, and high above, an intricate brass chandelier hung from the center rosette of the plasterwork in the ceiling. The sole item of furniture in the room was a small table, much too small for the space, to the right of the door.

"The hall," said Lucien, unnecessarily, as he pulled her along into a large drawing room, again bright with sunshine coming in through four windows along the length of the room. The walls were paneled in walnut boiseries, gleaming with polish. Once more, there was not much furniture, but a pair of armchairs flanked the fireplace, where the marble mantle was supported by an exuberant throng of cherubs.

Lucien regarded them, arms akimbo and smiling with pleasure. "I was afraid my memory might have played me false, but they are just as I remember them. Look here, this one, with his head tilted out. There is a space behind, and maman used to hide little treats for me there when I was small. Later I would hide my special fishing lure there."

A door in the paneling opened, and a maid stepped in, carrying a bucket of cleaning supplies. She gave a gasp when she saw them and promptly disappeared again.

Emily looked after her. "Are we so frightening, then?"

M. Bouchard chuckled. "The coachman must have been delayed in the stables or the news of your arrival would have spread throughout the house. Now, I estimate another five minutes before all is known." He turned more serious. "I hired only a minimum of servants, and they all know that they are on trial, so to speak. You must feel free to make any changes you desire."

"Well, I can certainly find no fault with the cleanliness of the house," said Emily with a smile. "It is all most welcoming."

The notaire suddenly looked distressed. "Speaking of welcomes…" His voice trailed off. With a deep breath he began again. "A message has come from La Boulaye." He reached into his coat and pulled out a folded sheet of heavy paper sealed with wax and handed it to Lucien, who received it with a frown.

Snapping the wax, he opened the missive, scanned the contents, and handed it to Emily.

She read it quickly and looked up with a laugh. "He *orders* you to appear before him immediately? How very peremptory."

M. Bouchard blinked. He had obviously never expected laughter as a response to the message.

Lucien, however, grinned at his wife. "Peremptory? Yes, it is that."

"I do not think we can appear quite as quickly as immediately," she said, tapping the letter on her cheek thoughtfully. "I, for one, am rather tired from all the traveling. Let me see, it is now Thursday. We shall need a few days to rest and settle in. Perhaps on Tuesday?" She smiled. "I will send a note, saying that if it is convenient to the comte, we will call on Tuesday afternoon at three."

"That sounds…unexceptionable." Lucien managed to restrain his laughter. "But why at three?"

"Too late for lunch, too early for dinner. That way they will feel under no obligation to offer a meal."

"And we will feel under no obligation to accept one."

M. Bouchard looked back and forth between them as they smiled at each other, and his worried frown relaxed into a smile.

❧

Another carriage ride, approaching another chateau, but this time Emily was filled with trepidation rather than eagerness. They rode past miles of vineyards, their neat rows stretching on and on, and a bleak village of gray stone but with no visible inhabitants. Not even in the café.

Emily would have asked, but Lucien seemed lost in thought. Or in something. He had withdrawn, and seemed to see nothing as they rode along. She looked down at her lap and smoothed the red silk with her matching kid gloves. Nervousness on her part was understandable, she supposed. It was not every day a woman was introduced to her husband's relatives.

But the red dress and the little black velvet hat perched on her head gave her confidence. She was no longer a sensible young girl, always doing what was expected of her. She was now a married woman, prepared to do whatever was necessary to support her husband.

Lucien's clothing had also been carefully chosen, she suspected. Instead of a formal cutaway or even a frock coat, he wore a loose sack jacket and a tie in a loose bow under a soft turned-over collar. His hat, resting on the seat opposite them, was the sort of wide-brimmed hat with a low crown that he had worn in Mesopotamia. It was an extremely casual costume.

They were dressed for battle.

The carriage turned into a gate and began to climb a long, steep drive. This time her gasp on seeing their destination was not one of pleasure. La Boulaye was a fortress, surrounded with high stone walls leading to round towers with arrow slits for windows.

"You are right. La Boulaye is designed to intimidate visitors, not to welcome them." Lucien's mouth twisted, almost in pain.

Emily sniffed. "How very pretentious."

He stared at his wife and gave a shout of laughter. "Thank you, chérie. That is precisely what it is."

He was still grinning when they drove through the imposing portal and entered the courtyard of a miniature Versailles. Emily looked at him in amazement. "Yes," he said, "I agree. Even more pretentious."

Six bewigged footmen in silver-laced black livery hurried out the door to help them from the carriage and line the steps as they ascended to the door, where a majordomo in more elaborate livery and a much larger wig awaited them. Lucien winked at him. "Don't worry, Alphonse. I'm not back to stay." He turned to Emily. "I used to bedevil poor Alphonse here when I was a child. I always wanted to find out if I could make him laugh or frown or grow angry, but I never succeeded."

"If you will come this way, M. de Chambertin," said the majordomo impassively as he turned to lead them into the house.

"You see?" Lucien whispered to her. He sounded amused, but as she rested her hand on his arm, she could feel the tension in his muscles.

Eventually they reached a pair of carved and gilded

doors, flung open by another pair of footmen as they approached. The majordomo stopped in the doorway to announce, "M. and Mme. de Chambertin," before he stepped to the side to allow them entrance.

Given what she had seen of La Boulaye so far, she should not have been surprised to enter a drawing room that looked more like a throne room than anything else. True, the comte did not sit on a raised dais, but other than that, the room could have held its own with Queen Victoria's throne room at St. James or the emperor's throne room at Fontainebleau. There was enough red silk damask on the walls and gilding everywhere to make any monarch feel at home.

She was almost disappointed that there was not a runner directing their feet to the foot of the comte's throne or even a railing. They could have wandered anywhere in the room. Well, perhaps not. The comte's obelisk stare drew them inexorably to him.

Looking at the old man, she wondered that those dark eyes could be so intensely alive when the rest of him seemed so desiccated. He was dressed in a uniform of some sort, with fringed epaulets, a blue sash across his chest, and an enormous starburst decoration pinned to his chest. Its high, stiff collar forced his chin up, and his legs were encased in gleaming black boots up to his knees. He sat on an armless chair whose high carved back looked decidedly uncomfortable, his skeletal hands resting atop a walking stick that stood between his knees.

The silence in the room was so complete that she could hear the faint silken rustle of her skirts as they walked toward him, coming to a halt about five feet away. Emily wondered if that was a prescribed distance or if Lucien did not wish to get any closer.

"Grandfather." Lucien dipped his head in greeting.

"So you have returned at last."

"Indeed." Lucien nodded again. "I know how delighted you must be to see me alive and well after the alarms regarding my death."

The old man's mouth twisted in a grimace of some sort—anger? She was not sure.

"And you need not concern yourself about that foolishness with the bankers," Lucien continued. "I spoke with them on my return from Fontainebleau. They have restored things as best they can, and I assured them that there would be no prosecution."

The comte flicked his eyes briefly at Emily and then returned his stare of barely repressed fury to Lucien. "The only foolishness is your failure to do your duty to la Boulaye." Without turning his eyes away from Lucien, he raised a finger in Emily's direction. "And this nonsense?"

Emily was unable to decide which nonsense caused the greatest fury, Lucien's casual dress, his return to Varennes, his remarks about bankers and Fontainebleau, or her own existence.

Lucien maintained an amiable smile. "Allow me to present my wife, Lady Emily." He turned to her. "My dear, this is my grandfather, the Comte de la Boulaye."

She smiled and offered him a brief but graceful curtsy. She did not claim that it was a pleasure to meet him.

The comte's full glare was turned on her this time.

"Impossible." He turned back to Lucien. "You knew that I arranged a marriage for you to Mlle. Fournier."

"Which, as you also know, I refused. I do hope no one expected the poor girl to wait. Indeed, I thought I had heard that she was married some years ago to a young man from the north."

The comte lifted his stick to thump it down. "You have disgraced the family. Do you expect the court to accept an English nobody as a future Comtesse de la Boulaye?"

Lucien laughed. "Too late, grandfather. The emperor invited us to Fontainebleau immediately after the wedding and welcomed us most graciously."

"The empress as well," chimed in Emily, using her pretty, insipid smile.

"Emperor!" The comte said it with a sneer. "That upstart. What of our court, the real court, that of the Comte de Chambord? Henri V?"

Lucien looked at his grandfather with pity in his eyes but said nothing.

Momentarily stymied, the comte recovered himself. "Mlle. Fournier had the estate of Colombe, adjoining La Boulaye. What sort of dowry does this one bring?"

"How vulgar, grandfather, to speak of money before my bride." Lucien shook his head in mock reproof. "Rest assured that my uncle de Marbot arranged all that with her father, the Marquess of Penworth. As you are doubtless aware."

The old man glared at them both, as if expecting some sort of surrender, but Lucien continued to stand, apparently relaxed, with a slight smile on his face. Emily smiled too, politely. Finally the comte sagged against the uncomfortable back of his chair, as if suddenly weary. He looked away from them. "Rooms have been prepared for you in the south wing."

Lucien's arm jerked in surprise under her hand, but he maintained his detached courtesy. "Thank you, Grandfather, but we are making our home at Varennes."

There was a hiss from the side. Emily turned, startled. She had not even realized there were any other people in the room, so completely did the comte dominate the scene. But there were half a dozen more people standing at the side. They held themselves so still in the shadows that their very existence seemed uncertain. Could these be the relatives her mother had feared might make difficulties? The idea seemed ludicrous.

In the forefront was an elderly woman in black, her hair covered by a black lace cap, and her lips pinched together in anger. She, at least, had some substance to her.

"Insolent boy," she spat out. "You will do as your grandfather tells you."

Emily drew herself up, ready to flay the old witch for daring to speak to Lucien in that tone, but he laid a hand over hers to restrain her.

"Grandmother, forgive me for failing to see you immediately and for not greeting you earlier." He turned to Emily. "My dear, as you may have gathered, this is the Comtesse de la Boulaye, my esteemed grandmother." He offered his grandmother a charming smile and a gracious bow. Those gestures had worked wonders on Empress Eugénie, but his grandmother seemed immune.

Her social smile firmly in place, Emily took her turn and dipped her head in greeting. "I thank you for your kind offer of hospitality, but, as my husband told you, we have our own home."

The comtesse glared at them in a silence that almost sizzled in fury. Arrayed behind her, the shadowy relations looked both fascinated by the exchange and extremely nervous.

"And now, I fear we must return home," said Lucien. "I wished only to assure you that I am well and happy. I hope the same for you all."

They turned and departed in the same silence that had greeted their entrance.

∾

She found Lucien sitting on the terrace. Evening shadows were beginning to create pockets of darkness in the garden, but the stones still held the warmth from the sun. He had discarded his jacket and even the soft bow tie. His eyes were closed, and his head leaned back so that the tan of his neck was exposed by the open shirt. Beside him on the table were a wineglass and an open bottle.

He must have recognized her footsteps, because without opening his eyes, he reached out an arm in invitation. She sat down beside him on the wide chair and settled herself against him, her head nestled on his shoulder, his cheek resting against her hair. She could feel the tension that had been coiled inside him ever since they set out for La Boulaye continue to ease.

He heaved a deep sigh. "I have been a fool. I

created a monster where there was only a deluded old man. A shriveled spider, trapped in his own web."

"You exaggerate." She was too comfortable here, with his arms around her, to lift her head, so that her voice was slightly muffled against him.

"No, you saw him. He is nothing. That silly uniform he wears is nothing but a sham of delusions, dreams of past glories."

She could feel the tension in him again, so she put her hand on his chest, just over his heart. "Hush. I meant that you exaggerate your foolishness. When you were a child, he was powerful. Powerful enough to dominate everyone in his family. Powerful enough to worry even M. Bouchard. You are the one who has changed, so that whatever power he had in the past, whatever power he had over your father—all that is gone. Finished."

He expelled a breath, half laugh, half sigh. "Yes, it is. And do you know what? I do not feel victorious. Not in the least. I feel only pity. His life has been such a waste. He spent years, decades, trying to revive a dead world, pretending that the past had not happened." Lucien shook his head sadly.

"It is over. Whatever war you two were waging, it is finished. It no longer matters."

He kissed her gently, peacefully, and then settled her comfortably in his arms. He filled his glass again, and they shared the wine, both sipping from the one glass, as they watched the shadows lengthen.

"There will be rain soon," he said. "Can you feel it?"

"Mmmm, yes. The air is soft with it."

He leaned back, his eyes closed. "I would dream of this, you know."

"Of Varennes?"

"Not just of Varennes. Of sitting here in the cool evening, of drinking wine from my own grapes. And of air soft with the coming rain. Ah, how I longed for rain at times."

She smiled, remembering the desert, the colorless plain. But then she tilted her head, curious. "Why did you not just come back? There was no need for you to return to your grandfather's house. You could have come here, could you not?"

He looked off into the distance, into the past. "Yes," he said slowly, "I could have done so. But I was too angry to stay still. I had to move, to travel. I was too restless, too uncertain to stay in one place. And besides…and besides, it would have been too empty, too lonely if I tried to live here alone."

He looked at Emily. "I was looking for you. I needed you, so we can make Varennes a home."

❧

Neighbors came to call, timidly at first. Gradually they began to realize that the old comte was indeed growing old, that he was no longer someone to fear. The future, they saw, lay with Lucien. Then friendships grew. Soon there were children, and more children. Family from England came to visit, as did family from Avignon. So many children, so many visitors that they had to add a wing to the gray stone house. A wisteria vine, like the one in Avignon, grew up the side of the house, filling the air with its spicy scent every

May. To the south of the house, a walled garden was created with a canal running down the middle, like an ancient paradise.

And the walls of Varennes rang with joyous laughter.

READ ON FOR AN EXCERPT FROM
*LADY ELINOR'S WICKED ADVENTURES*

*London, 1852*

CHEERFUL FRIVOLITY REIGNED IN THE BALLROOM OF Huntingdon House. The dancers swirled to the strains of a waltz, jewels glittering and silks and satins shimmering under the brilliant light of the new gas chandeliers. Even the chaperones were smiling to each other and swaying unconsciously to the music.

Harcourt de Vaux, Viscount Tunbury, an angry scowl setting him apart from the rest of the company, pushed his way to the side of his old schoolfellow. Grabbing him by the arm, Tunbury spoke in a furious undertone. "Pip, your sister is dancing with Carruthers."

Pip, more formally known as Philip Tremaine, Viscount Rycote, turned and blinked. "Hullo, Harry. I didn't know you were here. I thought this sort of thing was too tame for you these days."

"Forget about me. It's Norrie. She's dancing with that bounder Carruthers."

They both looked at the dance floor where Lady Elinor Tremaine, the picture of innocence, was smiling up at her partner, whose lean face and dark eyes spoke of danger. He was smiling as well, looking down at her with almost wolfish hunger.

"What of it?" asked Pip.

"He's a bloody fortune hunter and a cad to boot. How could you introduce him to your sister?"

Pip frowned slightly. "He introduced himself, actually. Said he was a friend of yours."

Harry spoke through clenched teeth. "You idiot. That should have been enough to disqualify him. Where are your parents?"

"Dancing, I suppose."

Harry caught a glimpse of the Marquess and Marchioness of Penworth on the far side of the room, dancing gracefully and oblivious to everyone else. Turning back to find Carruthers and Lady Elinor again, he muttered an oath. "He's heading for the terrace." When Pip looked blank, Harry shook his head and charged across the dance floor.

❧

Mr. Carruthers had timed it quite neatly, she thought. As the music ended and he twirled her into the final spin, they came to a halt just before the terrace doors. These were standing open, letting in the scent of roses on the breeze of the soft June evening.

"It is rather warm in here, Lady Elinor, is it not?" he said. "Would you care for a turn on the terrace?"

Before she could answer, a strong hand clasped her arm just above the elbow. "Lady Elinor, your mother wants you." When she turned to object to this high-handed treatment, she found herself staring up at the all-too-familiar scowl of Lord Tunbury. "Harry..." she started to protest.

"If Lady Elinor wishes to return to her parents, I will be delighted to escort her." Carruthers spoke frostily.

"Lady Penworth requested that I find her daughter." Harry's even icier tone indicated that there was nothing more to be said on the subject.

Lady Elinor looked back and forth between them and wanted to laugh. Carruthers was tall, dark, and handsome, or at least decorative, with a pretty bow-shaped mouth. Harry, equally tall, had broad shoulders and a powerful build. His square face was pleasant rather than handsome, his middling brown hair tended to flop over his middling brown eyes, and his wide mouth was more often than not stretched into a broad smile. Not just now, of course.

One would say the two men were not much alike, but at the moment they wore identical scowls. They did not actually bare their teeth and growl, but they were not far off. She could not manage to feel guilty about enjoying the sight. It was too delightful.

Carruthers stopped glaring at Harry long enough to look at her. He may have stopped scowling, but he was not smiling. He was stiff with anger. "Lady Elinor?" He offered his arm.

Harry's grip on her arm tightened and he pulled her back a step. His grip was growing painful, and she would have protested, but she feared it might create a scene not of her own designing, so she smiled. "Thank you, Mr. Carruthers, but if my mother sent Lord Tunbury, perhaps I should accept his escort."

Carruthers bowed stiffly and sent one more glare at the intruder before he departed. That left her free to turn furiously on Harry. "There is no way on earth my mother sent you to fetch me. What do you think you are doing?"

He caught her hand, trapped it on his arm, and began marching her away from the terrace. "I cannot imagine what possessed your parents to give you permission to dance with a loose fish like Carruthers."

"They didn't, of course. He at least had enough sense to wait until they had left me with Pip." Harry was dragging her along too quickly, and she was going to land on the floor in a minute. "You might slow down a bit," she complained.

"You little idiot!" He turned and glared at her but did ease his pace. "He was about to take you out on the terrace."

"Well, of course!" She gave an exasperated humph.

"What do you mean, 'Of course'?" By now they had reached the end of the ballroom, and he pulled her into the hall and swung her around to the side so he could glare with some privacy.

She shook out her skirt and checked to make sure the pink silk rosettes pinning up the tulle overskirt had not been damaged while Harry was dragging her about. She was very fond of those rosettes. "I mean, of course he was going to take me out on the terrace. That's what he does. He takes a girl out on the terrace, leads her into one of the secluded parts, and kisses her. Marianne and Dora say he kisses very nicely, and I wanted to see if they were right."

Harry made a strangled sound. "Marianne and Dora? Miss Simmons and Miss Cooper…?"

"Among others." Lady Elinor waved a hand airily. "He's kissed so many of this year's debutantes that I was beginning to feel slighted, but I think perhaps he is working according to some sort of pattern. Do you know what it might be?"

He was looking at her with something approaching horror, rather the way her brother looked at her much of the time. "You and your friends discuss... What in God's name are young ladies thinking about these days?"

She shrugged. "Young men, of course. What did you suppose? That we discuss embroidery patterns? Don't you and your friends talk about women?"

He closed his eyes and muttered a prayer for patience. Then he began speaking with exaggerated formality. "Lady Elinor, under no circumstances are you to even dance with a rake like Carruthers, much less go into the garden with him. You have no idea what he would do."

"Fiddlesticks! I know precisely what he was going to do. He apparently has only two speeches that he uses to persuade a girl to let him kiss her, and I want to know which one he is going to use on me. Then I'll know if I am generally considered saucy or sweet."

"Norrie, no one who is at all acquainted with you would ever consider you sweet."

"Well, I should hope not. You know me better than that. But I want to know how I am viewed by the people who don't know me."

He grabbed her by the shoulders and turned her to face him. "Norrie, I want you to listen to me. A bounder like Carruthers will try to do far more than simply steal a kiss."

"I know that. You needn't treat me as if I am simpleminded. But I am hardly going to allow anything more."

"It is not a question of what you will allow. Just precisely how do you think you could stop him from taking advantage of you?"

She gave him a considering look and decided to answer honestly. "Well, there is the sharply raised knee to the groin or the forehead smashed against the nose, but the simplest, I have always found, is the hatpin."

"Hatpin?" Harry looked rather as if he were choking as he seized on the most innocuous part of her statement.

"Yes. It really doesn't matter where you stab. Gentlemen are always so startled that they jump back." She offered him a kindly smile. Sometimes he sounded just like her brother.

He went back to glaring at her. "Norrie, Lady Elinor, I want your word that there will be no strolls in the garden with disreputable rogues."

"Like you?" she interrupted.

"Yes, if you like, like me! Forget about rogues. You may not always recognize one. Just make it all men. You are not to leave the ballroom with any man at any time."

"The way we just left it?"

"Stop that, Norrie. I am serious."

He did indeed look serious. Quite fierce, in fact. So she subsided and resigned herself to listening.

"I want your promise," he said. "If you will not

give it, I will have to warn your brother, and you know Pip. He might feel obliged to challenge anyone who tries to lead you into dark corners, and you know he is a hopeless shot. You don't want to get him killed, do you?"

He had calmed down enough to start smiling at her now, one of those patronizing, big-brother, I-know-better-than-you smiles. It was quite maddening, so she put on her shyly innocent look and smiled back. "Oh, Harry, you know I would never do anything that would cause real trouble."

"That's my girl." He took her arm to lead her back to the ballroom. "Hatpins indeed. Just don't let your mother find out you've heard about things like that."

She smiled. He really was quite sweet. And foolish. He had not even noticed that she gave him no promise. And then imagine warning her not to let her mother find out. Who did he suppose had taught her those tricks?

❧

Tunbury hovered at the edge of the ballroom and watched Norrie hungrily. He had not seen her in more than a year, and then two months ago, there she had been. It was her first season, and somehow the tomboy who had been his and Pip's companion in all their games and pranks had turned into a beauty. Her dark hair now hung in shiny ringlets, framing the perfect oval of her face. Her eyes—they had always been that sort of greenish blue, shining with excitement more often than not, but when had they started to tilt at the edge that way? And when had her lashes grown so long and thick? Worst of all, when had she gone and grown a bosom?

But she was such an innocent.

She thought herself so worldly, so knowing, when in fact she knew nothing of the ugliness lurking beneath the surface, even in the ballrooms of the aristocracy. That ugliness should never be allowed to touch her. Her parents would protect her and find her a husband worthy of her, a good, decent man who came from a good, decent family.

Not someone like him. Not someone who came from a family as rotten as his. The Tremaines thought they knew about his parents, the Earl and Countess of Doncaster, but they knew only the common gossip. They did not know what Doncaster had told him, and he hoped they never would.

Yes, Norrie would find a husband worthy of her, but he couldn't stay here and watch. That would be too painful. He had to leave. He would leave in the morning and disappear from her life.

# *Two*

*London, four years later*

WHAT FIRST CAUGHT HER EYE WAS THE WAY HE WAS striding along Oxford Street, so unlike the languid stroll of most gentlemen, even in the chill of late January. He was turned away, of course, and it was already starting to get dark, so she couldn't be sure. After all, for years now her eye had been caught by glimpses of men who might be him. It had surprised her, the number of tall, broad-shouldered, brown-haired men in the world.

At the corner he stopped and looked to the side, and Lady Elinor caught sight of the high cheekbone, the angle of the jaw. She grasped her mother's arm. "Mama, isn't that…" She couldn't finish.

Lady Penworth looked at the young man her daughter was staring at. "Good heavens, it is!" She stepped forward and called out, "Lord Tunbury!"

He had to stop and turn, of course. Even if he hadn't wanted to, her mother's call—her shout, to be blunt—had drawn attention to him. At first he just stared at them, almost as if he were afraid. As if Harry had ever been afraid of anything. Harry, who had always been the first to race down a cliff or dive into the water or send his horse flying over the hedge. Didn't he recognize them? But he had to know that he couldn't just stand there staring. He finally did move toward them, even if not quite as quickly as she and her mother were moving to him.

He looked the same. Well, no, he didn't. He had the same square, solid face, so familiar, so...reliable, that was it. But different, somehow. The set of his wide mouth was firmer, harder, and there were slight creases at the corners of his eyes, as if he had been squinting a lot. His shoulders seemed broader—was that possible? And he looked older.

He was older, of course. After all, it had been almost four years. Still, he seemed to have matured more than Pip had in the same time. But after that first moment of surprise when he just looked blank, he smiled, and she had to smile back. That was Harry, who had been her friend since childhood. She would know that smile anywhere. How she had missed it.

Beaming joyfully, Lady Penworth put out her hands to greet him and he took them in his.

"Lady Penworth, Lady Elinor, what a wonderful surprise."

His voice was deep, deeper than she remembered. A rich, man's voice. Elinor could almost feel it vibrate in her but couldn't manage to say anything herself. She just stood there, feeling foolishly glad that she was wearing her new blue velvet capelet with the fur lining and the matching bonnet.

Her mother, of course, had no trouble finding her tongue. "Harry, look at you, so brown and handsome! You look like sunshine in this gray London drizzle. When did you get back?"

"Just yesterday, as a matter of fact. I'm putting up at Mivart's Hotel."

Lady Penworth frowned slightly. "At a hotel? You are not staying with your family?"

Harry seemed to freeze up at that, and his smile vanished. What was the matter? And he spoke almost roughly. "No, no, I am not."

"Well, in that case, you must come stay with us," Mama said firmly, ignoring his tone. "No, I insist. We can't have you staying in a hotel. You can come with us now, and we can send someone to collect your things from Mivart's."

Elinor couldn't hold back any longer. She flung herself at him to give him a hug. "Oh, Harry, I am so very glad to see you."

Her mother uttered an indulgent "tsk," but after a moment of hesitation, when Elinor feared he was going to push her away, Harry's arms wrapped around her and he hugged her back. "I missed you too." His voice seemed a trifle thick, and he held her longer than she had expected.

Lady Penworth took charge, of course. She sent Harry to fetch a hackney, explaining that it would have been ridiculous to bring their own carriage into this traffic, settled them into the cab when it arrived, and had them on their way in no time. Harry seemed to have been struck silent by all of this, and Elinor was struck silent by the amazement of having her friend

Harry not just back in England after all his adventures but right here in the carriage, only inches away, so Lady Penworth chattered away, filling Harry in on four years' worth of family doings.

# *Author's Note*

Gentle Reader,

You will, I hope, be relieved to know that the Lion Hunt sculpture was not lost forever beneath the waters of the Tigris. That spectacular find was actually made earlier by Hormuzd Rassam when he was poaching on the section of Nineveh that had been allotted to the French. He uncovered not only the Lion Hunt bas-relief, now at the British Museum, but also a trove of clay tablets that, once translated, turned out to be the *Epic of Gilgamesh*, the great Sumerian tale. (You can understand why the French were annoyed.)

Even though the French were the first to begin serious excavations in Mesopotamia, they continued to be unlucky in their efforts. Not long after Rassam's discoveries, the French archaeologist Victor Place sent two hundred and thirty-five crates downriver from Mosul on four rafts and a barge, all overloaded. The flotilla was attacked by pirates on the river and only two rafts made it through. The other vessels sank, and the crates and their contents have never been recovered.

European archaeologists more or less lost interest in Mesopotamia after that. No serious work was undertaken there until the 1920s, when the British archaeologist Max Mallowan began excavations. You may recognize his name. He was married to Agatha Christie, who set several of her mysteries in that part of the world.

It is hard to know what remains of those ancient cities and palaces after the destruction brought about by the recent wars in that part of the world. Those nineteenth-century archaeologists may have seen more of Ancient Nineveh than will ever be seen again.

I have used the actual names of the British ambassador in Constantinople and the British consuls in Mosul and Baghdad in 1861, but all else about them is the product of my imagination.

# Acknowledgments

With grateful appreciation to all the artists, editors, copy editors, and proofreaders at Sourcebooks for all the work they do to make this book as good as they can. And special thanks to editor Hilary Doda, who not only identifies problems, but offers brilliant suggestions for their solutions.

Any mistakes that remain are entirely my own fault.

# About the Author

Lillian Marek was born and raised in New York City. At one time or another she has had most of the interesting but underpaid jobs available to English majors. After a few too many years in journalism, she decided she prefers fiction, where the good guys win and the bad guys get what they deserve.

# In Search of Scandal

## London Explorers

## by Susanne Lord

Introducing a brand-new series of lush,
adventurous Victorian romance

❧

In 1850s London, the city is abuzz with the news of a tragic expedition into western China. Only explorer Will Repton returns to England, plagued by injuries, insomnia, and a secret. He must raise funds as soon as possible and return to the site of the tragedy, but convincing investors to back this quest without telling them why proves impossible.

Buoyant Charlotte Baker is on a quest of her own—the discovery of a heroic husband. She has bachelors panting at her dainty slippers, but no aristocrat will have her to wed. When Charlotte meets the famous "Chinese Will," no other man will do. The only problem is, marriage is the last thing on his mind.

The mantel clock is ticking. The tides are changing. What if an explorer's greatest adventure doesn't lie across an ocean, but within his own lost heart?

❧

**For more Susanne Lord, visit:**
www.sourcebooks.com

# A Talent for Trickery

## The Thief-takers

## by Alissa Johnson

— ❧ —

### The Lady is a Thief

Years ago, Owen Renderwell earned acclaim—and a title—for the dashing rescue of a kidnapped duchess. But only a select few knew that Scotland Yard's most famous detective was working alongside London's most infamous thief…and his criminally brilliant daughter, Charlotte Walker.

Lottie was like no other woman in Victorian England. She challenged him. She dazzled him. She questioned everything he believed and everything he was, and he has never wanted anyone more. And then he lost her.

Now a private detective on the trail of a murderer, Owen has stormed back into Lottie's life. She knows that no matter what they may pretend, he will always be a man of the law and she a criminal. Yet whenever he's near, Owen has a way of making things complicated…

— ❧ —

**For more Alissa Johnson, visit:**
www.sourcebooks.com

# Wicked, My Love

## by Susanna Ives

---

### A smooth-talking rogue and a dowdy financial genius

Handsome, silver-tongued politician Lord Randall doesn't get along with his bank partner, the financially brilliant but hopelessly frumpish Isabella St. Vincent. Ever since she was his childhood nemesis, he's tried—and failed—to get the better of her.

### Make a perfectly wicked combination

When both Randall's political career and their mutual bank interests are threatened by scandal, he has to admit he needs Isabella's help. They set off on a madcap scheme to set matters right. With her wits and his charm, what could possibly go wrong? Only a volatile mutual attraction that's catching them completely off guard…

---

### Praise for Susanna Ives:

"A fresh voice that reminded me of Julia Quinn's characters." —Eloisa James, *New York Times* bestselling author

### For more Susanna Ives, visit:

www.sourcebooks.com

# *The MacGregor's Lady*

## by Grace Burrowes

*New York Times* and *USA Today* Bestselling Author

━━━━━━━━━━━ ✤ ━━━━━━━━━━━

### What if the steps he takes to avoid marriage...

Asher MacGregor, the new Earl of Balfour, refuses to choose a Society wife to be his countess, though he agrees to hot Boston heiress Hannah Cooper for one Season. When he's tended to that chore, he'll happily go home to bachelorhood in the Highlands.

### ...Lead instead to impossible love?

Hannah Cooper's stepfather insists she have a London debut, but she has no intention of surrendering her wealth to a fortune hunter. After she's endured one Season, she'll sail back to Boston and the siblings who depend on her.

The taciturn Asher suits Hannah's plans well—for if the Scottish earl and the American heiress fall in love, an ocean of differences will come between them.

━━━━━━━━━━━ ✤ ━━━━━━━━━━━

### For more Grace Burrowes, visit:
www.sourcebooks.com

How about we finish up whatever needs finishing, then meet somewhere and drive back here together?"

Vincent brought her closer, and she didn't resist. She liked the feel of him against her, even if it was way too distracting.

"What I really want is to get you upstairs in bed," he said, "but you're right. Duty calls."

"Sucks, doesn't it?" God, she'd love to stay in bed with him the rest of the day and night. She didn't want to have to face more time in airports and airplanes, starting from scratch on yet another case when this one was so close to cracking—and Vincent was smack in the middle of danger.

But, yes, duty called, and he was a big boy. He could take care of himself without her going mother hen all over him.

"Hey, promise me something," she said as he walked her out to her car.

"What?"

"Wear your gun, okay?"

Vincent nodded.

Claudia headed back to the hotel, taking a different route and checking her mirrors frequently. She spotted no sign of a tail but didn't let down her guard. Instead of going into the hotel's parking garage, she parked across the street. No need to make it easy for anyone to get the jump on her.

The envelope from Sheridan Express was waiting

for her at the front desk, and, Claudia grabbed it and limped to the elevator.

Up at her room, she opened the door slowly, alert for any sign of an intruder, but there were no ominous shadows, no blur of a body jumping at her. The room was empty, recently tidied by housekeeping, who'd left a little chocolate mint on her pillow.

With a sigh of relief, Claudia sat and thumbed through the contents of the package Ellie had sent. Vincent had guessed correctly: stolen church relics. Not much else beyond the expected itinerary and contact info, along with a new temporary cell phone. She was going to need to come up with a reliable way for Vincent to contact her. She couldn't expect him to program a bunch of constantly changing numbers into his phone.

After she'd gone over everything in the envelope, she gingerly examined her knees, wincing as she peeled back the bandages that stuck to the weeping skin. The scrapes and bruises looked alarmingly red and puffy, but as long as infection didn't set in, they'd be healing up within a few days.

She took a quick shower and reapplied ointment and bandages, dressing in jeans to protect her knees and double-padding the bandages at her elbows. Vincent's suggestion to leave the hotel was a good one, and staying the night with him appealed to her more than it probably should. She quickly packed her belongings, then buckled on the belt holster, her gun snugly inside, and slipped on the denim vest to conceal it.

From the doorway, she glanced back at the room, undisturbed except for an indentation on the bed where she'd sat and the pile of damp towels in the bathroom. It was like a hundred other rooms she'd stayed in, sterile and anonymous compared to Vincent's modest, cozy house.

There'd be more hotel rooms like this one as long as she was with Avalon, but the thought of "coming home" to Vincent's place sometimes made the situation a little more bearable.

After she checked out and got into her rental car, she dialed Vincent. He wouldn't be done with his work yet, but maybe she could join him.

She reached him at his office, surprised to hear that he *was* already finishing up forms and paperwork, and arranged to meet him at a small Italian restaurant a few blocks from the FBI building. She waited in a booth for almost a half hour, impatiently at first, then with worry. Just as she decided she should go look for him, she spotted a familiar figure in a black suit, white shirt, and skinny tie approaching the restaurant.

Only when she realized she'd stopped breathing did she admit how worried she'd been. Oh, yes, she was falling hard for this man. When and how it had happened, she couldn't say, but she'd been fighting her attraction to Vincent DeLuca from the first antagonistic second they'd met.

The door chime tinkled as Vincent walked in, and he spotted her waving at him. He slid into the booth opposite her, tugging his tie loose. "Did you get your package?"

"Yup. I leave tomorrow morning." He was plainly not happy about her answer, but accepting of it. "And you?" she asked. "Everything taken care of?"

Vincent nodded. "We've issued alerts and descriptions for the two women; and maybe we'll get lucky. I checked about Brody, but nobody's brought him in yet."

"So now what?" she asked.

"I don't know," Vincent admitted. "It could be this is the last we see of them. I hope so; I don't like the possibility that they're still out there, watching me. I just wish I knew what they wanted."

"For what it's worth, I don't think you've seen the last of them. They've fixated on you, for whatever reason, and they're going to want to try and make contact again." She reached across the table and pulled his coat aside, gratified to see the shoulder holster. "Good. I'll rest a little easier knowing you're properly accessorized."

He straightened his coat, looking around to make sure no one had noticed the gun. "I wanted a taste of danger. Guess I got my wish."

"And how'd you like it?"

"Can't say I care for it, but maybe it's an acquired taste. And you? I recognize that vest."

"I'm licensed up. For real."

"I don't believe the 'real' part, but it doesn't matter. You could be carrying a missile launcher under there and I wouldn't care."

"So much for those rules, huh?"

"Seems that way," he said, glancing away.

Claudia immediately regretted her words. "Sorry. I shouldn't have said that. I know how important personal integrity is to you, and teasing you about something that serious isn't fair."

"But it's the truth. I've learned a few things about myself over the past couple days."

"Is this good?" she asked, not sure she wanted to hear his answer.

"Mostly." He leaned back against the booth. "You busy right now?"

"Not really, why?"

"What do you say we head over to Champion and Stone and test-drive our theories about the theft? I called Arnetta Gallagher, and she was fine with it, as long as we were quiet and didn't upset any customers."

"Did you mention me? I get the feeling she likes you much better than she likes me."

"That's because I'm a nice, well-mannered Italian boy." Vincent grinned. "And yes, I mentioned you. I told her we're working together."

"Really?"

"Uh-huh." He gave her a smug look. "Do I get any rewards for good behavior?"

After waving off the approaching waiter, Claudia slid out of the booth. "If we had a few hours to kill, I can't think of a better way to pass the time than letting you ravish my poor body in thanks, but we shouldn't keep that nice lady at Champion and Stone waiting."

Vincent grinned. "Can I ravish your body after that?"

"I'm counting on it."

# Chapter Seventeen

Arnetta Gallagher met them with a warm smile directed at Vincent. When she took in Claudia's cuts, scrapes, and bruises she said, "Oh, my, what happened? You look like you got hit by a truck, poor thing."

"It felt like it, too," Claudia answered with feeling. "Thank you for letting us come by to walk through a couple theories. We'll be sure to stay out of your way."

She was on her best behavior, Vincent noted with amusement. "Yes, thank you." he added.

"It's a little slow right now, as you can see." Arnetta motioned to the empty gallery. "So if there's anything you'd like me to do, just ask. I'm happy to cooperate in any way I can."

"Appreciate it, Ms. Gallagher. For now, we're only going to walk around and take a look at things."

After Arnetta retreated to the cashier's desk, Claudia said softly, "Déjà vu, eh? We're right back where we started."

"Technically, we started out at the Alliance Gallery."

"Mmm," Claudia murmured, as she followed him to the next annex. "You were so mean to me."

"You were so intrusive and pushy."

"And here we are, making nice. Amazing, isn't it?"

"Yup," Vincent agreed, stopping at the empty display case that had held the Corinthian helmet.

Claudia moved up beside him. "They've got a new camera setup. It wasn't like this before."

"Looks like more cameras, period. That one"—he pointed to the hall entrance—"is new. This annex is under full surveillance now, but before you couldn't see this side of the case."

"Or this entire hallway." Claudia headed down the hall that led to the office. "At least not until you get to the back service door."

Vincent stopped to point to the doors along the hall. "This is the bathroom. This door's to the office, and this is the storage room. This one . . . the supply room, right?"

"Right." Claudia walked back to him. "The cleaning crew didn't go into the supply or storage rooms. They did clean the bathroom and office so I think we can safely rule out those two rooms as potential hiding places."

Vincent met her gaze. "You thinking what I'm thinking?"

She nodded. "People would be going in and out of the storage room a lot. The supply room, not so much, and probably not at all toward the end of the day. Is it locked?"

Vincent tried the doorknob. "Locked."

Claudia hunkered down to examine the keyhole. "It's a cheapie, and old. Pretty beat up, so it's hard to say if it's been jimmied recently. Did you check if it had been locked the night of the theft?"

"I asked Arnetta about it." He'd jotted down a few notes before coming over, and now he pulled them from his inside coat pocket and thumbed through them. "Basic office supplies inside, nothing valuable. Sometimes the door's locked, sometimes not. It was open the night of the theft. She couldn't remember if she'd locked it before she went home."

"It doesn't matter." Claudia straightened. "Both the office and storage room have secure locks. The bathroom only locks from the inside, and there's no place to hide in there."

"So we go with the supply room." When she nodded, Vincent called, "Ms. Gallagher, can you please open the supply room for us?"

A moment later, Arnetta's heels click-clacked toward them and she appeared with a jangle of keys. "Why do you need to go in there?"

"We're exploring a theory that the thief might have remained in the gallery, hiding, after you closed," Vincent explained. As Arnetta opened her mouth to protest, he added, "The cameras didn't cover this part of the hall, and it wouldn't be difficult to slip down this way unnoticed while you were busy helping customers. Both the office and storage room are locked down, and the janitorial service only cleans the office and bathroom."

"They never do this room unless I ask them. It doesn't really need cleaning often, just the occasional dusting." The lock clicked open, and Arnetta pushed the door inward. "To tell the truth, it's not a very good lock. I've known a few employees who've opened it with a paper clip."

The small room was dominated by industrial steel shelving units, filled with boxes of various sizes, and two older steel cabinets. Vincent motioned Claudia in. "After you." To Arnetta, he said, "Thanks. We'll come get you when it's time to lock the door again. And, by the way, let's keep this between just the three of us for now."

The gallery manager looked a little disappointed, probably wishing she could stay and watch. "Of course I'll keep quiet, Agent DeLuca. We have our reputation to maintain. Though I do have to say, it's highly unnerving to contemplate that someone might have been hiding in here all along. After today, we'll make sure to take any necessary steps to prevent that from happening again."

"Good idea. Some knowledge is hard-earned, but better to learn from mistakes than repeat them." Vincent waited until she'd left, then followed Claudia into the room. "Pretty tight in here."

"I know," she said as he brushed up against her. With a wink, she added, "Kinda sexy."

"A garden shed would be sexy, if you and I were alone in it," Vincent retorted. His body's reaction to touching hers was instantaneous—and very inconvenient, considering their situation.

"Heh. Makes us sound like horny teenagers. Ain't it great?" She grinned, then gave him a swat so that he stepped aside. "This is looking promising. You can squeeze behind the shelves here, see? And with all these boxes here and here, if you squat down, nobody sees you unless they come around the corner."

Vincent nodded, seeking out other likely hiding spots. He pointed toward two cabinets. "Either side of the cabinet provides cover . . . and there, the boxes on those shelves. You're right; looks promising."

He turned slowly. "Okay. If you were hiding here, and knew there was a chance someone could come in for a box of staples, where would you want to be?"

"Good question." Claudia joined him in the main aisle in the middle of the room. When his gaze tracked toward the far set of shelves and boxes, she followed it, her eyes narrowing. "Yeah, that would be good, right there. Mobility."

"Exactly. Someone comes in, you move quickly around to the other side without being seen, and, if things get worse, it's just a step or two to the cabinet there. It's a tight fit, but far back enough that you wouldn't be too noticeable if you were still standing, and not noticeable at all if you squatted down."

"Good observation," she said, smiling. "You're a credit to the badge."

Grinning, Vincent pulled two pairs of latex gloves out of his pocket and handed one to her, loving the look of surprise on her face. "I always come prepared for the job at hand."

She grinned back. "Oooh, a man with spare latex in his pockets. Sexy! I am impressed, DeLuca."

"As an encore, there's tweezers." He handed his extra one to her as she laughed, softly. "And . . . a penlight."

"Impressed once again. I didn't think to bring *my* crime scene kit." She pretend pouted. "That means you win all the smarty-pants points this time."

"Yay for me. Let's go look for evidence, shall we?"

"Aha! I get your master plan now. You want me bending and crawling around so you have an excuse to shine your flashlight at my ass or down my shirt. Just be damn sure you keep your tweezers to yourself, buddy."

His deep chuckle blended with Claudia's giggles.

A half hour later, Claudia sucked in her breath and said, "Hey, I think maybe I've got something. Come over here and take a look."

Backing out from where he knelt by one of the empty shelves, Vincent headed over to the door. Claudia pointed at the first shelf. "Hair strands. A couple of them . . . long and black."

Their eyes met, excitement flashing between them. "My dark-haired businesswoman—the one who walked out but never walked in the next morning."

"The Amazon."

"Yup," he said, grinning back at her.

"We're sure it's from a wig?" Claudia asked.

"We'll know if it's synthetic hair as soon as we get it back to the lab."

"It's not Arnetta Gallagher's; hers is gray and short. Any employees here with long dark hair?"

"There are only four employees including Gallagher, and two of them are male. The other's a forty-something woman with short brown hair. I think there's a good chance this could be from our thief. She put on the wig, and it caught on the screws here. She probably never felt the hair catch since it was a wig," Vincent said.

"Well, I'm assuming you brought baggies along with everything else."

He had, and produced one from his back pants pocket. "I think your finding the first piece of evidence evens the smarty-pants score. Let's finish up in here so we can do a review of what happened."

By the time he and Claudia finished scouring the supply room for evidence, Champion and Stone had closed for the day. They'd found nothing else of note, not even fingerprints on dusty shelves.

"Somebody was very, very careful not to leave anything behind," Claudia said, stripping off her gloves.

Vincent took off his gloves as well and went into the main gallery room, where Arnetta was cashing out the register. "When you're done there, Ms. Gallagher, could we borrow you for a moment?" he asked.

She raised a brow but nodded. "Of course."

They tossed the gloves in a wastebasket, which then reminded them to check the bathroom's trash can. It was a typical large, chrome canister with an easily removable top. It was partially full of paper towel waste.

"Plenty of room for a helmet," Claudia pointed out. "And lots of paper towels for padding and protection."

"Still, the helmet would likely be damaged in handling," Vincent said.

"Yes, but damage can be repaired. Given its age, a few extra dings might not even be noticeable."

"All right, then." Vincent nodded, feeling that familiar thrill of excitement when a case was coming together. "Let's do this."

Arnetta was waiting for them when they returned

to the main room, not even bothering to hide her own excitement. "So what are we doing?"

"We're going to talk through what we think happened the night the helmet was stolen." Vincent pulled out his notes again. "Remember, this is still only a theory. All we want to prove is that it's possible. It doesn't mean that it's fact. Okay?"

Arnetta nodded. "What should I do?"

"For now, nothing." He glanced down at his scribbles. "This is where you were at four-twenty-three PM, when the businessman in the gray suit walked in. He's got one of those oversize messenger bags on his shoulder. Gray Suit stops and talks with you for a few minutes."

"I remember that guy," Arnetta said. "He was a lot younger than I'd first thought."

Vincent nodded absently and glanced at Claudia. "The businesswoman in the tan suit comes in at four-thirty-six PM. She's got a big purse. She walks toward Ms. Gallagher, who breaks off conversation with the man to talk to her new customer. Gray Suit heads into the next annex. Less than five minutes later, at four-forty PM, the elderly couple comes in, and Ms. Gallagher here is probably gritting her teeth and wondering why everyone always shows up in the last minutes before closing."

"Actually, I *was* thinking something like that . . . along with hoping they'd at least buy something. Please, you can call me Arnetta."

He nodded. "Thanks. The businesswoman goes into the next annex as well. She's briefly off-camera, time enough to hide her purse in the trash can in the bathroom. The businessman is no longer on-camera. The couple buy a doll. While Arnetta's taking care of that purchase, the businesswoman leaves. She doesn't have her purse. Arnetta finishes up with the doll couple. After they leave, she does a quick walk-through of the gallery, sees no one else, and locks the main door." Turning to Arnetta, he explained further: "You assumed the businessman left while you were with the doll couple, but you missed actually seeing him leave."

"Right," she said, frowning. "But that didn't happen?"

"Maybe not. Theory, remember?" Vincent reminded her. "Arnetta does all the usual closing routine, locks the office, then sets the alarms for the night and goes home. Business as usual, as far as she's concerned."

"But," Claudia said, walking past him as she picked up the story. "All is not business as usual. The businessman is actually working with the businesswoman—and while that woman distracts Arnetta, Gray Suit slips into the hall here."

Vincent and Arnetta followed along with Claudia.

"We know this is a camera blind spot. No need to keep a hallway under surveillance, right? Or the office. Besides, there's a camera outside the back door, and that's what matters. You don't want people getting in; people getting out is less of an issue."

"Oh, my God," Arnetta said softly. "This is terrible. I feel so stupid!"

"Just a theory," Claudia echoed Vincent, then continued down the hall. "Gray Suit goes to the supply room, hoping it's unlocked. They've both been in the gallery before; they've already checked out these rooms. If it's locked, they're prepared for it. Gray Suit goes inside and settles down to wait in the corner over there. You close up and Gray Suit still waits, in case you forgot something . . . and keeps waiting until he's certain you're not coming back."

"They're aware of the janitorial service," Vincent said, motioning the others to follow him toward the annex where the helmet had been. "And they know their window of opportunity. Once enough time has passed, Gray Suit carefully crawls out to this corner of the annex. Again, this area is in a blind spot, and one small blind spot is all they need to steal the helmet."

"The fake helmet was in the woman's purse," Arnetta said, catching on.

"Probably. So Gray Suit very carefully raises the top of the case, slips in the fake plastic helmet, and takes the real one. The real helmet might be packed in the purse with lots of paper towels for protection, and then hidden back inside the bathroom trash can. Or the helmet's packed carefully into the trash by itself, cushioned with handfuls of paper towels. Once that's done, Gray Suit returns to the supply room to wait out the night."

Vincent caught Claudia's gaze and grinned. This was working; he could feel it, and she knew it, too. "At the usual time, the janitorial service arrives and cleans up. They empty the bathroom trash and leave the bag in the Dumpster. Claudia, your guess about what happened next."

She came up beside him, keeping a discreet distance between them, but he was still acutely aware of her body's heat, her scent.

"Very early in the morning, a woman—the business-woman from the day before—comes to the alley and removes the helmet from the Dumpster," Claudia said. "She's back at your door before opening, waiting when you arrive."

"The watch," Arnetta said, eyes wide and round. "She said she'd lost her watch."

"Yup, and while you were kind enough to help her look for it, totally distracted once again, a woman with long black hair, and carrying a messenger bag, walked out of the gallery. You never saw her leave. Even if you had, you probably wouldn't have recognized her from the day before. We've observed these two; they're very good at disguising themselves. The messenger bag had held a brand-new persona."

"So she was the man who'd been hiding in my supply room?" Arnetta blinked. "I'm feeling a little confused."

Vincent said, "That's our theory, yes."

Arnetta frowned. "I think . . . I might like your theory."

"We're liking it, too," Claudia assured her.

"I'll like it a lot more when it becomes fact. Thank you for involving me in this; I've learned quite a lot tonight," Arnetta added. "Something like this will never again happen at any gallery I manage."

A short while later, as they were walking back to their cars, Vincent let out a sigh. "That went a lot better than I expected. It came together perfectly, Claudia."

"I know! I'm so excited, I could kiss you right here and now."

He laughed. "Nothing's stopping you from doing that."

"Nope, I'm saving up. We deserve a really major celebration, just the two of us."

He'd been feeling the letdown after the big rush, but that comment brought all his energy charging back. "Yeah, we deserve to be really good to each other."

"Let's get back to your place, then. But don't drive too fast: if you get pulled over for speeding, I can't be held responsible for what I'd do to that poor cop."

# Chapter Eighteen

Claudia was barely inside Vincent's front door before he had her in his arms, hungrily kissing her. No need to waste what little time they had on small talk and foreplay.

On the same wavelength, they made their way up the stairs. All she wanted was to get skin to skin with him.

Stripping down took a little longer this time, mindful of injuries and two loaded guns, and while Vincent's touch was insistent, he remained gentle, so very different from last night's aggression.

He lowered her to the bed carefully, leaving a trail of soft kisses along her cheeks and chin and lips. His stubble rasped against her skin as he kissed the tip of each breast, and then he settled between her raised legs. She was more than ready for him, and she sighed with satisfaction as he pushed slowly inside her.

Hands braced beside her head, he rocked his hips against her, eliciting a short gasp. That he'd aroused her to this extent in so short a time, and with so little effort, amazed her. It was as if her body had been aching for this for so long, just the feel of him pushing inside her was enough to trigger all those tingling, hot, wonderful sensations.

He watched her, smiling, as he continued to move oh-so-slowly in and out.

Mmmm, yes, a long, slow ride. She could take him for hours like this, feeling the teasing friction, the pleasure gather gradually at the edges of her awareness.

"I love watching your face," he whispered. "How your mouth opens, the way your eyes go soft."

"I like watching you, too," she murmured. When he went a little deeper, a little harder, she closed her eyes with a moan. He kissed her, tongues stroking and touching in time to their bodies' movement. He was being so careful, so tender. And as much as she needed that, she also wanted more.

"A little harder," she whispered.

"You sure?" he asked, his tone tighter than before.

"Yes. I won't break."

"If I hurt you, tell me and I'll stop."

"Do me right, and I'll never notice." She laughed, but it ended in another gasp as he drove into her, hard and deep.

Just the one, deep thrust was all it took to push her

to the brink. She tried to hold on, to make it last a little longer, but it was too late and she lost herself in the orgasm, crying out and arching toward him.

Vincent followed a moment later with a guttural grunt and a final thrust. He kissed her deeply before carefully rolling off her.

"See?" Claudia said, scooting closer to his heat. "Not broken—just very, very satisfied."

He chuckled, draping an arm over his eyes. "That was really nice. Last night was great, too, but I liked having the chance to really get into it just now. This time it was . . . I don't know. Something more."

"More like making love," she said—and instantly wished she hadn't. Any mention of the L-word was asking for trouble. Claudia risked a quick look at Vincent and found him frowning.

Well, what did she expect? Only a few days ago they were harassing each other. Given their situations, the relationship didn't have much chance of developing beyond sex.

"Yeah," he said, interrupting her thoughts. "That's a better way to put it. Last night was all lust . . . this was making love."

She blinked, taken aback. "Well, we don't need to go that far. We have separate lives and priorities, and maybe anything more complicated is too much to manage right now."

He rolled over, hitching up on his elbow. "You have a problem with getting closer?"

"Vincent, I'm a realist. Anything more involved is going to take a hell of a lot of hard work, and even that might not be enough."

"So?"

She stared at him. "What kind of getting closer are we talking about here? Close like scheduling sex between cross-country flights, or close like a commitment?"

"It took me about five minutes to realize I'm falling in love with you. I don't know what you're thinking, but my getting closer means commitment. What does yours mean?"

Oh, God, he was serious. He was falling in love with her? What could she say to that? What *should* she say?

Tension hung between them, humming about the small bedroom with its off-white walls, hardwood floors, and king-size bed. The old oak headboard had carved spindles, and the beige duvet on the floor looked worn but comfortable.

She could imagine nights snuggled up in this bed with Vincent, reading books or making love, and she could imagine being part of his life.

"Someday I'd like to get married and have kids," she admitted. It was a truth she'd shared with only a few close girlfriends, and with Ellie and Shaunda since they also had the kinds of careers that made mixing marriage and family more of a challenge than usual. "I'm not ready for that yet, but I wouldn't mind settling down. I like my job and don't want to leave it, but I'm starting to feel like I need something more."

"I guess there comes a point when you're ready to share your life with someone else. I'm at that point, and I'm beginning to think you might be the one I'd like to share it with," he replied.

"And maybe it's just the sex talking, and you'll feel that way only until the odds against us drive us apart." She sighed. "Vincent, maybe it would be better to . . . you know, keep it simple for a while. Just to play it safe."

"Since when do you play safe?"

She met his gaze, seeing tight anger in the lines of his face. Feeling wholly out of her element, she looked away. "Maybe because, for once, something really matters to me, and I don't want to mess it up."

He sighed. "Look, I know it's going to be hard. I know we have differences, but I also know we're more alike than we're different. I'm willing to give it a chance. What about you?"

A *chance*. She'd had a few of those come her way, and knew what it really meant: this was the last offer, the last call, the last chance.

"I want to," she said, well aware of his gaze on her, waiting for an answer. "I really, really do, but . . . I need to think it through, because lying next to you like this, it's hard for me to get everything clear in my head. Maybe spending the next few days apart is good. We'll get a chance to really think about the problems we'd face—not only between us but with your people, my people. It's not like we're alone on an island. What we decide is going to have consequences."

"Okay."

He still didn't sound pleased, and she glanced his way, angry with herself for letting him down, and angry with him for pushing matters.

"Vincent, what is this?" She sat up, facing him. "What the hell did you think I'd do, fall at your feet and spend the rest of my life baking pies and changing diapers? *You* are not thinking this through, or what it might mean to your career, or—"

"No," he snapped, also sitting up. "Goddammit, I'm afraid that once you leave tomorrow morning, I'll never see you again. You'll decide it's just too damn much trouble to come back, and Sheridan will pressure you to stay away. You've told me over and over that you owe him. If he tells you to stay away, would you really tell him to fuck off and mind his own business?"

Claudia tried to imagine herself telling Ben Sheridan to "fuck off" and started laughing; she couldn't help herself. "I can't believe we're fighting about this. We barely have a relationship, yet already we're arguing about it. I promised you that I'd come back, didn't

I? I don't give my promises lightly, Vincent. I meant it. You'll just have to trust me, okay?"

Her laughter had defused some of the tension, and he smiled back a little sheepishly. "Yeah, you're right. I'm being too possessive."

"Control issues," she said lightly. "I warned you about that."

"So you did." He leaned over for another kiss. "It'll be a test of sorts, and if you don't—"

"If I don't come back, then you deserve better and you know it. Baby steps, Vincent. It's the only way—"

The doorbell rang, startling them into silence. Then Claudia whispered, "Were you expecting someone?"

"No."

"Careful," she said sharply as he rolled out of bed.

He went to the window, careful to stay out of view as he pulled the curtains aside and peered down at the front yard.

"Who is it?" Claudia asked.

"I don't know . . . I can't see anyone. There's no car in the driveway, besides your rental."

"I don't like this."

"Me, either," Vincent said grimly. He pulled on his pants and grabbed his gun.

"Hey! Wait for me!" Claudia scrambled out of bed, gritting her teeth against the pain as her elbows hit the headboard, and dragged on his T-shirt.

He was already at the bottom of the stairs before

she caught up with him and immediately veered off to look out the front window. Nothing; only the usual quiet street in a typical quiet, working neighborhood. This early in the evening, there wasn't much going on. Little traffic, and the distant sound of a few children playing outside before having to go to bed.

"Anything?" Vincent asked, tersely.

She shook her head. "If it was a car or truck, we'd have heard it pull up."

"If it's Jennie's boys doorbell ditching, I'm going to feel really stupid," Vincent muttered, then slowly opened the door.

Claudia was at his side in a heartbeat, gun drawn and ready to defend him, only to look down, sharing his bemusement, at a cheap vase of wilting white daisies that sat on top of a blue, card-size envelope.

"What the hell is that?" she demanded.

Frowning, Vincent pocketed the gun and gingerly picked up the vase and envelope. "Too small for a mail bomb."

"Be careful anyway. Give me that," Claudia said, taking the vase as Vincent cautiously opened the envelope.

The vase was warm, as if it had been sitting in the sun—or a hot car—for a long time. She cast another quick look around: no lurking Amazons or Arty Asses, no cars, no cops. Nothing.

"What does it say?" she demanded, impatient and still tense enough that she wanted to yank him back inside the house, slam the door shut, and lock it tight.

He turned to her, his expression oddly blank. "It's a letter from our thieves. They said . . . Hell, you read it."

Vincent thrust the card at her—it was one of those obnoxiously cutesy ones with bug-eyed bunnies and fat bees buzzing around impossibly perky cartoon flowers—and went back inside the house.

Claudia followed more slowly as she read the neatly printed note with the little hearts dotting the i's:

> Hi, Vince!
> It's been fun but that's over now, because it's not just the three of us anymore. We wanted to see if you would ever catch on, but you never did. Not as smart as you think. What a disappointing performance.
> Bye,
> Sindy and Susie

"A *game*. All along, it's been a fucking game!" He kicked a chair across the kitchen floor and then, taking a deep breath, leaned against the sink counter.

"The stolen property is still missing, Vincent. You can't give up now."

He grunted, clearly struggling to keep his temper under control. "Who said anything about giving up? There's no way in hell they really expect me to believe they've called it quits. This is *their* game, Claudia, not mine—and now they're starting to seriously piss me off."

# Chapter Nineteen

By the time the crime scene team arrived, Claudia had freshened up and pulled on a pair of Vincent's cargo shorts.

She recognized one of the detectives; he'd been at Champion and Stone after the helmet was stolen. His eyebrows nearly reached his receding hairline when he saw her; then he glanced at Vincent, snorted, and returned to talking shop with the other cops and an FBI agent.

"Sindy" and "Susie" had left behind a final "gift," one she and Vincent hadn't seen right away because they'd stayed inside until the crime techs could secure the area: a neon-pink smiley face spray-painted on the back of Vincent's house. From beneath the kitchen window, it overlooked the investigation with mocking amusement.

Claudia saw Vincent's gaze drift toward the hot pink

paint, and he scowled. "What the hell did they have to do that for?"

Claudia thought the reasoning obvious enough: embarrassment. She suspected Vincent knew the answer, as well, and was only letting off steam. He was actually handling the situation fairly well.

She couldn't blame him for being upset; she wasn't too happy, either, because it made them both look bad. The officer patrolling the area had driven past Vincent's house only fifteen minutes before the doorbell rang, and so far, the officers going door to door had found no one who'd seen either woman.

Two young boys reported seeing a woman on a bicycle, but they hadn't been able to provide a useful description: they'd been absorbed in a game of basketball and weren't close enough to notice details. It had been determined that the flowers and card were purchased at a nearby discount store, but the clerk could remember only that a tall woman had paid cash for them.

As if picking up on her thoughts, Vincent leaned over and said, "One left the flowers and the card to distract us while the other spray-painted my house. Same tag-team approach they've used all along."

"It works because they're willing to wait for the right moment," Claudia said. "And that alone raises them above the spur-of-the-moment, grab-and-run thieves."

"Maybe I should file this case away as a lost cause." Vincent folded his arms across his chest. The scowl eased into an irritated frown. "Even if we catch them, prosecuting them will likely be a waste of time. We're lucky if minor charges stick in these cases, and that's assuming the insurance companies or owners even bother to press charges. Way too many of my cases never make it before a judge."

"And I bet that's something else these women have picked up on—our tendency to focus more effort on re-trieving stolen items than on prosecuting thieves." She sighed. "Litigation is expensive in time and personnel, as well as money. I kinda get why they shrug it off once the property is recovered, but it sure as hell makes our job a lot more difficult."

The detective—she remembered his name was Matherson—sauntered over to join them. "Some crazy shit, huh?" he asked, shaking his head. "In all the years I've been a cop, I don't think I've ever seen anything like this."

"They wanted to be noticed," Vincent said, his tone neutral. "I'd say they succeeded."

"I guess these mousies wanted to tease the cat." Matherson glanced at Claudia. "Or cats. We'll run the story in the news with Ms. Cruz's descriptions; maybe someone will call in a useful tip. Aside from that, though, we got nothing. We're not picking up any prints. The card and vase were clean."

"Have you sent anyone to question the kid at the bar I told you about?" Vincent asked. "He had a con-versation with the short woman."

Matherson flipped through his notes. "It's on the list. I'll check. We're still looking for Digger Brody, by the way. So far, no luck."

"If we're lucky, he'll turn up dead," Claudia said. When both men stared at her, she went on, "Murder changes the whole scope of things, right? Juries can shrug off stealing expensive knickknacks, but dead bodies mean serious business."

"Me, I'm thinking Brody will be showing up a little worse for wear after a bender," Matherson said. "Could be he's with his buddies in Miami or Jersey, and I'll look into that, too. But even if he turns up dead, you'd have your work cut out for you trying to prove they did it."

"There's always the chance they'll contact me again," Vincent said after a pause. "I suppose that's our best chance of catching them."

Claudia didn't like that thought at all. It seemed far too risky for the women, but they'd proved they liked their games on the risky side—and there was always the possibility there were more than two of them.

"They better not try it while I'm still around," she said with feeling. "I swear, I'll shoot them on the spot."

Matherson's eyebrows rose yet again.

"Claudia," Vincent said, but his tone told her he was fighting back a grin.

"Just a figure of speech." She shrugged. "Sorry."

*     *     *

Vincent's subsequent sour mood sank Claudia's plans for their romantic evening. She knew he wasn't angry with her and didn't even blame him for his temper, but after a few attempts at kissing and cuddling led nowhere, she settled for simply being with him. The humiliation had hit him harder because it was directed at him specifically, but it didn't sit so well with her, either.

She'd had a few nights like this after the bad guys had gotten the better of her and understood what he was dealing with, so she didn't try to coddle him or talk him out of his mood. It would only make matters worse.

A little snooping around revealed that Vincent owned an Xbox, so she split her attention between keeping an eye on him, working at his desk, and Halo's Master Chief. Shooting the shit out of everything made her feel a little better. After a while, seeing how much fun she was having at killing pixels, he joined her, and they played together. He slowly began to relax again, and by the time they hit the sheets, utterly exhausted, he made up for his earlier bad mood by making love to her with a lazy gentleness that was a perfect send-off to deep, dreamless sleep.

She'd set the alarm early to allow plenty of time to get ready and drive to the airport. In Texas she'd meet with her contact, review the files, find a moment to sneak off and visit the family—her mother would never forgive her for not visiting if she was in the area, even if the "area" was the entire state of Texas. Then she'd spend the rest of the week, if not more, visiting churches and interviewing outraged priests about missing relics.

It was still dark outside when the alarm blared, and she quickly rolled away from Vincent and shut it off, not wanting to wake him. She eased out of bed, holding back a groan: she was much stiffer this morning. Being stuck in an airplane seat for hours, even in first class, wouldn't be fun.

She made it to the bathroom without turning on any lights, bumping into a wall only once, and as she stood under the hot water, swearing under her breath at the stinging in her knees and elbows, she decided she needed a vacation. After this Texas job she'd ask Ben for a week off. Maybe he'd even allow her a few sick days, if she flashed her injured elbows and knees at him.

Either way, she'd get back to Philly as soon as possible.

The shower curtain was pulled back, and she yelped in surprise until she saw a stubble-scruffy Vincent standing outside, yawning.

"Want company?" he asked. "You might need some help washing those hard-to-reach spots."

She grinned, tipping her face up for his kiss, and motioned him in. He shucked his shorts—revealing a most impressive morning erection—and stepped in beside her.

He stuck his head under the running water, making a rumbling sound of male contentment as he rubbed his hands vigorously over his face, then ducked back out.

"Washed the hair yet?" he asked.

"No, but that's not exactly a hard-to-reach spot," she pointed out, still grinning. He was furry as hell in the morning, but in such a cute manly-man way. She wanted to explore the texture of the beard stubble, then rub along his erection, but decided to hold off and see what he had in mind.

All those delicious little fantasies she'd entertained would have to wait until she healed, but in the meantime she could give that arching, aggressive piece of male muscle a decent workout. Sex in the shower was so practical: you could have a little fun and get clean at the same time.

After Vince gave her head a soapy massage she returned the favor, lathering his chest hair with extravagant swirls. Then, palms slick with suds, she lavished attention on his erection until he turned her around and, bracing their hands on the wall tiles, thrust into her from behind for a thoroughly satisfying quickie.

Afterward he made coffee while she dressed, and served her a plate with two warm, gooey Pop-Tarts. Not the pseudo-healthy fruit-filled kind, either, but the frosted chocolate fudge kind.

"Sex *and* chocolate. Dear God, where have you been all my life?" She broke the pastry in half. "But please tell me you don't seriously eat this kind of stuff for breakfast. It's worse than pizza."

He yawned. "I bought these the last time my nephew and sister-in-law dropped by for a visit."

"A family man, too," she said, taking a tenuous bite. Mmmm, yummy, if a bit too rich this early in the morning. "That earns you even more points. I'm big on family."

"I'm Italian. It comes with the genes."

"And I'm Mexican. I know exactly how that works." She paused, then asked, "How many siblings do you have?"

"Three brothers and two sisters."

A silence fell between them, then Vincent said, "Where's your family?"

"They're all in the Dallas area. Mom, Dad, brothers and sisters, grandmother, aunts and uncles, a small horde of nieces, nephews, and cousins . . . it can get pretty crazy during the holidays."

"It sure does." Another silence, this one longer. "You'll give me a call when you get settled in tonight?"

"Definitely. I'll be checking to make sure you're okay. I don't like leaving you, knowing those two are still out there somewhere."

"I can take care of myself, Claudia, and the police are aware of the situation."

"I know, I know. . . . But I can't help worrying about you anyway. Promise you'll keep yourself properly accessorized?"

Vincent laughed. "I promise, but I seriously don't think there'll be any more trouble. The police have added an extra patrol to the area at night, and I can't see those two women storming a federal building."

"Fine, but I'm still calling whenever I get the chance."

"And I'll keep you posted if there are any new developments. Or if somebody finally runs Digger Brody to ground."

They were working up to good-bye, dancing around actually saying the words, but it was time for her to go. The only thing she could be happy about was that an early flight meant less traffic.

"I have to get going," she said finally.

"Wait a sec while I grab my briefcase, and we'll leave together," he said. "I'll follow you until your turnoff."

A flurry of activity followed: car keys jingling, pockets checked and double-checked for all necessities, her suitcase bumping against his briefcase. When she opened the door, he slammed it shut with his palm, took her shoulders, and pulled her against him for a long, deep kiss.

When Claudia broke away, gasping for air, he traced the line of her jaw. "For the road—and because I can't be there to see you off."

"Maybe next time," she said as tears welled, stinging and hot. "Not that you really *need* any excuse to kiss me like that."

She'd never cried over a man before and hoped he hadn't noticed her rapid blinking to clear the tears away. Tears achieved nothing and only made an awkward moment all the more difficult.

Neither spoke as they walked to her car. Vincent took care of her luggage, and she thanked him quietly. She waited until he pulled out of the driveway before putting her car in gear, and watched him from her rear-view mirror until she reached her turnoff. He honked and waved as she drove away.

"I hate good-byes . . . hate them, *hate* them," she muttered, wiping at her eyes again.

The drive to the airport didn't take long, and she checked her bags and went through security, then bought another coffee as she waited for her flight to begin boarding.

Maybe it was only the lingering mood from their good-byes, but she couldn't shake a sense of unease. She knew that the police and the FBI were doing their job and that Vincent would be more careful than usual. Besides, there wasn't anything she could do that he couldn't do for himself. If he were fussing over her like this, she'd be annoyed, and he'd feel exactly the same at her fussing. That kind of behavior would kill any chance for a relationship.

Still, she couldn't get over the feeling that she was letting him down just when he needed her most.

An intercom crackled, and she glanced up. "*Good morning. In just a few minutes, we'll begin boarding for American Airlines flight number 1057 to Dallas/Fort Worth International Airport, with intermediate service to . . .*"

Claudia finished off her coffee, still uneasy.

# Chapter Twenty

Exhausted as he was, Will managed to keep up with Mia as she seized his arm and dragged him from the Knightsbridge tube entrance into Harrods to buy a small thank-you gift for her boss, who was babysitting her ferret back in Boston. It was their final day together, and there was no way he could've refused her.

At slightly over one million square feet, the old department store was massive, squatting along an entire block on Brompton Road. It offered everything: haute couture for people and pets, cheese and chocolate, electronics and furniture, banking services, hair salons, and, of course, the mouthwatering Food Halls. No other department store boasted décor that ranged from opulent Egyptian themes to Art Nouveau, much less a life-size memorial to a dead princess hovering over an escalator. Anyone who thought the Mall of

America was the epitome of shopping had never been to Harrods during the annual January sale. Will had endured the cutthroat chaos once and swore he'd never do that again.

"So where to first?" he asked.

"I thought we'd just wander a bit and see if anything strikes my fancy. I'm hoping we can eat while we're here?"

He laughed. "I can swing that. It all goes on my expense report anyway." He took her hand, noting there were enough security guards around to fill the police force of a small town.

A sign of the times, unfortunately.

Mia had collected an impressive number of shopping bags by the time a display rack of shirts caught Will's attention. If he was going to badger old Mrs. Whitlea, a nicer shirt and tie would be a good idea. Had she been an average sweet little old lady, he could've played the part of the charming, nicely respectable-looking man. At this point, though, he could safely eliminate "sweet" as applying to anyone, old or young, who gave Ben Sheridan his orders. As an interloper— and likely an unwelcome one—the only way he'd score any points with Mrs. Whitlea would be by giving her the respect she deserved, and part of that was to dress up, not down. As he browsed through a staggering assortment of shirts, Mia pitched in to help and headed a few aisles over to check out the selection of ties.

*     *     *

"Hey! Don't do that, it hurts." Rainert stopped short, wincing as Vanessa's fingers dug into his arm. He looked down to see her all but crawling into his suit coat, hiding. She'd been doing so well, and now this. She must've spotted someone she knew.

Dammit, if she panicked, he'd have to ditch her. "What's wrong? Vanessa, do—"

"Sssh!" she hissed into his chest. "It's him! That's *him*!"

Rainert knew better than to turn and look. "Stop acting like this. Stop it now," he ordered quietly. To mislead anyone who might be watching them, he bent and kissed her, pretending they were embracing. She stiffened but had the good sense not to fight him.

"Kiss me back. Make it look like you're kissing me because you're excited, not scared."

She did as he told her, with more force than he expected. Though it was terror fueling her intensity, not desire, it wasn't a bad kiss.

"Who is here?" Rainert asked, pulling back enough to see her face. She was flushed, but that was due to fear not desire. From the corner of his eye, he pinpointed the nearest security guards. They weren't watching, luckily. "I need you to calmly tell me who and where, and do not look around. Look only at me. At *me*, Vanessa. Focus."

Nodding, she moistened her lips. "Will Tiernay—the bastard who killed Kos! He's looking at shirts behind you and to your right. Oh, God, I can't believe this!"

So much for his earlier cockiness about moving as

freely as he wished. Still, what were the chances he would run into an Avalon agent *here*?

"Is he alone?" Rainert asked.

"Noooo . . . She's with him. Mia."

No more Avalon agents, then. Mia was Tiernay's girlfriend, the museum reproductionist from Boston. Apparently, they'd found time for a little tryst.

"What are we going to do?" Vanessa whispered, frantic. "He's right *there*!"

"Right there" was between them and the quickest exit, and Rainert again discreetly tracked the location of the security guards.

Reviewing his options, Rainert realized the surest way to get out of this mess would be akin to yelling fire in a crowded theater. Messy, but effective.

"Stay with me, and when I tell you to run, you run. Got that?"

She nodded, her skin shiny with perspiration.

"Smile. You need to look calm, simply another shopper grazing the Harrods acres."

The smile she gave him wasn't entirely convincing, but it would have to do. "We're going to walk right past him toward the street exit. Hold on to my arm and don't let go."

"I won't."

"Trust me?" Rainert asked, smiling.

Anger flashed in her eyes. "Of course not, but I don't have much of a choice, do I?"

"True," he said blithely and then turned and walked toward Will Tiernay.

Rainert didn't know this agent and had no idea how dangerous Tiernay might be, but he marked the man's face in his memory. If he were to deliver this Tiernay to Vulaj's kin—if not today, then some other time—that might get them off his back.

Rainert could feel Vanessa trembling, trying to pull away as they came closer to Tiernay. "Stop that," he murmured. "You're free. You have every right to be here. Show it to them. Show it to everyone."

It seemed to help; her shoulders straightened and she quit dragging her heels. He wasn't sure which of the women in the department was Tiernay's girlfriend and asked, "Which one is your old friend?"

"She's back by the pillar," Vanessa whispered, and he didn't miss the quaver in her voice.

A quick glance showed him a pretty, slender woman with a lot of dark hair, wearing a red T-shirt. Earthy, gypsylike, and not quite what he would have expected of the conservative-appearing Tiernay.

A few feet more, and Vanessa's hands tightened on his arm, her nails digging once again into his muscles. He ignored the pain, keeping his attention on Tiernay, who was comparing two ties against a shirt: one a navy tie with a chevron print and the other a lighter gray satin with a subtle stripe.

"The navy one is a better choice," Rainert said

as they walked past, then added, "I'd buy that one."

Tiernay smiled as he looked up. "Thanks, I—"

His eyes widened, and as he said, "Sonofabitch!" Rainert bellowed, "Bomb! This man has a bomb! Terrorist! Run, run!"

He dragged Vanessa with him while the entire men's department erupted in a churning, screaming panic as shoppers stampeded for the exit. Security guards flew past them, heading in the opposite direction toward Tiernay.

"Oh, my God," Vanessa gasped, looking back.

"Keep running," Rainert ordered coldly and steered her toward the door, ruthlessly shoving through the terrified throng. Someone nearby fell with a high-pitched scream, but he didn't stop, didn't care. He risked a quick glance backward only once, gratified to see his heavy-handed plan had worked: Tiernay was on the floor, buried beneath a pile of uniforms as the wild-haired woman, shouting in anger, was restrained by several others.

Outside he continued to move fast, knowing he didn't have much time. They'd have to clear out of the hotel, and then he'd have to make a few phone calls. Dammit, he still had work to do in London; this was going to cause all sorts of unwelcome complications.

"That was brilliant!" Vanessa exclaimed.

Her exultant shout reminded him of her presence, and he was surprised to see the sparkle of laughter in her eyes and bright spots of color on her cheeks.

Quite pretty, really. In her own way.

"Simply *brilliant*," she repeated. "I never would've thought of that. Do you think they killed him?"

The eagerness in her voice also surprised him. His meek little kitten was rather bloodthirsty.

"Keep quiet! And no, it's unlikely he's hurt, but he'll be stewing in jail for at least a few hours. When he gets out, they'll be looking for us, so we need to leave London now." Still amused by her response, he said, "And thank you for the compliment. It helps to be able to think fast."

"I loved it! Did you see the look on his face? Bastard—I hope they hurt him anyway." She glanced up as they hurried to the tube station. "From here on out, I won't doubt your word, Rainert."

"I'm flattered." Oddly, he was; as if he'd needed to prove something to this woman, and he had no idea why. "Stick with me, and I'll show you what it's really like to be free."

# Chapter Twenty-one

*Saturday, Dallas*

Claudia met her contact at a small ice cream parlor in downtown Dallas late in the afternoon. If Philly in August was hot, Texas was hellish.

The contact was an impeccably dressed youngish Asian-American named Jeff Chu, who worked for a major insurance agency. He didn't tell her which one; she didn't ask—and didn't care. Most of her clients were insurance carriers. A number of them had long ties with Ben Sheridan, and it was a beneficial alliance. He charged them a lot to find wayward art and collectibles, but that was still cheaper than settling a claim for millions of dollars.

"I never thought about churches having insurance. You'd think faith in God or something would handle all that," Claudia said, slurping up the dregs of her malt.

"Don't be flip, Ms. Cruz. This is serious business."

"It's pretty much routine for me. You just tell me how many churches were robbed and what's gone missing, and I'll take it from there."

Chu slid a half dozen fat, file-size envelopes toward her. "All the information you'll need is here. Contact me if you have any questions or need additional information. Otherwise, I don't expect to hear from you until you've found the missing relics." He stood. "Good day, Ms. Cruz."

Claudia watched him leave, walking like his boxer shorts were stuffed full of porcupine quills, and shook her head. Not just unfriendly but rude.

Or maybe she'd been a little rude herself. It was hard to be enthusiastic on only a few hours of sleep. All that frantic sex and operating at full speed had caught up with her, and, despite the lengthy nap on the plane, she needed to crawl into bed and sleep away the rest of the day.

Her gaze fell to the packets on the table. Ugh, paperwork—and lots of it. Not her favorite part of the job. If she tried to read all that right now, it would only put her to sleep.

She checked the time on her cell phone, wondering if she should try Vincent again. Her first call had bounced to voice mail. She'd left a message that she'd call him back tonight, so she should do exactly that. The last thing she wanted was to go all clingy on him.

Slipping the phone back into her pocket, she let

out a huff. She already missed Vincent something terrible, a sure sign that she was getting too emotional
over him. Maybe this little break *was* a good idea. It'd
help her think over the situation without his distracting nearness—and her crazy need to jump his bones
given the slightest opportunity.

Again, she eyed the monster pile of papers. Whether
it put her to sleep or not, she had to read it over. She
grabbed the files and headed to her rental car, grimac-
ing as the heat blasted her outside the shop.

As she left the parking lot, she tried to remember
when she'd last been in Dallas. It had been a long time,
for sure. She didn't have a lot of fond memories of the
city after what had gone down here, and she had no
reason to come here now that her family had moved
outside the city.

She was tempted to drive to the Dallas *barrio* where
she'd grown up, to revisit the Tex-Mex culture she'd
known for so much of her life, but in the end she
headed toward the highway, driving away from downtown and its unique skyline: a self-conscious huddle of
skyscrapers smack in the middle of what she'd always
sworn was the flattest land in all the United States.

Heading south on 45, she lowered the windows and
let the wind blast through her hair. Her family lived in
the tiny town of Bellefleur, and now was as good a time
as any for a quick surprise visit.

The town was home to a largely blue-collar Mexican-

American population. No McMansions here, only boxy little houses popular during the sixties and seventies, showing their age but still well-tended. It might not be much, but it was better than the poorest parts of Dallas. If nothing else, her job with Avalon was helping her to keep her family in safer neighborhoods.

She pulled up to a drab green ranch and parked under the carport awning. The grass needed mowing, the concrete on the front porch could stand some patching, and toys and small bikes littered the lawn. But the flower gardens ringing the house were impeccably tended.

Her grandmother Consuela sat on a lawn chair on the porch shelling fresh peas, each little round green pea making a *ping* as it hit the big metal bowl between her bare feet. After Claudia's grandfather died two years ago, Granny Consuela had moved in with her parents. She wore a flower-print tee and a long, baggy skirt that emphasized her frailness. The old lady was squinting at Claudia's rental car as she pulled up, trying to see who was driving such a nice, new vehicle.

"*Abuelita!*" Claudia grinned, waving, as she got out of the car. "Surprise visit!"

Her grandmother grinned back—Claudia was delighted to see that someone had finally persuaded her to buy new dentures—and motioned her over to sit beside her. The old woman spoke just enough English to get by, and now she let loose with a rapid string of Spanish.

"Whoa, slow down," Claudia protested, laughing, as

she took a seat in the other lawn chair. "I speak English most of the time these days, remember? I'm a little rusty."

"You don't forget something like that," her grandmother said, her tone frosty.

"I didn't say I forgot, only that I have to get my head and ears used to it again. There's a difference."

"You should have called ahead to let us know you were coming."

"Yes, but you know how my work is: sometimes I don't know where I'll be until I'm there."

Granny Consuela shook her head, long gray braids swishing back and forth. "Crazy life. Crazy, crazy."

Not in the mood for a disapproving lecture on her work, Claudia quickly changed the subject. "Where's everyone?"

"This is why you should have called. Your mother and father are in the city. Tía Adela is in the hospital. She has a bad heart, you know."

No, Claudia didn't know. "Oh. I'm sorry to hear that."

"Bah, she's a tough old woman, like me. She'll be with us awhile longer yet."

"How come you're not visiting, too?"

"Your tío Manny took me to see her yesterday. Those hospital rooms are so small, it's easier to take turns. His wife left him, you know."

"What?" Claudia asked, startled. "Who?"

"Fabiana, Manny's wife. She left him. He's a good boy. Too bad about that, yes?"

"Yes," Claudia said automatically. She'd forgotten the way all the little dramas constantly played out like this in the "real" world. Funny, how she could miss even something so mundane.

Without warning, the old woman dumped a pile of pea pods on Claudia's lap. "A good price on peas at the market today. I'm going to freeze some of them," she said.

They sat in a companionable silence, shelling peas to the accompaniment of traffic and the muffled sounds of music and TV from the neighboring houses. Claudia tried not to think what this was doing to her manicure. A rush of screaming, laughing children came running down the street, waved at them, then veered around a corner of the next house. After a while, their shrieks and laughter faded.

"The Iturbide family put in a pool. I think maybe they are having second thoughts about that." Her grandmother pointed at Claudia's knees. "So what happened to you? Somebody beat you up in this crazy job you have?"

"No, I fell down."

The old woman snorted. "Looks like you fell down very fast and very hard."

Claudia grinned. "It's a long story, but I'm fine."

"How is that nice young man you work for? The one who helped out your grandfather and me?"

Nice young man? Well, Sheridan *was* a man. One out of three wasn't bad. "He's fine. Busy making money, I'm sure."

"Are you working around here, then?"

Claudia nodded. "I may be around the Dallas and Houston areas for a while, on and off. It seems someone's been breaking into churches and stealing reliquaries and other things."

"No!" Her grandmother hastily made the sign of the cross. "Stealing from churches! What is this world coming to? I don't even listen to the news anymore. It just scares me. I stay with my game shows."

"There are days when it seems nothing good ever happens, *Abuelita*."

"What's some thief going to do with church things? TVs and cars I understand, but bones, bits of old cloth, or vestments?" Her grandmother shook her head, a look of disgust drawing together the many seams and wrinkles of her face. "God will cut them down for that, you'll see."

"Fine by me if He does. It'll make my job a lot easier."

More peas pinged into the bowl, then her grandmother sent her a penetrating look. "Have you been going to Mass?"

Damn; she should've seen that one coming.

"When I get the chance," Claudia said.

Her grandmother heaved a dramatic sigh, clearly not fooled. "And still not married, I see. I would like great-grandchildren."

"You have twelve already!"

"You think I can't find room in my heart for more?"

Claudia managed not to scowl or roll her eyes. "Of

course not, *Abuelita*. Stop trying to make me feel guilty. You know I hate that."

"You're a good girl," Granny Consuela said, reaching over to pat Claudia's hand. "You take good care of your family. That's important. We worry about you, though. Your mother would like to see you find a nice man to settle down with. Babies or no, she worries that you are lonely. Your father agrees. If you have to put yourself in such crazy work, you should at least have a husband around to help take care of you."

If Claudia thought it would do any good, she'd have reminded her grandmother that she could take care of herself. But Granny came from a different generation.

"I did meet a nice man recently."

"This is very good news! What kind of work does he do?"

"He's an FBI agent."

"FBI!" Granny Consuela rapidly crossed herself again, and then once more for good measure.

"He's not a border agent, *Abuelita*. His work is the same as mine—going after people who steal art and collectibles."

"Aha! Then you have a lot in common. This *is* very good news."

"Well, it's not like we're getting married or anything. We just met. I like him, but work is going to keep us busy. That's always the hard part."

"Work, work, work. . . . All you young girls these days,

it's all you worry about. Work is good, but you need to be good to yourself, too. And remember, a good man is hard to find." Granny Consuela paused. "So . . . is he a good man?"

"They don't get much better than him," Claudia said with feeling—and realized with dismay that the real reason she'd come to visit was that she wanted to talk about Vincent. Just talk, to anybody who would lend an understanding ear.

Her mother might have been more sympathetic—and a little less set in the old ways—but her grandmother could make a good sounding board, too.

"If he's a good man, then you should keep him."

"It's not that easy, *Abuelita*."

"Yes it is, if you want it enough. Your problem, Claudia, is you still don't know what you want. A troubling thing, in a woman as old as you are."

"I'm not *that* old." Exasperated, Claudia accidentally shot a few peas over the top of the bowl and down the porch steps, where they were lost in the weedy grass. "And besides, it's not the same as when—"

"I know you girls are different today. It's a bigger world than when I was your age, but some things do not change. You find someone who is for you, and you stay with them. You make it work. Maybe it's hard, but you make it work."

The words—and her grandmother's firm tone—rang true. Claudia sighed and sat back, tossing away a pile of empty pea pods. "I'm trying, *Abuelita*. It's just that . . . it's not easy for me, you know?"

"You always were a very distrustful child."

"I think I prefer the term *solitary*," Claudia protested, a little stung. "I preferred to do things on my own terms, and everybody else was into group-this, group-that, and they got mad at me for not wanting to go along."

"Yes, but sometimes you could have done it your way, and other times do what others asked of you. There's no shame in meeting someone in the middle."

"I do have a hard time with compromise," Claudia admitted, grabbing another handful of pods. Silence gathered again, except for peas pinging in the bowl, until she said, "How do you know if it's real? What you feel for someone . . . that it's real?"

Granny Consuela stared at her. "Well, what else would it be?"

Discussing specifics of sex, lust, and love was not what Claudia intended, even if her grandmother had given birth to eight children and surely knew what transpired between a man and a woman.

"Well, sometimes when you first meet someone, you get carried away by the moment. You're not really thinking with . . . your head."

"Ah. *Those* feelings." Her grandmother sat back and waggled her gray eyebrows as Claudia laughed. "Yes, they are nice, but nicer yet when there's also respect and affection. If you respect this man, if you care for him, you can build something more from that."

"You make it sound so easy."

"It can be." Her grandmother popped several raw peas into her mouth. "Sometimes, it's not. We all have that kind of trouble, not knowing if we make the right choices. Did you think it would be any different for you?"

Well, this was a new low: having your *grandmother* tell you that you're acting like a whiny, melodramatic brat and complicating matters more than necessary.

"No, *Abuelita*. I don't think I deserve any special treatment. But I was hoping you'd take pity on me and spill the secrets of the male universe."

Granny Consuela grinned. "Here's a secret: men are easier to manage when they get older. You don't have to shake a broom at them or threaten to whack them nearly as often."

Claudia laughed, remembering her grandmother shaking a broom at her grandfather. A lot.

"And I have faith that you can work out this man trouble on your own." Her grandmother looked down, surprised. "No more peas. We made short work of that, yes?"

"Glad I could help, but it's time for me to head back out."

"You can't stay?"

"No time. I could only make time for a quick visit today, but I'll come by again as soon as I can."

"Call ahead next time."

"I will, I promise. Tell *Mami* I was here, okay?"

"You should stay for dinner, tell her yourself."

"I really can't. I have a lot of work to catch up on, and—" Her cell phone started vibrating. "Hold on. I've got a call."

She pulled out her phone and smiled when she saw Vincent's number. "Hey, you. Did you get my message?"

"Yeah. Thanks for letting me know you arrived safely."

Just hearing his voice stirred a delicious little tingle, which she quickly squashed. One should *not* feel such tingles while sitting with an eagle-eyed grandmother.

"But I also wanted to let you know they found your buddy Digger Brody."

"Alive?"

"Yup. The cops had hauled him in on a drunk and disorderly."

"I'm shocked, I tell you. Shocked."

"You still want to talk to him?"

"Absolutely." She glanced at her watch, already justifying the trip in her mind. She would've spent what was left of today and most of tomorrow in her hotel room reading files, and she could just as easily do that on a plane. "Tomorrow morning, I'll get the earliest available flight back to Philly. Will you have any trouble keeping him in lockup until I get there?"

"I'll make sure he's going nowhere. But won't you catch hell from your boss for coming back here?"

She heard his surprise. "Not if I make the trip short enough, and it's for an ongoing case. It's not like I'm returning just for—" She cut herself off. While Granny barely spoke English, she had no trouble understanding it. "I have to behave. I'm here with my grandma."

"Your *grandma?*" Vincent sounded startled.

"Why so surprised?"

"Not surprised, just . . . it's nice of you to visit your grandma. That's very sweet. Say hello to her for me."

Grinning a little sheepishly, Claudia glanced at her grandmother sitting beside her all but vibrating with curiosity, and said, "Vincent says hello, *Abuelita.*"

"Is this Vincent your new boyfriend?" When Claudia nodded, Granny Consuela smiled and said, "He sounds like a good man, to think of an old lady like me. You tell him I said that."

Grin widening, Claudia said, "*Abuelita* said to tell you that you're a good boy."

"No she didn't; I heard what she said and I know enough Spanish to tell the difference between *hombre* and *niño*. But I'm flattered. I know how hard it is to impress grandmas. They're a brutal bunch." She could hear the humor in his voice. "All right, then. I gotta run. Give me a call when your plane gets in. I'll pick you up at the terminal, and we can go have a little fun with Digger Brody."

# Chapter Twenty-two

*Saturday, Seattle*

Ron Levine's latest update about the missing guide in Peru—still missing, and with every hour less likely to be found alive—had left Ben in a foul mood.

Lately he'd been finding it harder to shake the encroaching frustration. Pacing up and down his office, past the wall of windows, he tried to work out his tensions. When he heard the door open, he spun so fast that Ellie took a step back in surprise.

"What?" he snapped.

"Ben, I've got Mia Dolan, Will's fiancée, on the phone, and you need to talk to her right now. Will's in jail in London, something about him threatening to bomb Harrods and —"

"He threatened to bomb *Harrods*?" Ben interrupted, incredulous, as he strode toward his desk. "Why? Didn't he like the selection of cuff links? What the hell was—"

"Ben!" Ellie's uncharacteristic sharpness stopped him short. "Mia says von Lahr and Vanessa Sharpton started the trouble."

Ben snatched up the phone handset. "Mia, this is Sheridan. What's going on?"

"Thank you for speaking with me. Will said I had to get this information to you immediately because he's going to be in custody for a while and he couldn't tell you himself."

"You did the right thing. Is he all right?" Terrorism threats were taken very seriously these days. Tiernay was lucky if he hadn't been beaten within an inch of his life.

"Security was rough on him, but he's okay." Ben could hear the trembling in her voice.

"What exactly happened?"

"I didn't see everything. A man started shouting about bombs and terrorists, and next thing I knew people were screaming and running all around. I looked for Will and saw him struggling with the security officers. He was trying to explain, but they wouldn't listen. They kept shouting at him to get down, and they pushed him to the floor. God, I thought they were going to kill him. I've never been so frightened in my life."

Considering only a few short months ago she'd been held captive in a building rigged to explode, that said a lot. "Are *you* all right? Did they take you into custody?"

"No . . . well, I had to go with the constables, but after they searched Will and me and didn't find any bombs, they let me go. I'm not sure why they're still being so difficult, but Will thinks they're just being cautious and I shouldn't be too upset about it."

"Did he explain the situation to the constables?"

She sighed. "He tried as best he could. He said it was this von Lahr who yelled about bombs to get Will into trouble. They didn't believe him. I suppose it sounds a bit far-fetched."

"You've done everything you can. I'll take it from here." Ben hesitated. "By the way, did either Sharpton or von Lahr see you? Think carefully, Mia. It's very important."

"I don't think so," she answered after a moment. "But I can't be positive about that. All my attention was focused on Will."

"Can you verify it was Vanessa Sharpton?"

"No, sorry. By the time I realized what was happening and why, they'd disappeared. But Will is positive it was Vanessa. He had a good look, and there's no way he could've made a mistake about this."

"Get on a plane back to the States right away. I have associates in London who'll get Will out of custody as soon as possible. In the meantime, you need to take yourself out of the picture. Do you understand?"

"Yes. Will already told me the same thing. I'll be on the next available flight to Boston."

After disconnecting, Ben stared at the phone for a moment.

Von Lahr. What was that sonofabitch doing in London? He was well-known by British law officials, so it was an incredible risk for him to be there, especially if he was hauling around a woman who was supposed to be dead.

Ben squeezed his eyes shut briefly. Jesus, this was going to be a mess, and by now von Lahr had certainly hightailed it out of the city.

Of course, that's what von Lahr would expect him to think. Frowning, Ben looked up. "Did you already log that call from Mia?"

Ellie looked puzzled. "Of course, it's the—"

"I know. SOP. It's okay." He mulled over his options, few as they were, then said, "I'll take care of this myself. Please hold all calls until I say otherwise."

He waited until she'd closed the door behind her before pulling up his email program and swore softly when he saw the message already waiting for him.

"That was quick. Don't trust me to behave, do you?" he muttered and clicked it open.

As always, it was short and to the point:

> You will not go to London. Until we determine how VL was able to find WT, we will assume this was an attempt to draw you into the open. The encounter with WT may have been accidental,

*but we feel this is unlikely. We will take care of the matter. You need do nothing on your end.*

Ben understood the cautious reasoning behind the email order, even if he didn't like it.

Had Tiernay been careless enough to allow von Lahr to tail him? That was unlikely, as unlikely as an accidental meeting in one of the world's most exclusive department stores.

Then again, both von Lahr and Tiernay were fastidious dressers. If they were to accidentally encounter each other, it *would* be over a rack of expensive clothes.

He reread the email message. Orders were orders, but this was bullshit. If he wanted to go to London, he'd go. She couldn't fire him. If von Lahr was trying to draw him out and start a fight, fine by him. It was a long time coming.

Decision made, he quickly called several acquaintances in London, one of whom promised to get Will Tiernay out of jail—and then keep him out of any more trouble until Ben could have a chat with him. Ordinarily Ben would cut Tiernay a little slack with this recent habit of mixing work with his personal life—the man was on a private project *and* newly engaged—but any encounter with von Lahr was a game changer.

Once he finished up with Tiernay, Ben intended to take a little more personal interest in the hunt for von Lahr.

When he'd finished his calls, he jabbed the intercom button. "Ellie, I'm going to London."

"Okay, I'll call and get your plane ready. Would you like me to come along or have Shaunda—"

"No, I'll be going alone this time."

Silence, then, "All right. Anything else? What about the situation in Peru?"

"I'm not planning on being away for long, and I trust Levine to take care of it. If there's an emergency, you know how to contact me." He frowned as he recalled his conversation with Mia Dolan. "I'm also going to need someone to do a babysitting job in Boston on the QT for a few weeks."

"Hmmm, the field's a little thin. I'm not sure if we have anyone to—"

"Can you spare Shaunda?"

Another silence, this one slightly longer. "Yes. I can always ask Nolan to help me out if things get crazy. What do you want Shaunda to do in Boston?"

"I'll get the details to you later today. For now, I want her to keep on eye on Mia Dolan, but to keep quiet about it. No need to worry anybody yet; I just want to know if someone takes a sudden interest in Mia. Von Lahr's identified her and knows she's with Tiernay. Von Lahr's also with Vanessa Sharpton. I don't know what's up with that, and I don't like it. I've got a gut feeling we haven't seen the end of the fallout from the Vulaj incident."

"You're worried Vulaj's people might use Mia to get to Will?"

"Something like that."

"Don't worry. Shaunda will take care of things."

Ben disconnected and sat back with a sigh. It was his responsibility to anticipate these situations and intervene before things went veering out of control. Of course, it would help if some of his operatives were a little less impulsive.

Frowning, he hit the intercom again. "And Ellie? Give Claudia a call tomorrow and make sure she's in Dallas."

# Chapter Twenty-three

*Sunday, Philadelphia*

By the time her plane touched down, two hours late, Claudia was sick and tired of crowded airports, crowded planes, and crappy coffee. Get on a plane, get off a plane. Turn around and get on another one, get off . . .

She'd be boarding a plane for Dallas at the crack of dawn tomorrow, before Ben could find out she was in Philly and chew her ass out.

On the positive side, at least she'd have a few more hours with Vincent.

Speaking of her FBI Man, where was he? He'd promised to meet her at the gate, and she didn't see any familiar black suit and skinny tie.

"Claudia! Over here!"

She turned and spotted him waving at her. Grabbing her luggage, she hurried toward him with a smile and an extra bounce in her step.

Vincent didn't even give her time to say hello. He

wrapped her in his arms and pulled her close for a long, hard kiss that left her gasping.

"Wow. If you kiss me like that after I've been gone only a day, I can't wait to see what you do when it's been a couple weeks!"

He turned red, which she found utterly enchanting: men who blushed were too sexy for words. He cleared his throat and said, "I guess that would be one perk of a relationship like ours. Sex would always be phenomenal."

That he spoke so matter-of-factly about their relationship scared her as much as it thrilled her. "That's one way of looking at it. So where's your car? Are we heading right over to talk to Brody? Have you run into any trouble with our cross-dressing stalker babes?"

Vincent blinked, then grinned as he grabbed her luggage. "Car's parked. Yes, we're heading over immediately to talk to Brody, since we're both short on time. No, I've had no more stalker trouble. I'm hoping that's the general trend."

"I'm still really worried about you, Vincent."

"And I keep telling you not to be." He looked down suddenly, frowning. "What the hell do you have in here? It weighs a freakin' ton."

"Files on the church thefts. My contact is, to put it kindly, very thorough."

"You look great, by the way," he said, his gaze skimming along her body. "How are the knees and elbows?"

"Fine, if a little sore and itchy. And you . . . you look

like you always look." She winked at him. "Totally attackable. I'd use a more descriptive word, but we're in public."

"If we're lucky, maybe you can squeeze in time for an attack or two before you fly back out."

He was grinning, open and honest like a kid, and it made her feel a dozen kinds of sexy-sweet-hot things, along with a simple need to just hug him.

So she did, taking him by surprise and nearly tripping them up, since he was juggling her luggage. He hugged her back fiercely and landed a kiss on her temple as he said softly, "Missed you, too."

For a terrible minute she was afraid she'd sniffle, but she managed to get her unfamiliar, alarming emotions back under control and followed him out of the terminal without making a fool of herself.

Once they were heading downtown, Vincent said, "I don't think you can keep up a schedule like this; you're going to run yourself ragged if you're not careful."

"You sound like my grandmother," she huffed, though she was strangely pleased by his fussing over her. "Don't worry about me, I know my limits."

He glanced at her, then back at traffic. "I do worry, like you worry about me. Get used to it. And don't forget that you're not the only one capable of hopping on a plane."

Claudia smiled. "Noted and filed away for future trysting."

After a brief silence, he asked, "What were you doing at your grandma's?"

"I went to see my parents, since it's been a while. My grandmother lives with them. They weren't home, just Grandma. So we shelled a few peas, talked a little girl talk. Nothing too exciting."

"Sounds like you had a nice time, though."

"It's always good to see family." She looked over at him. "Anything new on our case? Or anything else I should know about Brody?"

Vincent grinned. "I laid out our theory to my supervisor, and he agrees we've nailed it down. We're still trying to ID the photos from the surveillance data. That's been slow going."

"But no more flowers on your front porch?"

"Nope. Seriously, Claudia, they won't be back. It's too dangerous, and they've made their point that I'm not infallible." He paused, focusing on a quick lane change. "As for Brody, I've got no more than I told you yesterday. There was a fight and the cops arrested nearly half the bar, Brody included."

"I want to ask the questions."

"Go for it. He's yours, not mine."

"You're welcome to try and scare him, if you want."

Vincent laughed. "That probably won't be needed after you're done with the poor bastard." He glanced at her. "Do you think he knows something?"

"Pretty sure he does. I have a feeling there's more

behind his seeing one of our girls in the alley by chance." She spotted the city building up ahead. "And we'll find out soon enough. You know, I was hoping I wouldn't have to see the inside of this place again for a very long time."

"Sorry. If it helps any, I still feel guilty about that."

"Don't. I had it coming. Pride goes before a fall, and all that shit."

He eyed the simple cotton shirt she was wearing with her pants. "Gun?"

"Safely locked away in a Texas hotel. And you?"

"Still accessorized."

Good. "Then we're covered," she said.

Vincent had to turn over his gun before they could enter the interrogation room, where Donald "Digger" Brody waited for them, handcuffed and slumped in a chair, looking bored and badly hungover.

When Claudia and Vincent walked in, Brody sat up and she noted that he also sported a nasty black eye. And, dear God, did he stink!

"Must've been some fight," she said as the door closed behind her. "I'm assuming you got a punch or two in yourself before the cops showed up."

"Shit, yeah." Brody stared at her for a moment. "What happened to you?"

"I was running and fell down."

The man smirked, then glanced at Vincent. "Okay, her I know. You, I don't."

"Special Agent DeLuca, FBI," Vincent said tonelessly and held up his ID.

"FBI? What the hell? All's I did was drink a little too much and get in a fight. I didn't even *start* the fight. What's with the FBI?"

"I'm with her," Vincent answered, taking a seat. "Don't mind me."

Brody snorted. "Don't mind a Fed. Right." Then, to Claudia, "What you want with me now? And why bring this guy in here? You trying to bully me again and—"

"I think you know what I want." Claudia sat. "Why didn't you show up at our meeting, Brody?"

He shrugged. "Changed my mind."

"Why?"

"Not a crime to change my mind, is it?"

"I didn't say it was, I just asked a simple question."

"I don't have to answer any questions. I know my rights."

"I'm not a cop, remember? I'm not here to charge you with anything. I don't have the authority for that."

Brody inclined his head toward Vincent. "He does."

"But he's not here investigating you, either. He's here so that *I* can be here, asking questions. Not a cop, and not a lawyer, see?" She sighed and leaned across the table toward him, trying to breathe through her mouth. "Brody, like I said the last time, let's just cut to the chase, okay? You didn't intend to show up, did you? How much did they pay you to lure me out into the open so they could get a good look at me?"

"Don't know what you're talking about."

"The night Little Otis was arrested for assault, you were down by Champion and Stone meeting with the woman who had the box. It wasn't an accidental encounter at all. Was it a business deal, or were you already planning on setting me up?"

Brody laughed. "That's some imagination you got. You should write books."

Claudia glanced at Vincent. "Brody, the women ripping off galleries—you know who they are, and I want you to tell me their names. I already assured you I'm not going to cause you any trouble over this, and Special Agent DeLuca is currently inclined to agree with me. However, these two women have shown a disturbing interest in Mr. DeLuca, and by not talking to me, you're endangering the safety of a federal law enforcement agent. I guarantee that if anything happens to Mr. DeLuca, the FBI will come after you. Unfortunately for you, I'll have gotten to you first."

She sat back, crossing her legs and smiling. "You see, I'm not a cop. What I am is kinda like a mercenary. You know what mercenaries do, right? You're small-time, Brody. You don't want to get tangled up in something that involves the FBI. You know the people you work for won't like that."

After a furtive glance at Vincent, Brody slumped

back in his chair. "Fuck no, that ain't my kind of trouble. If I talk, you promise you won't get me arrested for any of this?"

"I promise."

"And him?" Brody tipped his head toward Vincent.

"If you cooperate, I'm inclined to let it go this time," he said.

It wasn't a straight yes-or-no answer, and Claudia watched Brody as he weighed his options. Several minutes passed before he repeated, "Not my kind of trouble. Yeah, I know these girls. I know their names, know what they're doing, and I know why they're interested in him."

"Smart move, Brody," Claudia said approvingly as she pulled a legal pad from her bag and clicked open her pen. "Let's start with the basics. Is it just the two of them, or are there more?"

"Just two that I know of."

"Names?"

"One's called Shai Lewis. She's tall, has light hair cut short like a man's. The other one's Candy Bartowski."

"Okay, so we've got Shai Lewis and Candy Bartowski. They're stealing lots of little bits and pieces, mostly from art galleries and antiques stores. What do you know about that?" Claudia asked.

"I know these girls like you know friends of a friend of a friend, that's all. They asked me to help 'em find buyers if they could provide a steady supply of merchandise. I expressed an interest, as long as they weren't stupid about it. Part of what I do is to make sure nothing causes trouble for the people who pay me, understand? To move that kind of product, in that market, you have to go through me first."

"You work for the mob." Claudia looked up from her notepad. "I know organized crime makes a fortune on stolen art, because that's *my* job. Let's get to why they're so interested in Mr. DeLuca."

"Well, first off, they wanted to sell because they needed money for a good lawyer to get Shai's brother out of jail. They were short on time, since your Mr. DeLuca over there was working on putting the brother, and a couple of his buddies, in prison for ripping off a bunch of antiques in Chicago and selling them here and over in Jersey for twice what they were worth."

Claudia glanced at Vincent, catching his frown.

"But things didn't happen fast enough, and the judge sentenced the brother, who's also Candy's boyfriend, to twelve up at Rockview," Brody continued.

"The brother's name?" Claudia asked, but it was Vincent who answered.

"Johnny Lewis. I remember the case. Straightforward theft and fence. I didn't even have to testify at the trial."

"Yeah, petty shit like that ain't worth your time, right? Too bad for you that Johnny's sister and his girl don't see it that way," Brody retorted.

In the heavy silence that followed, Claudia stared

at Vincent. "I knew it," she said tersely. "I *knew* it was more serious than some stupid game, Vincent. They want revenge."

Vincent turned to Brody. "Did you set up a meeting with Ms. Cruz so that Lewis and Bartowski could then identify her?"

Brody shrugged. "Yeah. I didn't like how things were playing out. Too hot for me, and I figured if all of you were mixing it up, nobody would be bothering with me. If they're stupid enough to fuck with FBI agents, I want none of their business. I mean that."

"Does this also mean there were no business transactions, as you call them, between the three of you?"

"Nope."

"You're sure about that? Because if you're lying, all promises are off."

"I'm sure. We'd been talking, negotiating details and all that, but then Johnny got his ass sent up to Rockview, and that was the last I'd heard from them until a few weeks ago."

"So why didn't you move anything for them?"

Brody didn't answer right away. "My associates, they keep me around because I make the business easier for them. I keep out the troublemakers and those who don't take the work seriously. I shake out the good from the bad. It also has to be worth *my* time. I wasn't convinced they were worth my time, but I was willing to give 'em a chance. Just because *they* were in a hurry don't mean I was in a hurry. I told 'em to stop fucking around with all that little crap and get me a big sale to work with. The Greek piece, that had potential. Too bad they didn't go for it earlier."

"You think selling it would've given them enough money to get Mr. Lewis off the hook?"

"Doubt it, but that wasn't my problem. They had a window of opportunity and blew it. When they told me they were going after the Fed over there, that's when I knew it was time to cut 'em loose. And that's it. Nothing more to say."

Claudia put down her pen. "All right. You answered most of my questions. I don't suppose you know where they're keeping their merchandise? Or where they're staying?"

"No idea. They kept giving me different addresses and phone numbers." Brody grinned unpleasantly. "I don't think they trust me."

"Imagine that," Claudia drawled. "Okay, how about giving me the addresses they gave you, if you can remember. Phone numbers, too."

Brody could remember only two hotel names, no room numbers. Claudia knew Vincent would check the leads out, even if they would prove to be of little help.

"I think we're done here," she said, standing. "Unless there's something else burdening your soul that you feel a need to share?"

"After you go, I don't see you ever again, right? That's the deal?"

"That's the deal, Brody. I seriously hope to never see your sorry ass again."

"That's a promise? You made a promise."

She gave a dramatic sigh. "Pinkie-swear, I promise it."

As she headed for the door, Brody asked, "And you?"

"Me?" Vincent said. "I never made any promises, asshole."

# Chapter Twenty-four

"I don't like this. At all." Claudia snapped her seat belt buckle with more force than necessary.

"I know."

Vincent started the car, its engine rumbling louder in the confines of the ramp where they'd parked, and wished he knew how to make her believe once and for all that she didn't need to worry. But in all fairness, if their positions were reversed, he knew he'd be acting the same way.

"So what are you going to do about it?"

"For starters, I'm going to make a few calls before everyone heads home for the day."

He called his office first, relaying the information they'd learned, asking the agent on the other end to pull up whatever she could find on the two women. Then he called his police liaison, Matherson, and repeated everything to voice mail since the detective didn't answer.

Then he got back on the phone to his office. "Hi, Annie, it's me again. I forgot to ask if you could call the warden over at Rockview for me. Let him know that I'd like him to get in touch with me at the office tomorrow morning, or as soon as possible, and that I'll need to have a long talk with an inmate named John Adam Lewis, who began serving his sentence back in April."

After he'd disconnected, Vincent shifted toward Claudia and wasn't surprised to find her watching him with a frown.

"That's it? Vincent, these two women are not—"

"I've done my part," he interrupted, his tone terse. "Now it's up to the police to do theirs. We have names, and we'll soon have decent photo IDs. It's *over* for them, Claudia. If these women are still in the area, it's only a matter of time before the cops pick them up. Until then, I promise to be even more cautious than usual. That's going to have to be good enough for you."

Her expression, even her body language, reflected the struggle to back off and trust him. "This is hard for me, okay? I don't usually work with a partner, and we've that going here, among other things. And you're not used to living with this kind of trouble. I don't mean to imply you're not strong enough or brave enough, or any of that crap," she said, staring straight ahead at the concrete wall rather than at him. "I don't . . . I don't know what to do or think."

Vincent took a deep breath to steady his temper.

"Maybe I don't face high-risk situations on a regular basis, but I *am* a trained FBI agent, not some car salesman or tax accountant."

At that, she met his gaze, then reached over hesitantly and brushed her fingers along his face. "It's just that I want to be *here*, for *you*, and it feels like a betrayal to get on that plane again."

Vincent squeezed her hand, smiling faintly. "Isn't that laying it on a little thick? It's not a betrayal, it's your job. You need to go back to your assignment, and I need to get busy with my own caseload."

"True." She looked away again. "People are depending on me . . . not to mention *paying* me. Still, I'll feel so much better when those two are locked up."

Her cell phone chirped, and she pulled it from her pocket, checked the number, and grimaced. "Uh-oh. Sorry, I have to take this one. It's Ben."

Vincent had already guessed as much from the flash of alarm in her eyes.

"No, no, Ben, you're right . . . I'm not in Dallas at the moment. I'll be there soon." A pause. "No, soon as in tomorrow. I'm in Philadelphia, and I—"

Vincent frowned. While he couldn't clearly hear every word, Sheridan's tone of voice left no doubt about his displeasure. It was bad enough getting chewed out by your boss, even worse when it happened in front of your boyfriend.

Claudia concisely explained why she'd come back,

and while it seemed perfectly reasonable to Vincent, Sheridan must've felt otherwise.

"It *is* important information, and now we know— Yes, yes, I agree the locals can handle it from this point, but—"

Sheridan cut her off again, and she glanced at Vincent, frowning. "I've already made plans to fly out first thing tomorrow. I have both situations under control. I can take care of me. You just take care of that other problem. Right. I understand." She glanced at Vincent again. "*Yes*. Okay. Bye."

She tossed the phone on the seat beside her. "I *hate* it when he yells at me. It makes me feel like when I was a little kid and got caught doing something wrong and my mom and dad would look so disappointed. I don't know how he does that. I mean, he doesn't even have any kids to practice on! And I have no idea how he knew you were with me. It creeps me out sometimes, that he always *knows*."

Not sure what to say, Vincent put the car in gear, backed out of the parking stall, and headed for the exit.

"He told me I'm off the case," Claudia said once they were on the street, her voice still tight with anger. "It's the Art Squad's from here on out."

"I can't believe I'm saying this, but he's right. You've been a lot of help to me, but there's not much you can do from here on out."

"I know, I *know*!"

Vincent drove through city traffic, keeping quiet and letting her temper cool. When he thought she looked calmer, he said, "So, where are we going? I could drive around Philly for the rest of the day, but seems to me we could make better use of our time."

"I'm still really mad. For the record."

"I see that."

"I'm mad at me, at Ben, at you, at pretty much *everything*." She nodded. "Yessiree, a genuine hissy fit."

He suppressed the urge to laugh. "And is it making you feel any better?"

"No. All it's doing is getting me all worked up and frustrated." She scowled. "Sex might help with that."

His body eagerly agreed. "Anger sex, huh? Could be fun."

She smiled ruefully. "No matter what I throw at you, you take it, and somehow turn it around and make it better. You're way too good for me."

"That's debatable." Vincent switched lanes and headed toward his place. "I heard you say there's trouble. I hope it's nothing serious."

"Oh, it's trouble, all right. You'll love this." Claudia turned to him, and he didn't miss the glint of ironic humor in her dark eyes. "Ben's in London because von Lahr's popped up there."

"London? That's pretty damn ballsy. What's von Lahr done now?"

"I didn't get all the details, but apparently he ran

into Will Tiernay, there was something about yelling 'Bomb!' in a crowded department store, Tiernay got busted by the locals, and von Lahr slipped away."

"I'm beginning to understand why you people hate this guy so much."

"The kicker isn't so much that he got away—we've gotten kinda used to that part—but that he ran off with Vanessa Sharpton. Remember her?"

"The woman you people blew up in Boston four months ago?"

"Guess we didn't blow her up as much as we thought."

"That's not good news?"

"Not sure. Get back with me on that one later."

Vincent grinned. "Well, it's good news that Sheridan's in another country. He's less likely to call while I'm stripping off your clothes and then getting down to business on your smokin' hot body."

Grinning back, she pulled out her cell phone and pointedly turned it off.

The ride home passed in record time. Vincent barely made it inside before he was locking the door with one hand and unbuttoning her shirt with the other. Claudia quickly unbuckled his belt and slid down his zipper while kissing him, hungry and demanding and insistent.

With a groan, he lifted her up, spun, and braced her against his front door. In seconds, he'd sunk himself in her slick, welcoming flesh, shuddering from the near painful pleasure of her inner muscles tightening around him as he started thrusting.

No control this time. He couldn't hold back, already poised on the edge of release while she made high, gasping moans of pleasure as his body slammed against hers. He came fast with a low growl of pleasure and felt her follow, leaving them both shuddering. Vincent tightened his grip, keeping her from sliding down the door, and met her gaze.

"If we keep up this kind of pace," he said, still breathing hard, "I think it's gonna kill us."

"Or you'll need to get a stronger front door."

He laughed. "Feeling better?"

"Oh, yes." She licked her lips. "Thank you."

"Any time."

"How about we . . . try to get to the bed next time?"

"Okay. But just in case, you ever do it on the stairs?"

Lying in his bed with Claudia curled against him, Vincent began to drift off to sleep, lulled by the pleasant, regular sensation of her fingers lightly caressing his chest and the satisfying weight of warm, naked female skin pressed against his own.

"So what do you think they want from you?"

At her soft question, he opened his eyes. It was late, the room dark, and whenever the air conditioner cycled off, he could hear crickets chirping outside and the sound of passing cars.

"I have no idea," he said at length. "Maybe revenge of some sort, like you said."

"But in what way? I'm not getting a feel for what they're trying to accomplish beyond annoying the crap out of you."

"If that's the extent of it, they've succeeded." Even dog-tired and distracted by Claudia's nearness, he couldn't stop thinking about it either. "If what Brody told us is true, a symbolic 'fuck you' was likely part of it. Mostly, they needed to make a lot of money fast and only knew of one way to do that. I bet we'll find out they learned a few tricks from Johnny Lewis about ripping off art."

"Maybe they were even involved in some of the thefts he pulled off."

"It wouldn't surprise me at all."

"I kinda have to give them credit for the sheer nerve of stealing art to raise enough money to buy a lawyer in order to clear a guy on charges of art theft."

"That's one way of putting it. I'd say they got a cheap thrill from following me around and ripping off galleries and museums where I'd given talks. Initially they might not have been trying to get my attention. I'm thinking the focus shifted from the money to me after Lewis was sentenced."

"I don't see how stalking or threatening you is going to help this guy out. If anything, it'll get him into more trouble. Everyone will assume he's behind their plans."

"Who's to say he's not? I have a lot of questions to ask Johnny Lewis, and that's definitely one of them."

Claudia pushed herself up, meeting his gaze. "Good catch. I didn't think of that."

Lazily, he reached over and captured an errant curl, toying with it. "Seems a stretch. What were they going to do? Kidnap me and hold me for ransom? Like that would ever work out."

"I'm more worried they want to put a few bullet holes in you to make a point that you're not their favorite person." She bent, pressing a soft kiss to the side of his mouth. "One of them had the guts to follow you into a bar, Vincent. If she'd wanted to, she could've killed you right there. You wouldn't have been expecting it."

The realization chilled him, how easily he could've been shot to death over his burger and a beer. "Assaulting a federal law enforcement agent is a hell of a lot more serious than lifting a few collectibles. If Lewis behaves himself, he'll be out in a few years. Do you think they'd try something so risky rather than wait out his sentence?"

Claudia lay back down, her bare breasts distracting him all over again. "Beats me, but for whatever reason, they've taken this to a personal level. It's not logical or smart, and to be honest, that's what worries me most. People who are a little crazy aren't exactly predictable." Turning her head, she said, "I hope you're properly worried about all this."

"Absolutely."

"Good. Even though I'm worried enough for the both of us . . . and then some."

Another unwelcome thought came to him. "They also seem to have taken an interest in you. Don't forget that."

"I won't."

"Another reason to be glad you'll be in Dallas."

"True." She grinned at him. "We'd just get in each other's way here, trying to protect each other's back. Like Laurel and Hardy, but with gun fights instead of pie fights."

Vincent laughed, despite the seriousness of the moment and the fact that, in only a few hours, he'd have to drive her back to the airport. Already anticipating the loss of her comfort, of her presence beside him, he pulled her close and kissed her. When she responded with hungry eagerness, he slid his hands over her breasts. She pressed even more tightly against him, and he welcomed her smooth, warm heat, the rush of desire burning through him, chasing away the unease and the worries.

"One for the road?" he whispered against her throat.

She laughed, a deep, throaty sound that made him even harder. "Why not? Who needs sleep, anyway?"

"Why is it," Claudia said early the next morning, as Vincent pulled up to the Southwest Airlines terminal at Philadelphia International, "that the good times pass by so fast, but the hours crawl all those other times?"

"Don't know," he said. He looked tired, she thought, and worried it wasn't only because they'd passed the night shagging until they could barely move. "Things'll settle down, Claudia. We'll see each other again soon, and work through whatever needs working through."

"You'll call me?" she asked, as she opened the car door. "Keep me in the loop?"

"Of course."

She bit her lip. "I don't know when I'll get a chance to get back here."

"Don't worry about it." He gave her a quick kiss. "I'll be heading out to South Carolina soon. After that, we can make plans. Remember, it's as easy for me to get on a plane as it is for you."

Time to do the good-bye thing again—and it was harder than before, with these new, unspoken worries.

"You be careful," she ordered and didn't miss the brief flash of irritation in his eyes because she'd already said this one time too many. "Keep wearing that gun."

He nodded, then pointed his chin toward the terminal. "You better get going. We cut the timing pretty close."

Right. Go, before she said something stupid again. After a last, quick kiss, Claudia grabbed her bag and backed out of the car. He waited until she was inside before he drove away.

After passing through security, Claudia bought coffee and a donut and sat down in her gate area, wishing she could shake her persistent dread. Revenge was messy, and people with a vendetta could be alarmingly unpredictable.

In the end, it didn't matter how many times he told her not to worry. It didn't matter how often she rightfully told herself that he didn't need protecting. When she loved someone, she worried. When she loved someone, she wanted to be there when he needed her, no matter the consequences.

But she *had* to leave. In a way, this was a first and crucial test. If he couldn't believe that she trusted his intelligence, his ability and training, and his instincts for self-preservation, then their budding relationship was dead before it ever had a chance to bloom.

# Chapter Twenty-five

"So, I hear you've got another lead on the Champion and Stone break-in."

Vincent, fighting off a tension headache and pretty much losing the battle, looked up from a pile of paperwork—which he'd been working on for much of the morning while waiting for the Rockview warden to call—and nodded at Ed Cookson.

"It looks that way, yeah."

His supervisor pulled up a chair. "Want to fill me in with the condensed version?"

Vincent did, including Claudia's part in the investigation of Brody's information. Cookson raised a brow but only said, "What do you want to do about Brody?"

"Turn him loose. I can find a way to use him again, and for a bigger catch than these two."

"How are *you* feeling about all this?"

"What do you mean?"

"I mean, do you feel safe? Do you want to take some time off?"

"No, I'm fine. I want to drive up to Rockview and have a long chat with Johnny Lewis. I'm waiting for the warden to call and clear it with me."

"You could just head up there."

Vincent shook his head. "I know that guy. He's a real stickler for the proper channels, and if I show up without calling first, he'll keep me cooling my heels for as long as he dares. This way I'm saving myself the trouble."

Cookson nodded. "So the police are on top of things?"

"Yeah. Matherson's pulled picture IDs from the DMV on the two suspects, and he's issued an alert to bring them in for questioning. He's also checking last-known addresses and acquaintances. We'll have them in custody soon."

"Good job. Do you want us to keep up the watch in your neighborhood until the suspects are brought in?"

"For maybe another week or so. I'll know by then if they're still interested in me."

"You might want to wear a vest. Just to be safe."

The idea of wearing bullet-resistant body armor didn't appeal to Vincent, and not just because of the ungodly heat wave. "I could do that," he said reluctantly.

"No harm in stacking the odds in your favor." Cookson stood to leave. "So I take it you found a way to work with the woman from Sheridan's outfit."

"Yes."

Cookson waited for more, and when it didn't come, he cleared his throat. "Off the clock, I have no problems with any relationship you two develop."

"Especially since you wouldn't mind cultivating a closer connection to Sheridan?"

"Sure, why not? I'm a pragmatist, and Avalon has resources we could use. The FBI has resources Avalon could use. Consider yourself an ambassador for the cause."

As if Vincent hadn't seen that one coming. "Why do you think Sheridan would be interested?"

"That's a complicated question."

Vincent grinned. "The condensed version is good."

Cookson slipped his hands in his pockets and jangled keys and change—a habit whenever he was busy thinking. "I know enough to understand that what Sheridan wants may not be the same thing that those who fund and support him want. But what worked for Avalon a hundred years ago isn't working as well in the twenty-first century. It's more difficult to pull off the secret boys' club derring-do in view of today's technology. I think Sheridan wants to bring Avalon out of the shadows and make it a legit business. We can help with that, and I think it would be good for all parties concerned."

"Especially since they'd be subject to rules and regulations like anybody else."

"That's part of it, yes. It would also afford his people

more government protection. In Avalon's old days, all they had to worry about were knives and pistols. Now the bad guys are armed with automatic weapons, pipe bombs, and grenade launchers. Sheridan's been scaling back his operations in the Middle East for this reason. They're not an army."

It made sense, and the idea of bringing Avalon—and, by extension, Claudia's work—under tighter conditions of lawful conduct appealed to Vincent's conflicted sense of justice and fair play. If nothing else, it would make their relationship a little easier in those messy gray areas.

"What about Sheridan himself? What's your take on the man?" Vincent asked.

"Again, it's complicated." The change in Cookson's pocket jangled with a vengeance. "In his early twenties, he was heavily involved in Avalon's effort to repossess stolen art. At some point, that abruptly changed and he took control of the operations, and surprised a lot of people when he made little effort to hide that fact. I don't know why this change occurred, but it's also no secret that most everyone who's aware of his extracurricular activities knows he's not in it for the sake of the art."

Intrigued, Vincent leaned back. "So what is he in it for?"

Cookson shrugged. "I have no idea, though I've long suspected it's connected to the suspicious deaths of two

British citizens some twenty years ago. We also have conflicting reports of his part in an incident in Britain that involved multiple shooting deaths when he was only seventeen. Looks to me like the British authorities covered up something irregular about it. We also have files documenting his frequent inquiries into the unsolved murder of an Italian woman in the early nineteen forties. But, again, that was some twelve, fifteen years ago."

"Why would he be interested in any of that?" Vincent said, thinking out loud.

"Again, haven't a clue." The sudden gleam in Cookson's eyes hinted he might not be telling the truth—or, at least, not the whole truth. "If you want to look into any of it, I can arrange for that to happen."

Vincent raised a brow, understanding what his supervisor wanted. Well, why not? Having any leverage over Sheridan couldn't hurt. "I might be interested."

"I hear Italy is nice this time of the year."

"I hear Italy is nice any time of the year," Vincent said drily.

Another loud jangle of keys and change. "You could probably use a vacation anyway."

"There's a few meetings I can't reschedule and the court case in South Carolina, but after that, I might want a few days off." Vincent grinned, sitting back. "By the way, I have it on excellent authority that Rainert von Lahr was recently spotted in London."

"Really?" Cookson's brows shot upward. "How recently?"

"A couple days ago."

"I haven't heard anything about this."

"You should check with personnel in London. I know for sure he was there, and he was with Vanessa Sharpton. You'll remember her from the Boston factory incident a few months ago?"

"She's alive?" Cookson looked genuinely surprised. "And with von Lahr?" When Vincent nodded, he added, "And you know this how?"

"From Sheridan himself, via Ms. Cruz. Sheridan's in London as well. Or was; I have no idea if he's still there."

"That's very interesting." Cookson smiled grimly. "Thanks for the tip-off. Maybe we can still pick up his trail, and if von Lahr's traveling with the woman, he might be easier to track. Nailing that bastard would be a real feather in our cap."

Claudia wouldn't be too enthused he'd passed on this information, but she'd understand. They were on the same side, after all, and arresting Rainert von Lahr was more about scoring a win for the good guys than about staking out exclusive rights.

"See?" Cookson continued. "Already we can anticipate the advantage of a working relationship between—"

Vincent's desk phone rang. "Excuse me," he said as he picked up the handset. He hoped it was the Rockview warden. "Hello, this is DeLuca."

It *was* the warden, and Vincent mouthed "Rockview" to Cookson, who nodded and turned toward his office.

"Thanks for calling back, sir," Vincent said politely. "I'm assuming you received my message that I need to speak with one of your inmates, John Adam Lewis—"

"This inmate is deceased," intoned the warden's flat voice.

For a moment, Vincent was too surprised to respond, certain he'd misunderstood. Then he said, "I'm sorry, what did you say?"

Something in his voice must've caught Cookson's attention, because he turned back, frowning.

"I said, that inmate is deceased. You were sent a notification of the death, Agent DeLuca."

"I didn't receive it," Vincent said, meeting Cookson's gaze. "When did he die, and how?"

"Exactly two weeks ago. Mr. Lewis was involved in a fight, which is hardly an unusual occurrence in prison. He fell and hit his head on a table, hard enough to fracture his skull. By the time we realized the seriousness of his injury, it was too late. It's unfortunate," the warden added in a slightly more defensive tone, "but such freakish accidents happen. Would you like me to resend the death report to you?"

"Yes, that would be good. Thank you for your time." Vincent hung up. "Shit. This isn't good."

A massive understatement, as a dead Johnny Lewis changed the entire situation.

"Bad news?" Cookson asked.

"Lewis died in a prison fight two weeks ago, which explains why his sister and girlfriend have suddenly developed such an intensely personal interest in my whereabouts. They blame me."

That Lewis was in prison in the first place because he broke the law wasn't an issue for Shai Lewis and Candy Bartowski. No, it was Vincent's fault for prosecuting him—and if that skewed line of thinking was an indication of their general frame of mind, these two women would have their pound of flesh no matter what.

"Maybe you should reschedule those meetings," Cookson said. "And head to Columbia a little sooner than you'd planned."

"Maybe."

"We could assign an officer to you around the clock. That might be enough to scare them off."

Or simply get someone else killed. "No, let's up the priority of finding these two. Get their faces on the news. They've gotten close to me before because my guard was down and I made it easy. They're not master assassins; they're likely as frightened as they are angry, and acting irrationally. Behavior like that is going to get them noticed faster. But it also makes them more dangerous. I recognize that, and I'm not taking the problem lightly."

"Good. So what are your plans?"

Vincent rolled his chair closer to his desk and pulled

out a thick folder. "Right now, my plans are to get caught up with the piles of paperwork threatening to crush my desk under their weight, and to pull together my case file for the Columbia trip."

"Fine. But if you need anything, Vince, you let me know."

"Will do," he said as Cookson left the office.

Pen in hand, Vincent focused on the comforting, mindless task of filling in blank lines and checking boxes. He'd barely made a dent in his pile when his phone rang.

Snatching it up, he said, "DeLuca."

"Hey, it's Matherson. Got your messages, and I have some good news for you."

Vincent straightened in his chair. "Please tell me you picked up Lewis and Bartowski."

"Not exactly but close."

"Matherson, I'm in a fuckin' lousy mood, so would you get to the point already?"

"Love life a bit rocky, son?" The detective gave a bark of laughter. "We had a little scare over at the airport this morning."

Thinking of Claudia, Vincent snapped, "What kind of scare?"

"An unattended box at the United terminal; had to close down that part of the terminal until the tactical team determined the box was clean. When they saw what was in the box, they called me right away."

Vincent knew where this was going. "Let me guess: an old Greek helmet, some photo negatives, things like that."

"Exactly. Our two girls dumped all the hot goods and took off. They're probably on a plane to who knows where by now, but we've got their names and pictures out to federal authorities across the country. If they're on a plane, we'll get them as soon as they land."

"Goddammit," Vincent said.

A moment's pause. "Uh, this isn't good news?"

"Not for my investigation. Once the stolen items are returned, the galleries, museums, and insurance carriers are less motivated to press for a trial and conviction. The end result is wasted hours of work on my end. Pisses me off."

"I can see how it might make you feel that way. So what do you want me to do with all this?"

Vincent glanced at his watch. "Do you have time later this afternoon to meet with me? I can drop by and talk about what we can do next."

"Sure. I'm in the office for the rest of the day. Just give me a ring before you show up so I can find you a clean chair."

Grinning, Vincent said, "Thanks. I appreciate that. So will my dry-cleaning bill."

"You still going after these two?"

"Yup. Even if the insurance carriers bail on me, I think I can make charges stick once we bring them in."

"It would be nice if we good guys won for once."

Vincent disconnected and slumped back in his chair. He wasn't pleased that all his hard work and Claudia's could amount to nothing, but in a way he welcomed the news. The situation was coming to a head, and the next few days, maybe even the next few hours, would see its end. Either Lewis and Bartowski had given up on fantasies of revenge and were running scared or else they just didn't give a damn anymore and would come after him without a care for the consequences. He hoped it was the former but was prepared for the latter.

Or as much as anyone could be prepared for an unknown type of attack that could come from anywhere and at any time. A little self-consciously, he judged his closeness to the nearest window—and wheeled his chair to the side to make sure he wouldn't be visible.

All right, so it turned out a spice of danger wasn't much fun after all. Mostly irritating, with an edge of unease, where he found himself actually looking forward to something happening just so he could get the thing over and done with.

The only positive spin he could put on his whole shitty day was that Claudia was in Texas by now, probably busy terrifying a bunch of priests.

The thought made him smile a little.

He was glad she was safely out of it, but he really missed having her around. A *lot*.

At the end of his lousy day, there'd be no Claudia to chase away the weariness, no Claudia sitting with him, talking shop, or poking and prodding at his comfort zones, assumptions, and general ruts. Funny how she'd made such a difference in his life in so short a time. He regretted wasting most of their last full day together on an angry funk, but even that had its silver lining: if he hadn't been moody, he wouldn't have discovered she played a killer game of Halo.

Beautiful, sexy, great in bed, smart, she actually laughed at his jokes, and she played video games. What more could a guy ask from a girlfriend?

His phone went off again, this time his cell. He didn't recognize the callback number and frowned as he answered. "Hello?"

A man's voice responded: "Am I speaking with Special Agent DeLuca?"

"Yes. Who is this?"

"Ben Sheridan."

Surprised, Vincent asked, "To what do I owe the honor of this call, Mr. Sheridan?"

"Where's Claudia? Is she with you?"

A dread washing over him, Vincent sat forward. "Last I saw her was when I dropped her off at the airport this morning. She should've been in Dallas hours ago."

"She never got off the plane. As far we can tell, she never got *on* it."

"Oh, Jesus," Vincent whispered, running a hand through his hair.

How could he have made such a rookie mistake? *This* had been their plan all along: to confound and distract the opponent, to make a move no one expected—and he *should* have expected it; he should have known.

An eye for an eye, a tooth for a tooth . . . a loved one for a lover.

"They have her," Vincent said. "Goddammit, I could kick myself for being so fucking stupid! I thought for sure they'd make one more attempt to get to me, but I didn't think they'd go after Claudia."

Sheridan was silent, but Vincent could practically feel the tension crackling across airwaves. Then Sheridan said, "I'm not entirely sure what's going on here, but do you really believe someone could grab a trained operative who fights like an alley cat out of a public airport without anyone noticing?"

"I don't know," Vincent snapped. Cradling the phone between his shoulder and ear, he unlocked his desk drawer, pulled out the shoulder holster and gun, and shrugged into it. "And I'm not taking any chances second-guessing them. They'll kill her if they have her."

Saying the words out loud, making them real, filled him with such rage and fear that, for a moment, he couldn't move or speak. He could only stare down at his hand, crushing the drawer key in his palm so tightly that a bead of blood appeared.

Slowly, he became aware that Sheridan was speaking: ". . . I said, where are you now?"

"I'm not one of your people, Sheridan. I don't answer to you."

"Stay where you are. Don't—"

"Fuck that! Do you think I'm going to sit on my ass while the woman I love is in trouble?"

"Shut up and listen to me," Sheridan snapped. "I'm in Philadelphia right now. If Claudia has her cell phone with her, I can track it. Tell me where you are, and I'll meet you. We'll find her."

By now, Vincent had left the building and was running for the parking ramp and his car. "I'll be at the parking ramp outside the federal building."

"Where exactly in the ramp?"

"Second level from the top, toward the back." Skipping the elevator, he took the stairway two steps at a time.

"All right. I'll be there as soon as I can. Stay put."

It wasn't until the call ended and Vincent pushed open the stairwell door and was running for his car, that he wondered how Sheridan had gotten his cell phone number in the first place.

He'd worry about the implications later; he had bigger problems now. Jesus, if they hurt her, he'd kill them. To hell with the consequences.

Even angry and worried, he kept a wary eye on his surroundings. Lewis and Bartowski knew where he lived and worked, the car he drove, even where he liked to have a beer after a long day. The police had beefed up the drive-bys of his neighborhood and security at the federal building was tight, but once outside those zones, he was laying himself wide open.

He slowed to a walk, taking in his surroundings as he made his way to his car, keeping his gun hand close to his holster. He should've taken the time to grab body armor. A gun would be little help if either Lewis or Bartowski were preparing to take him out with a well-placed bullet. And he'd be no use to Claudia dead.

The thought of Claudia dead, along with the possibility of a high-powered rifle aimed right now at his head, made his skin crawl. Still, he couldn't shake the suspicion that an impersonal hit wasn't their intent. They were all about revenge, and if they meant to kill him, they'd want him to see it coming.

If they were going for maximum humiliation and pain, they'd keep the specifics personal. If they were going for messing with him, game playing, they probably wouldn't make it too hard to second-guess them. They couldn't; every cop in the city was on the lookout.

He approached his car cautiously, half expecting to see a taunting note duct-taped to the windshield. But the car sat there, looking harmless. A sense of urgency compelled him to hurry, but he forced himself to slow down, to not take any more chances. Gun in hand, he carefully checked for signs of an explosive device while trying not to stand out in the open any longer than necessary.

His suspicion that they'd make their move up close and personal didn't guarantee he was correct.

Vincent got in the car, placing the gun on the seat in easy reach. Where would they take Claudia? The greatest insult would be to take this deadly game to his home. It wouldn't be easy, but they could conceivably find a way to dodge the patrolling squad car, then get inside his house to wait for him. If they did that, they'd keep Claudia alive and use her against him or as a bargaining tool.

He started the car, cell phone in one hand as he speed-dialed Matherson. If his hunch was right, there was already a squad in the area that would get there before he would.

The detective answered on the third ring. "Hey, Vince. You on your way over?"

"No." Vincent quickly filled him in. "I have a feeling they might go to my place. I'm on my way home now. Meet me there as soon as you can. And if she didn't board her plane—"

"On it. I'll get some uniforms to the airport to check it out. Be careful. I'm on my way."

God, he hated feeling so helpless.

Then Vincent remembered Sheridan, supposedly on his way to the federal building. He couldn't wait for that. He quickly hit the callback button, and Sheridan answered immediately.

"I don't have time to explain," Vincent said, before Sheridan had a chance to speak. "I'm on my way to my house and can't wait for you. I have reason to believe they might take Claudia there. If you have my cell number, you have my address. Meet me there."

Then he tossed the phone aside and backed out of his parking spot so quickly that he narrowly missed hitting an SUV parked behind him. He headed for the exit as fast as he dared, keeping a constant eye on his mirrors, on the gun beside him.

If he didn't get to Claudia in time . . .

Suddenly the car jerked violently to the right, just as he registered the sound of a gunshot. The car jerked again, and he fought the wheel, trying to steer away from the rapidly looming exit wall. Then his windshield exploded inward.

# Chapter Twenty-six

Vincent slammed forward into the stinging hail of safety glass shards.

As another shot shattered the passenger-side window, he rolled down onto the seat. Outside he could hear shouting, the thud of running feet close by.

*Goddammit! Innocent people were out there!*

He groped for his gun, but it was no longer on the seat beside him. Where was it? And where were those shots coming from? He didn't think the shooter was in the parking ramp.

A sound caught his attention, and he looked down to see drops of blood hitting the floor mat in a steady drip drip.

Had he been hit? He didn't feel any pain; it had to be from the safety glass. Wiping the blood from his eyes, he slid his hand under the seat, trying to locate his gun. In the car he was a sitting duck.

As if to prove his point, another bullet hit the car with a muffled *thump*. Quickly, he sized up his options. The passenger side of the car had hit the exit wall; no escape that way. His side was clear but would leave him wide open to another shot.

They'd either kill him while he huddled in the car or get a lucky shot at him as he dashed for cover on the other side of the ramp. Neither option appealed, but they'd find it harder to hit a moving target than a stationary one.

No gun under the seat, no time to find it. The police had to be on their way; all he had to do was stay alive long enough for them to get here. Taking a deep breath, he eased the door open, then kicked it wide, rolling out to the floor in a crouch, only to find his sprint to safety blocked by a pair of legs in jeans and running shoes.

He looked up, registering the barrel of the gun, then the face.

Candy Bartowski.

"Hey, Vince," she said, her tone flat and hostile, the twist of her lips more a sneer than a smile. "Do I have your attention now?"

Drip drip, the blood kept coming. "You've had it for a while. Where's Claudia Cruz? What have you done with her?"

Bartowski stared down at him with those wide, pretty blue eyes. "Misplaced your girlfriend, huh? How sad for you. Get up."

Furious anger made him want to tell her to fuck off, but his common sense and training persevered. "I know what happened to Johnny. I am very sorry for your loss."

"No, you're not. Shut up and get up."

"I can understand why you blame me, but please don't put any other innocent people at risk. Killing me, or anyone else, won't bring Johnny back. Put the gun down, and let's talk—"

"I said, shut up!"

Still crouching, half-hidden by the open car door, he could hear the chaos and panic outside, as well as the rapid thuds of footsteps. Someone running fast. No sirens yet, no local security, but a car engine gunned to life close by. Whoever it was, Vincent hoped they had the sense to go like hell in the opposite direction.

"Is Claudia still alive?"

"I don't feel like answering that question. For the last time, get up."

Slowly, Vincent stood. A detached part of him registered that he was covered in blood, yet he still felt no pain. Senses sharpened, he could smell the coppery tinge of his own blood, her sweat and perfume, the hot, cloying air around them, and he took in even the smallest of details of the woman standing inches away from him, with a small handgun pointed at his face. The freckles, the hint of lipstick, the weave of her jeans and the stitching on her yellow T-shirt, how her fine blond hair shifted in the sluggish breeze.

He spotted Shai Lewis running from across the street toward them, rifle in hand—and knew in that moment they weren't expecting to escape this alive and had every intention of taking him down first.

He wouldn't make it out alive. Claudia . . . Claudia was probably already dead. Pain twisted deep inside him at the thought, but a calmness settled over him. Maybe he wouldn't walk away, but he wasn't going down without a hell of a fight.

The noise of the car engine rumbled closer, moving fast behind him. He heard the car slow . . . and then the sound of squealing tires—a rubber-burning, fishtailing, pedal-to-the-metal squeal as the car roared around the corner and down the main lane at top speed.

Bartowski's eyes widened as Lewis screamed a warning, bringing up her rifle, never breaking stride.

Vincent ducked and crouched low just inside the open car door. He heard another scream, high-pitched and terrified, and felt a rush of air and the heat of a racing engine. A split second later, his car door was torn off with a wrenching groan that nearly drowned out the sickening *thud* of a body against metal, then the nerve-rattling squeal of brakes and more screaming.

And another rifle shot.

Still crouched, he spotted a dark gleam at the back of his driver's seat. His gun! He grabbed it and spun as Claudia's voice shouted, "Watch out! She's got a rifle and she knows how to shoot!"

Vincent stared, shocked. "What the *hell* are you doing here?"

"Being your partner and guardian angel!"

Relief rushed over him with such force that he almost laughed out loud.

Her bright blue Toyota, engine still running, sat at an angle to his own car, mostly blocking the exit and providing him a triangular wedge of cover—or as much cover as it could against an enraged woman with a rifle.

Claudia was slouched as low in the seat as possible, her hand on the steering wheel. "Gun?" she asked.

He raised it.

"Good boy. Now take her out before she shoots us." She grinned. "I'd do the honors, but my gun's in Texas."

Again, he almost laughed.

"Bartowski's down but not dead. She's trying to get up. I don't see her gun. . . . Oh, shit, the other one's here."

Vincent heard Shai Lewis frantically calling Candy, who answered in a string of raw cursing that culminated with a shrilly escalating "Kill them, kill them, kill them!"

Claudia's eyes locked on his, shining with fierce emotion as her hands tightened on the wheel. "I'll cover you as much as I can. Make your shot count."

He nodded once.

Still slouched down, she mashed the gas. Engine racing, tires shrieking, she backed up fast, then spun the car around as Vincent stood.

Lewis was raising her rifle, face contorted with rage, with Bartowski on her knees beside her, gagging blood.

He fired a split second before Lewis, hitting her shoulder. She jerked aside, her own shot going wide. His second shot hit her in the neck, and she fell in an ungainly heap, like a doll dropped by a child.

Vincent ran, gun still raised, toward Bartowski. She didn't look like she'd be much of a threat, but the rifle was within her reach. "Hands on your head! Now!" he shouted.

From the corner of his eye, he saw Claudia run toward him, yelling, "Don't move! Don't you fucking move!"

Bartowski's gaze caught his, her eyes brilliantly blue in the paleness of her bloodied face. Then she smiled and lunged for the rifle.

*Ah, shit.*

Claudia stopped in her tracks as Vincent fired again. Bartowski jerked to the side, then slumped against the pillar, looking down where bright red blood bloomed on her yellow shirt. She touched it as if puzzled, then her head fell back, eyes rolling upward as her body went limp.

Vincent stood still, staring at the two bodies, unaware that Claudia had moved until she touched his shoulder. He startled, then turned.

"You look like hell," she said softly. "You okay? Hurt anywhere?"

It was enough to snap him back to his senses. "I'm fine. You?"

"A little shaken, but that's all."

In an unspoken agreement, they both hurried toward Bartowski and Lewis. Bartowski was still alive, her pulse fast and weak under his searching fingertips. Lewis was dead.

Before he could process the reality of what he'd done, Claudia said, "Put your gun down and raise your hands."

He stared. "What? I don't—"

"The cops are here." She sounded so calm, as if this was something she did on a regular basis. Her hands were already raised. "Just *do* it. Some cops are more quick on the trigger than others."

Now he heard the sirens, ear-piercingly close. He quickly dropped his gun, kicked it well away from Bartowski, and raised his hands.

Not a second too soon.

"Police!"

The shout came from the exit, quickly followed by a swarm of blue uniforms aiming guns their way.

"Federal agent! Don't shoot!" Vincent shouted back. "We need an ambulance. The woman with the yellow top is alive, but she needs immediate medical assistance. The woman beside me is unarmed and a private citizen."

The cops didn't take his word for it, and he hadn't

expected them to. But the tension dissipated, and he stood in stoic silence as he was roughly searched. Claudia was also searched, and she neither protested nor spoke.

Once his identification was found, the officer in charge called out, "It's okay. He's FBI." The cops holstered their weapons but remained watchful. Several moved to assist Bartowski, gently easing her down as they assessed her wounds.

"Officer Bachman, sir," said the officer in charge. "I'm sorry, but you'll have to stay here awhile."

"I understand," Vincent said and motioned Claudia to come to him. "Is the ambulance on the way?"

"It's here now," answered another officer. "The blonde's in rough shape. The other one's gone."

More cops swarmed in, along with security guards, agents from the federal building, and, finally, the EMTs. The officer asked Vincent a few terse questions to establish the basics of what had happened.

"Anybody on the street hurt?" Vincent asked.

"Can't say for certain yet, sir, but there are no reports of any other casualties."

"Thank God for small favors, huh?" Claudia said quietly, and Vincent turned toward her.

It was the first chance he'd had to really get a good look at her since the shooting began, and aside from a few new scrapes, she looked beautifully safe and sound. Not caring about the staring cops or his fellow agents, he kissed her hard on the mouth, then hugged her close.

"You scared the hell out of me. When Sheridan called to tell me he didn't know where you were and that you hadn't boarded your plane this morning, I thought those two had killed you. It felt like I'd been hit by a Mack truck, thinking that you—"

"Sssh, it's okay. I'm okay." She kissed him back, quick and breathless. "I'm so sorry I scared you like that, but I had no idea— Oh, God, did Ben really call you?"

"You were missing. He thought you might be with me."

She briefly squeezed her eyes shut. "Oh, boy. He's gonna be so pissed at me."

Maybe it was relief at seeing her alive and well, or maybe it was relief at not dying like he'd expected, but the mix of panic and frustration in her expression struck him as funny, and he chuckled.

"Then this is probably a bad time to tell you he's here in Philly, most likely sitting in a car outside my house." Vincent recalled who else he'd asked to go to his place. "And most likely surrounded by cops, too."

She blanched. "I'm dead. He's seriously gonna kill me."

"Not while I'm around," Vincent told her. "And don't take this wrong, but would you care to explain why you're here and not in Dallas?"

"Yeah . . . but how about we wait until we're alone? This mess is going to take a while to clean up." Leaning closer, she whispered, "I'm so, so sorry you had to shoot. If I could've done that for you, I would have."

Vincent closed his eyes. Her words seemed to release something within him, and all the fear and anger and sorrow rolled over him in a smothering wave as the full implications of what he'd done hit. He wanted to laugh, he wanted to cry. He blew out a breath instead, and said, "I could really use a beer."

The cop sent him a sympathetic look, then politely averted his gaze as Claudia leaned forward and rested her head on his shoulder.

"Me, too."

"I don't regret it," he added, watching as the EMTs loaded Bartowski onto a stretcher with quick efficiency. Two others stood by another stretcher, a folded body bag waiting on top for Lewis's body. "There was no other choice."

"I know," she said, still softly. "And I know how sometimes not even that makes it any easier."

# Chapter Twenty-seven

What a rotten day.

Ben sat in his rental car, seat back and windows open, as a local news station played quietly on his radio. The updates on the shootings at the federal building sounded less chaotic by now, but it didn't improve his mood. From the moment he'd pulled up to DeLuca's house, things had not gone well. Too many cops, and no one with any idea what was happening. He was lucky not to have been arrested in the midst of all the confusion, luckier yet that a detective believed his explanation because he'd just had a similar conversation with DeLuca.

When all hell broke loose at the federal building, the detective and the small army of cops had rushed off, leaving behind a single disgruntled-looking patrolman to keep an eye on Ben.

A glance at his side mirror revealed the cop still

parked across the street, still watching him. A nuisance, but a useful one. The cop had informed Ben that Claudia and DeLuca were alive and unharmed. Two others were not so fine, but the cop refused to pass along any more information.

From what Claudia had told him the day before, he figured the two shooting victims were the women who'd been after DeLuca. Which meant he could file this assignment under "Closed" and "Near Disaster."

Settling back, he tried to ignore his shirt sticking to his sweaty skin, the weariness pulling at him, the frustration and anger nipping at his raw nerves.

London had been . . . tense. No sign of von Lahr or Vanessa Sharpton—and that she was traveling with von Lahr piqued Ben's interest. She didn't fit von Lahr's usual type, so what did he want with her?

The inevitable argument with Will Tiernay had been particularly unpleasant. Something was wrong there, and Ben wasn't quite sure what, although he had his suspicions. Mostly they'd argued over Will's girlfriend, and how their secretive little trysts may have placed her in danger once again.

Then came Ron Levine's call from Peru, confirming Ben's fears. Stuart Wilcox's body had been found. Cause of death was a gunshot wound to the left temple. And the additional details made it clear that locals weren't responsible. The news cut Ben's London trip short, and he immediately flew back to deliver the news of Wilcox's death personally to his wife and family.

They'd been in Bangor, refueling, when Ellie finally contacted him with the alarming news that Claudia had apparently disappeared. With the details of Wilcox's death fresh in his mind, Ben had immediately assumed the worst, and he'd decided Mrs. Wilcox could remain blissfully ignorant of her husband's death for a few hours longer while he tracked down Claudia.

Instead he sat here in the blistering heat, under the sour gaze of a Philly cop, contemplating how one of his smartest operatives could've fallen for an FBI agent she'd been bitching about for months. And wondering how he could turn this unwelcome development to his own advantage.

What a rotten, rotten day.

# Chapter Twenty-eight

An hour later, Claudia slid into the backseat of Detective Matherson's car beside Vincent.

"Thanks again for giving us a ride," she said.

"No problem." Matherson glanced back at them in his rearview mirror. "Vince's car didn't look like it was going anywhere"

"Between the bullet-ridden car and the Day-Glo paint job at my house, my insurance company is going to jack my rates up through the roof," Vincent said ruefully. "So I could really use some cheering up. How about you tell me a nice story, Claudia, and explain what the hell is going on?"

Claudia leaned back and finally allowed herself the luxury of relaxing. *Exhausted* didn't even begin to describe how she felt.

"I couldn't get on that plane. I just knew you were in danger, and I had to stay, even if it made you very angry."

When he didn't deny the anger part, she shot him a quick look. "Are you mad?"

"That you cared enough about me to risk getting into big trouble by staying? Not really. Do I look that stupid?"

"Well . . ." After a quick peek at Matherson, she lowered her voice. "There's that male pride thing. And the trust thing."

"That's a lot of 'things,'" he said, his tone mild. "You'll have to believe me when I tell you my life is worth more than my ego. You were right, and I was wrong. Lesson learned."

Relieved, she said, "I kept thinking about what they might do, looking at it from their viewpoint. I couldn't shake the feeling that they were desperate, maybe even suicidal—and no matter how prepared you are, you can't prepare for that kind of crazy. I figured it would be easier for them to get you on your way home from work than at your house, since the police were already watching the area. I parked close enough that I could see your car, and once the shooting started, I got to you as fast as I could."

"That was some fancy driving. And quick thinking," Matherson said.

"Thanks. I used to be a cop."

"It shows."

Claudia was glad Matherson didn't ask why she wasn't a cop anymore. "It still ended up a big mess. We're lucky no one else was hurt."

"Yeah," Matherson said. "Good shooting, Vince. I know you wish it could've ended differently, but they didn't give you a choice."

When Vincent didn't answer, she searched his face, trying to gauge how he was responding to what he'd done. You could train all your life for the possibility of having to shoot someone, and it still didn't help you face the aftermath of actually ending a life. "You really okay about what happened?"

"Yeah," he said after a moment. "If Bartowski dies, too, I might feel it more, but right now there's nothing except maybe anger. Such a waste, you know? To throw your life away over something so stupid."

"Are you going to talk to her, if she pulls through?"

"Yes. I want to know if there was something more than grief that pushed them over the edge. If that's all it was, so be it. I'm expecting more, though. Maybe Johnny Lewis had something to do with it all. Maybe he asked them to go on a private war against me. Maybe they made a promise, and kept it even after he died." He paused. "Mostly, I want to understand."

"Well, good luck with that," Claudia said, still a little worried. He acted calm, but his saying such things made her realize he was pretty shook up. "Don't be surprised if they turn out to be a little crazy."

"I'm voting for crazy," Matherson said. "Did Vince tell you they returned everything they'd stolen? We found it in a box at the airport."

No, he hadn't. Must've slipped his mind while he was busy not getting killed. "The airport?" she asked.

Vincent nodded. "That's one of the reasons I thought they'd kidnapped you after Sheridan said you never got on your plane. Instead, it drew a big chunk of cops to the airport for much of the morning. That was probably their intent—to thin out the blue line."

"Are you going to prosecute her for the thefts?"

"I'll try."

"There's always the fact she tried to kill an FBI agent. That's a federal offense."

"If she lives, she's going to prison. There's no doubt about that."

Claudia gently touched his arm, and after a moment, his rigid muscles relaxed. "It'll get sorted out. In a few weeks, you'll be living your life just like it's always been," she said.

"I hope not."

Taken aback, she asked, "What do you mean?"

"I think your presence has to be factored into any happily-ever-after for me. You seem to be a chaotic force."

Not one of the more romantic things to tell a girl. "Well, excuse *me*."

"Not a chance." He smiled. "I wouldn't want it any other way."

His warm smile banished her worries. "We did okay. We make a good team, huh?"

"I think so."

"We should do this more often." At his stare, she added quickly, "Work together—not get into shoot-outs in parking garages."

"Okay, you two. Cut that out until you get behind closed doors. Have pity on me, okay?" Matherson sounded grumpy, but Claudia had a sneaky feeling he was smiling. "My wife's visiting her mother, and I'm probably the only cop in Philly who doesn't have a decent porn collection."

"The old lady won't stand for that, eh?" Vincent asked, smile widening.

"Just you wait—you'll see. They're all sex kitten and tease before you marry 'em. Then they fill the house with cute kids, fattening food fit for a king, and civilize all your brutish ways. No more farting while watching TV. No more sleeping in on weekends. No more living on pizza and beer. It's sheer hell, I tell ya."

Claudia laughed, and Vincent joined in. She knew what Matherson was doing, and silently sent him a thank-you.

Ten minutes later, she wished someone could ease *her* nerves. She spotted the large, dark SUV outside Vincent's house and knew with a sinking feeling that Ben hadn't gotten bored waiting for them and left.

She hadn't really expected him to let her off that easy, though—and the presence of a police cruiser warned her he'd be in no mood to be nice. Then there was the matter of the wrecked rental car he didn't even know about yet.

"I think you can send that cop on his way," she said.

"Will do," Matherson said as he pulled up behind the SUV. "Look, I didn't know this Sheridan guy, and even though his story made sense and he was cooperative enough to let us search him and his vehicle, I didn't want to let him hang around unattended. I still wasn't clear on what was happening at the federal building."

"It's all right. I appreciate all the trouble you've gone to on my behalf," said Vincent.

"So you owe me one. I'll find a way to make you pay me back."

After they got out of the car, Claudia watched the detective jog across the street to tell the patrol cop he could leave. Then, with a sigh, she looked back at the SUV. How could fiberglass and rubber look so ominous? "I am *so* not looking forward to this. I should've called and explained myself, but . . ."

After a moment, Vincent prodded, "But . . . ?"

"But I'm such a chickenshit," she whispered, not wanting Ben to hear her. "I knew he'd refuse to let me stay, so I didn't call and figured I'd deal with the fallout later. I'm almost glad we got shot at. If I'd been wrong, I'd be in even more trouble." She straightened her shoulders. "But I made the decision; I'll take the lumps. Ben's really not that bad, but he didn't get where he is today by being a nice man."

Vincent frowned. "Why the hell is he just sitting in there?"

"Terror tactics," Claudia said with feeling. "He's probably waiting until Matherson leaves."

Vincent grunted. "Or maybe he just fell asleep."

"I don't think he sleeps. My theory is that he's really a robot."

The patrol cop drove off. A moment later, Matherson followed with a jaunty wave.

Claudia sucked in a long breath. "Okay. Let's get this over with."

She walked over to the SUV, Vincent close behind her, as the door swung open and Ben Sheridan stepped out, his clothing wrinkled from a day's worth of traveling and sitting in hot vehicles. He'd no doubt started out with a tie and suit coat, but now his shirt was opened at the collar and the sleeves rolled up. His short, dark hair was as perfectly trimmed as ever, but, like Vincent, he was one of those men who went through life perpetually in need of a shave.

"Glad to see you finally made it," Ben said, his tone uncomfortably mild. His gaze dropped briefly to her bandaged elbows, but he said nothing. "I was entertaining the idea of betting the cop which one of us would have heatstroke first, me or him."

What could she say, except, "Sorry, Ben."

Ben's gaze shifted to Vincent. "You must be DeLuca."

To Claudia's surprise, Vincent held out his hand. "Pleased to finally meet you, Mr. Sheridan."

Ben shook his hand. "I'm here for my operative. She goes to the airport with me."

Oh, boy. Beyond awkward. To nip any tense stand-offs in the bud, Claudia deliberately moved between them and made a show of peeking inside the car—she was genuinely surprised to see no one else inside. "Isn't Ellie or Shaunda with you?"

"No," Ben said, shortly. "They do sometimes let me off the leash."

Claudia saw Vincent perk with interest. "Who's Ellie and Shaunda?"

"My bodyguards."

Vincent blinked. "Do people try to kill you very often?"

"Not as often as they'd like. Let's go, Claudia. I've waited long enough, and you've neglected your work long enough as well."

Ben and Vincent were of a similar height and build, but Ben was heavier. More intimidating. They stood eye to eye, evaluating each other in that familiar male territorial way while Claudia mentally squirmed in discomfort.

"And I hope you have a very good explanation for neglecting your responsibilities."

At that, all her guilty feelings vanished. "But Vincent is more important than any of that! He's a friend." She felt a blush heating her face. "More than a friend, obviously, and he was in trouble. I'm sorry for not calling, but I had to be here for him. If something had gone wrong, I never would've forgiven myself."

After a moment, Ben said, "You know the protocol. A missed check-in means I get involved, no matter what, even if it turns out you were only bailing out your boyfriend's careless ass."

Vincent stiffened, but she grabbed his arm, nails digging into his muscles in warning as she repeated, "I am sorry."

She couldn't promise that it wouldn't happen again, though, and by the look in his eyes, Ben hadn't missed that finer point.

"I respect your dedication and loyalty. It's one of the reasons I value you as an employee," Ben said, although his focus was on Vincent.

After that long, measuring glance at Vincent—with a shade of calculation that made Claudia nervous—Ben added, "I apologize if I'm short-tempered. One of my tour guides went missing in Peru last week, and his body was recently discovered. I have good reason to believe it's an atypical murder, and I was concerned that his disappearance might've been linked to your situation. I'm very relieved to see you safe, but now it's time to go. The jet's waiting, Claudia, and you *do* have responsibilities elsewhere."

The guilt came creeping back. She had no answer to that—she'd been unprofessional and knew it, and understood now the worry behind Ben's gruff mood. He hadn't explained everything, but Claudia could tell there was more going on than a tour guide's disappearance, although that was bad enough.

She hated feeling torn between the man she was falling in love with and the man to whom she owed a tremendous debt. But she and Vincent would face separations like this over and over again. If they couldn't deal with it now, they never would.

"Sorry," she said quietly, meeting Vincent's gaze. "I really do have to go."

He nodded, his expression closed. "Sure."

Claudia frowned, not liking his sudden change of mood. "I will be back. I already promised you, and nothing about that has changed."

Ben, picking up on the awkward tension, said, "I'll be waiting in the car. Make it quick. And, DeLuca? I believe you owe Avalon a favor, since my operative put her life on the line to save yours. You can rest assured I will collect eventually."

Claudia squeezed her eyes shut, trying not to think evil things about Ben and wishing he'd kept his mouth shut. He was only making matters more difficult between her and Vincent.

"I don't like the way he talks to you," Vincent said bluntly when Ben was out of earshot.

"Ben doesn't own me. What you're seeing is me feeling guilty as hell for letting down anyone who depends on me, no matter how good my reasons for doing so. We've been through this already, haven't we? I will come back as soon as I can. Please trust me." Leaning toward him, she kissed him softly, then added, "Believe in me. I'll see you later."

Claudia had begun to turn away when Vincent tugged her back and kissed her, a long, deep kiss that was also more than a little angry or desperate . . . or, more likely, both.

"Don't keep me waiting too long, Claudia."

Or what? He'd give up? Not sure what to say, or that there even *was* anything more to say, she turned and headed over to the SUV, its engine now humming quietly.

She climbed in beside Ben and snapped, "You said we were in a hurry, right? So let's go."

Ben put the SUV in gear and drove off. An uncomfortable silence settled between them until he sighed and said, "So you're really serious about that asshole."

"Who said he's an asshole?" Claudia shot back, still angry. Anger was good; it held back the weepies.

Brow arched, he glanced at her. "You did. Quite frequently, as I recall."

Belatedly, Claudia remembered that she had indeed called Vincent an asshole—and a whole lot worse. "Well, it so happens he's *my* asshole, so nobody else can call him that. Got it?"

She'd never acted like this with Ben before, but maybe standing up for what she wanted, for the first time in a long, long time, had made the difference. All of a sudden, she didn't feel half as intimidated in his presence.

To her further surprise, her boss said nothing more, and the ride to the airport passed in silence.

# Chapter Twenty-nine

❖

*Thursday, Marseille*

Rainert von Lahr leaned out the window of the small, quaint house that was temporarily providing him a safe hiding place. As the hot sun streamed down on his face, he closed his eyes and took in a deep breath smelling of the sea. Marseille was one of his favorite cities, old and sprawling, with an overall impression of bright blue water and stately white buildings crowding the curve of the port.

In another few days he'd have a new identity and travel papers for himself and Vanessa, and then they'd fly to Jamaica. Once there, he'd decide where to go next.

Bad luck, that business in London. He'd managed to turn it to his advantage, but barely. It would be wise to lay low for a short while. All the plans he intended to set in motion over the next few months could be handled from anywhere, but a place where he could take off and land his own small plane would be best. Before long, he'd have to move around various countries in South America, and he'd need to do so quickly.

"What are you doing?"

He turned slightly from the window as Vanessa came up beside him. She was wearing his undershirt again, a habit it seemed she wouldn't abandon, no matter how many clothes he bought for her. Nor was she wearing a bra, another habit that was beginning to bother him.

"Thinking," he said, turning back to the view of the sea.

"Am I going to like the results of all this thinking, or are they going to terrify me to death?"

He shrugged, not really caring. "I know where to find Ben Sheridan. That's never been an issue, even if getting to him is all but impossible. He guards himself too well."

Sheridan Expeditions tour guides were easy pickings, however, if not quite as satisfactory catches as Sheridan's operatives.

"In the past, I found it difficult to anticipate where any Avalon operative might turn up. As you can imagine, this is a constant source of frustration to me. But now, I'm thinking about how your little friend in Boston might provide me a way to work around that problem."

Vanessa glanced at him, her expression filled with unease. "Mia, you mean? Are you going to do something to her?"

"Would you care if I did?"

"No, of course not," Vanessa said, a little too quickly. "But I don't see why you'd want to bother with her. She's not with them, even if she is sleeping with one."

"Precisely, and she was with Tiernay in London. Chances are she'll meet up with him again or he'll come to her, giving me the perfect opportunity to follow one or both. I'm going to have her watched. I'm confident that several of Vulaj's associates, who are still in the area, would be willing to do their part in memory of their dear departed friend."

She disliked it when he talked mockingly of Vulaj but this time didn't react. Instead she asked, flatly, "And then what? You'll kill them?"

"No, my bloodthirsty dear, I will not kill them." At least, not for a while. "I will use them to gather information against Sheridan and, more important, against whoever is holding his leash."

"I could care less about this Sheridan. I want Tiernay dead."

"Yes, I know," Rainert said, drily. "And so do Vulaj's people. However, I need him alive for a while longer yet. Anything I can learn will be of use to me, and since I'm somewhat at a disadvantage—being a wanted criminal has its drawbacks—I need all the extra leverage I can get."

"So your grand plan is get rid of these Avalon people?" She looked skeptical. "And then you can merrily go your own way once again?"

"I think *merrily* is too optimistic, but yes, I will be able to move somewhat more freely. They have been my primary opposition up until now." He paused, frowning. "The Carabinieri have given me some trouble as well."

"Why does Avalon want you so badly?"

"I've killed a few of them," he said and shrugged. "Sheridan seems to have taken it personally."

"Imagine that," Vanessa drawled.

He looked over at her again, and noticed how the sunlight brought out the blond highlights in her hair and that the edges of her eyelashes were a paler color. She had freckles, along with a few lines of exhaustion marking her face, but he had to admit that the pale, thin British look suited her well.

"Sheridan is smart, but he has a weakness. Everyone has a weakness."

"Even you?" she asked, a touch too impertinently.

He focused again on the water, on the mesmerizing sparkles, the near-blinding brightness of it. "Even me."

"So are you going to tell me what it is?" From impertinence to teasing, in a matter of seconds.

"Not likely," he answered, unable to hold back his amusement. "Have you ever heard of Sun Tzu, Vanessa?"

"Of course. He's reputed to have written a treatise on war called *The Art of War*. Stupid title. Only those with a Y chromosome would consider bloody carnage to be an art."

He smiled and admired the soaring and swooping rhythms of the seabirds as they hunted over the ocean. Would she miss the art in that, too? "You wouldn't say this if you'd met some of the women I've known over the years. You really need to get out more."

"I assume you're trying to make some sort of point about nobly killing people in this war you've declared on Avalon?"

"They declared war on me first," he said, stung a little by her scorn. She had quite the sharp tongue when she was of a mind to be disagreeable. "Sun Tzu wrote, and forgive me if I misquote him, 'It is said that if you know your enemy and know yourself, you can win a thousand battles without a single loss. If you only know yourself, but not your enemy, you may win or you may lose. If you know neither yourself nor your enemy, you will always lose.' "

"Sun Tzu was a wise old bugger."

"Very much so, yes."

"Okay," she said at length. "I take it you're stuck at the second point, where you know yourself but don't know squat about your opponent."

"Precisely, and I intend to learn as much about them as possible." One of the seabirds dove with breathtaking speed, skimming the water, then rising again with a fish in its beak. "I'm also a believer in another of his maxims: 'If his forces are united, separate them. If sovereign and subject are in accord, put division between them. Attack him where he is unprepared, appear where you are not expected.'"

Vanessa leaned farther out the window, squinting against the bright sun, her warmth brushing against him.

He eased away. "Over the years, I've come to understand that Sheridan isn't running Avalon because he considers himself to be like his predecessors—some crusading knight, righting the wrongs of plundered art and antiquities. He's after something. Or someone."

"But you don't know what that something or someone is, I take it?"

He watched as she closed her eyes and tipped her face toward the sun, as he had earlier, and admired how the light made her hair almost glow.

"Yes, that about sums it up. But I will find out what it is he wants. And when I do, I'll use it against him like a knife and make him bleed."

# Chapter Thirty

*Friday, Philadelphia*

In the days since Claudia had been whisked away by Sheridan, she'd called twice, both times in a hurry. She didn't say much about what she was working on, and Vincent knew better than to ask. The conversation stayed strictly on mutually common concerns.

He'd updated her on Candy Bartowski's condition when she'd asked—serious but expected to live—and passed on the disappointing news that several insurance carriers had already accepted the return of their clients' stolen property and then declined to press charges. She made the appropriate noises of sympathy, which he appreciated, even though they'd both expected as much.

Vincent had asked her only once when she'd be back, and when her response had been vague, he'd let the matter drop, reminding himself that she'd said she would be back.

"Believe in me," she'd pleaded, and he was trying. If it weren't for the force of Ben Sheridan's will and his sway over Claudia, Vincent wouldn't have doubted her at all.

But after the week passed and she hadn't called in several days, he resigned himself to the possibility that he wouldn't see her again because it really was just too damn hard to make a relationship work.

Vincent never doubted it would be difficult, but if he'd been willing to try, why couldn't she? He'd pegged her for a stronger woman that this, one who wouldn't give up so easily.

By Friday—how could only a week feel like months?—Vincent was more than ready to fly to Columbia. Even long hours in court sounded better than waiting for his phone to ring or staring moodily into a beer. After his trip to Columbia, he'd take that vacation Cookson had suggested. He needed to get out and do something for himself. Maybe visit his folks; he hadn't seen them in a while, and they weren't getting any younger.

He'd already packed for the flight, so he didn't need to go home first, and Joey Leone had promised to water the yard and garden. As he walked to his car in the parking garage, mulling over how he'd evade his eagle-eyed mother's questions—she could always tell when he was in a blue funk—he noticed a human-shaped shadow shift against the ramp wall.

Memories, still fresh, rushed back, and he tensed, adrenaline pumping, until the shadow moved again and a shaft of sunlight glinted along copper curls.

"Hey. I was beginning to wonder if you were going to pull an all-nighter in that joint."

All the knots of tension, of doubt and frustration, loosened in an instant and then vanished, leaving him almost giddy.

"You ever hear of calling a guy ahead of time?" Vincent demanded. Maybe his tone was a little belligerent, but he couldn't hold back his smile.

"You sound like my mother. And my *abuelita*." She made a face and pushed away from his car to meet him. "It was one crazy assignment. I'll fill you in later on why, but I hardly had any free time at all. When I did, it was way too late to call. It was only a week, anyway. Don't tell me you thought I was—"

He quickly said, "Why are you standing out here, anyway? You look hot."

He stopped then and looked at her, really looked. She was wearing shorts and a tee, and, yes, she looked hot and sweaty—and so damn beautiful, it felt like a punch to the gut.

"And I mean that in every sense of the word," he added, grinning, crazy-happy to see her.

She eyed him, a smile playing at the corners of those full, luscious lips. "You look surprised to see me. Did you think I wouldn't keep my word?"

How could he have forgotten her persistence? Rather than dodge the question, he shrugged and said, "I was beginning to have a few doubts. Never claimed to have the patience of a saint."

"Well, here I am. Making my point."

Vincent wanted to take her in his arms, hold her close, and kiss her—and a whole lot more—but he sensed she had something else to say, so he waited.

"Me being here is making a point to my boss that I'm a good little worker bee and worth every penny he pays me, but that I also have my own life and I'm going to live it. Me being here tells *you* that I keep my word, and you should do a better job of trusting me." She took a deep breath. "And me being here is my way of telling myself that I can do this—that *we* can do this, if we really want to be together."

Again, a rush of relief, along with a sense of smugness. "Told you so."

At his answer, she visibly relaxed. "There you go again, having to get in the last word."

"Who's keeping score? Not me."

"Score?" She shook her head at him. "See? Control issues."

He opened his arms, and she went to him, clinging a little more tightly than before. He was holding her more tightly than usual, too, judging by her sudden squeak, and he loosened his hold. It was so good to have her back in his arms, to feel her close against him.

"Maybe you can do something about all those imaginary control issues of mine," he said after a quick kiss and unlocked the car door.

Claudia arched her brow. "Now?"

"Not exactly. I'm on my way to Columbia. You feel like hanging around South Carolina for a few days?"

"You want me to go with you?"

"Well, yeah. Unless you have other plans?"

"If I did, I sure as hell wouldn't be standing out here waiting for you in ninety-degree weather." She took his tie, and unknotted it. "There. Much better. Did I ever tell you that you have the sexiest neck? It makes me want to do wicked, evil things to your body."

"That's cruel. I have a plane to catch."

"Planes fly out all the time, day after day. Maybe we can catch a later flight. Or an early one tomorrow."

He *had* padded his schedule with an extra couple days in case of any last-minute work. "We could do that."

"Smart man." With a small smile, she said, "So . . . how about we go back to your place and find out just how happy we are to see each other?"

Vincent grinned as he helped her into the car. "I like the sound of that."

"I thought you would."

# Epilogue

Ben was staring out his office windows, hands in his pockets, when Ellie buzzed him on the intercom. "A courier's here with a package for you."

Just what he needed—more drama. His trip to the Wilcox household had been even more difficult than he'd anticipated, and he'd set the bar pretty low on that.

Maybe he'd get lucky and it would be another pile of boring spreadsheets with sticky notes full of demands for explanations.

"Does he need to see me?"

"Yup, she does. It's Beth, and she says it's urgent and she has to return with your response."

Ah, Beth. Not his favorite courier, since her arrival always signaled trouble. "All right. Send her in."

As he sat, the courier walked in, wearing the usual

dark blue Sheridan Express uniform. A cap with the company logo covered long blond hair drawn back in a ponytail.

"What have you got for me?" he asked as she shut the door behind her.

She dropped the flat envelope on his desk, then sat in the opposite chair, leaned back, and propped her boots on his desk. "We have a problem, Benjamin."

"No shit. We always have a problem. Did Tiernay finally track down your mother and grill her about your great-great-uncle?"

"Yes, but that's trouble we expected." She motioned to the envelope. "This is not."

He ripped open the envelope and drew out its contents. He'd already seen the photos, but that didn't make looking at them again any easier.

Stuart Wilcox had been a big man in his early thirties, fit and alert. It wouldn't have been easy to overpower him, so he'd been shot from a short distance away by a high-powered rifle. It had been a clean head shot, and he'd died instantly. Not that this would be of any great comfort to his grieving family: a wife, three kids, parents, a sister, and who knew how many friends.

The look in his wife's eyes was still keeping Ben awake at night.

The third photo was the main point of interest, however. It showed a note affixed to the dead man's back by a large hunting knife. The note read: *Tag! You're it.*

The note, and its method of delivery, were all too familiar.

"It wasn't von Lahr who killed him," Ben said. "We know without a doubt that he was in London when this happened. I bet our knowing that throws a kink in von Lahr's plans, because he clearly intended us to think he'd killed Wilcox and that he's still somewhere in South America."

"It doesn't matter. I don't like the implications of this one bit."

"Nor do I," Ben muttered.

"We're going to have to handle the situation carefully, and to do that I'll need your absolute cooperation." The woman fixed him with an unblinking, pale-eyed gaze. "So we need to make one important matter very clear here: Who gives you your orders, Mr. Sheridan?"

*Ben, if anything happens to me or my father . . . can I ask you to promise me something?*

He returned her stare. "I'm not ever allowed to forget that, am I?"

"Answer the question," she said coldly. "Whose orders do you solely obey?"

As he always did, Ben replied, "Only yours, Izzy."

*Promise to take care of Izzy. Watch over her and keep her safe.*

Ben had kept his promise to Gareth for twenty long years. Too bad the sweet little girl he'd nearly died for, way back when, had grown up to be such an icy, controlling bitch.

"So tell me what you want me to do," he said flatly. "And I'll do it."

# Author's Note

The FBI recently added an Art Theft Program to the bureau, since art theft, looting, and forgery have become a complex and worldwide problem. Over the years, a few police departments in the United States and in other countries have created specialized units for art theft, most of them flourishing or fading depending on funding and available personnel. Italy's Carabinieri, a paramilitary police force, has a long involvement in investigating and prosecuting art-related crimes. Avalon, however, is a total figment of my imagination, and any dramatic license taken with factual organizations was done for the sake of adding a bit of "ye olde derring-do" to the plot.

# *Sexy suspense that sizzles*

## FROM POCKET BOOKS!

Laura Griffin
### *THREAD OF FEAR*
She says this will be her last case.
A killer plans to make sure it is.

———•———

**Don't miss the electrifying trilogy from
*New York Times* bestselling author Cindy Gerard!**

### *SHOW NO MERCY*
The sultry heat hides the deadliest threats—
and exposes the deepest desires.

### *TAKE NO PRISONERS*
A dangerous attraction—spurred by revenge—
reveals a savage threat that can't be ignored.

### *WHISPER NO LIES*
An indecent proposal reveals a simmering desire—
with deadly consequences.

Available wherever books are sold or at www.simonandschuster.com

**POCKET BOOKS**
A Division of Simon & Schuster
A CBS COMPANY

19582